DISCOVERY

DARK NEBULA
BOOK 2

SEAN WILLSON

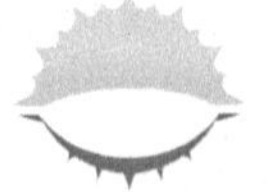

WELCOME TO DARK NEBULA

Thank you for buying this book!

If you're interested in a free novella entitled **Dark Nebula: Contact**, hearing more about the series, seeing new cover art as it's released, or getting exclusive access to sales as they happen, then you can subscribe to my newsletter online at:

seanwillson.com/subscribe

You can also drop me an email at:

author@seanwillson.com

I always love hearing from my readers.

DARK NEBULA SERIES
Novella: Contact (FREE)
Book 1: Isolation
Book 2: Discovery (This book)
Book 3: Generations
Book 4: Beacon
Book 5: Graveyard
Book 6: Nursery

PORTAL SERIES
Book 1: Drowning Earth
Books 2-4: Coming Soon…

CONTENTS

DATA SHEET
TAU CETI

Target: Tau Ceti
Alternate Designation: Sol 3
Distance from Sol: 11.905 light years
Number of Planets: 6
Habitable Planets: 1 - Tiān
Terraformed Planets: 1 is eligible

System Population:

- *Tau Ceti b, Adi*: 0
- *Tau Ceti c, Tiān*: 31,082 planetside, 326 orbiting
- *Asteroid Belt*: 125 orbiting
- *Tau Ceti g, Métis*: 0 planetside, 11 orbiting
- *Tau Ceti h, Hepa*: 0 planetside, 0 orbiting
- *Tau Ceti e, Laniger*: 0 planetside, 205 orbiting
- *Tau Ceti f, Fumis*: 0 planetside, 141 orbiting
- *Dwarf Planets*: 0
- *Other*: +/- 10

Description:

The current year is designated 3 AC (After Colonization). Tau Ceti is the home of humanity's second colony and was established after a fifteen year voyage to the system aboard the colony ship Spērō. The colony's planet, designated Tiān, was visited several centuries ago and confirmed to have the natural resources to both sustain human life and establish a colony.

The colony's primary focus is on solidifying and expanding their presence on Tiān and within the star's habitable zone. The planet's single colony has grown substantially since arrival, adding thousands of humans, driven by pre-departure agreements by travelers to focus on population expansion. They've had tremendous success in both their mining and farming operations, which has allowed rapid expansion of population and physical area.

1

BRADLEY OLIVAW
TAU CETI, TIĀN

It was the first of the month, colony requisition day. Bradley found the entire process extremely monotonous. Had Nathan not required his attendance, he'd have sent someone else on. That reminded him, he needed to pick up some coffee beans to bribe Cynthia to attend next month's meeting.

The binary suns of Tau Ceti were both rising in concert this morning, framing the billowy pink clouds in the distance. Tiān's orbit was nearing aphelion around both Tau A and B, an astronomical first in their young colony's history. Their golden sunlight glistened in the dew on the native plants in front of the council building like jewels resting on a velvet canvas.

He reached down and rubbed his fingers over the leaves of the orange and red fronds. The fine fur covering their surface reminded him of his childhood dog, Cheddar. Their thin strands were strong enough to withstand the wind but rubbed off like Cheddar's winter coat.

"Are you killing time again, Olivaw?" Nathan asked walking up behind him. He was the colony's mayor. They'd met early in their careers at the Jovian Academy and worked closely over the past twenty years developing the Tau Ceti colonization plans.

"Guilty as charged," he said with a chuckle. "These meetings are a tad pointless if you ask me. The less I'm there, the more we get done." He stood up and rubbed his hands, struggling to shake the fur loose. The plants were beautiful, but they shed like the dickens.

"Well, they're expecting me, and I'm expecting you," Nathan nodded his head sideways toward the stairs. "The meeting starts in two minutes. I'll see you inside." He turned and made his way up the sea of steps.

He should've hung out around the other side of the building facing the community center. Then he could've held back longer. He reached up and tapped his ear to check his schedule, hoping something more important had come up. It hadn't.

Resigned to losing the morning, he spun around and trudged up to the top of the council building. Fifty-eight steps, one for every year mankind spent planning the colony before departing for Tau Ceti.

The doors slid open as he approached the top, and he nodded at the security detail flanking the chamber entrance. That was weird. It'd been a few months since he'd attended one of these, but they'd never had security before.

As he entered the council chamber, all hell broke loose. The sleek and clean designs of the room would usually set his mind at ease and help him relax, but that was lost over the shouts of disagreement and confusion from down below.

"What the hell," he muttered staring down the funnel-shaped room.

"Like I said, we won't be reviewing inbound personnel or the pending supply requisitions this morning," Nathan began. "Please exit at the rear and check your comms later today for a new date and time for this meeting."

Nathan reached into his pocket and pulled out a strange-looking device Bradley had never seen before. With one hand holding the base, he turned the top clockwise and a set of blue glowing bands lit the device's perimeter. A moment later the lights in the room flickered.

Bradley slowed his descent into the funnel and glanced around. The guards positioned at each exit had stepped inside and were now holding their weapons.

Nathan cleared his throat and addressed the council members who were now standing and raising their arms in disagreement. "Anyone who doesn't have security clearance alpha, please gather your things and head toward the exit so we can continue."

Voices from council members murmured around the room. Their frustration over the divergence from the normally smooth process was apparent.

Nathan continued and calmly addressed everyone. "It's alright, folks. Once we figure out what this is about, we'll reconvene to handle requisitions. Right now though, it's important that unless you have alpha clearance you leave without commotion. We appreciate your patience, and we'll keep everyone in the loop where possible."

Bradley smiled. He finally had an excuse to leave. Nathan was staring directly at him so he nodded in return. "Good luck!" he said as he pivoted to leave.

Nathan reached out and placed a hand on his shoulder, stopping him. "Where are you headed?"

He sighed and turned. "Thankfully I don't have alpha clearance like the rest of my family. It's one of the reasons I refused that Director promotion you tried to force on me." Something was up and he wasn't about to be coaxed into staying.

"Don't you go anywhere. You need to listen to this comm."

He cringed. So close. Maybe he could find an out. "I have

a batch of recruits waiting for their readiness check, and I really should get back before they go off—"

Nathan's grip tightened. Not to hurt, but with concern. "Please, Bradley. I need you here."

"Sure, Mayor. Whatever you need." He turned and headed back to his seat. Reaching up to his ear, he activated his retinal comm to subvocalize a message to his recruits, but it wouldn't send. It had worked outside. Nathan's glowing device must somehow be blocking their comms.

He slid down one of the rows and was about to sit when Nathan waved him over. "Let's move together into the center of the room. It'll be easier."

As he worked his way back to the front of the room, he realized there were only four people left: Nathan, Janine, Tyre, and himself.

Secure comms from Sol weren't a normal occurrence. Something big must be up to interrupt this meeting. Glancing around at the other faces, he could see they were sensing it as well. Janine was staring at the closed door, already guarded from the outside. Her hands were fidgeting with a Taser baton on her belt. Tyre was tapping a rhythm under the table, something Bradley recognized, but he couldn't quite place it.

Nathan sat down, placing the mystery device in the center of the table. He then pressed his forefinger on the top and removed it. A residual drop of blood remained on the surface before a faint puff of smoke expanded and expunged the evidence. That was a new feature. Maybe it was doing a DNA scan in addition to verifying the nanites from Nathan's blood.

"Identity confirmed; Mayor Nathan Clarke," a voice enunciated from the device. "Three additional personnel are present. Please touch the scanner to confirm your identities."

Everyone's eyes focused on the device. "Don't worry," Nathan said. "It doesn't hurt. It's protocol for this level of secure comm."

One by one, they went around the table, pressing their

fingers. "Identity confirmed; Director of Security Janine Cooper. Identity confirmed; Director of Colonization Tyre Baley."

Bradley stared at Nathan, raising his hands up as if to ask, "What do I do?"

Nathan merely nodded his head looking down toward the device.

Still hesitant, he reached forward and gently touched it, as if doing so might somehow change the answer. There was a slight prick of his finger and it was over. That wasn't so bad. It didn't matter though, they'd oust him in a second.

The machine seemed to pause for an eternity analyzing the results, but it was really only as long as the others.

"Identity confirmed; Doctor Bradley Olivaw. All present personnel identified and confirmed with clearance level alpha. One moment while the communication payload is decrypted."

He tilted his head and glanced toward Nathan.

Nathan leaned forward and whispered. "We upgraded your clearance after leaving Sol. Like I said before, I need you here for this."

The room descended into silence except for Tyre's continued musical foot tapping. Quiet, yet tense moments like this reminded him of the annual review process they went through at the Jovian Academy back in Sol. During those examinations he'd become proficient at remaining calm and stoic on the outside, while on the inside he was a mess of doubt and discomfort.

"Thank you all for meeting like this," began a familiar voice. It was his sister Abigail, the President of CoPE. What the hell was this about? "We've enacted the Omega Security Communication Protocol to broadcast emergency information with the CoPE Colony Leadership. On this day, March 15, 2278, at 14:20 Sol Standard Time, CoPE has declared an emergency under the Ring Alliance War Act. Six unknown alien ships have appeared between Jupiter and Mars in the main asteroid belt. Approximately twenty-four hours after their arrival, they advanced through the Inner Ring asteroid defense perimeter and are heading toward Earth. Because of this unforeseen event and the unknown nature of our enemy's technology, we have henceforth cut all imminent colony bound personnel and supply ships. We've also stopped broadcasting all data feeds toward your colony. This is an effort to protect you by doing whatever we can to mask your location. Our goal is also to act with the utmost of caution to manage Sol's resource flow during this critical time."

She paused and stared off into the distance as if she'd heard something. This was a joke, right? Abigail always loved her zingers. She'd pop back on in a second and they'd all have a laugh.

He glanced over at the others. Everyone was staring wide-eyed at the projection, shock on their faces. When he turned his attention back to his sister, it seemed like she'd changed. Her posture had stiffened and she'd regained her composure.

"I know this comes as quite a shock, but rest assured we will take emergency measures to continue colonial aid as often as possible. You're still at the outset of your colonization efforts and I know that the coming days, months, and perhaps even years will be trying. You must have faith in your training and most of all in your people. It's imperative that you not only continue your colonization but your explo-ration efforts, as well. The future of your colony and possibly humanity hangs in the balance."

There was a long pause as she looked down at her desk. Maybe she's done? Her brows drew together as if she were contemplating something. He'd never seen her look so tired and why were her cheeks pink? Had she been crying?

She raised her gaze and stared straight into the camera. "Life is like the Great River. Sometimes it sweeps you gently along, and sometimes the rapids come out of nowhere. May the ocean of stars guide us safely through these rapids to the river's end."

The audio and holographic display cut out, leaving the room in silence. All that remained was the hypnotic blue throbbing light from the center of the table. Everyone remained motionless, staring at it as if in a trance.

He wasn't sure how to react. Abigail was in trouble, Sol was under attack by an unknown alien force, their colony was cut off, and that odd speech at the end about the Great River. It was familiar, but he wasn't sure from where.

2

———

PLANETSIDE

TAU CETI, TIĀN

Nathan's assistant reached forward and paused the comm. When the screen blurred, she let out a screech. The officer wasn't listening to what she was saying, and she was about to lose it. She took a few deep breaths to calm her nerves and resumed the call. "I'm sorry, officer, but as I've said twice already, I cannot interrupt Mayor Clarke. He's in a meeting with the Directors at the colonial council chambers. I can connect you to his message queue if you'd like to record a comm for him."

"You don't understand!" The officer's face reddened and he raised his voice. "This is a matter of colonial security. I'm the officer in command onboard Spērō, and we've had an incident that needs his immediate attention."

"I understand but—"

"You don't! You don't understand at all. Spērō's been compromised. Someone has detached the ship's drive and launched it into Tau Ceti. There has to be a protocol to reach him in situations like this, doesn't there?"

"Y—Yes," she stammered as she checked the Director's status again. Still no connection. "There is a protocol, and we've actually been trying to reach him for several hours. The solar storms are causing comm issues."

"I hate to be blunt, ma'am," the officer said. "But if there were comm issues, would I be talking to you right now?"

Just then she realized what he was saying. He was in orbit and they were communicating without issue. "Frak, you're right. I'm sorry. Can you please tell me your message for the Director? I'll deliver it." She reached forward and pressed a button on the console to summon a security detail.

"It doesn't make sense," he muttered as he rubbed his chin. "Who'd want to destroy the drive? I was only asleep for a few minutes—"

"Officer! You have my attention. Dictate your report and I'll deliver it personally with an escort." She turned and nodded at the security detail arriving behind her.

The officer stared at the assistant and the security detail for a moment before speaking. "Yes... certainly... you're right, I'm sorry ma'am." He paused and then came to attention. "At precisely 14:32 Tau Ceti Standard Time, someone gained access to the navigational computers aboard Spērō. They then locked down all levels, internal hatches, and external airlocks. The crew onboard was a skeletal security detail and most of them were asleep. Anyhow, the emergency klaxons went off and there was an announcement that the ship's drive was being detached. I tried to override the lockdown, but the system kept telling me that my security clearance was denied and that zeta clearance was necessary. All attempts at a manual reboot or even external ship to ship communications failed. Approximately ten minutes later, the computer started the countdown to engage the ship's drive and then it launched toward Tau Ceti. It took me a few minutes to confirm the trajectory, but it was aimed dead center. After the collision, Spērō exited lockdown, and that was when my attempts to reach Director Baley began."

The assistant glanced up from her tablet. Her mouth

opened, but words failed her. The security detail had stepped into the room and were listening to the comm, as well. They were both white knuckled and wide-eyed.

Grabbing the tablet with her notes, she sprung from her chair and sprinted toward the exit, her security escorts in pursuit. She didn't care if they had to blast through the door, Director Baley and the Mayor needed to see this note.

3

BRADLEY OLIVAW
TAU CETI, TIĀN

He and the top leadership of the colony stood patiently in the council chambers. The room that two days earlier was used to deliver a message of isolation and fear, was now waiting on Mayor Clarke to deliver one of hope and camaraderie. This time the audience wouldn't be four people with alpha security clearance; it'd be the nearly 32,000 colonists of Tiān.

They were standing in the center of the expansive room flanking the podium on each side. The holoprojector had been removed, and all that remained was the CoPE crest and the Tiān colonial flag as a backdrop to the event.

Everyone on stage was wearing their day-to-day clothes, which for him was a simple, yet stylized blue jumpsuit. It was easy to clean and you could wear it under an exo-suit or to crawl through machinery, something he did almost daily.

The goal of not dressing up, while not obvious to the audience, was to keep everyone at ease and comfortable. The smallest things could be critical to the success or failure of this speech, and they'd attempted to plan every angle as best they could, leaving nothing to chance.

Media from every news outlet in the colony packed the

first few rows near the stage. Colonists filled the remaining seats and overflowed into the aisles. There were parents with their children, teachers, doctors, politicians, and officers. A cross-section of the entire colony was crammed into the massive chamber. He studied the colonists, eavesdropping in on their conversations as they discussed what they thought was going to be announced. This scene was repeating throughout the colony in every home, office, and public gathering place.

The mayor's speech would break into all media outlets at the same time. Nathan had also sent a colony-wide notification of the event. He requested that everyone tune in, and if people had a location where they communed with neighbors and friends, that they go there to watch.

It was a risky approach, and the result could either be a spectacular success, or a devastating failure. News like this could tear the colony apart. There'd been intense debate about internalizing the news and not telling anyone at all. Sure, it might leak someday, but it could be months or years from now and they could deal with it then, after they were better prepared. Nathan was adamant the colony had to know soon, and it couldn't be from a leak. Without the trust of the people, there was no hope for their future or the future of humanity.

As he glanced around the room, people were joking around trying to figure out what the mayor had called the colony together to say. He overheard them making guesses based upon who they saw on stage. Things like expanding to a new city or the arrival of a new colony ship. He shook his head slightly to not draw attention. They had no idea how far from the truth they were. Overall though, he'd say it was as successful and non-confrontational a lead in as they could have hoped for.

"Audience, check," he muttered to himself.

The clock ticked over to 19:00 hours and the lights in the

room flashed. Everyone quieted down. The doors on the west side opened and Mayor Clarke strode in. He was dressed in a modern, yet understated blue suit without a tie, something that was now trendy. As the crowd applauded his arrival, he smiled and waved toward everyone. Taking his time approaching the stage, he shook hands and chatted with a few random folks. About halfway from the stage, he stopped to pick up a small child and playfully tossed her into the air. Everyone seemed comfortable and it set the tone.

"Entrance, check," he muttered.

The mayor stepped onto the stage and took a moment to shake the hands of Janine and Tyre. Bradley studied the audience's reaction as Nathan was shaking everyone's hand; they seemed confused and began whispering when he finally came to Bradley. His presence was certain to be a much talked about angle in the pundits' theories after tonight's speech.

It felt odd shaking Nathan's hands at an event like this, but he was trying to not show his nerves. They both nodded and smiled at each other. Bradley leaned in and whispered, "Good luck." He thought he caught the briefest glimpse of nervousness in Nathan's eyes, but it disappeared as quickly as it arrived.

Nathan had practiced the speech multiple times in front of a virtual audience, but the real thing was always different. He couldn't imagine the pressure Nathan was feeling right about now. He was glad to be standing on the sidelines rather than in the crosshairs. Every gesture and movement they made was being recorded and would be endlessly analyzed in the coming days. It was important that the speech feel natural and not rehearsed.

His muscles tensed as Mayor Clarke approached the podium. He had to focus on his breathing and relax his shoulders to not draw attention. The Mayor raised his hands one last time to wave and then gestured downward for everyone to sit so they could begin.

The audience settled, all eyes on Nathan.

There was an uncomfortably long pause as Nathan seemed to be gathering his thoughts at the podium. Was he imagining it, or was time slowing? It felt like right before a crash or fall, when time slowed to a crawl and you could sense every movement before it happened. The audience was whispering between each other. They were unsure what was happening.

He wasn't imagining it; Nathan was choking at the most critical moment.

"First, I want to thank everyone for taking the time out of their evenings to come together and listen in. As I stand before you, I can't help but see a strong, happy community and an even stronger colony. One filled with friends and growing families." Nathan gestured toward the child and the people he passed moments earlier.

He swallowed hard, struggling to not look at Janine and Tyre. This wasn't the speech Nathan rehearsed. Was he going to improvise the whole thing? This could go sideways quickly.

Nathan turned and gestured toward the people behind him on stage, as if he were reading Bradley's mind. "One full of amazing scientists and engineers, doctors and teachers, farmers and officers." He nodded toward Bradley as if to say, "I've got this."

Turning back toward the front, Nathan paused for a moment looking over the audience. "Clear leadership and a strong community is something we'll be needing now more than ever. I stand before you today to share a grim message. One that no leader could ever prepare for. One that I sincerely hope doesn't tear us apart."

Nathan stared down at the podium. He was struggling to compose himself.

The audience was so silent and captivated that they could hear a stylus drop. People were shifting in their seats and glancing back and forth at each other, with looks of concern and shock on their face.

Nathan raised his eyes up and across the audience, settling on the central clump of camera drones. "Two days ago, the Sol supply shuttle contained a message from President Olivaw. An alien force of unknown strength entered Sol, broke through the Inner Ring defense perimeter, and advanced toward Earth. As a precaution and to minimize our exposure, CoPE has broken off all communication and future shuttles with the colonies."

Bradley nervously shifted back and forth on his feet. He caught himself and stopped. This didn't feel right at all. Nathan should've stuck to the script. The audience seemed to be collectively holding their breath. A few had even brought their hands up to their mouth in shock. An instinct even he'd fought when he first heard the news.

"As you all know, this shuttle was sent from Sol nearly fourteen years ago. While our first instinct is to come to their aid, the interstellar distances and timeframes involved are insurmountable. Whatever's been done is now out of the realm of our direct influence." He paused again to let that thought soak in before continuing. "We know the people of Sol are strong and resourceful. If there's a way to defeat this alien force, they'll find it."

The mood of the audience was sliding further downhill. Frak, he'd lost them. They're off the rails. Most of the people were crying, some uncontrollably. Nathan had to turn this around, and quickly.

"While we're all rooting for Sol's survival, we must also plan our own. It's imperative, now more than ever, that we come together as a colony, as the future of humanity. We must build our defenses and continue to develop technologies that foster innovation. We must support our children, communities, and industries. Growing across Tiān and Tau Ceti is of the utmost importance. We can no longer depend on supply shuttles that may never arrive."

What Nathan did next was even more unexpected than going off script. He stepped out from behind the podium and down off the stage. Walking past the cameras, he worked his way toward the crowd, stopping just outside the jammed aisles. The people sitting there rose and parted as he approached.

The camera drones repositioned, scrambling to catch a better angle of the Mayor. Nathan reached down and gently took the hand of the woman to his right and the child to his left. They then, as if on cue, reached for their neighbors' hands. This same action cascaded throughout the room, everyone hand in hand with their neighbors until they were all a single intertwined human fabric.

Bradley reached over to hold Janine and Tyre's hand, closing the loop on the stage with nearby onlookers. Their palms were as sweaty as his own. Apparently, everyone's nerves were being frayed.

Nathan continued his speech as he stared at the crowd surrounding him. "These hands represent the bonds and dependency we now have to one another. They represent the closeness of our colony, the strength and support of a community motivated. One driven to not only survive, but to thrive and prosper. To ensure the long-term strength of Tiān and all of humanity."

With that last word, the crowd erupted in cheers and tears. Everyone shook hands and hugged one another. People weren't sure if it was a celebration or a wake, and they didn't care. They weren't only expressing the emotion of potentially lost friends and family; they were expressing the emotions of entire planets and asteroid communities in Sol.

As the commotion continued, Bradley found himself overcome with emotion like the people surrounding him. Everyone had tears in their eyes. Hugs were passed from one stranger to another and others were shaking hands. The conflicting emotions of fear and hope didn't seem appropriate to mix, but the strength of their communal bonds made it work.

After several minutes of this, Nathan returned to the podium and held his head down as if he were praying amongst the chaos. Members of the audience took notice and quietly returned to their seats, putting their heads down as well. He'd somehow managed to subliminally coerce the entire audience from sitting, to holding hands, to tears, and now finally prayer. He was clearly more talented at this than he led on.

Once he'd completed his prayer, Nathan looked up and straight into the cameras. His eyes were piercing and his voice strong. "Make no mistake, fellow colonists. We won't survive these rapids; we will master them and arrive stronger to the battlefield ahead."

With that, the crowd erupted with cheers and chants of "Long Live Tiān!"

At the same time, the media erupted, pelting Mayor Green with questions and demanding details on the message. He took it all in stride and with a strength Bradley hadn't seen before in Nathan. He saw now why his sister had chosen him as the colony's mayor.

"Speech, check!" he muttered to himself, as he applauded alongside the crowd and joined in the chanting. He glanced to his left when he heard a particularly loud whoop from Janine. Both her and Tyre were smiling and cheering with everyone else. The collective stress and concern over the speech had lifted from the group.

HE STEPPED out of the simulator and stopped for a moment to let his body adjust to the change in reality around him. He could watch the cadet's data streams overlaid into his retinal comm, and he took a moment to see if they were taking his advice. While they were getting better at using the reduced gravity to creatively influence their designs, they still weren't trusting the limits built into the automata.

They were wasting precious time.

He tapped his ear and set his comm to broadcast to everyone in the sim. "No no no, stop simulation! Reset event to T minus 120 minutes. If this squad doesn't solve this the next time around, I want all of you back in here practicing tomorrow morning at oh seven hundred hours."

The groans and protests were audible even through the closed simulation doors. "These are ridiculous mission parameters, Brad. There's no way—"

"Enough!" he interrupted. "I don't want to hear your excuses any longer cadet. I'll remind everyone one last time; this is not a contrived simulation. This is the actual start of a situation we faced during the first month of our arrival at Tiān. The space elevator was malfunctioning, we didn't yet have ramjets, and we hadn't extracted enough propellant to use chemical rocket jump ships to get supplies to the colonists. Now start again and stop thinking like you're in an Earth gravity well."

Most of this batch of cadets came from humanity's home planet and he could tell. Their structures were rigid, they had no creativity in method, and they were constantly triple checking their systems rather than trusting their programming. Generations of political mistrust in computers and technology were leaving them behind. It was no wonder the Outer Ring was kicking their ass in technology and science.

He shook his head. Even he had to watch himself and work to retrain his thoughts. There was no Inner and Outer Ring here. There was only Tau Ceti, and it was up to him to help shape this class into the best possible colonists.

"Don't you think you're being a bit harsh, Bradley?" Tyre asked.

He'd seen Tyre walking toward him but kinda hoped he'd keep going. "No I don't, Director Baley. There were lives in the balance down on the surface in this simulation. Someone needs to crack these cadets Earthly mold before it kills us all. It might as well be me."

Tyre raised his hands in submission. "I agree. They have a lot to learn. But I'm sure you remember how this played out. You were the one who got us through the crisis on that day."

He gestured to wipe the cadet's streams from his comm. He couldn't watch it anymore. Instead, he focused on Tyre. "I remember the event vividly, sir. I'm sure I don't need to remind you that other people were close to solving the problem; I merely helped connect some dots faster. No one in this squad is even remotely close."

Tyre made a lopsided smile and chuckled. "Let's agree to disagree on this one. Your faith in your peers, especially when they've hit rock bottom, is one of your best leadership qualities. But this wasn't why I stopped to talk. I need your help on a project we're spinning up."

"Sure boss. What's the project?"

"Actually, I'm headed into a meeting on it now. Mind coming along?"

The training session wasn't over, but these cadets needed some latitude to learn and fail on their own. He reached up to his ear and paused the simulation, opening a comm to everyone inside. "You're all on your own until the end of this sim. If you fail, you're welcome to try again. Whichever attempt is your last, I'll watch it later and grade you according to your results. Good luck!"

He cut the comm and turned to face Tyre. "I've got a few hours before I need to check on the hydroponics fabrication progress. Where's this meeting?"

"Let's walk." Tyre turned and headed toward the lift tube.

He did a small skip jog to catch up. When he entered the lift tube, he instructed the system to follow Tyre. They'd dropped below ground level, so they must be headed to the transport tunnels.

The lift exited under the dome into a large transport terminal where the tubes encircling the colony interconnected. If you didn't travel above ground on the maglev, you usually took these faster below ground tubes to get around. Most of the infrastructure was over-engineered for colony growth, something they'd be thankful for at some point.

They stepped into one of the two seated personal cars, sat back, and the seats automatically adjusted to their weight and body shape. As the car accelerated, he glanced over to Tyre. "So, are you going to tell me what this meeting's about?"

"In due time, Bradley, in due time." Tyre was smiling.

"Perrrrfeeect." He was too nervous to not talk; unknowns freaked him out. "How about that speech yesterday? Nathan knocked it out, didn't he? I can't imagine going off script like that, especially after all that prep."

"Sometimes it doesn't feel right. No matter how much you try, the words feel forced. I'm sure he wouldn't have taken the risk if he didn't know what he was doing. You must get gut feelings like that?"

He nodded. "Of course. But it's one thing to have a gut feeling about a cadet or fabricator. It's quite another to stand in front of tens of thousands of people and improvise the delivery of news that changes the course of humanity."

"Point taken, but it's like any muscle. The more you use it, the more you trust it, the easier it gets. President Olivaw wouldn't have nominated him to become the colony's mayor if he hadn't exhibited some talent to lead and inspire."

The mention of Abigail brought with it a flood of emotions and memories of her speech the other day. He'd been struggling to uncover its meaning. Why was she so distracted? And then something changed in her before she went on a tangent and started talking about a river. What was that about? It could have been nothing, but something was off, he knew it. He reached down and brushed the stone in his pocket.

"We're here," Tyre said.

He hadn't even realized they'd stopped. That's odd. The station was eerily silent when they climbed out of the car. Silence was an unusual sensation to encounter in a tube station that was usually bustling with activity, especially nowadays with the colony in overdrive.

He touched his ear and subvocalized a command to bring up a map. Tyre had taken them all the way out to ring fourteen. It was a new ring and dome along the perimeter of the colony and was still under construction. The build projections were showing the ring wouldn't be habitable for another six months. He could have sworn it was half that a few weeks ago when he'd visited here to work on construction automata. "What are we doing in fourteen?"

"All of your questions will be answered shortly. Just give me another minute."

Stepping away from the departing car, they entered the lift and shot up to the top floor of the dome. In what was usually the communal dining area of most domes was instead a command-and-control center, or at least what looked like one.

He paused as he stepped from the lift tube. In the center of the expansive space was what appeared to be a three-dimensional holographic projection showing the state of everything in the colony. Every building, person, robot, transport, etc. Nothing that most colonists couldn't access if they wanted, but still impressive at this scale.

As he spun around the domed common room, taking in the space and studying how they'd transformed it. There was an active chatter of voices and a life to the room. Nothing like the lively dining hall atmosphere customary to this place, but the pulse was still there. There were multiple temporary projection walls, almost like officer stations around a battle room. They were positioned around the perimeter and each one was clearly marked along the top. The labels read Communications, Transportation, Health & Safety, Food, Environment, Mining, Fabrication and several that ominously read Defense and Contingency.

"Well, this wasn't here a few weeks ago," he said glancing back and forth around the control room. "You guys have been busy."

Tyre walked them around to the far side of the ring of projection walls, all with officers busily working. As Bradley came around the last wall he paused on seeing both Nathan and Janine. They were talking in front of the wall marked Health & Safety.

"Hey, Bradley!" Nathan reached forward and shook his hand. "Welcome. I assume Tyre already filled you in?"

He chuckled and shook his head. "No, let's not assume that."

Nathan peered over at Tyre and smirked before returning his attention to Bradley. "Classic snatch and grab, aye?"

"Something like that."

"That's two times in as many days we've caught you off guard. Are you getting enough sleep?" Nathan patted his shoulder. He searched around for his assistant who scrambled when they made eye contact. "Let's get Bradley some coffee. Actually, unless I'm mistaken, I'm sure we could all use some."

There were nods of agreement all around, and his assistant disappeared out the side entrance.

"Alright, officer. It looks like we're all here. Let's start with Health & Safety, shall we?" Nathan asked.

Bradley guessed he'd wing it. Apparently, no one was going to tell him what the heck was going on. The less he knew, the less he was ultimately responsible for. Sometimes it's better to be a cog in the machine rather than sitting in the pilot seat.

"Yes, Mayor Clarke," the officer began. "There are no reports of AWOL officers, community uprisings, or mobilizations. The message delivery was managed without incident, except for a few hospital visits because of heart and panic attacks."

"Heart attacks?" Tyre asked. "Why didn't the person's body & blood nanites take care of that?"

The officer brought their hand to their mouth and cleared their throat. "Both incidents came from members of the anti-nanite contingent. They're rare but vocal... well, they were. Those were two of their three leaders. The third showed up to a clinic this morning for his first nanite injection treatment."

"Well, that's one less conspiracy contingent to worry about," Janine said. "Please continue."

"Yes, Director Cooper," the officer said. "Our stores of medical supplies are stable. They were refreshed by the recent Sol supply shuttle. We've been working with Bradley to increase the fabrication of some rarer medicines, but ran into issues."

Everyone turned toward him.

"I guess that's my cue." He took a deep breath. He was ill prepared for this, but gestured to take control of the display from the officer and brought up the chemical schematics of the rarer medicines. "Our primary problem is that most of these medicines are grown or fabricated. We don't have the necessary source materials to grow them, so we're left to fabricate. To do that, we need more medical grade printers. That's why we've commandeered the specialized nanites that weren't mission critical and put them to work on building more nanometer scale components for these printers. There are other issues after we get past this one, but one step at a time."

"Fabricating fabricators." Nathan shook his head. "There's a joke in there somewhere."

Everyone chuckled, which seemed to be a cue to Nathan's assistant to show up with the coffee. They'd guessed everyone's preferences to a tee, and after handing them out disappeared to wherever they were hanging out in the shadows.

"So what are we doing about source materials?" Tyre asked.

He and the presenting officer began speaking at once until the officer gestured toward him to continue. "Well, again we're short on collection and recon automata. They weren't as high a priority with the supply run refreshes coming in from Sol. Once we're able to fabricate more, we believe we can both scout for and collect most source materials locally. The early mineralogical scans from a few decades ago showed several large pockets a hundred clicks away. We can recycle the rarer ones until we can mine these native sources."

As he was talking, the officer at that wall had been leading them through visuals following what was being said. These included projections for when they'd be able to meet fabrication demand.

"Is this right?" Janine asked pointing at the wall. "We're not projecting to meet the demand for another year?"

He turned to study the data; he wasn't sure. "I've not done any formal projections Janine, I mean Director. This is the first I'm seeing this."

The officer at the wall jumped in. "They're correct, Director Cooper. This is as of moments ago from our current fabrication rate and prioritization. At the moment, this effort is being impacted by Defense and Contingency planning."

"Well, that's our cue to talk about them then. Thank you, officer," Nathan said.

They all walked over to the next set of command walls.

He wasn't sure what to expect approaching this wall. He'd never been involved in defense planning outside of colony security measures for crowd control. Building a military wasn't something they'd planned to tackle for several decades in Tau Ceti. He thought they'd left the military industrial complex in Sol.

"Alright everyone," Nathan began. "We're new at this, but as you already know, we have what we believe is the impending arrival of an unknown alien force. We'd like to put up a decent fight if we're forced to. Ok officer, what have you come up with?"

The officer was at attention with her hands behind her back. "Thank you, Mayor Clarke. We've been digging into the archive of military schematics we—"

He shook his head. "Wait! Did I hear you right? Did we bring an armament catalog with us from Sol, Nathan? You're not serious are you?"

Nathan turned to face him. "No, we didn't, though I kinda wish we had. That and some Outer Ring defensive armaments would be nice right about now. These schematics were included in the data payload beamed with your sister's message from Sol."

People rarely referred to her as his sister. It wasn't a surprise to anyone, but it was more common to refer to her as president. Why in the hell hadn't she talked normally? Why the code and mysterious ending in that message? It was like they were kids playing one of their camping games under the stars, telling stories, and trying to confuse each other. Was that it...

"What do you think, Bradley?" Janine asked.

He'd totally missed everything the officer had said. Glancing at the screen, he quickly tried to deduce what they were attempting. They couldn't be serious? The colony didn't have the resources to build a battlecruiser in orbit. What were they thinking? And why the frak would they send battlecruiser plans? Sol knew they didn't have these capabilities yet.

"Sorry Director, I was taking it all in," he said.

"And?"

"It'll fail, and more importantly, it's a waste of resources and manpower at a critical juncture in the colony's stabilization."

Nathan glanced between the presenting officer, Janine, and then back to Bradley. "Do you have a better suggestion? We're not going to sit here and do nothing and let the aliens waltz in and take us out without a fight. If you're taking the pacifist route, then the door's over there." He pointed toward the far side of the room.

His back tensed up and he stared at the ground. He hated it when people jumped to conclusions with his statements. "I didn't say I'd do nothing, Nathan! And don't you stand there and insult my allegiance to the colony or humanity. My family has done more for colonization than nearly everyone in Tau Ceti combined." He was pointing at Nathan by the time he finished talking.

You could hear a pin drop in the dome. Every officer present had left their post and was staring at the group. They'd never heard anyone talk to the Mayor like that.

"You want to know what I'd do, Nathan? I'd realize that Sol knows we don't have the capabilities to build anything in this data payload. This was one hundred percent a diversion in case the message was intercepted." He paused for effect and to make sure they were following. Seeing nods from both Janine and Nathan gave him hope that maybe he wouldn't be escorted away in handcuffs.

He walked over to the central holo-display and gestured to take control. "First, we walk before we run. I'd start with fabricating some rail gun armaments to build a defensive perimeter around Tiān here, here, and maybe here." He was highlighting a Lagrange point around Tiān and locations on both of the planet's moons.

"That should hopefully give us some basic form of

defense. It might be old school but it's a start. After that's established, I'd build out some early warning systems. We wouldn't know for quite a while if aliens entered Tau Ceti right now. We need active scanning and covert visual monitoring throughout the system. Something that took centuries to build in Sol, we need yesterday."

He hadn't noticed it, but everyone in the room was now crowded around the holo-display. It reminded him of lecturing to his cadets. This could be going well or a complete disaster. Might as well keep riffing with it.

"And then I'd play dead," he said.

Nathan shook his head and raised his hand forward. "You'd do what? I thought—"

"Hold on, give me a second. Well, maybe playing dead isn't the right analogy. How about hide and never seek?" He gestured and zoomed into one of the asteroid groupings near the second of two gas giants in Tau Ceti. It was a Trojan grouping, one that led the gas giant through space because of its immense gravitational forces.

He continued. "We need to find a well sized Trojan planetesimal out near Tau Ceti e. It has to have a crazy dense crust and ample raw materials. Then I'd build the mother of all bunkers."

"Why a bunker?" an officer asked.

"I can only assume the meaning of that…" he pointed at the wall marked Contingency. "Is to plan for the worst-case contingency scenario in a last-ditch effort to prevent humanity's extinction. We'd move most of our cryo-pods from the colony ship to that bunker, and as many supplies as we can spare. Enough to give whoever hunkers down there a chance, however minor, to survive and return to Tiān at some later point."

Everyone was staring at the holo-display and his amateur riffing on how he'd defend and save the colony and humanity. There were murmurs between many of them as they began to nod and whisper.

A smile spread across Nathan's face as he slowly paced around the holo-display, studying the crude plan Bradley had created.

Bradley's retinal comm alerted him to a short-beam message being sent from Tyre. He accepted it and was greeted with a hushed message from across the room.

"Twenty minutes ago, you were telling me you couldn't improvise the delivery of an important message that could change the course of humanity. You realize what you just did, right?"

He glanced toward Tyre, he was making a pumping fist gesture in the air. He'd nailed it, apparently. Maybe he wouldn't be sleeping in the brig after all.

4

____

BRADLEY OLIVAW
TAU CETI, TIĀN

His head jerked off the table. The water was everywhere and it burned. Wait… no. The haze and vividness of the dream lingered but the fogginess of his mind was clearing. He'd been drowning in boiling water. When he reached up, his face was still warm to the touch.

He wasn't underwater. No, he'd fallen asleep working in his lab last night. The holographic planisphere threw off some serious heat, and he was soaked in sweat. There was a nice watery outline on his desk where he'd been resting. He rubbed his eyes and ran his hand down his face. That must have triggered the dream.

Lifting his arms over his head to stretch, he retched at his own stench. He desperately needed caffeine for his pounding head and a shower for his stink. When he stood up, his back ached and knotted muscles screamed at him from the contorted posture he'd held for hours.

He reached down and grabbed his toes and held the position. A little movement should help. His muscles were tense but soon gave way and started to unknot.

After a few minutes of stretching, he stood back up and

twisted around, glimpsing the planisphere. Usually he used it for mission planning, orbital trajectories, or exploring planetary mission data. For the last week, however, he'd been using it in a fruitless attempt to scratch a nagging itch.

He'd spent every free evening wracking his brain on this problem and was getting nowhere. No matter how hard he tried, he couldn't put a finger on what she was saying. She was always a fan of layered meaning and hidden messages, he just wasn't sure what this one was saying.

He'd been using the planisphere, trying to shake loose some old childhood stories hoping it would shine some light on her speech.

Some of his fondest memories were of his childhood and camping under the stars with his family in North Carolina. They'd setup one of his father's telescopes and stay up late peering through it. They had fun making up their own stories about the constellations and wild adventures they'd undertake exploring them someday. Abigail loved speaking like ancient people who assigned names to stars to honor gods, aid in traveling, and explain things they didn't understand.

The most esoteric and out-of-place phrase that gnawed at him from his sister's speech was:

Life is like the Great River. Sometimes it sweeps you gently along, and sometimes the rapids come out of nowhere. May the ocean of stars guide us safely through these rapids to the river's end.

The passage was familiar. He recognized it from one of their family adventures, but he couldn't quite place it.

Shaking off the image, as he had countless times before, he had to focus on more immediate problems like his pounding headache and his smell.

He shuffled out of his lab and secured the door behind him. As he worked his way through a maze of halls toward the locker room, he passed lab after lab bustling with activity and discussion. So many things had changed in the last week on Tiān.

Soon after the initial shock of the announcement wore off, the colony changed. People stopped complaining about previously petty things such as working extra hours or in hard environments. They stopped acting entitled and instead put their collective heads together working toward the common good.

People were coming up with creative new solutions to supply deficiencies and energy constraints. From how to manufacture products with less waste to miniaturizing things using fewer materials. Another interesting change was the re-evaluation of why robots weren't leveraged for more of the tasks that humans had previously fought to perform. Things like final inspection spacewalks that a few weeks ago were a rite of passage and an adrenaline rush were now seen as an unwarranted risk. Jobs and habits inherited from a bygone era of space exploration and human expansion were suddenly being questioned.

It'd only been a week since their isolation, as some people were calling it, but things were... different. It was amazing what became possible when you were forced to adapt to a new normal. Previous stagnation and lack of innovation needed a fresh perspective or, in this case, a forced adaptation response.

Walking into the locker room, he stopped when he saw his disheveled appearance in the mirror. He reflected back to his time at the academy and during the colonization planning. Back when everything was meant to be. When he was on top of things and his life was moving forward. Heck, he even showered regularly back then.

Now... everything was chaotic. He couldn't remember

when he'd showered last. His lab was a mess, and like his appearance, he wasn't in control of anything. He was drowning. While everyone around him was rising to the challenge, he seemed to be spiraling out of control.

He didn't recognize the face staring back at him in the mirror. "Baby steps," he muttered as he undressed and placed his clothes into the laundry tube. Grabbing the misting sprayer, he doused himself with the water soap mixture and made sure to completely cover his body and hair. Finally, he put his earplugs in and stepped into the ultrasonic shower.

He rotated and lifted his arms, taking cues from the androgynous wall display. The sonic vibrations worked the dead cells and dirt from his skin and slowly his smell returned to publicly acceptable levels. As he let the shower wash the sweat and grime from every part of his body, he thought about the colony he'd helped create.

The sprawling heights, density, and lack of community common on Earth were the same problems they hoped to address on Tiān. They designed the colonies with simplicity and a strong community in mind. The concentric rings and spacious domes intertwining recreational, business, and residential areas allowed for a comfortable and sustainable lifestyle.

Each of the domes was a microcolony unto itself. They depended on the farms for food, and engineering for core goods, but were able to handle everything else themselves. Their power came from solar elements embedded in the external surface of the domes, through geothermal vents, and in extreme situations from wind power. Water came from aquifers deep in the planet's crust and each dome had its own pumping units. The goal was to have as few single points of failure as possible, something the early Sol space colonies learned and most populated cities on Earth were still battling to this day.

He finished up in the shower and stepped out refreshed, hungry, and ready to take on the day. There was a clean change of clothes waiting for him in the laundry tube, and after he put it on he headed toward the cafeteria. "Baby steps," he muttered.

He weaved his way through the halls of the dome and his mind wandered back to the message from his sister. He couldn't imagine what she must be going through, what Sol must be going through. As president, she was sure to have some secrets up her sleeve, but a Sol wide defense system wasn't likely to be one of them. Sure, all the planets had nukes but an alien armada, that was certain to have something a wee bit more powerful.

His last conversation with Abigail had been a fight, the final blowout. She'd blocked him out of the family business, and the week before he left she attacked him for having second thoughts about leaving. She claimed he couldn't hack it, said they couldn't afford a know-it-all or coward when lives were on the line. That was nearly two centuries ago. He'd proved her wrong, he usually did. She'd...

Shaking away the bad thoughts, his mind switched to his brother. They also hadn't spoken in over a century but theirs was about distance, not insane family delusions. Zachary had left for Epsilon Eridani before Bradley had left for Tau Ceti. The two colonies were nearly five and a half light years apart, so catching up wasn't as simple as tight beaming a comm. He'd sent one after their arrival, but it was still en route to the colony. Their relationship was filled with brotherly one-ups and goofy antics, at least when they weren't bickering about trivialities. Bradley had always been the chatty in-your-face one but Abigail was a close second. Right about now he could use to see either of their faces.

As he approached the cafeteria, his melancholy lifted, and the skip returned to his step. The energy of the space was palpable. The smells of food wafted through the open space perfectly framing the noise and vibrant colors of Tiān in the background. It was an explosion of humanity. Crossing from the threshold of the clean and sterile engineering labs and into the cafeteria was comparable to crossing from a hospital birthing room into a waiting room full of family and friends. That unbounded happiness when you told them it was a girl, or a boy was the standard greeting when people entered the cafeteria. You were leaving behind your messy life-transforming projects and returning to the people you were doing it all for, your friends and family.

His mates were in their usual place near the far window and they were waving him over. He grabbed an egg casserole and a healthy mug of coffee before he weaved his way to their table. Setting down his tray, they welcomed him with a cacophony of high fives, hugs, and fist bumps. Most everyone here had met at the academy, but a few joined their colonial family after the isolation.

"Hey, Bradley! How've you been? It's been days. You camping out in your lab again?" Dwight asked. As a biochemist, he was no stranger to long periods of lab time isolation.

"Guilty as charged. I'm struggling with those nano fabricators still. Their structures are fusing together under electrical current. It's maddening." He hated not being entirely honest. He wasn't up to facing their ridicule over his late-night research. "What about you, still eating the mush I see?" He gestured toward the bowl of colorless porridge in front of Dwight.

Dwight poked numbly at his bowl with his spoon. "We're still working on the smells. They break down after a few minutes, but it's nearly perfect nutritionally. There are a few small side effects left to be worked on, but otherwise, it's getting there."

"Side effects? I don't even want to know." He smirked

and glanced around the room. He couldn't help but think back a few months. To some, the isolation was an end, a final act for mankind. To him, it was a reawakening, a reigniting of mankind's drive to explore and learn. If you put a large number of passionate and smart people on a distant planet and cut them off from the outside, you're bound to witness something great form. That or absolute chaos. He chuckled as he watched Dwight choke down his breakfast.

Cynthia, never being one to ease into anything, let alone a personal question, jumped right in. "Have you made any moves on Janine yet?"

He glanced across the table and caught her blush and then smile mischievously at him. Her dark hair and cinnamon complexion glowed in the dome's sunlight. He couldn't help but wonder her motives in asking.

Cynthia was a hydroponics engineer who constantly fought with Dwight about nature's intended use for plants and animals. She relentlessly jabbed him over man's failed attempts at artificial replacements.

She knew he was interested in Janine but the time was never right. He was nervous she wouldn't reciprocate.

"I can't say the opportunity's presented itself between the fabricators, training recruits, and readiness checks," he said toying with his food. He had to change the topic. "When's the next field trip to The Edge? I could use to get away for a few hours."

The Edge was a favorite recreational spot a few clicks from the colony where the world seemed to fall off and end. It'd formed millions of years ago when the plate tectonics of the area caused one plate to drop straight down for thousands of feet creating a vertically sheer cliff for kilometers. The attraction wasn't only to the drop; it was the horizon. When the Tau Ceti suns set near where The Edge met the horizon, it made for a spectacular visual show of shadows and colors.

Cynthia yipped in excitement. "Oh yes, I'm in! I'll bring the drinks. How about tonight?"

The chorus of voices agreed enthusiastically.

"It's settled then," he said sharing a reminder with everyone. "Let's meet near the south entrance at around 19:00. That should give us plenty of time to get out there and toss a few back before the show."

As if on cue his comm buzzed, it was Tyre. Reaching up to his ear he activated it. "Bradley here, what's up, Tyre?"

"I need your help with something."

He closed his eyes and sighed. Last time Tyre came calling like that, he ended up getting yanked into that secret meeting out at ring fourteen. He was never going to make progress on his other work at this rate. "Sure thing, boss. Where do you need me?"

Tyre lowered his tone as if someone could eavesdrop in his ear. "At the L1 orbital transport hub. Can you get up here ASAP?"

"Yea… sure. Is everything alright?"

"We'll talk more when you arrive. And Bradley, not a word to anyone about this, ok?"

"Affirmative. I haven't been topside in a while, this ought to be fun. I should be there in a few hours."

He cut the comm. What was so secretive about going topside? He couldn't understand why anyone would care where he was headed, but orders were orders. He'd have to eat quickly and head to the space elevator if he had any hope of getting back in time for the evening festivities.

He snarfed down his breakfast in a few bites while his friends laughed at his feat. "Sorry," he said between bites. "I hate to eat and run but duty calls."

After he stuffed his face with the last morsel of his casserole he stood to leave and reached for a piece of fruit on Cynthia's plate. She slapped him back playfully. "Get your own! I've been waiting a week for this berry crop."

He shot her his patented smile pout, but she didn't budge, so he shrugged and turned to leave.

She relented with a sigh. "Oh ok, but only a few." She handed him a handful of berries, and he leaned in to thank her with a quick hug. Her body melted into him, lingering a bit too long. When he pulled away, she smiled coyly toward him. After bidding everyone else a farewell and reaffirming their evening plans, he headed to the exit.

The cafeteria was always located in the middle, at the apex of each dome. The only thing more central was the staircase circling down the center through all the aboveground and subterranean floors. The cafeteria and staircase gave people amazing circular views of the entire colony and allowed sunlight to spill into the lower levels.

As he spiraled down the seven floors of translucent metallic glass stairs, his mind drifted to the other colonies. The initial waves of colony ships were planned to spread within fifty light years of Earth. The target of the first waves were G type stars with Earth-like planets. While they'd debated over other star types with liquid water, it was eventually agreed that G type would be the best bet for initial success.

When he reached the ground level, he paused to gaze upward. Clouds passed high above the large hexagon window directly over the apex of the dome. Each of the stair treads protruded outward from within the nearly seamless cylindrical surface of the stairway walls. They rose skyward from the three levels below ground and continued seven more above. The effect combined with the sky above gave a celestial aura to the space. People were constantly stopping to take it all in, and at times they'd lie on their backs to stare upward.

"Shit," he muttered as his retinal comm chimed. He only had fifteen minutes to make the morning space lift. As he turned down the south hall, he leaned forward and began to jog. The transport hub was only a few domes over. There was a direct maglev route through engineering, but it was used primarily to transport raw minerals from space. The minerals that jetted overhead were destined for engineering and other manufacturing domes for further refinement, fabrication, and experimentation purposes.

He'd have to double time it to reach the elevator before it departed. Tyre wouldn't be happy if he missed it. Whatever he'd summoned him for must be important.

Exiting the dome, he hit a rhythm jogging down the radial arm of the colony to its southern edge. It was a beautiful and comfortable morning with light wispy clouds passing overhead. When he glanced skyward, his destination bisected the view ahead, the space elevator.

It was a simple-looking structure that consisted of six independent carbon nanotube cables. The cables could be used in pairs or combined with others to ferry larger freight to and from orbit. They reached skyward from an inverted dome-like structure, or bowl as people called it. It ended at the orbital L1 transport hub. The climber, or ferry, depending on who you asked, ascended and descended the cables using a combination of power fed through the cables, lasers, and good old-fashioned gravity.

The cables reminded him of a spider's thread. Not only were they indiscernible from the background sky at times, but their fragile appearance gave them a feeling like a strong gust of wind would topple them. It wasn't until you approached the structure, that the sheer size of the ferries and the freight they transported became apparent. Much like spider silk was stronger and more ductile than steel, these nanotubes were sturdier than they appeared.

He arrived at the bowl and headed straight for the security checkpoint. If he was lucky, passing through would be as easy as his other recent checks. He'd been helping Janine and Nathan on several colony projects and was surprised at the level of access they'd granted him with alpha security clearance. His security wait time went from minutes to mere seconds nowadays.

As he approached the checkpoint, he did a double take. The line was way longer than usual. It didn't seem to be moving, and for some reason several people were having animated conversations with the gate staff. Their arms were flailing toward the guards flanking the door but they weren't even flinching.

He kept his head down and guiltily walked to the head of the line. He then placed his fingers against the security sensors beside the door marked *Authorized Personnel Only*. There was a brief pause and everything went green. The security guards shifted from their usual stiff disregard and gave him a nod.

"How the hell is he allowed through?" one of the people shouted. A murmur of agreement cascaded down the line of waiting colonists.

Bradley pushed open the doorway into the bowl's terminal and hurriedly walked inside. It felt weird skipping to the head of the line. He'd worked hard for what he'd accomplished and never wanted special treatment or the watchful eyes that came with it. It was what he hated most about being an Olivaw.

According to the departure schedule inside the door, the next ferry was leaving from terminal six. He'd made good time getting there, and with his new clearance he had time to spare. The terminal was strangely vacant except for security. It was strange seeing them inside near the elevator. They usually remained in position outside the entrance.

The terminal was a minimal space with seating for several dozen. Its windows were along the inside of the bowl and had seating configured to observe the actions within. Most people sat silently, mesmerized by the orchestrated flow of mining ferries. Each arriving ferry would detach from the descent cables and reattach to the neighboring maglev line only to accelerate into the distance heading towards nearby domes for refining. This was usually closely followed by a departing ferry that reversed the same process climbing skyward.

There were manned ferries arriving and departing from Tiān four times per day. These were usually full of crew members, pilots changing shifts, or people heading off on missions within the Tau Ceti star system. When a ferry was preparing to depart, the terminal was usually bustling with activity. This morning, however, the terminal was eerily silent.

He walked up to the boarding door. There were two guards standing like statues positioned on either side of the ferry entrance. "Good morning." He nodded toward them.

The guards were silent and resolute in their duties. He placed his fingers on the security scanner and after the customary pause, it glowed confidently green. The ferry's boarding door silently slid aside, welcoming him inside. The guards each made eye contact and nodded at him.

Walking through the boarding door, he continued down a featureless tube and then stepped inside the ferry. Its design was like everything else on Tiān, simple and functional. The cylindrical ferry was divided into eight circular levels with the boarding tube penetrating it at its base. Each level wrapped around the cable used to climb into orbit, giving passengers a full 360-degree view of the world they were arriving or departing from.

He glanced around. It appeared he was the first person aboard. Where the ferry was usually a hum of conversations, the eerie silence of the terminal seemed to have overtaken it. He worked his way around the perimeter and found a seat opposite the boarding door and sat down. The chairs engulfed his body in a gel-like padding when he leaned back into them. They were specifically designed to absorb the effects of the planetary acceleration and often induced sleep in weary passengers with their cradling comfort.

An automated announcement interrupted the silence of the ferry. "All passengers are now aboard. Please prepare for departure in sixty seconds."

That couldn't be right. Why was he the only person aboard? There were so many people in line outside the terminal. Certainly, some of them should have boarded as well. Something must be wrong at the orbital transport hub to shut down all outbound personnel ferries.

With little to go on, he could only lean back and enjoy the trip. His mind was so preoccupied playing through the problems he might encounter that he hardly noticed the ferry slide out, grasp the cable, and launch skyward.

The only sensation he felt was the chair countering the G-forces. Millions of microcontacts actuated to both support and cushion his body. The contacts were like tiny masseuses working the stress from his muscles. He swore he could sense his nanites communicate with the chair, struggling to make his body comfortable from the inside. The crick in his neck was all that remained from the prior evening's fitful sleep and that melted away within seconds of their departure.

Despite his mind manically jumping through the possible situations he'd encounter in orbit, he dozed off.

BRADLEY ROSE out of his slumberous nap in a fog, and it took a moment before he noticed he was still on the ferry approaching orbit. He must have dozed off during the ascent.

A yawn crept out as he attempted to stretch, but the chair pressed him into place. He was far more tired than he'd realized. All the fitful nights of sleep in his office were taking a toll.

"We're finalizing our approach to the L1 orbital platform.

Please stay seated during the deceleration and detachment," came the announcement overhead. The chair constricted slightly as the ferry decelerated toward the station.

Out his window, Tiān was below and the L1 platform above. He marveled at the engineering of space elevators. Their simplicity and elegance made the years of rocket-propelled launches seem barbaric and misguided. Every lesson mankind had learned was costly and excessive. Hindsight was twenty-twenty he supposed, and besides, you needed a rocket to get into space to lower the elevator… chicken and egg.

He sat upright and stared out the window toward the orbital platform. Something was amiss. The regular bustle and constant flow of shuttles and elevators was practically nonexistent. Instead, the platform sat silently perched atop its needle-like threads of life, each quietly cascading toward Tiān.

The potential causes of the problem burst through his mind. Nothing short of a catastrophic loss of gravity, power, or worse could have caused a complete shutdown in traffic flow to the colony. Tyre should have properly warned him ahead of time, he would've gathered some tools and supplies to repair whatever was wrong.

His comm buzzed in his ear. Reaching up, he accepted the call; it was Tyre. "Once you detach and finish taxiing to your terminal, head over and meet me at gate C7."

"I wish you'd warned me you were experiencing problems up here," he said, rapping his knuckles against the window. "I could've helped remotely diagnose from below, plus I'd have brought tools and equipment suitable to the task."

"Hold your rocket. There's nothing wrong with the station. Just head over to C7 and we'll discuss more. Until then, maintain comm silence." Tyre cut the comm.

It was difficult to discern which gate was C7 studying the

station from below. He worked his way visually around the circumference of the station starting at the top which was torus A. The first gate that was polar aligned was A1, so he visually walked down to roughly the third torus, and around to the seven o'clock position. There, docked at C7 was a single lone mining shuttle. At least the age and size of it resembled a mining shuttle.

As his elevator detached and worked its way toward A7, his mind was spinning with conjecture and theories about the nature of the problem, each more elaborate than the next. "Cut it out," he muttered to himself. "This is crazy and getting nowhere."

The ferry docked without a sound, and he felt his ears pop as the pressure inside equalized with the station. When the exit lights went green, and the doors opened, he leapt from his seat before the automated voice even told passengers they could disembark. The seamlessness of the artificial gravity would usually have caused him to ruminate about the science and engineering involved in making it work, but this time he barely noticed. He had other things on his mind as he jogged through the eerily empty terminals toward the lifts.

Arriving at torus C, an armed squad of guards greeted him. His arrival had put them on edge. "Stop and identify yourself," they called out. Their stun pistols were raised and directed at him.

"At ease, Sergeant!" Tyre said walking out of a nearby office. "We've been expecting Mr. Olivaw. Now put down your pistols and go back to guarding the shadows!"

The guards having put a face to his name shifted back into their neutral defensive posture staring into the distance.

Tyre walked forward and reached out to shake his hand. "Sorry about that, mate. I told Janine we didn't need her people to handle this, but you know her, she insisted. We're the only ones aboard the station right now. Everyone else was evacuated early this morning and no one can board. I don't know what they think they're protecting us from."

"Forget them," he said. He didn't care about the guards, they were doing their job. "What's up with the Sol relic you've got docked outside?"

Tyre eyed the guards and then put his arm on Bradley's shoulder, gently guiding him toward the gate. "That's what I brought you up here to figure out. We detected it a few days ago as it entered the Tau Ceti system. Our visual warning systems in the Oort Cloud recognized its thrust signature on entry. It was reversing direction and decelerating."

They both walked up to the gate and Tyre placed his fingers on the security console to authorize their access. There wasn't a faint blue puff of smoke like in Abigail's briefing, but otherwise, it was nearly the same. He shook off lingering memories of the speech. He had to focus on the problem at hand.

Outside the windows at C7 he got a much better view of the shuttle. It was docked to the station from its aft end and was battered and charred from something, a planetary reentry perhaps. Its external identification markings were freshly painted over and out of place compared to the rest of the shuttle's aged exterior. There weren't any other markings that indicated prior mining operation, but CoPE used this hull design to haul massive ore shipments between planets. It also had the markings of both CoPE and Tau Ceti freshly painted on its bow and stern.

"I don't understand," he began. "Where was it returning from? Why would a Sol mining shuttle be out near our Oort cloud? This class of ship isn't typically equipped with a subluminal drive. I wonder if its drive was destroyed like the one from Spērō. Were we expecting any additional supply shuttles from Sol?"

"That's what we're hoping you can help us figure out," Tyre said turning to face him. "We weren't expecting anything from Sol for quite a while after the isolation message. Our people are spread thin with Janine's security projects and expanded mining operations on the Tiān moons. We're still struggling to build up our mineral reserves. If this shuttle contains supplies, we could definitely put them to good use."

The freshness of the paint and the odd missing drive didn't make sense. It set him on edge. Something about this whole thing seemed staged. "Has anyone boarded yet or touched anything?"

"The regular supply crew here on station hadn't seen the orders to hold off in time. It took them a bit before they realized what they were dealing with. They started the standard Sol supply shuttle boarding procedures, but I stopped them before they cracked the crew airlock. They'd already begun opening the cargo hold, though. We reversed the opening process and nothing was ever disturbed inside."

"I'll take it from here." He turned and glanced around at the station and the nearby guards. First things first, clear away unnecessary eyes. "Guard! As a precaution, I need you to sweep and clear this level back to the first emergency airlock. Hold your position there until you hear from me."

"Yessir!" the guards said. They began systematically closing the airlocks clockwise and counterclockwise of the gate.

He opened a nearby maintenance locker and donned a lightweight EVA suit in case the ship didn't have proper environmental controls or if things went south. The helmet was a lightweight transparent nano-composite polymer that was flexible and yet stronger than steel. The suit's pressurization allowed it to take shape. Putting it on was a bit like putting your head into a plastic bag, but once pressurized, it was spacious. Its simplicity added to the utilitarian design of the suit.

After he interfaced with the station's computer, he ordered the service bots to do a scan of the shuttle's exterior and cargo hold. That should give him enough time to walk through the interior before he decided on the next steps.

His retinal comm mated with the suit and was reporting all systems green. He then opened the station's airlock and transitioned to the shuttle. The hatch closed automatically behind him and the pressure adjusted to match the shuttle to prevent blowback. Normally, they'd open the ship to the station and walk straight in, but he was being cautious. The last thing he needed was to expose everyone to a contagion from the mining site.

The shuttle's airlock wasn't registering any pressure leaks, so he reached out and rotated the handles, swinging the door inward. The clang of the releasing latch eerily echoed through the interior of the ship. It sounded unusually large for a mining shuttle.

His suit was reporting normal oxygen quality with no foreign particulates detected. Mining shuttles weren't designed for superfluous things like life support. They're essentially autonomous mineral storage lockers. The station it docked at usually supplied any oxygen aboard, but this shuttle had its own.

He stepped across the airlock threshold and the station's gravity disappeared, replaced with the weightlessness familiar to most colonists. The shuttle didn't have its own gravity because, like oxygen, it wasn't necessary to transport minerals. At least something was coming up normal.

The sole purpose of this class of ship was optimal ore transport. Its massive cargo hold was designed to be filled to the brim. If for some reason the ore haul didn't fill the hold then the ore was held in place with a flexible graphene netting designed to withstand planetary accelerations. The only remaining usable space within a mining shuttle was a small control room for brief astronaut excursions and in case of emergencies.

Entering the shuttle, it was clear that while it was externally a mining shuttle, internally it was a different beast entirely. Inside the airlock, he found an empty maintenance bay with lockers stocked with EVA suits and tools. His suit was detecting high saline levels in the lockers, likely remnants of human sweat. This usually meant it'd been used recently and vacated.

Maybe they had a smuggling situation on their hands. He'd never heard of such a thing in the colony, but if it existed, they'd need some type of ship like this to get goods into and out of the colony.

Above the airlock, if there were an up in space, was the cockpit. He did a double take. This thing was huge. It was large enough for multiple crew seats and control systems but was presently void of anything except a small navigation console. He tried using his comm to interface with it but it wasn't working.

Touching the screen caused a crude targeting system to come online. Someone had repurposed a missile guidance system to navigate the shuttle to Tiān. It was rather ingenious actually, especially if you wanted to cover your tracks because it didn't have memory to store past events. Mark a point for the smuggling theory.

Below the central maintenance bay was a decent sized galley. At least he imagined it was, since it was nearly empty. Except for a few mounts along the floor typical for heavy equipment like a food reconstituter or waste processor, there wasn't a piece of furniture in sight.

This made no sense. Why would you need a galley if you were automating the inbound flight using a targeting computer? Maybe this was some type of mobile drug lab.

He pushed off from the galley and transitioned through the maintenance bay to the starboard and port side of the ships. Both sides had crude crew quarters with the sleep sacks typical of a short haul ship.

Wherever they were going or coming from, they weren't

expecting to be there long. More support for smuggling he supposed. These weren't the types of bags you lived in. A drug lab was looking less likely.

Continuing astern from maintenance he floated into what resembled a cryo chamber without the pods. As he inspected the space, his suit's sensors pointed out that the lighting units were duller and emitting more vitamin D than normal. There was also a grating and ventilation system embedded in the walls typical of a zero-g cryo-pod drain. The space was large enough to hold about a dozen pods in four sections of three pods using all dimensions of the room.

He reached up to rub his hands through his hair and crashed into the helmet. He chuckled and shook his head. This didn't make sense. Why would someone take a mining shuttle and rehab it for subluminal travel? So much about this ship didn't add up. Subluminal smugglers was looking more and more likely by the second.

There was another airlock astern of the cryo chamber. It was on the exterior of the ship, at the point where it expanded dramatically in size. Where the crew quarters and cryo-pods were positioned was normally a space reserved for housing mining robots and other automata typical of an automated mining operation. Like the ore, these types of machines usually traveled on the ship as they required constant rotation and maintenance.

The stream of data from the exterior service bot scans was in the corner of his retinal comm. The hatches usually used for the mining robots were perfectly aligned with where the cryo-pods were placed. This was an ingenious design. It allowed for easy external pod maintenance and removal.

His suit was still reporting full pressure. You could never be too cautious with suits from a random locker. He floated into the airlock, and once it cycled, he gently pushed off into the cavernous cargo hold. Instead of being full of netting and ore, it was packed from starboard to stern with supply cubes.

The service bots were already in the hold scanning for anomalies and uploading inventory details from all the cubes. He brought up the cargo distribution schematic and a list of the contents on his retina comm. There wasn't anything unexpected or out of the ordinary. An entire shuttle packed to the gills with replacement parts for fabricators, robots, comms, new biotech crops to rotate in, etc. Everything a growing colony needed.

He subvocalized a recorded comm to Tyre. "There's nothing here that would prevent us from unloading the cargo bay. The initial inventory scans check out and there's some equipment here we could use. Make sure the supply drop teams planetside do detailed inspections while opening them. I want to know as much as we can about every item in these containers. I suspect there may be some illegal contraband inside. This ship has a full crew cabin for some reason. My guess would be smugglers, but I've never heard of anything like that on Tiān. I'm keeping it locked down until I investigate further. Make sure the station security detail keeps that airlock secure. I'll have a report to you by the end of the day. Bradley out."

His hand was grasping a handle outside the airlock. He spun around and pushed off into the hatch. Using his retinal comm, he guided a few of the service bots inside to begin an internal scan. Once he'd floated inside, he manually locked down the airlock so no one from the cargo bay side could board without compromising the door.

So much didn't add up about this shuttle. Why retrofit it to hold cryo-pods but then gut it? Why rig up a weapons guidance computer to navigate it to Tiān? It didn't appear to be decelerating from a subluminal jump when it entered Tau Ceti, so where was it coming from? Was there a smugglers' nest somewhere out in the Oort Cloud? And most of all, why all the cloak and dagger masking this ship for subluminal travel as a mining shuttle? The questions were mounting without any answers in sight.

He diverted his attention one more time and quickly composed a message to his friends planetside. He wouldn't make tonight's trip to The Edge after all.

BRADLEY OLIVAW
TAU CETI, TIĀN

He'd always enjoyed using a planisphere. It reminded him of playing a vid-sim game. He'd been an avid gamer as a kid, but as he grew up, games switched from fun time sinks, to part of his job. He'd spent thousands of hours in planetary and city planning simulators. From helping with the design of Tiān, mission planning, or readiness drills; he'd spent much of his adult life in simulations.

As he manipulated the controls of the planisphere, it overlaid the possible orbital trajectories of the mining shuttle within the Tau Ceti models. Each of the different planets, moons, asteroids, shuttles, and space habitats was rendered in three dimensions. Based on the supply routes from Sol, there were only a few viable routes the shuttle could've arrived on. Depending on how far off course the shuttle was when it disengaged its subluminal engine, only a few trajectories could have placed it where it was initially detected.

While the mission parameters were simple, the shuttle mods weren't. It wasn't obvious why someone designed it to hold cryogenic pods, nor why they were missing. And then there was the subluminal drive. If they'd ejected it like Spērō had, they still should have seen the shuttle decelerate; otherwise it would have flown right through the Tau Ceti star system.

Perhaps there was a problem with the communication gateway at the edge of Tau Ceti. Bringing up the gateway's diagnostics and service logs, it appeared to be operating well within parameters. So, why hadn't it detected this shuttle's arrival? It should've been tracking the deceleration signature years before it made its way to Tiān.

He'd left the missing drive signature out of his report to the mayor. He didn't know why he'd withheld it, but until he couldn't explain it, he felt it was important to not disclose. Maybe the system optimizations they'd put in place after their arrival had malfunctioned. Maybe it was cycling through a positive feedback loop, or they'd inadvertently introduced a software bug.

He'd ordered repair drones to the relay station a few days ago. They were instructed to record and check every centimeter of the primary and secondary relays and to scan the memory for corrupt sectors or suppressed failure codes. So far, everything was green. No abnormalities, no bugs, no nothing. The drones also didn't find any deceleration signatures in the raw telemetry over the past several months.

Eliminating the field of view of the relay station from the planisphere left no viable path for the shuttle. Unless it had veered light years off course, stopped or course corrected, and then came in from an alternate path. He even conjectured that it could've deployed some type of cooled sunshade between Tau Ceti and itself to mask the deceleration signature. It made no sense to hide from the colony. If they'd been trying to protect the colony from the alien threat in Sol, they'd instead deploy a shade toward Sol to reduce detection not toward Tau Ceti. There's also the little fact that this shuttle was launched well before the isolation message was broadcast. It wouldn't have been prepped with a massive cooling stealth shade.

The frustration of dead end after dead end had taken a toll

on him. He lifted the planisphere into his hands and hurled it across the room. It shattered into thousands of starry shards. As the pieces fell to the ground, the light within each shard slowly disappeared, throwing the room into absolute darkness.

"End simulation," he muttered.

The ambient lights embedded throughout the room raised. He was standing in the center of his office surrounded by random piles of rations, shipping manifests, and unfinished gadgets.

It made no sense. Everything about the shuttle was illogical. He was missing something obvious. He had to be. It was right there staring back at him and he couldn't see the missing piece. It was fraking killing him. He hadn't slept in days, and like the investigation into his sister's message, he'd hit another dead end both mentally and physically.

His office door chimed and he turned, blankly staring at it. He didn't have time for interruptions. He shook his head and went back to his immediate problem. Bending over, he shuffled through a pile of shuttle manifests. He preferred physical documents and their tactile benefit for finding patterns in data. Few people appreciated print nowadays. Even if it was reusable micro ink enhanced by his retina computer, his mind and fingers couldn't tell the difference.

Whoever was outside began pounding on the door, startling him and pulling him from the holes gnawing at his mind.

"Persistent, aren't they?" he muttered. "Enter!"

"Here he is!" Dwight shouted down the hall as the door to Bradley's office slid open. "Where've you been, mate? We've been waiting for nearly an hour out front in the ground car."

"Waiting? Waiting for what?"

"The trip to The Edge, man. Did you forget already? We've moved it twice for you. There's no way we're moving it again." Dwight glanced around at the mess in his office and then back at him. "Is everything okay, buddy? Your office… you… look like shit."

"Yeah, I'm fine. I'm just tired. Tired of dead ends, tired of riddles, and tired of these awful rations." He kicked over the pile of empty cartons. "I'm not sure I'm up for a trip tonight. I need to catch some shut-eye and attack this… fabricator issue with fresh eyes in the morning."

"I'm not about to make excuses for Earth rations. They're nearly inedible and don't get me started on their degraded nutritional value after our voyage. I personally can't stomach them." Dwight peered at the pile of papers on the ground that Bradley had failed to conceal. "Please do me a favor though. Don't lie to me. You know you're horrible at lying. Everyone knows you're working on a secret project."

"I don't know what—"

"Dude, please! Don't worry; no one wants you to break protocol. We do, however, think you've burned your wick from both ends and are a shell of your former self. You need to take a few hours to unwind, and then go check your eyelids for holes in your quarters. Let's go, no excuses!"

Dwight stared at him and he stared back, unsure what to do next. There was so much to do and so many unknowns, but Dwight was right. His mind hadn't been clear in days, and he could use to unwind.

He touched his ear and subvocalized a command. Within seconds bots were cleaning up documents and straightening his room. His micro ink sheets were wiped, and by the time he'd made it to the door the details of his investigation were expunged. He couldn't afford to leave any details behind. Most people had bots constantly cleaning and scouring their workspaces and homes. He preferred his thought processes and brainstorming to overflow, even if it meant clutter.

He smiled and rested his hand on Dwight's shoulder. "You're right. I'm sorry I kept y'all waiting. Let's get out of here."

"No worries, mate. You made me a few bits and I'm happy you're getting out. Clear some of that moon dust from your head." Dwight turned and walked down the hall.

"What do you mean I made you a few bits?" He turned and checked his office door, confirming it'd closed behind him.

Dwight smirked. "Providence had twenty bits on you not being ready and canceling again. I lost the twenty but bet fifty I'd be able to get you to go. She also had odds on you having not showered or shaven in days. You can't blame them. You've fallen off a crater since that shuttle inspection."

They walked out of the dome into the sunlight, and he raised a hand to cover his eyes. The sun was blinding. As he approached his friends, they cheered his arrival. Well, except for Providence.

His spirits were already turning as he came up alongside the ground car.

"Thanks, everyone. I appreciate y'all waiting. Except you, Providence." He grinned and slapped her on the back. "It sounds like you're buying drinks for The Edge tonight. Assuming we can find any I suppose."

"We're hours ahead of you," Cynthia said. "Dwight made some elixirs of relaxation in his lab, and we have a backup in case that goes its usual direction."

"Hey!" Dwight said as his face turned red. "Except for a light itch, I believe everyone was delightfully intoxicated on the last trip."

They erupted in laughter as the car accelerated up and onto the maglev track. It would take them to the city's edge and from there they'd travel offtrack.

Everyone was in great spirits, and joked with him about the state of his office and his hair. Cynthia's eyes hadn't stopped watching him since he'd sat down next to her. He rested a hand on her leg and leaned into her. "Thanks for rescuing me from my office."

She smiled and tilted her head into him, resting it on his shoulder.

The car disconnected from the maglev and dropped near the ground, continuing toward the setting suns in the west.

The Edge wasn't far outside of town. It was in the direction the colony didn't actively expand. While it wasn't forbidden, people weren't motivated to move closer to it.

Despite assurances from geologists that there was no risk of The Edge collapsing, the taboo was pervasive. A ridiculous amount of debate went into choosing the colony's location for its other benefits, one of which was geological stability.

The car floated above the ground using controlled jets of air. It usually flew higher on unknown terrain, but this was a path well-traveled. They'd positioned their seats three by three facing each other.

As their joking and volume reached a crescendo, the car notified them they'd arrived at their destination.

He stepped out of the car and glanced across the sea of people. He'd never seen so many colonists here before. "What happened? This place is a zoo."

"You really do live in a cave, don't you, Olivaw?" Providence said. "The colony's freaked out over the news from Sol and our uncertain future. People need places to unwind and blow off some steam. If they aren't heads down working like you, they're splitting their time between The Edge or sports at the dome. I've never seen so many Zero-G Disc or Crolo leagues in my life."

He hadn't thought about that. He'd been living in a cave and hadn't bothered to watch any news feeds since the shuttle inspection. "I suppose that makes sense. But last I remember there wasn't anything about The Edge that would address people's acute stress levels. What are they doing, just getting plastered?"

As if on cue, he watched four people in the distance jump off The Edge into the void below. "What the frak?" He rushed up to the railing. People around him were watching the jumpers fall. "What's wrong with you?" he yelled. "Those people just jumped to their death and you're just standing around like nothing happened."

Cynthia ran up and pulled him away from the railing and the staring colonists. "Ignore him. He doesn't get out much." She guided him back toward their party and then leaned in and whispered, "Social," while tapping the side of her head.

He rarely had the public social feed enabled on his retinal comm. It was too distracting, and the experiences too banal.

"Social layer on," he subvocalized. In his peripheral vision, he saw dozens of video experiences nearby. Scrolling through them, he noticed several people looking over The Edge watching the jumpers fall and a few were from the jumpers themselves. He enabled a feed from a jumper and took it full view, so he was seeing everything the jumper was seeing, experiencing it as if from his own eyes.

A few seconds later the free-falling jumper grasped their opposing wrists. This signaled their suit to deploy small wings from under their arms. When the wings caught the wind, faller became flyer as they instantly transitioned from careening through the air to gliding through the sky.

Each of the jumpers had done the same thing in unison. Were their suits networked together or did they somehow signal to each other? The fliers transitioned to doing tricks and began spiraling and spinning in intricate patterns.

Dwight reached out and grabbed Bradley by the arm, pulling him backward a bit. "Careful! You know you can't go full experience first time. Take it windowed or you'll go tumbling over The Edge yourself."

"Windowed," he subvocalized and regained his center of balance, taking a few steps backward. "Thanks. It's been a while."

They walked down along The Edge until they found an open set of tables to set up their party. He hadn't noticed the bots following them carrying a cooker, cooler, and supplies. This was exactly why the social layer scared him so much. Time, and all semblance of what was going on around him slipped away when he linked in. It was like when he was in the planisphere or doing an EVA in an exo-suit, but at least that was his reality and not someone else's.

"I'll take one of those drinks now, Dwight." He smiled. "I think I owe it to everyone to be the guinea pig for this batch. What're we calling it?"

Dwight smirked as he reached into the cooler and grabbed some bulbs. "Considering Bradley as subject zero, how about we name this mixup The Stumbler?" He handed a bulb to him.

"Done and done!" He slammed the first drink down. "Yum! It's fruity and..." His mouth puckered. "Love the flavor, D. So how long until the suns set?"

"Around thirty minutes," Cynthia said. "Plenty of time to catch up. I feel like we haven't seen you in weeks. You've been MIA since the mystery shuttle's arrival. What've you been doing locked up in your office?"

He knew they'd all been wanting to ask, but you could hear a pin drop as everyone stared between each other. No one was expecting Cynthia to rip off the bandage so quickly. She was never one to beat around the bush.

As he lowered his second empty bulb, his stomach had that warm and cozy sensation he found so relaxing and always proceeded intoxication. Strangely though, he felt oddly focused. "Say, Dwight. What's in this batch? I feel like I'm getting drunk, but I also feel... I don't know... alert. How's that work?"

Dwight held a bulb up to the light and shook it. "It's the Xybathal plant we found growing natively near the colony when we arrived. I crushed it, and slowly infused it into the later stages of the fermentation process. I was hoping the effect would be delayed rather than the usual instant focus people have grown used to. I thought it would be interesting to engineer a positive side effect to being intoxicated instead of a hangover." He shook the bulb some more. "I'm still working out the kinks with the timing of the delivery."

He'd heard some good and bad things about Xybathal. It was extraordinary at providing near instant focus, but the more you used it, the less its effects worked. Shuttle pilots and security teams had been experimenting with delivery mechanisms they could use in emergency situations. He'd never experimented with chemical enhancements before so this was a new experience.

The binary suns of Tau Ceti danced toward the horizon and he sat back in a chair. Were the jumpers enhanced or was he buzzed?

Cynthia walked up with some food, jabbing the plate into his stomach. "Stop changing the subject. What's Tyre got you locked up in your tower working on?"

"Nothing much, actually," he said staring at the plate of food, struggling to not make eye contact. "After I gave my shuttle report I've been working on coordinating supplies and repairs on the ground. We've been having technical issues with the mods we made to the fabricators, and the supplies helped fix some of what we broke."

"Come on, Bradley," Providence said. "There's no reason to lock yourself up to handle that. Anyone could help with fabricators. You didn't even enter hermit mode when your hacked maglev mods went haywire and catapulted your new recruits into Hilder Pond. I'm not buying that excuse at all. Who's got odds that Bradley faked the Isolation message and it's all a huge prank?"

Was she fraking kidding? Did she really think he'd do something like that to the colony he'd given up everything for? He turned to face Providence and sprung out of his chair to close the space between them. Grabbing her by the shirt, he lifted her into the air, leaning threateningly toward The Edge.

"If you ever accuse me of treason again, I'll have you jettisoned into Tau B faster than a muon through ice."

Providence's face went from smiling to white with fear in the blink of an eye as her back leaned closer to the sheer drop of The Edge. She reached out and grasped his arm with every bit of strength she had. She wasn't struggling to get loose; she was fearing her own death.

"Hey, cut it out, you two. Stand down, Bradley!" Laruy yelled, forcing his arms between the two of them and pushing Bradley back away from The Edge. "You know she was kidding, right? And seriously, Bradley. A muon through ice? That's the best you've got, Olivaw? You really gotta work on your trash talk. That was so bad. Now let her go."

She mouthed the words sorry toward him before glancing behind her and then forward again, grasping him even tighter.

The last thing he'd ever be was a traitor, and while she might have been joking, her words stung. He'd made his point. There was no sense in ruining the evening over this.

He stared into her face for another moment before he shook his head rapidly, transforming himself from aggressive to laughing uncontrollably in an instant. He set her back down and then reached his arm around her shoulder, pulling her in playfully and giving her a noogie. "Sorry. Between work stress, my sister, and the alcohol, I'm not in my right mind."

"That's a surprisingly lucid comment from a drunk," Providence said.

"I blame Dwight's fruity Stumbler concoction. It's hard to mumble and blame being drunk when he's got me hopped up on stimulants. At least he kept the stumbling though." He reached out to catch his balance on the railing and leaned over The Edge.

He could see kilometers downward. The geological changes required for such a sheer drop were hard to imagine, let alone the tectonic stability of the region that ensured this cliff didn't collapse. The geologists still couldn't explain it. Their models weren't even close to aligning with reality.

As he studied the horizon, he realized it was about to happen. "It's starting!" He waved his hands for everyone to come over.

Each of the suns in the binary system of Tau Ceti moved through the sky at different rates. From time to time, they crossed the horizon together. The Edge was a place where that crossing was both regular, and spectacular.

During the autumn, the equatorial region on Tiān reached aphelion around Tau B. At the same time, they were also nearing aphelion with Tau A. This meant that both suns were close to each other in the sky. They rose and set together, in sync, but slightly offset. The effect of the two different spectra was beautiful.

The clouds tonight were wispy. They painted the horizon in greens and pinks and were dense enough to allow people to see the binary suns without needing to adjust their retinal lenses. The shape of the valleys far below was like V grooves, and channeled away from The Edge. These cavernous grooves added to the wonder and effect of the sunset.

They were like the grooves of the antique music players he'd read about in history books. What sort of needle would you need to play these, and more importantly, what tune would they play? He tilted his head. It was needles they used, right?

He glanced across the valley and studied the grooves. Tonight they were fortunate. The suns were setting into one of the wider deeper valleys at The Edge. As the gaseous globes of light set over the horizon, darkness descended, and their light spilled into the network of valleys far below. It was like someone spilled lightning onto the ground. Bolts of jagged light bounced through the grooves toward them, and seemingly into the base of The Edge itself. It helped that the rocky materials that made up the valleys had a vitreous luster which made it highly reflective.

He watched as The Edge jumpers sailed out and over the grooves below. They'd stopped their acrobatics and were staring at the sunset event. Despite their rapidly descending situations, they were as enamored with the visuals as he was. The perspective from the lower squad's cameras was similar to the higher, just a bit more in their face.

How far could the twin suns be apart and have the same visual effect? Surely, someone must have already measured this. Did anyone actually see a visual difference most of the time? Aphelion was ideal, but any of the weeks leading up to and after it should have the same visual impact. Could you tell where the sun was further down the groove? His mind was racing with ideas, and angles of incidence and reflection.

Maybe... he'd been thinking about it wrong. What if the shuttle was coming from the ideal delivery route? He'd thought the path of entry into the Tau Ceti system was weird, but what if it wasn't? What would it mean if that was the direction of Sol?

"That's it! It has to be. I've been looking at it wrong. I've gotta go. I've gotta go." He ran up to Cynthia lifting her into the air and spun her around. "Thank you," he mouthed as he set her down and took off, sprinting toward the ground cars.

BRADLEY NODDED and froze just inside the entrance into Nathan's office. He wasn't expecting to see Janine. This was a last-minute emergency appointment, but he specifically noted that he wanted to meet alone. "Good morning, Janine. Um... no offense, but I was hoping to speak to Mayor Clarke alone."

Janine chuckled. "None taken, Bradley. Also, no offense, but you look awful. Are you feeling well?"

What was she talking about? He glanced down at his

clothes. They were a mess and judging by his odor, he seriously needed a shower. He shrugged and looked back toward Janine. "I feel fine enough, thank you. I'm tired, but nothing a half dozen coffees can't handle." He turned toward Nathan. "Sir?"

"Relax, Bradley." Nathan gestured to the chair in front of his desk.

He glanced from Janine to Nathan. "But—"

"No. Seriously, have a seat." Nathan walked behind the desk and waved his hand over a globe of Tiān off to the side. It opened a comm to his assistant.

"Yes, sir," the assistant said.

"Can we please get some coffee, and perhaps some breakfast pastries for Mr. Olivaw? Actually, on second thought, make that three of us," Nathan said.

"Right away, sir."

"Seriously, Bradley. Ass in seat. I insist." Nathan gestured forcefully to the chair in front of his desk. "Given everything going on right now, I'm sure whatever you want to talk to me about is also fine for Director Cooper to hear."

He stared at the chairs and then toward Janine. Why couldn't even the simple things just go his way? Was it so hard to schedule a conversation with someone alone? He walked forward to the chair on the left and sat down.

Janine sat next to him.

"So what brings you here at this ungodly hour, Bradley?" Nathan asked.

He spun around in his seat, and took in the layout of the room. There was a security panel near the wallboard. He hopped out of the chair and practically skipped over to it. When he rested his left hand against the panel it glowed a confident green and he turned to face the others, tilting his head toward the panel.

They both sighed and rose from their seats to do the same. The secure blue glow trimmed the room and the soothing voice of the computer confirmed that security protocols were in place.

He swallowed hard. "Sorry, Mayor. I just had to—"

"No worries," Nathan interrupted waving his hand. "It's fine. What's on your mind?"

They all walked back to their chairs and sat down.

He nodded and paused, looking away toward the now translucent window. The shadowy outline of a passing maglev shot past. He wasn't sure where to begin and he couldn't just blurt out his questions. Janine and Nathan both wore expressions of concern. "Sorry. I was just trying… to find a good place to… I suppose at The Edge makes the most sense."

"The Edge?" Janine asked furrowing her brow. "As in the cliff outside the colony?"

"One and the same. So, I was out at The Edge with my peeps the other day after spending several days of dead ends in orbital sims. They yanked me out of my office for some fresh air and relaxation. You see… after the message from my sister last week something never sat right with me. It was something she'd said. Ever since then, well, except for my excursion to look into the supply shuttle—" he paused, glancing from Janine to Nathan. He wasn't sure if she knew.

Nathan nodded. "She knows. Like I said, you can say anything."

"Ok, well, except for that side project, I've been spending a lot of time thinking about my sister's message."

Janine leaned back in her chair and crossed her arms. "What about it?"

He stared at the globe behind Nathan's desk. Why was this so hard? The interrupted days and too many sleepless nights were throwing him off. "The last part of the message. It seemed… off to me." He subvocalized a command that brought up the text of the message on the wall screen behind him.

Life is like the Great River. Sometimes it sweeps you gently along, and sometimes the rapids come out of nowhere. May the ocean of stars guide us safely through these rapids to the river's end.

"Yeah," Nathan began, "that was an odd ending, wasn't it? I thought it was the symbolism she was going for. You know, something to uplift everyone."

Janine was nodding.

He reached up and scratched at his face. It'd been days since he last shaved and the stubble was thick. "You're right, Mayor. My sister loves her uplifting speeches. But this one… this one struck a different chord with me. You see… my sister, brother, and I used to go camping with our family on Earth when we were kids. We'd spent many an evening lying on our backs staring upward at the stars and making up stories. We'd talk about what it would be like to visit those far away suns."

He brought up a flat version of the constellation Eridanus on the wall. The constellations outline and name were visible along with its English name, *The River*. "Several of our stories spoke of this river."

"I'm confused," Janine said, adjusting her position in her chair. "Why would President Olivaw mention this in her speech? Why wouldn't she just come out and send you a message?"

He leaned forward, placed his elbows on his legs and his head in his hands.

Nathan cleared his throat. "Bradley and Abigail aren't exactly on speaking terms."

"She didn't want me on this voyage," Bradley said. He sat up and slid forward to the edge of his seat. "I needed to get away from my family, for my sanity, and theirs. I saw this opportunity so I—"

"He pulled some strings to get here," Nathan interrupted. "But that's ancient history. That was over seventeen years ago. You're a fixture here. What does this have to do with the message?"

"Put a pin in that, Mayor. I'll come back to it. So back to my office. I was buried in my simulations around Eridanus and something didn't make sense." He brought up another label on the constellation at the furthest end, the label *Achernar* came up along with *The River's End*. He paused again, staring at the words on the wall. They'd spent so many hours telling those stories.

Janine interrupted the silence. "I don't know what we're supposed to be seeing, but that isn't helpful."

He shook his head. "Sorry, I was lost in thought again. Anyhow, this is the river's end she mentioned in the message. It's something we'd talked about many times as kids. What's weird though, it means nothing to the colonies or anyone else. It would only make sense to Zachary and I, so it just felt like she was talking directly to me.

"So there I was, sleepy and at a dead end. Fast-forward to my peeps, they asked me to The Edge for some… levity. While we were there, I was watching these Edge jumpers. They were leaping off the cliff and flying. One of the groups jumped just as the suns set. The suns lit up the chasm below. If you ever get a chance, it was an awesome and truly breathtaking view. I'd highly recommend it. Anyhow, the suns' and the jumpers' points of view, they made me see the whole problem differently. You see, I was looking at them wrong, both of them."

"Both of what?" Nathan was shaking his head. "Am I the only one who's confused?"

Janine chuckled and shook hers, as well. "No, I'm right there with ya."

"Ah yes, sorry. I forgot about the supply shuttle." He jumped out of his seat and started pacing around the room. "When I went up there to investigate the shuttle, I found some weird stuff, all of which were in the report I shared. The oddities didn't sit well with me and I couldn't stop thinking about them. The shuttle was a rigged mess and the whole thing made no sense. It clearly hadn't decelerated from a subluminal jump, or we'd have detected it. So, where'd it come from? We knew the general direction, but it could've jumped from anywhere and then slingshotted.

"So I dug deeper, and started redirecting some dish time toward Sol. Then I noticed something odd. Since the message from my sister, our signal from Sol had dipped slightly. I don't know why. So, that made me wonder if perhaps they'd adjusted it to help protect us from the aliens. I started digging deeper to see if any of our visual resources could detect anything unusual in or around Sol. That's when things really started falling apart."

He brought the visuals of Sol up on the wall, and let them sit there for a second. He stared at Nathan and Janine, waiting to see if they noticed it.

"I'm sorry. I'm not an astronomer," Nathan said. "What exactly are we looking for?"

"That's not Sol," Janine interjected.

"Correct!" He pumped his arm and pointed his finger at the wall screen. "That's not Sol! Not only is the spectral type off, but the surrounding stars aren't correct."

Nathan was shaking his head. "I'm going to sound like a broken record here, but I don't get it. How's that possible?"

"It's not." Janine rose from her seat and walked toward the wall screen. "Did you cross check this with the imagery from our catalogs? Surely something's amiss. Maybe the telescope's guidance is off. It must be pointing at the wrong star field."

"My thoughts exactly." He subvocalized the command to

bring up the star catalogs from their computers. There in the catalog was Sol, with a slightly different star pattern than the one their telescopes had taken.

"Now watch this." He subvocalized a command and then spoke aloud. "Computer, please compare these two images."

The computer replied. "They're a match. These images are of Sol, home of humanity." Its tinny computer voice echoed throughout the room.

The overhead lights flashed and the screen blurred as Nathan's assistant entered the room. He was holding a tray of coffees and fresh pastries. Setting them on the table he could see he'd interrupted something important, he turned and exited without a word. The blue glow returned, and the screens brought back the same imagery.

"I'm confused again. Why would it say the image matched? It's clearly not the same," Nathan said.

"I was just as confused myself, so I rolled up my sleeves and pulled out some of my hobby wares. Before I'd left Sol, I was into Astronomy, but I just hadn't had time on Tiān to mess with it. Anyhow, I had some old tools that I used to plan observing sessions. You could use them to fly around other stars, see different skies from different locations, nothing fancy. It's been around for centuries. I took the data from this image and started a brute force search from Sol, to find a matching pattern taking the spectral types of nearby stars we observed." He spun around to face them. An epiphanic grin was on his face. "Here's what it returned this morning, just before I scheduled this meeting."

He subvocalized a command and brought up an image on the wall. It was from his tool, and it matched the image taken from their telescopes around Tiān.

"It's a match?" Janine said, confusion in her voice. "Where's it from?"

"Great question. Before I answer that, let me jump back to the river message." He brought the message back up on the screen. "After I realized where this image was from, I pulled the message from Abigail back into the fold.

"You see, when we told the story about the river, we never told it by itself. It was always a much bigger story arc about Hydrus the snake attacking Pavo the peacock." As he was talking, he was zooming out the planisphere of constellations on the wall that had been showing *Eridanus* the river.

"An important part of our story around the river was the animal that defended it. In our story, the river brought life to the sky. You see, it was the water that fed everything and enabled trade and a certain way of life. There was also a guardian of the river, a great beast. An unbreakable thread created by dwarves bound it near the river, to defend the riverbanks."

He zoomed a bit further out, and showed the constellation named *Lupus* with a label just beneath it that said *The Wolf*.

"You see, this was always the true river's end in our childhood stories. It was this beast, the great wolf of the sky that guided friendly people to safety." With that, he highlighted that passage from Abigail's message.

...guide us safely through these rapids to the river's end.

"So if I'm following you, and I'm barely doing so at this point... are you saying we're actually somewhere in Lupus?" Janine asked.

He adjusted the wall screen again, and a star brightened. A label beneath it appeared, *Zeta Lupi*.

"Okay... so we're in Zeta Lupi?" Janine was half asking and half telling. "But why? Why all the subterfuge? This seems like someone went to great lengths to conceal that fact from us."

He turned to face Nathan, not wanting to miss his reaction

to this. He subvocalized another command. On the screen below Zeta Lupi appeared the distance in flashing yellow, *117 Light Years*.

Nathan froze. He didn't say a word, but there was something. A spark. His eye twitched, and he deflated ever so slightly. It wasn't much, but something about that number had made Nathan connect a dot.

"So tell us, Nathan. How can we be 117 light years from Sol if we've been getting comms for two years that clearly say they're fifteen years old?" he asked.

Janine glanced from Bradley to Nathan. It was dawning on her what he was asking, and why he was here this morning.

"She... we'd talked, but..." Nathan stammered as he stood abruptly and walked toward the window; it was still securely blurred. After a few seconds, he turned and faced them. "Ok, let me first start by saying I had no idea that we weren't at Tau Ceti. I just want to set that record straight."

When neither he nor Janine said anything, Nathan continued. "I'd met briefly with President Olivaw a year before we'd departed. She wanted to make some changes to the colony ship's subluminal drives. She said they had a breakthrough which could get us to Tau Ceti sooner. I was against any last-minute changes despite her adamantly claiming they'd tested them out and it was perfectly safe. As far as I knew, Abigail's team never made the changes."

Nathan glanced back and forth between them. "By the time we arrived, I'd forgotten all about it. We were in cryostasis for fifteen years. I swear, I had no idea!"

He nodded his head. "I believe you."

"You do?" Janine was wide-eyed. "Why?"

"Because that's how my sister rolls. We were on a need to know basis, and from her perspective we didn't need to know."

"Ok, so let's assume for a minute he isn't lying." Janine

shot Nathan a dubious look. "How'd they make the changes, and why didn't we notice this star wasn't Tau Ceti before now?"

"I have no idea how they swapped our drives. Maybe they did it mid-flight. We never noticed because our star is actually remarkably similar to Tau Ceti. They're close spectral types, both have distant binary companions, and both have similar planetary configurations. They'd worked hard to mask the particulars if you compared everything side by side. But otherwise, if you weren't looking for it you'd never notice. And why would someone look for something like this? No one in their right mind would change our destination star."

Janine was squinting at the wall screen. "But what about the shuttle?"

"It means that if my theory is correct, we need to venture here." He circled a region of Zeta Lupi space out near their Oort Cloud.

"Why there?" Janine asked.

"It's the line of sight to Sol from Zeta Lupi. If there was something weird related to that shuttles missing subluminal drive, then I'd guess it would be out there somewhere."

"So how can I help?" Nathan asked.

"I've redirected some project alpha probes to scope out a route," he said.

"You did what?" Nathan's face was screwed up into a scowl. "You shouldn't have done that without talking to us first."

"I'm also taking a ship. The mystery shuttle. I'm taking it with a crew, and we're going out there," he said in a matter-of-fact tone. He was standing resolutely staring down Nathan, daring him to say no.

"Now listen—"

"No, you listen!" he interrupted. "I believe your story but that doesn't mean I trust you. I have to think you knew more than you're letting on. You must've seen some other hints of this and chose to ignore them. I'm doing this with or without your help. Without either of your help if I have to. So, if you want to do this together, great. Otherwise, you can make this hard if you want, but you'll lose."

Nathan walked closer to Bradley; his chest was out and his back had stiffened. "Stop threatening me! It's not your style, seriously. I'd have backed this mission if you'd only asked. I'm actually disappointed that you resorted to doing it this way, but to be honest, I guess I don't blame you."

"Whatever you need, Bradley. Just ask," Janine said.

"Can we all just work together on this from here out?" Nathan glanced between them both.

He nodded. "Yeah, but no secrets from here on out. None! No matter how big or small. Anything that's ever nagged at your subconscious concerning this mission, we need to turn it over and see what crawls out. It could be a clue."

They both nodded in agreement.

Bradley reached down and picked up one of the cooling cups of coffee. He breathed in the bright aroma and smiled. "Ok, let's talk about the crew I'd like on the mission."

6

BRADLEY OLIVAW
ZETA LUPI, OORT CLOUD

They'd been following the planned route for days, scanning every millimeter of space as they went, and so far they'd come up empty. No stray emissions, signals, or visual sightings. If there's something out here, it was hidden well.

He and the team repurposed the previous supply run mining shuttle from the week before. They swapped the targeting computer for a traditional bridge control set up for five. The galley was rebuilt and stocked with supplies for a few months. Finally, they added EVA suits for the entire crew, a contingent of probes, and cryo-pods just in case.

The crew quarters lacked the personal space needed for a long-haul mission. It felt like a kid's space camp with everyone bunking in the same rooms. They'd had fun with it so far, but maybe after a few more weeks they'd have another viewpoint entirely.

Floating onto the bridge, he glided to his seat, and his suit automatically locked him into place. He brought up the status of the continuous lidar scans on his console. They'd traveled three times further than where they'd first detected the mining shuttles deceleration into Zeta Lupi. That felt strange to say, Zeta Lupi. In the few years since their arrival, they'd grown comfortable calling their new home Tau Ceti. It would take a while getting used to a new name.

Before they'd sent off, Nathan called the colony together again to share the news of where they'd actually colonized. As expected, it shook things up but to be honest, people seemed relieved. To most, it was comforting. It meant that they were further from the aliens than everyone originally thought.

A side effect of sharing the details of their situation with the colony was that many people came forward with anomalies in dates they'd noticed over the years, but shrugged off. Supply shuttle products with dates of only two years in the past. Signals from the real Sol location that were somehow being canceled out were now being amplified and confirmed their theory. The ancient broadcasts were nearly 120 years old.

Based on the available data, they estimated their travel time to Zeta Lupi at under a year and a half. They'd somehow traveled at nearly one hundred times the speed of light from Sol. That was assuming this wasn't some ridiculously large-scale practical joke.

"Hey, Bradley. I have an idea I wanted to run by you. Do you have a second?" Isaac asked. He was their pilot and expert in all things robotic.

He dismissed the lidar data and turned toward Isaac. "With all these empty scans, I've got nothing but seconds to spare. Whatcha got?"

Isaac brought up a simulation of the Zeta planetary system on the wall near his station. "I was killing time and tried to run some new sims. I took into account the trajectory we assume the shuttle followed and added the distance Zeta Lupi has rotated in that time. It's not much, but I ended up with this huge space over here where we should also be looking."

"Wait, isn't that—"

"The Barycenter Lagrange Point, yep!" Isaac interrupted. "I was hoping you'd notice that."

"That'd be a perfect place to hide a base of operations. Let's reroute there and send some forward probes to scope it out. How long till we arrive?"

Isaac brought up the flight plan. "Two hours tops. We'll have probes there in a quarter of that."

"Awesome find!" He gently patted Isaac on the shoulder and pushed off aftward to share the news with the others.

He found Cynthia and Amir working in the central maintenance bay on the teams' EVA suits. Amir was their security assignment from Janine's team. They'd been over these suits a dozen times already and were itching to find something that warranted investigation.

Isaac's voice came over everyone's comm. "Lock in while we reroute! Thirty seconds until I burst."

The three of them scrambled to lock into nearby acceleration harnesses. Once they'd leaned against one, it engulfed the extremities and head of the person, bracing them against the attached surface.

"Hey, Bradley," Cynthia said, smiling when she noticed him strapped in nearby. "I didn't realize you... awe shitttt!"

The burst came hard and fast. The harness tried to compensate to make them more comfortable, but it didn't matter, acceleration hurt. This was why cryo-pods and acceleration drugs were invented.

After two minutes of pain, the acceleration let up.

Isaac's voice came over their comm again. "That's all for now. Expect a deceleration in T minus ninety minutes."

A countdown clock appeared in the corner of everyone's field of view.

Amir reached up and started massaging his neck. "I'm out of practice with high-g maneuvers like that. I've been spending too much time planetside."

Cynthia gently pushed off from her harness and headed

back toward the EVA suits. Grasping the torso of a suit as she floated past, she adeptly countered the momentum and rotated toward Bradley. "Why the course correction, boss?"

He glided in, touching down next to the EVA suit. "Isaac found an interesting coincidence reanalyzing the projected route of the mining shuttle. Apparently, we're close to a Barycenter Lagrange Point between Zeta Lupi A and our binary, Zeta Lupi B. It'd be an ideal location to hide something like a shuttle relay facility."

"So we'll finally get a chance to take one of these babies on an excursion?" Amir slapped his hands on the EVA suit. The force threw him off and he started to rotate.

Bradley and Cynthia chuckled.

"Damn this zero-g skill attrition. I need to get upside more often."

"We all do, Amir, we all do," he said. "I'm going to head over and check if Dwight's awake. See how he managed the acceleration."

"I'll join you." Cynthia floated alongside him toward the starboard crew quarters.

Entering the cramped quarters, he could tell that Dwight wasn't here. As he stopped against the wall to rebound Cynthia collided into him, and they tumbled in a mass of giggling arms and legs.

Cynthia stared at him as they came to rest and didn't give him a chance to say a word; she started passionately kissing him. She made a brief hand gesture behind his back, and the door to the quarters closed.

THE DOOR to the crew quarters opened after they'd finished the deceleration. Bradley floated out toward the bridge first, and Cynthia soon thereafter.

Last week he announced the crew for this mission, but

Cynthia refused to join. When he pushed her on why, she broke down and told him about her feelings for him. She'd apparently been hiding them for a while and didn't know how to broach the topic. That was all it took for him to kiss her. She changed her mind about joining after that.

After he entered the bridge and locked into his seat, he brought up the data from the forward probes. There were several planetesimals stuck in the Lagrange point, but they hadn't detected anything foreign in their scans.

"Alright. Let's start with the bigger one in the middle and spiral out from there," he said.

Amir adjusted course. In a few minutes, they were nearing the largest planetesimal. It was roughly four hundred kilometers in diameter and was primarily composed of metals with trace ice water and other minerals.

"So what details are we looking for that the probes didn't already show?" Isaac asked. "I can make adjustments to future scans to improve their detection rate if I know."

Everyone on the bridge looked at each other and then finally at Bradley. He laughed. "Suddenly I'm the OPS expert? Ask Amir, he's from Security. I thought for sure we'd recognize something on the surface. Some right angles or maybe a cavity would show up on the scans. There should also be radiant energy signals from man-made structures."

"I'd expect the same—" Amir began.

An alert chimed. Their sensors were picking up something on the surface near the planetesimals north axis.

Was he seeing this right? The surface was dilating open revealing a previously unseen inner chamber. From their current angle of approach, there seemed to be guide lights on the inner walls. "Isaac, can you—"

"Already on it, boss. I'm redirecting a probe toward the entrance and adjusting our course." Isaac was frantically issuing commands into his console.

"That wasn't there a second ago, right?" He brought up

the earlier scans on his retinal comm. There was no sign of this opening nor an inner chamber anywhere. Only hills and small craters spread randomly over the planetesimal. The deeper scans were reporting back kilometer upon kilometer of empty regolith.

"I'm looking at the surface and ground penetrating scans from the approaching probes and it's still not there. Nothing shows up except for the hole from the new opening." Cynthia shared the new feed with everyone's control panel.

Sure enough, it looked like the planetesimal was both absorbing and scrambling their scans. This wasn't uncommon for pockets of metal rich asteroids, but it was unusual this close to the surface of a planetesimal.

They intently stared at the cameras from the approaching probe until he broke the silence. "Amir, Cynthia, prepare the EVA suits."

"Hold on a second, boss," Isaac interrupted. "If I'm reading this right… there's gravity inside that chamber."

"Gravity? How's that possible?" Dwight asked.

"It's theoretically possible, I suppose. The principle would be similar to the lift tubes we use on the colony," Cynthia said. "I've never seen it implemented at a scale of a planetesimal though."

"So if there's gravity, how do we get inside?" he asked.

"Maybe it's a controlled gravitational field like the lift tubes, and we just fly in," Cynthia said.

"Bossman," Isaac began, "we're being given approach vectors. It's being broadcast from inside the planetesimal over standard CoPE tight-beam frequencies."

They glanced around at each other, their faces blank. Bradley half expected something like this. The other half expected aliens, which still wasn't out of the question. "Well, I guess that solves that. Amir, please round up some firearms. Just in case."

"Yessir!" Amir pushed off hard toward the aft section of the ship.

"Isaac, route the probes toward the entrance. I want every square centimeter scanned before we enter that thing. Redirect them toward scanning other portions of the entrance radiating outward after they complete their baseline scans."

"Yessir!"

"Also, as a precaution, let's drop a beacon. Once we head inside, if we aren't out in two hours, I want Tiān updated on our location."

"Done and done!" came the replies.

The clang of a beacon launch echoed in the distance.

Everyone worked in silence from that point forward. The probe scans showed a long shaft leading deep inside the planetesimal. On the other side was either a dead end, or another door that would dilate open; they couldn't tell. The walls of the chamber were standard nano-polymers like the ones used throughout the colonies. Only the outer material was unknown. No matter what they threw at it, nothing came back. As far as they knew, it covered most if not all the planetesimal.

"All the ground penetrating scans are complete, sir," Isaac said. "We can't scan past the far end of the tunnel. It's likely made of the same material as the outer surface."

Amir returned from the storage lockers and passed sidearms to each member of the crew. He also had a shock rifle and a few TMS grenades that launched specialized nanites at nearby enemies. They used magnetic stimulation to knock out the target's motor cortex, incapacitating them.

He shook his head, struggling to review all the data. "Alright everyone, I have two minds here and I need your help choosing a path. Do we send in a small EVA away team and leave everyone else out here, or do we head in together? Candid thoughts only please."

"They're using CoPE communication protocols," Dwight said. "That's gotta mean something, right?"

"Easily spoofed, yo," Amir said as he fiddled with the rifle.

"Fair enough," Cynthia said. "But it's not like we're armed to the nines in this mining shuttle. What're we gonna do out here other than cut and run? Assuming whatever's inside doesn't blow us out of the vacuum before then. The beacon we launched will warn our fellow colonists without leaving someone alone out here to shat themselves."

He chuckled. She had a point. "Alright. Unless there's an objection, we head in together?" He glanced around the bridge, they each gave him the thumbs up. "That settles it then. Isaac, let's follow our mystery host's approach vectors into the belly of this beast."

"Yessir!"

Their ship passed silently through the entrance of the planetesimal. Guide lights along each side of the tunnel shut off, darkening the space behind them as they passed. The spacious tunnel was designed to allow both inbound and outbound traffic, that or movement of some other type of massive ship. Either way, their tiny mining vessel fit easily inside.

"Boss, the outer entrance is closing." Isaac brought up the rear camera view on their control panels. It was an eerie feeling watching the iris close, knowing the space beyond was out of reach.

"We're detecting some smaller tunnels off the side of this chamber." Amir shared the scans with everyone's controls.

"Perhaps they're service tunnels or for launching probes without opening the inner chamber?" Dwight asked.

"Should we stop and explore them?" Amir asked.

"Too late." Bradley pointed toward the forward cameras on their controls. "Our hosts are opening the inner doors."

The doors dilated open to the largest spaceport hangar

he'd ever seen. Their ship crept across the threshold of the tunnel into the expansive space beyond. They went from being alone inside this planetesimal seconds ago, to suddenly being insignificant.

There, spread throughout the hangar were hundreds of alien-looking ships in various stages of construction. At first glance, they had a consistent central design and the only difference was the variety of sizes. Some were wide and long, and seemed intended as shipment vessels with vast empty cargo holds. Others resembled small nimble fighters or shuttles. They were all shaped like a droplet or a tear, but the part that came to a point seemed to be expandable, like the plume of a peacock or the feathers of a badminton birdie.

He stared wide-eyed at the ships. This had to be a dream. "Are we recording this?"

At first, there was no response, but then Amir realized Bradley was talking to him. "We are, but unless I'm mistaken, none of our signals are making it out. I've lost contact with our beacon. I haven't detected any external signals since the outer doors closed."

"Look at that!" Dwight was pointing at one of the gigantic cargo ships.

Thousands of robots were swarming the skeletal ship from the ceiling and floor of the hangar. Some were moving massive black panels into place, covering the ship in that same mysterious dark material. Others were positioning themselves into the superstructure of the ship. They seemed to disappear, to be absorbed and become part of the ship itself.

"I've never seen such a highly scaled and orchestrated construction process," Isaac said, his eyes darting around. "It's... beautiful."

Amir brought up the active lidar scans on the wall screen. "That black material seems to have the same properties as the outer doors that absorbed our scans. I can't penetrate the surface of ships with that material in place on any frequency."

"Have we performed enough scans to get an idea what the internal layout is?" he asked.

"For the most part," Amir said.

"Should we keep following the approach vector they transmitted?" Isaac asked.

"You could try asking," Cynthia smirked.

Isaac shrugged and opened a comm on the same frequency the approach vector was transmitted on. "Hangar control, this is mining shuttle Ibdac Prime on the assigned approach vector. Requesting taxi guidance."

Cynthia reached toward Isaac. "Wait, I was joking! And who's Ibdac Prime?"

Isaac chuckled. "I figured it was worth a try. Ibdac is our first initials all strung together. We hadn't discussed a ship name, so I winged it."

"Ibdac Prime, this is control," said a friendly female voice over the open comm. "We'll guide you on your assigned approach vector until you reach hangar berth two. Please disengage your impulse drives. You're wasting fuel at this point."

Isaac disengaged their drives and sure enough, they continued moving along their original vector.

"That's something you don't see every day." Cynthia brought up their sensor array on the wall screen panel. "Check this out. They're shaping the gravity around our ship to guide us through the hangar. A safe and precise docking experience that saves fuel to boot."

This all felt too convenient. "Do we have any idea where berth two is, or when we'll reach it?"

"Judging by the numbers on the ceiling we appear to be at berth 251, and the numbers are going down." Isaac was pointing in the distance at the numbers above the nearest ship.

"I guess we'll learn how big this place is. They don't seem too concerned about showing us around. That can't be all bad, right?" Dwight asked.

He got a knot in his stomach. "Unless we're insignificant to them. Let's hope they're friendly, shall we?"

It took them nearly half an hour to taxi to hangar berth two. At last count, they'd passed eight different ship configurations during their voyage through the hangar. Each ship had a common design with a wide range of sizes. Only a few appeared to have completed construction, but based on their build rate that was rapidly changing. It was almost like whoever was in command of this outpost was preparing for something.

"Assuming a linear build time and our observed rate of completion, I'd conjecture that these ships started construction under a week ago." Cynthia shared her calculations with everyone over their retinal comms. "This hangar though, it's been here a lot longer."

"That's extraordinary!" Dwight said. "The scale of this operation is staggering. They must be strip mining this and nearby planetesimals for construction. There's gotta be enough minerals for thousands of ships."

Isaac turned and glanced at Bradley. "Boss, we've finished docking at berth two, and control has extended a catwalk to our starboard side. There appears to be normal gravity on the catwalk, slightly less than Tiān but otherwise it's normal."

He had an odd sensation looking at the external cameras. The catwalks and nearby gantries were vacant of people. Except for a few robots attending to nearby construction, there wasn't a human in sight. He adjusted the cameras to examine the ship next to them. "Did anyone notice that our berth mate in slip one has a different design than all the other ships we've seen? It's wider in diameter than the other ships and isn't as fluid of a design. It sorta looks like the tip of a Phillips head screwdriver mated with those droplet ships."

Cynthia nodded. "I noticed that."

"Scans show the same external material but the shape seems more purposeful." Isaac brought up a zoomed in view of the ship on their control panels. "Unless I'm mistaken, those appear to be launch tubes here and here near where the cross-shaped head of the ship converged."

"They seem like they could fold back into the outer panel," Amir said.

"Indeed," Isaac said. "The inner surface of the launch tube is lined with the same material as the exterior, so except for being visible in this direct light, I'm not sure you'd detect them. I wonder what other toys are hidden under that black shell."

"Why don't you come out and see?" came a voice over their comm.

He looked around his team and pointed at his ear. "Who is this, and how did you get on our comm frequency?"

"Aw, quit your whining, Olivaw. Come out and say hello," the voice said.

They all looked at him. He shrugged and mouthed. "No idea."

"Well, they clearly have the upper hand, so why don't we find out what's going on?" Cynthia asked. "What do we have to lose?"

He always saw Cynthia as the voice of reason in whatever group she was in. By the time she spoke up, it was usually fairly irrefutable. "Cynthia's right. Let's meet our hosts, shall we?"

"If we might make a small request, Mr. Olivaw," a second mysterious voice began. "Please leave your weapons on board. I'd hate for there to be an accident with those grenades."

How was that possible? Their level of insight into what was going on inside the ship was uncanny. They'd had that conversation about the grenades outside the planetesimal. Were they compromised?

Without a word they passed their weapons to Amir for re-stowing in the lockers. It was only when they handed them off that they noticed gravity in their ship. Until then, they'd been preoccupied and locked into their stations.

The crew converged at the starboard exit hatch and waited for Amir. He could sense the fear in everyone's body language. They felt as naked as him entering the unknown with no defenses. He'd never imagined he'd lead an away team boarding an unknown ship during a war with an alien power. There was a first and last time for everything.

He slid open the hatch, and they walked as a group across the catwalk to the main walkway. No one was there to greet them. He wasn't sure what to do next.

The hangar felt larger standing in it than it did from the cameras. It was expansive, easily several kilometers long and wide. There was a constant buzz of motion and noise coming from the distant ships as robots hurriedly worked to complete their construction.

The clang of a hatch opening behind them at berth one echoed in the nearby space. They all turned in unison. Out of the ship hopped two human women. The one was a head taller than the other, completely bald, and remarkably tone.

At first glance Bradley didn't recognize either of them, but as they approached, he realized he'd seen the shorter one before. He thought perhaps at the maiden voyage of Spērō, the Tau Ceti colony ship. She'd been with his sister in a small contingent of dignitaries. He couldn't put his finger on her name.

"Doctor Green? Doctor Libby Green... is that you?" Dwight stepped toward the approaching people.

"Doctor Santos, it's good seeing you again." Libby walked up and shook his hand.

"I prefer Dwight nowadays, but yes... it's good to see you.

What… are you doing here?" Dwight stammered as he gestured to the surrounding hangar.

"I'm sure you have a lot of questions. Blazes knows I do," the tall familiar voice said from their comm. "I'm sorry, I haven't introduced myself. I'm Pluto."

Amir chuckled briefly and then blushed, embarrassed at his faux pas. "I'm so sorry. But… as in the cartoon character?"

Pluto laughed aloud. "Bloody hell no! I prefer the original ninth planet in Sol, but whatever helps you remember it I suppose."

Bradley gestured out at the hangar and then back at their greeting party. "So, what exactly is this place and why's it hidden out here?"

Libby made eye contact with Pluto and then returned her focus to him. "For that answer, we're better off heading inside and talking it over. Follow us and don't fall behind. It's super easy to get lost here."

Their two leaders turned and walked toward the hangar exit and his team followed close behind. "I guess I'm following," he muttered.

Isaac subvocalized a message to him. "Sir, should we do something about the beacon?"

"No, let's leave it. We know nothing about these people or their mission. It's the only chance the colony has for an early warning if this heads south."

Passing over the threshold from the alien construction space into the rest of the planetesimal was grounding. The walls and designs were nearly identical to that of the colony. There weren't any mystery materials here. They spotted a few other humans in the distance during their long walk and tube rides, but for the most part, the space was empty.

He glanced at Cynthia and smiled. He could sense she was anxious; she was biting her lip. She hated tense silence.

"So how many people do you have here?" Cynthia asked.

"Several hundred," Libby said without skipping a beat.

"Most of them came with you aboard Spērō. Without your knowledge, of course."

Amir tripped up slightly. "Stowaways?"

Pluto laughed out loud. "No, nothing like that. More subterfuge than stowaway. It was all a part of the stanley."

"The what?" Cynthia tilted her head toward Pluto.

"The mission, the quest, the plan," Pluto chuckled and continued smiling at their confusion.

"Exactly what plan are you referring to?" he asked.

Libby stared at Pluto, their eyes met widening slightly and then returned forward. "Best that we answer that in a few minutes."

Cynthia pushed on. "So how many ships are being built here? We counted 254 in our passing, but some of those smaller ones were challenging to keep track of."

"That was one of our sixteen hangars here in the vicinity of the Zeta Lupi Wheel. That's what we call this place," Libby said.

Cynthia froze in place, the others dodged her to prevent colliding. "Wait, you're telling me there are fifteen other hangars like that one? Where'd... you hide them all?"

"Indeed." Libby tilted her head and started walking again. "This one has more ships in later stages of development. As you've already noted during your tour, we've only recently ramped up production. The other hangars are in other parts of The Wheel and some are being built in the nearby planetes-imals while we hollow them out for materials."

"Yea, we noticed the production here would complete soon. Judging by the exponential appearance of new construction robots and the observed growth rate, you'll be out of space here in a few weeks."

Libby paused for a moment and turned to study Cynthia. Eyeing her for a moment with a smile. "That's a keen obser-vation, Dr. White. I like how your mind thinks." She resumed walking, the crew all briefly eyed each other as they followed on. "As I mentioned already, we exhausted this planetesimal's raw material and pulled those other asteroids into the Lagrange point for mining and reuse. It's slow-going with the mining and all, but we've started general construction on ships in all fifteen of the other hangars."

"You'd almost assume you were getting ready to invade somewhere," he interjected as his crew shot looks at him. He had a steely eyed gaze directed at Libby and was trying to judge her reaction.

Her smile faded and she suddenly became serious. "Those words aren't far from the truth, Mr. Olivaw." She turned her head to confirm the signage beside the door and then back toward them. "I believe we've arrived. Please follow Pluto. I'll be rejoining you momentarily."

They cautiously entered into the meeting room behind Pluto. There were seats for a few dozen and multiple wall screens showing various views of The Wheel hangars. At the center table was food and drinks prepared for them.

They all turned to face him. He could tell by the looks on their faces they were as hungry as he was. When he nodded, they sprint walked forward and grabbed something to eat and drink. He hadn't realized how much the stress of the last few hours had masked his hunger until he smelled real food. He swore he could hear everyone's stomach growl in unison.

They all ate together while pointing and talking quietly beside the wall screens. No one heard the door open behind them.

Zachary walked into the room. "Welcome to The Wheel!"

Bradley spun around and recognition dawned on his face. He hadn't seen Zachary in nearly twenty years, since he'd left for Epsilon Eridani. This was impossible. He couldn't be here. The timeline… the distance, none of it made sense… unless they'd lied to him.

Zachary turned to face him and grinned. "It's good to see you again, bro."

Seeing his brother in front of him resurfaced every painful frustration about his family that pushed him to leave Sol in the first place. He'd neatly packed the pain away years ago, determined never to see it again, and now it was exploding to the surface. It was too much anger, too much pain, too much disappointment for anyone to hold back. He leapt forward and rounded on Zachary, laying a hard left fist to his face. "You bastard!"

7

ZACHARY OLIVAW
ZETA LUPI, OORT CLOUD

The guards appeared out of nowhere and restrained Bradley. They pulled him off Zachary who wasn't even attempting to fight back. He'd instinctively shifted into a defensive posture, fending off all but the initial blow to the face until the guards arrived.

"I can't believe you're part of this!" Bradley screamed. He was restrained in the corner of the room, flanked by two guards and struggling to break loose. "I should've known you and Abigail were at the heart of this mess. I suppose you made up the alien nonsense to control the narrative?"

He rubbed his face with his hand, moving his jaw to relieve some of the pain. "That's gonna leave a mark," he mumbled to himself.

"I'll leave more than a mark if you take these blasted goons off me." Bradley spat and squirmed violently, unsuccessfully trying to force his shoulder loose.

His jaw throbbed to his heartbeat as he watched Bradley struggle. "I deserved that. I'll admit it. You always did choose fists before words."

Bradley lurched forward again, but he didn't get far being held by the muscle. His face was flushing and his temper overflowing. The room of people were in shock over the emotion and physicality of his actions. Everyone on all sides was frozen in place, unsure what they should do next.

"Once you calm down, I'll be happy to explain everything to you." He glanced around the room. "I'll explain it to all of you."

"More of your lies, I'm sure." Bradley was still struggling to break his arms from the guard's vise-like hold.

He shook his head and his jaw vibrated. "No, Brad, we're well past lies and deceit. Right about now we're deep into regret, and scrambling for a hint of hope. Without each other, I'm afraid humanity may fade slowly into the night." He subvocalized a command to display pictures of the alien vessels in Sol on all the wall screens.

There in the center of the picture was the President's ship, their sister's ship. It was dwarfed by the six alien vessels surrounding it. His crew had seen these pictures before, but no one from the colonies had. The room, while still fresh with the shock of the earlier outburst, was now wide eyed with fear.

Bradley leaned forward. "Is this—"

"Yes," he interrupted. "These are the alien ships in Sol. These six are out near Neptune, where the President lured them away from the inner ring. Another six arrived shortly thereafter and are headed toward Earth. We also received intel that these appeared throughout Sol, soon after President Olivaw boarded the alien flagship." He brought up pictures on the wall screen of what appeared to be moons.

"What... what are those? They look like they're as big as —" Isaac said.

"A moon," Libby interjected. "They're each over 1,000 kilometers in diameter. We're not entirely sure what they are but... we have a really good idea what they're for." She looked toward him and nodded an apology for interrupting.

Bradley appeared deflated. His posture had relaxed, and

he was no longer struggling with his handlers. "Abigail… she's… on board. But why?"

Nodding in response, he brought up a video of a shuttle passing between the ships. "They demanded a representative of humanity be present before something they called a Galactic Tribunal."

"Did they state the charges?" Cynthia asked stepping toward the wall screen to get a closer look.

He turned to face her. He'd forgotten anyone else from Bradley's ship was present. "You must be Cynthia White, my brother's girlfriend. It's so very nice to meet you." He walked up and held out his hand.

Cynthia shook his hand in return, her face barely moving a muscle. She looked toward Bradley and silently mouthed "How do they know?"

Bradley shrugged.

"We've been monitoring you for nearly a week," he said. "We know everything that's happening on the colony and throughout Zeta Lupi."

Cynthia was still frozen, her mouth wide open. "But… how?"

He gestured toward the nearby table. "Why don't you all have a seat. I can start from—"

"The beginning please!" Pluto walked to the table and flipped a chair around. Throwing her leg over, she straddled it and made eye contact with Zachary.

The Zeta Lupi colonists let out a small gasp, stunned that they weren't the only ones in the dark.

"Yes… yes, the beginning… the very beginning." He nodded. How far back should he go? Abigail would kill him but he didn't see another way. "This could take a while." He glanced around the room but didn't see anyone here that could help so he just spoke out loud. "Can someone get us some coffee, please?"

"Right away, sir!" Shauna said overhead.

"Is that Shauna, your A.I. assistant?" Bradley pointed upward. "You still have her after all these years?"

"It's only been a few years, bro."

"Oh yea, that's right. We're all still adjusting to that whopper of a lie." Bradley glanced left and right at the guards still restraining him. "Would you mind, brother?"

He eyed both of the guards and made a slight nod toward them. They released Bradley and stepped backward, careful to keep a safe distance in case he tried something again.

"Please, everyone have a seat." He gestured to the table in the center of the room and walked over to the wall screens. He subvocalized to Shauna. "Bring up some of the imagery from the first contact probe. I want to—"

"We can't share that information with these people," Shauna interrupted. "It'll put the broader plan at risk."

He replied subvocally. "I will not hide this any longer. We need Zeta Lupi on our side. It's the only way."

"This wasn't part of Abigail's plan. We're supposed to—"

"I said everything, Shauna, and I meant everything!" He shouted out loud. "No more lies and no more secrets. If we're getting through this mess, it'll only work if we do it together. I don't give a shit if Abigail wouldn't approve. I'm doing it my way from here on out."

Shauna's voice spoke aloud. "Alright, Zachary. If you're confident there's no other viable approach."

He looked upward. There was only one way to truly expose this information. "Harold, if you're also here listening, I'm activating the Zeta Contingency."

Harold's voice spoke from overheard. "Are you positive, Zachary? There is no undoing this. Once activated, we will have... eliminated many of our available options. This was only to be used in a dire situation."

He stared down at his hands. Memories of the screaming matches with Abigail flashed through his mind. They'd spent countless hours arguing over who should know about their plans and how they should lie to people to keep the secret. They'd spent so many years keeping their family secrets, told so many lies, and left so many people in the dark.

"Z…" Pluto whispered, trying to get his attention.

Still lost in thought, he tilted his head shaking off the cobwebs of the past, and looked up at her hazel eyes gazing at him. The others having heard her whisper in the quiet room did, as well.

Pluto blushed at the attention but collected herself. "The truth is rarely clear and certainly never simple. You can do this. I believe in you."

He smiled and winked at her. "I'm positive, Harold. Please execute the Zeta Contingency. Authorization code pente deka dodeka."

"Very well," Harold said overhead.

For several minutes, the room fell into a heavy silence. The crew of the Fountainhead and the members of Bradley's crew were unsure what was happening.

He was engulfed in his comm, deep in preparation. If he was going to do this, he had to do it right.

Amir was antsy and had been squirming in his chair. He broke the silence. "I'm sorry, but if no one else is going to ask, I will. What exactly is the Zeta Contingency?"

He ignored the question and instead focused on gathering his notes. Libby could answer it. He glanced toward her and nodded.

Libby swiveled to face Amir. "That's a fair question. It's Dr. Amir Sonn, correct?"

Amir nodded slowly.

Libby smiled. "The Zeta Contingency is a broadcast protocol. Everything that is said, once we begin, will be broadcast live to all of Zeta Lupi. There will be no delay except for transmission speeds. The broadcast will break into all programming on all devices throughout the colony and cannot be dismissed. We designed it as an emergency broadcast override for the President... or in this case whoever needed it." She gestured toward Zachary.

He looked up and his eyes darted randomly around the room. Some of this stuff was going to piss off Bradley, and a lot of other people in the colony. There was no easy way to deliver this much information without just ripping back the lie, and hoping the wound underneath would heal. He glanced back toward his brother. "Bradley, I know some of this will sound familiar, and some of it... not. All I ask..." He paused and sighed. "All I ask is that you hear it out and try to understand where it's coming from and why we did it."

Bradley didn't say a word. His face was still red with anger. He merely leaned back in his chair, his arms crossed over his chest.

Looking down at his disheveled appearance, he adjusted his shirt and attempted to smooth the wrinkles. There wasn't much he could do so he just straightened up and looked across the room. "Alright, Harold. Let's begin the broadcast."

WITHOUT A SOUND, a tiny camera drone flew out of a hidden recess in the far wall and moved to within a few meters of his face. It hovered at his eye level, awaiting his words to begin.

"Colonists of Zeta Lupi, formerly of Tau Ceti, my name is Zachary Olivaw. I'm the brother of CoPE President Abigail Olivaw and your fellow colonist Bradley Olivaw. I stand before you today from a previously undisclosed base of operations at Lagrange point two between Zeta Lupi A & B. I'm interrupting your transmissions to clear the slate of the past and because I need your help in shaping humanity's future.

"Many lies have been told to you over the centuries. Some of them cut deeper than others. Well, I'm exposing everything to you today. Not out of malice, but because these lies have ultimately led us to where we are, and I fear they may have caused more harm than good. I know their intent came from the right place so many years ago, but I've often wondered if we'd be in a better place had everyone known the truth. We'll never know for sure, but I want to move forward confident that everyone is operating with the same information, the same motives, and the same dreams. It's only then that we can truly define our destiny and not live someone else's vision of the future."

He paused and reached over to pick up a globe of water that somehow had appeared in front of him. His hands were shaking as he squeezed it down and cleared his throat. He'd never done anything like this before, and the thought of tens of thousands of people watching him was frightening.

He stared straight at the camera drone and paused, struggling to find his next words. "Humanity is not originally from Earth." The people in the room let out an audible gasp and quiet murmurs broke out. He imagined this reaction was repeating elsewhere throughout the colony.

"I know everything you're thinking right now. I once thought it myself. I also know that you've heard this same yarn time and time again from fringe conspiracy groups and cults. Please, just give me a moment to present the evidence before you rush to judgment." He subvocalized a command and on the screen in the room, and on every display throughout the colony, pictures of the first contact probe appeared.

"This alien probe was discovered under the ice of Antarctica in the year 2036 by my Olivaw ancestor during an exploratory environmental reconnaissance mission. After they realized it wasn't something of Earth, they covertly took it to a research facility for further analysis. Over the decades and centuries that followed, we mined it for technology and knowledge. For inside this probe was information central to unlocking the origins and the future of humanity.

"After we reverse engineered the probe's computers and unlocked the languages within it, we discovered that it contained a warning. The information within explained why the probe had ventured to Earth. You see, the Galactic Alliance, a group of alien species united to control the galaxy, was hunting down a species that had escaped their judgment. Members of this species had escaped to Earth, and they sent the probe from their homeworld to warn them of the judgment made by the Galactic Alliance."

He brought up some archival footage of a simple species catalog taken from the probe. Dozens and dozens of species pictographs appeared on screen, all marked with the words "Extinct." Some had question marks with notes of corrupt data, some had pictographs of aliens with strange names, and still more had pictographs only. On the final view, he brought up the last species labeled "Nanil" with the word "Extinct" but followed with a question mark "?" and an oddly human pictograph.

"Apparently, each and every species you see on screen had done something forbidden. Something considered so heinous and so revolting that the Galactic Alliance had only one punishment for it, complete xenocide of their species.

"So what crime could lead to such a brutal final judgment? The Nanil were found guilty of giving technology that enabled faster than light travel to an uplifted species. Superluminal technology was protected by the Galactic Alliance and was reserved for non-uplifted species who had independently developed it. It could not be obtained through theft, sale, or gifted.

"Based upon the biological records, evidence extracted from this damaged probe, and subsequent analysis, we believe that humanity is, in fact, the Nanil."

He gestured at the wall screen and a picture of a Nanil appeared. It looked anatomically identical to a human male. The room erupted into a cacophony of voices as everyone was openly processing the information and its implications. Their eyes were wide with fear and confusion.

After a moment of commotion, he glanced around the room and gestured with his hands for everyone to settle down. His hands were shaking. The first hard part was done. He took a deep breath and reached to take another drink of water and composed himself. He then returned his attention back at the camera drone and continued.

"So with this information, my family debated and fought for decades before finally deciding what to do. One group wanted the information destroyed to give humanity whatever time it had left in peace. The other group wanted to use the information to return humanity to the stars. To give us a fighting chance to not only escape the Galactic Alliance but one day, perhaps, defend against them.

"I stand before you today the byproduct of that second group. We took the information and knowledge from the probe, and over the past two hundred years struggled to guide humanity to the planets and the stars. We have once again taken our rightful place within the galaxy as explorers.

"The information was costly to withhold, but we knew that humanity had a history of wars and disputes that tore it apart. At one point, we thought humanity was past those conflicts, so we prepared to share the information. But then the Inner and Outer Ring wars broke out. The resulting bloodshed and divide caused by that conflict lingers to this day and prevented the information from being shared more broadly. Until now.

"After the conflict passed, we made one final push to the stars. We focused our family wealth on helping to both guide and fund multiple colony ships to both Epsilon Eridani and Tau Ceti. To explore and expand humanity to new alien worlds. At the same time, we aggressively expanded our own facilities and exploration without informing most of humanity.

"We sent probes to other stars, searching, and hoping to find our home world. We created a vast network of hidden storage and manufacturing facilities hoping one day we would use them to springboard humanity into a new era of exploration and growth.

"I stand here today in one of those facilities. Its heart is beating with that same mission. One filled with hope and discovery. Yes, this solar system is not the one you thought you were headed to. You see, several years before Spērō was scheduled to depart for Tau Ceti, one of our probes found humanity's home system. The Nanil's home system.

"It was then that we changed the original mission of this colony. We changed its destination from Tau Ceti to Zeta Lupi. This system is en route to our home world. I will not share the name of that system with you today. Not because I want more secrets but because we're at war.

"Let us not forget the message you received from President Olivaw several weeks ago. That message marked the point in time the Galactic Alliance rediscovered humanity."

On that, he brought up the same view he'd shown the others of the President's ship surrounded by six alien vessels. Even now, after everything that was said, audible gasps could still be heard.

"President Olivaw boarded this vessel one week ago to answer before a Galactic Alliance Criminal Tribunal. These ships, also known as Nebula Ships, arrived in Sol soon after she boarded."

He brought up the images of the moon size vessels that had appeared throughout Sol. They were received in silence, everyone transfixed by the visuals and the weight of their implications. He let the images rotate through familiar locations throughout Sol so the colonists could appreciate the scope of the arrival.

"I spoke a moment earlier about hope, of a new future for

humanity. These pictures are not ones of hopes and dreams. They are of impending destruction and fear.

"I need to take a moment and step back in time again, to explain this dichotomy of futures. You see, at the same time we started planning colonial expansion, we formed a small group of scientists set out to reverse engineer the faster than light technologies from the first contact probe. We did this to both preserve humanity by giving us a head start and to also see what we could accomplish when left to our own devices.

"My scientists worked within The Wheel, the name we all called our research lab since we were re-inventing the space travel wheel. We didn't give ourselves access to any of the technologies from the probe. We could only observe the results of their movement and subsequently attempt to create our own mechanism of travel. I'm sure you're asking yourself why we did it this way.

"Our hope was that if we didn't steal the technology then perhaps, perhaps, we could convince the Galactic Alliance that we weren't Nanil. We thought it was worth a shot. What else did we have to lose? Fast-forward to last year and we had a breakthrough."

His excitement was glowing and a smile spread across his face from ear to ear. "You see... something amazing happened. Something extraordinarily unexpected. After decades of attempts and failures to create an alternative faster than light technology, we hadn't just matched the Galactic Alliance speed limit. We destroyed it! Voyages like yours from Sol to Zeta Lupi would have taken humanity 146 years using subluminal technology. Your colony ship Spērō made that voyage in 428 days using Galactic Alliance superluminal travel." He paused and swallowed hard. "Using our latest breakthroughs, my team and I made that same voyage in 5.2 days."

The room erupted with voices of contention and doubt.

Those voices from Zeta Lupi were rebutted with excitement and nods of assertion from his crew from the Sol Wheel.

"What you're hearing in the room with me now are both your and my colleagues learning some of these truths together. Ladies and gentlemen, not only do we have more advanced drive technology than the Galactic Alliance, but we now possess an advantage. A very strategic advantage that we need to leverage in this war."

He reached down and took another drink of water, trying to steady and ground himself from the excitement. He cleared his throat once again and brought up pictures from the hangar.

"We've been working the past few weeks at the Zeta Lupi Wheel to build these ships, humanity's ships. They're a mix of freighters and fighters, destroyers and shuttles. They're equipped with our advanced drives and will enable the people of Zeta Lupi to grow your colony and, more importantly, help to save humanity.

"We need your help to make this happen. We need pilots to return to Sol to bring more colonists here. We also need pilots to venture to Epsilon Eridani to see if they have survived what we believe was the beginning of a Galactic Alliance attack on their system. We need tacticians to help us develop new weapons to defend our worlds. And if the Galactic Alliance attempts to destroy our homeworlds... we need battle ready individuals to defend our people.

"I should remind you, the Galactic Alliance does not yet know about this colony. They, like you, were unaware of its location. We have executed disinformation campaigns that we believe will buy us months or years of time in conjunction with some extreme diplomacy and subterfuge by President Olivaw. Let us not forget about her and the billions of people in Sol whose lives are in the balance.

"Our time is limited and humanity needs our help. We can choose to hide here in Zeta Lupi and watch humanity's fate from afar, or we can step into the challenge and do everything possible to ensure the future of Zeta Lupi and humanity.

"I know this is a lot of information to take in, and I assure you every single piece of history and evidence we have dating back centuries will be transmitted along with this message. There's no more room for lies nor anything but the truth. What we don't have, however, is time. I implore you, I beg you, to join the battle to save humanity."

On those last words, he cut the transmission to the colonies. He walked over to the table and sat heavily in an empty seat. His shoulders slumped and eyes were shaking from the emotion of the speech. It'd taken more out of him than he'd realized.

A guard shuffled in with some coffee for him and others to drink.

Bradley was still seated across the room. He'd stopped crossing his arms early in Zachary's speech and was now leaning forward on the edge of his seat. "I don't understand, Zach… why… why didn't you or Abigail tell me any of this?"

He stared down at his coffee, unable to make eye contact with his brother. "I'll only say that Abigail and I fought for a very long time about withholding this from you. If you didn't have that huge fight with dad so many years ago, and if you didn't have a propensity to over share information when you were emotional, then I'd have told you. But some people felt that those two things could be the downfall to everything we'd accomplished."

Bradley got up to sit next to his brother at the table. "I thought you joined the Epsilon Eridani colonization?"

Tears welled in his eyes and his cheeks burned as he continued to stare at the table. "I needed you to believe that. I needed you to put your all into this colony. To help it grow and succeed. Abigail and I haven't spoken much over the last few years. Because of the distance between us and the wall she thrust between the family with her decision."

He peered upward meeting Bradley's gaze. Tears were running down his face, as well. They chuckled in unison and leaned into one another for a hug. The sort of hug you can only give someone who's both punched you in the face and saved you at the same time.

While everyone else talked through the data feed shared by Harold, they sat in comfortable silence enjoying each other's company and some good coffee. The burden of the information had long been weighing on him and its pressure had finally lifted.

Bradley stood and strolled over to his colleagues to join their conversation. While enjoying the moment from afar, Zachary caught Cynthia smiling coyly at Brad several times. He could tell they were smitten with each other and made a note to have a talk with him about that later.

After a few minutes of discussion, Bradley walked back over to him and faked a quick left jab. Instead, he ended with a rustling of his hair. "So what's next, bro?"

He tilted away from his brothers jostling and uselessly adjusted his short hair. "Well, now that the information sharing is in motion, I hope they react positively when they respond to the message."

"You say that as if you're not going to be here to find out," Bradley said, scrutinizing his response.

He fixed his gaze on his brother. "We won't be. Well, some of us won't be. We have a mission to complete. There's this little thing about our home world that we discovered. We need to go there."

Bradley slammed his fist on the table, shocking everyone nearby. They'd jumped and were now watching the conversation. "Why would you leave? What could that world tell us that we possibly need to know? I thought you said we needed to rally to defend humanity? Or was that just another famous Olivaw speech to pull at the heartstrings?"

"I missed your passionate honesty, Brad. I really did." He

smiled at his brother and held it. It was something their mother used to do with them whenever they got mad or frustrated with something. No matter what, so long as she held the smile or laughed, she could get his brother to laugh as well. After all this time, Bradley was still Bradley, and he, too, started smiling and laughing out loud.

After taking a moment to calm down, Bradley asked again. "Seriously though, why are you leaving?"

"First of all I'm not leaving, we're leaving." He pointed to himself, his brother and several others in the room. "We're hoping to find important information in the Lupus Dark Nebulas that can help us."

"What's this Lupus Dark Nebula and what can it help us with?" Cynthia asked. She'd silently walked up with Pluto in tow close behind.

He glanced at Bradley and he merely shrugged and tilted his head toward Cynthia. "Don't look at me. She asked the question."

The two ladies were smiling in response.

"Do you remember how Libby mentioned earlier that we know what the Nebula Ships were for?"

"Yep, she never told us though," Pluto said.

He nodded. "They're used by the Galactic Alliance after a species cannot prove its innocence. They use matter from the planetary system to form a Dark Nebula barrier around one or more stars, thereby separating the guilty species from all the surrounding systems. No ships can enter and none can leave. We've tried passing through the nebula barrier and the results were instant destruction."

There was a silent realization that those same ships were already in Sol.

Pluto prodded on. "So, what again is the Lupus Dark Nebula?"

He took another long sip of his coffee and then set it on the table. Looking at Pluto, his brows knitted. "From our first contact probe translations, subsequent calculations and missions, we believe it contains the birthplace of humanity, of the Nanil. We need to understand our history, our complete history. We need to go there to find out about the Galactic Alliance and their evidence behind the initial Nanil tribunal."

———

ISAAC SLAMMED his fist on the table, rattling everyone's breakfast trays. "What in the hell do you mean our ship's gone? We've only been here a few days and you lost it already?"

"That's an incorrect assumption." Shauna's voice was coming from the speakers built into the table. "We didn't misplace your ship. We dismantled it."

"Zachary! Get over here. Your A.I. is on the fritz," Isaac shouted across the Zeta Lupi Wheel galley as he waved his arm toward Zachary who'd just entered.

He chuckled and shook his head, raising his finger and gesturing that he'd be there in a minute. Touching his ear, he opened a comm to Shauna. "What's he on about?"

While he waited, he ordered his breakfast from the food processor. It suggested his last few breakfast choices and the other crew's morning favorites. "Chicken and waffles, huh? That had to be something that Brad ordered," he muttered. He glanced around and didn't see Brad but shrugged and ordered the same.

"I presume you're asking about Isaac and not the waffles?" Shauna asked.

He smirked. "Obviously. What does he mean you're on the fritz?"

"He seems to be in a rage over our dismantling of the dilapidated mining shuttle they flew here in."

"How long had it been in service? Maybe they had an emotional attachment." The food processor chirped a quiet little ready tune, so Zachary grabbed the tray and made his way over to the coffee and tea bar. There was quite an array of choices today, at least a dozen fresh coffees and teas. He poured a coffee pod with a dark roast that had light cherry notes and headed toward the table.

"We dispatched that supply shuttle from this station a few weeks ago. Except for the crude retrofits they made to fly it here, it's a pile of scrap. All of their personal belongings are en route to their quarters here on the station or the Fountainhead."

"And you told them this? They're only human. Our possessions have sentimental meaning and importance to us. That's something that might be hard for you to remember, but real nonetheless." He arrived at the same table as Isaac. When he noticed Pluto was there, he sat across from her instead.

She glanced up and smiled at him. "Good morning, Z." Her cheeks turned pink and she returned her gaze down at her plate.

Sweat covered Isaac's forehead, and he had a glazed over look on his face. He turned to face Zachary. "So tell me something, Z. What's your A.I. on about? It said it dismantled our ship. Now, that can't be right." His hands were shaking, and he'd raised his voice enough that people at the surrounding tables stopped their conversations to stare in his direction.

Pluto snapped. "Don't call him—"

He raised his hand to stop Pluto and turned to glare at Isaac. "It's Isaac, right? Not I, Aac, or Issa? My name is Zachary, not Zach nor Z to you. Are we clear?"

A muscle in Isaac's jaw twitched and his face reddened. "I don't give a shit what I need to call you, bossman. I wanna know where my footlocker is, and I want to know it now!"

Pluto flew from her seat, did a one hand hop over the table, and pulled a laser blade from somewhere. She held it across Isaac's neck before anyone could speak another word.

"Swear or talk to him like that again, and you won't breathe another breath. Is that understood?"

Isaac's eyes bulged in surprise and his crew sprang from their table nearby to his defense.

The veins on Pluto's bald head were pulsing with energy and the muscles on her arm were flexed and ready to slit his throat.

"Y... ya... yes," Isaac stammered, his face turning white with fear.

Zachary rose from his seat and gently placed one hand on Pluto's shoulder and the other on the hand holding the blade. She relaxed under his touch and the hint of a smile flickered at the corner of her mouth, only to disappear a second later. Her gaze remained piercing at Isaac.

"Thank you, Pluto." He carefully pulled the blade hand back from Isaac's throat.

Pluto nodded and returned it to the sheath on her hip. She stayed close to his side just in case.

Shauna's voice came over his comm. "I believe Isaac is freaking out because he had several ounces of an illegal narcotic called Humm in his footlocker. I had security confiscate it before they transferred his personal effects to his quarters at The Wheel. Apparently, people use Humm to heighten their senses and reduce reaction times. It's a favorite of pilots and gamers alike. I've been watching him and I noticed that he's also exhibiting the classic symptoms of Humm withdrawal, like sweats and facial twitching."

"Everyone, may I have your attention please!" He spoke loud enough for the others in the galley to hear. "If you came in with the crew aboard the mining shuttle from Tiān, we've transferred all of your personal effects to your quarters. We apologize for the confusion, but we recycled the ship you arrived in for raw materials."

Isaac's crew seemed to be content with his explanation

and returned to their seats, though there were still several concerned stares toward the knife on Pluto's hip.

He stepped forward and leaned close to Isaac to whisper. The stench from his withdrawals wafted into Zachary's nostrils and almost caused him to gag. "You won't be joining us on our voyage. We've scheduled an appointment for you in medical in five minutes where you'll begin treatments for your Humm addiction." He paused for a second and glanced around the table to ensure no one was eavesdropping. He turned again toward Isaac. "Since you're Bradley's mate, I'll give you this one freebie. If you ever get caught again, or if you fail a random drug test, then you're gone for good. Is that understood?"

Isaac glanced from him to Pluto and back again. "Yes, sir." He adjusted his shirt and his eyes darted over toward his friends who were still watching him. He nodded at them, forced a brief smile, and then turned to leave.

"Make sure he arrives at medical," he subvocalized. "And Shauna, where's Bradley?"

"He's in his quarters with Cynthia," Shauna said.

He grinned and chuckled. Reaching over to his plate, he made a quick chicken waffle sandwich from its contents. He and Pluto met each other's gaze and both blushed. "Thanks for that. I'm gonna go talk to Brad about," he tilted his head, "this and the mission. Catch ya in a bit on the Fountainhead."

He turned and headed toward Bradley's quarters, briefly brushing hands with Pluto while passing. Her fingers instinctively moved toward him in response before returning to her side.

THE IBDAC PRIME crew quarters were close to the galley and the meeting rooms at The Wheel. He walked up to Bradley's door and gestured over the door controls to hail the occupants. The door opened with a swoosh a moment later and he stepped inside.

Bradley walked out of his bedroom wearing only his underwear. "Hey, bro. I heard you had it out with Isaac in front of everyone. What's that all about?"

He glanced around for an empty seat, but they all seemed occupied with clothes. "Yea, well, I wouldn't have had to if he wasn't making a public scene while dealing with his Humm withdrawal."

Bradley stared blankly for a second and then nodded. "I didn't know him well, but he was a solid pilot. He arrived at the colony a few transports back and wasn't part of the original crew. He was a dedicated and fast learner. Apparently, too fast it seems. I'd be interested to hear how he bypassed his nanite illegal substance detection, but we can worry about that later. What's the status of the voyage? Are we still on track?"

He stared again at the clothes everywhere and his eyebrows raised. "We're set to depart in four hours. Are you ready?"

"We are. I already spoke to my crew members I thought would be helpful, and they're excited and ready for the challenge." Bradley started walking around the room, picking up the clothes littered about and straightening up.

"You did what? I don't believe I ever gave you the authority to invite crew members."

Bradley laughed and put a hand on his shoulder. "Relax, bro. Want a coffee?"

"Sure."

"I wasn't trying to undermine your authority." Bradley handed him a coffee globe and then walked over to sit on the couch. "Despite what happened earlier with Isaac, we have some extremely talented and dedicated people. They'd be a huge asset to this mission."

He took a drink of the coffee; it was bitter and didn't have his usual additives, so he walked over to the kitchenette for some cream. "You mean like Cynthia?" He took a sip and peered over his bulb to gauge his response.

"Exactly like me." Cynthia walked out of the bedroom with a bag slung over her shoulder. She tossed it onto the couch and walked up to face Zachary, her hands on her hips. "I graduated with a mechanical engineering degree from the Jovian Academy. Top of my class. I know every square inch of our colony and I helped build most of it. I optimized our hydroponics production to leverage the native ecology and introduced my custom nutrient mixture that allowed faster environmental adaptation. I've worked on all of our ships, mining—"

"Relax, Cynthia. Seriously." He raised his hands in a stop gesture. "I was just jabbing my brother a bit. Giving him some shit. I don't have any qualms with you joining the mission. In fact, you'll find that both your and Brad's personal effects from the shuttle are already onboard the Fountainhead, in the same quarters."

Cynthia's mouth curved into a smile. "It's weird hearing you call him Brad. He doesn't let anyone else call him that."

"I'm sure he'd let you call him Brad. Right, bro?" He walked up and nudged Bradley as his face was turning a bright shade of red.

"She of all people knows she can call me whatever she wants." Bradley turned around to glance at her and their eyes met before he returned his focus down to his bulb of coffee.

Zachary shook his head gently. Shauna was right. They were smitten with each other. After another moment, he broke the silence. "So, Mr. Olivaw, who else did you have in mind for this mission?"

"Before we get into that," Bradley began, "first things first, the Fountainhead? Really? After all the years reading literature, classic sci-fi, and playing vid-sim games and you couldn't think of a cooler name?" Bradley had a smirk on his face.

He chuckled. No one appreciated a good name. "Oh come on. You're one to talk. Did you already forget Blue Motto Fotto and Abdiga?"

Bradley shot up off the chair. "Dude! That's not even close to the same thing. I was like five or six! You were still in diapers back then."

"You can argue all you want."

Cynthia brought her hand up to her mouth, muting a chuckle. "What's a Blue Motto Fotto?"

He smiled at her and tilted his head toward the door. "I can tell you on the way to the Fountainhead. Why don't you finish packing, bro? Cynthia and I are gonna catch up on the way."

"Sounds great," Cynthia smirked and gave Bradley a kiss on the head as she grabbed her bag and walked out of the quarters beside Zachary.

Bradley raised his hands and shouted after them. "Seriously? Don't you go spreading any canards, Zach!"

8

BRADLEY OLIVAW
ZETA LUPI, OORT CLOUD

He and Zachary were standing side by side looking out over the expansive hangar in front of them. They both had their hands clasped behind their back and their shoulders squared. He was taking in the scale of the starships neatly spaced and in various stages of construction as far as the eye could see.

Nearest to him was the Fountainhead, the only ship without robots swarming around it. While the other ships were covered in a sea of robots seemingly moving at random, he knew they were assembling them with daunting efficiency.

He cleared his throat. "Harold, how many robots are currently in this hangar assembling ships?"

A spherical robot rolled up next to them out of nowhere. Harold's voice projected from its pearly white form. "That depends on when you ask. A large percentage of the nanites used during construction ultimately reconfigure themselves as part of the superstructure of a ship. Presently, there are 10^{16} robots in operation in this hangar or ten with fifteen zeros after it. If you were to ignore nanites, then there are approximately 2.4 million construction, welding, fabrication, and other robotic forms."

Zachary turned toward him. "The sheer scale of the effort is hard to get your mind around. We've had nearly fifty years to plan and thirty years to create this place, well before anyone arrived. Remember, our original location wasn't Zeta Lupi. We only changed the colony's target star system after a forward probe found Tiān. In fact, a large chunk of the robots were moved here from Tau Ceti. We put a lot of time and effort into coordinating subterfuge to leave room in the forward supply ships for these metallic miracle workers. Some were left behind in Tau Ceti as a hedge and are still working there to build ships we'll add to the fleet before our assault. We weren't as aggressive in Tau Ceti because of its proximity to Sol and the possible need to destroy them at a moment's notice."

He crouched down and brushed his hand over the smooth surface of Harold's robot. This material was strange. He stared closely. It somehow absorbed the smudges his hand made. "With all these robots, what was their original purpose? I mean, had the Galactic Alliance not arrived, I assume we'd use them for something else."

Harold adjusted the ambient color of his robotic form and like a mood ball it blurred from white to green. "The plan was to build more and more colonization ships to prepare for when the colonies reached their critical mass of population growth. Our goal has always been humanity's rapid expansion throughout the stars, unimpeded and aggressive. The further we spread and the faster we accomplished it, the harder we'd be to contain."

He shook his head and smirked and then leaned into the little green robot, pushing hard against it. It didn't budge. "You wanted us to expand through the galaxy like a virus? Perfect. It all sounds like a crazy science fiction story except in this one the Galactic Alliance appears to be an obstacle we didn't expect."

"Yes, they really fraked things up." Zachary's irritation

flared and his hands were shaking as he spoke. "Instead of peaceful expansion... now... now we're preparing to fight for humanities very survival. We'll start by bringing that fight home, but if we need to, we're preparing to take it anywhere in the galaxy if they get in our way."

He stood and placed one foot on the top of the robot. "Well, let's hope it doesn't come to that. Perhaps Abigail can still pull off a diplomatic Hail Mary."

Zachary turned to face the view of the hangar and slowly nodded his head in agreement.

"I was checking out the designs of this place earlier. If I remember correctly, there are sixteen hangars in Zeta Lupi, right? How long until we have an operational fleet and how long until we can make our first strike?"

Zachary gestured at the windowed wall screen and the view changed to a top-down outline of every hangar in Zeta Lupi and a few extras in Tau Ceti. Outlines of the crafts being constructed, the class of ship, and a color coded heatmap from green to orange to red splashed across the wall. The key in the corner indicated that green was complete and red was starting construction. Most of the colors, except for those in this hangar, were a sea of red or orange.

Zachary pointed to the far corner of the display where the raw materials were reported. "We just finished tugging a few smaller metal rich asteroids nearby and into the Lagrange point. Now that we don't care about being stealthy, we can be much more aggressive about resource extraction. We should still try to minimize external system broadcast leakage, though. You never know when an alien probe might be nearby. All things being equal, and assuming we stay on track, we should be ready with a reasonably sized fleet in... 90 days."

His eyes widened. "Three months! That's an eternity. Surely, the Galactic Alliance will reach a final judgement before then. We can't mobilize anything sooner?"

"We have to trust that Abigail can delay them. If she can't, then this war was over before we started." Zachary brought up the last data from Sol on the wall screen. "We're getting data every day from Sol via the probe network. What you're seeing now arrived yesterday morning and is about eight days old."

The data on the wall transformed to show images of the alien nebula ships throughout Sol. Zachary continued. "I don't see how we can launch small skirmishes to scare off a fleet of over a thousand nebula ships or their flagships. These guys are playing for keeps, and we don't understand their offensive or defensive capabilities yet. If the solar system darkening power of a single nebula ship is any indication, then their other weapons will be formidable. No, we need to be ready. We only have one chance at this. Our goal, worst case, is the complete overwhelming annihilation of their fleet. Only that will send a message to the Galactic Alliance to not frak with humanity. It's us or them, take no prisoners. Unless, of course, Abigail can negotiate us out of this."

He studied the wall screen. "I thought Sol was only five days away? Where's the extra three days of comm lag coming from?"

Zachary brought up the star charts between Sol and Zeta Lupi. He overlaid the probe network waypoints. "We don't jump in straight lines. We take multiple different indirect routes and design gaps between our relays to throw off anyone that might be in a nearby system. This means we tight-beam to a nearby relay and then jump from there. OPSEC is of the utmost importance concerning Zeta Lupi."

He subvocalized a command and brought up a view of the Lupus Dark Nebula. "I was thinking about our conversation the other day. How are we planning on traversing the unpassable nebula in Lupus that these nebula ships created? Last I checked, unpassable meant one couldn't pass through it." He chuckled.

Zachary shook his head no and gestured to wipe the wall screen. He motioned his hand across his neck and glanced around to be sure that no one else had seen the map.

He tilted his head to the side. What the heck? He didn't know why, but apparently the topic was off limits here.

"Let's talk about the inbound recruits from the colony," Zachary said. "We've sent a few transports to pick up early volunteers for the war effort. Apparently my speech resulted in a huge wave of enlistment applications. People are already talking about refocusing our engineering talent from colony expansion to weapon testing. They had to end the council open session today after discussions of cloning got out of hand.

"Anyhow, the transports coming in contain several hundred recruits. They're people we've identified as having a pilot aptitude or have specific engineering skills we need. We knew we'd be short pilots, so we're planning to use military A.I. guided by humans for the final assault."

"Aren't we worried about the Galactic Alliance having more advanced systems? They could just take over or disable our ships?"

"We won't know until our first skirmish, but we don't plan on dogfighting their ships. Our plan is coordinated shock and awe. After the first assault, it's unlikely a similar approach will work again. We'll be creating advanced thousand megaton explosive devices hooked up to a small gate drive enabled delivery system. These differ from our gate ships because, rather than gating the missile through with the drive attached like our ships do, we're planning to propel them through the gate and then closing the gate before detonation."

"Then why do we need ships at all? Can't we launch them from anywhere in Sol?"

"Great question." Harold had been silent most of their conversation. He brought up the overview of Sol again on the wall screen. "Unbeknownst to President Olivaw, she's chosen one of the worst locations to convene the alien armada out near Neptune. Add to that the fact that the nebula ships are all positioned near raw energy sources from which they generate their nebula field. These gravitational bodies warp the gate field, which prevents us from precisely and predictably transitioning anything, let alone a warhead to their exact location in space across such a huge distance."

The simulation on the wall screen replayed multiple jumps attempted from a distant point in space to one near a gravitational body. The results appeared to be random and mostly failed. When they were successful, they were catastrophic with the warhead appearing within the body itself.

Harold continued. "We believe we have a viable warhead delivery strategy. If we gate short distances, especially when the angle of attack is parallel to the nearest gravitational vector, we can reliably and with tolerable precision deliver the payload."

The simulation replayed again delivering the payload repeatedly from points in space much closer to the simulated nebula ship. There were still some failures, but they were far less frequent.

"The probability of a successful warhead delivery goes from 0.34% to 98.5%. A much more acceptable tolerance for failure," Harold said.

He was shaking his head in confusion. "I don't understand. What do we even need pilots for then? Can't we automate the entire attack? I mean, we automate the probe network, right?"

There was a long silence and he turned to Zachary. He was expecting an answer from him if not from Harold.

"Short answer?" Zachary asked.

"Lay it on me, bro."

"Redundancy and the Zeroth Law."

He continued to stare at Zachary and chuckled. "I'm gonna need a little more than that I think."

"We need a redundant system in place. One not susceptible to outside hacking and one with manual overrides to deploy the warheads. It has to be a self contained deployment system."

"So they're a glorified bombardier?"

"Sorta, they'll adjust the tachyon particle fields to compensate for external gravitational influences as well but, yes, I suppose."

"It's worse than that if I'm understanding the plan," he said. "They're kamikazes right? They won't be able to gate away once they're near their target ships."

Zachary nodded. "Like I said earlier, it's us or them, take no prisoners. We get one chance at this and we can't risk those ships having gate drives and it falling into the hands of the Galactic Alliance. We design the warhead gate deployment mechanism in each ship to self-implode if an alien gets too close to it."

His eyes went wide. "Yikes! We're asking a lot of these pilots, aren't we? And you mentioned the First Law. I assume you're referring to our A.I. laws. That comes into this how?"

"We're unable to put humans in harm's way when we can't calculate an acceptable probability of success," Harold began. "Even with the zeroth law allowing this course of action, it's by the slimmest of margins. If the battle turns against us it's unclear how the A.I.'s would react. We'll need the pilots to issue military overrides before we gate to allow their A.I.s to disable their laws. This means the A.I.s will only handle diversionary tactics and defensive countermeasures with decoy ships. The pilots can choose to ramp up their A.I.s aggressiveness however they see fit."

"Would we even include A.I.s in the mission if we had enough humans?" he asked.

"No," Harold said. "We're a liability in a military exercise like this. There's a reason we've never used A.I.s in times of war. They either fail at interpreting or differentiating concerns or they're extremely aggressive and wipe the entire battlefield like during the Antarctic War of 2089."

He laughed out loud. "So let me get this straight. We need a human to drop the bomb, but we can't get close enough to our target without a robot who won't put us in harm's way without a direct order. Perrrffeecct... what could go wrong?"

9

ZACHARY OLIVAW
ZETA LUPI, OORT CLOUD

"All systems are green, captain. The ring drive is charged and we're ready to gate," Pepper said.

"All crew members are accounted for," Pluto began, "and we're clear of any nearby gravitational bodies. Our fast follow comm probes are ready and will relay information every twelve hours after our departure."

"Excellent! Weapons, Amir?" he asked.

"Yes, sorry, sir. I'm… still getting used to this." He gestured through the screens in front of him and on his HUD and then turned to Zachary. "All systems are green, defenses are ready, and our offensive systems are 100% captain. We're clear to gate."

"So, Zachary McCrackery. When are we going to learn about the rest of this ship?" Bradley asked.

He turned toward his brother. Irritation pricked at him. You could read the expression on his face. Some things shouldn't be said on the bridge, and family nicknames were one of them.

"In due time, Bradley, in due time. OPSEC and keeping people on a need to know basis give me joy sometimes. Today, me knowing and you not knowing is giving me a whole lotta joy right about now," he said and a smirk crossed his face.

Given the time crunch they were under, they'd done everything they could to prepare for this part of the mission. Every piece of data that Abigail had collected and transmitted through the network was being processed by Libby. Pepper and Pluto, their pilots, were ready and edging to enter unchartered space. Amir had finished his crash course on their navigational, defensive, and offensive weaponry. Brice and Dwight were sifting through the years of archives they'd collected from the colonies and their exploration probes to understand as much alien biology and fauna as possible. And finally Cynthia, well, she was the only other person he'd talked to about the Fountainhead, and she'd been sworn to secrecy until they needed to tell the others. She was down in engineering digging through system and environmental schematics hoping if something went sideways, she'd be able to help.

He hadn't been keen on including Bradley's crew on this mission, but he'd refuse to join without them. It worked out for the best, though. They needed more people to complete the crew. He just preferred they be his own. He had to trust Bradley's gut at some point. They'd have left days before had Abigail not demanded Bradley be brought along.

Before the mission departure, he sat the entire crew down and talked to them about information security. While they were free to record things during the mission, they were operating in a military command structure and absolutely nothing would leave their ship until after their return to port, and then only after Harold and Libby had reviewed it. Any attempt to bypass this would result in immediate arrest and possibly death. They took this last bit by surprise, as they should have. He had to reinforce the importance of security.

"Alright everyone. We all know why we're here… to find the ancestral home of humanity. We need to understand when humanity left for Sol, gather as much intel on what we're facing in those nebula and Galactic Alliance ships, and, if possible, prove our rightful place within said Alliance. There's a lot resting on this mission. I need not remind you of that." He was turning his head around the bridge to make eye contact with everyone and his voice was being broadcasted throughout the Fountainhead.

The speech was redundant, but he wanted everyone as focused as possible on this mission. The peaceful path came down to them executing this part of the plan successfully.

He sat back and adjusted in his seat and then glanced to his right. Pepper was awaiting his order to engage the gate drive. He gave her a nod. "The only way we can discover our past is to push beyond the assumptions of our present. Let's see if we can't uncover our impossible past, shall we?"

Lupus Dark Nebula

WHERE WAS IT? The blasted ticking noise was driving him crazy. Zachary sat up and turned his ear toward the sound. This one was coming from the environmental ducts.

He touched his ear to activate his comm. "Shauna, can you please check out that infernal ticking noise in the ducts? It sounds like it's aft of my quarters."

"I can take a look," Shauna said. "We've talked about this before. They're normal noises for any new ship to have."

A small pair of octopod shaped robots sprung to life from Shauna's workbench and storage area in the corner and clambered up the wall toward the ceiling ventilation duct. They made short work of the duct cover, swinging it aside and shot into the darkness in search of the noise within.

"Would you like me to adjust your hearing while you sleep to cancel out the noise? It might help you rest better."

Shauna's voice was coming from her white robotic humanoid form docked in the corner.

He brought his hands up and rubbed his head. "No. You know I don't enjoy filtering reality."

"But you could really use—"

"I said no! I can't fix this ship if I can't hear what's wrong with it. Now stop coddling me and get me some coffee."

"It's 3am. Are you sure you want coffee right—"

He shot a glare at Shauna's robotic form in the corner. "Never mind. I'll get it myself. I could use to get away from that goddamned ticking anyhow. Some of that eco-pure Alaskan blend we brought from the Zeta Lupi Wheel would do wonders right now."

The faint ticking noise started again. It was like a tiny woodpecker was trying to work its way out of the walls.

He slid out of his bunk and headed toward the ship's galley. He recognized he was being ridiculous about the noise, but if he couldn't fix something this simple, then how the hell was he going to help with the bigger issues they were facing?

They'd been at the Lupus Dark Nebula for nearly a week and hadn't found a way through the veil of darkness. In his gut he knew there had to be a way inside. The nebula would naturally ebb and flow. Gravity would form pockets and pathways through the blackness. They just had to find the trail.

Their probes had mapped out most of the exterior of the nebula. The last set of them returned last evening. They'd sent out dozens of waves in all directions and each one returned with the same results. The density of the nebula was uniform and consistent. Whatever this stuff was that the Galactic Alliance had laid down was amazing. It not only worked to keep its shape, but it did so over millennia and it acted as an impervious barrier to boot.

Another challenge they hadn't made progress on was

analyzing the nebula material itself. They couldn't risk trying to bring any of it aboard. They only had one ship and if they couldn't contain it, then this mission would end before it began.

They'd tried sending a probe through the veil of the nebula when they'd arrived and had interesting results at first. It made it nearly a tenth of an AU into the nebulosity before being destroyed. They thought they'd make it through, but then everything went haywire and fast.

The probe reported uniform structural degradation as the nebulosity swarmed it. There was no other explanation for it. The density of the surrounding particles converged around the probe, and within seconds it disappeared. All signals were lost, and none of their scans returned anything.

As he turned down the corridor leading into the galley, the ship's fire alarm started wailing and an audible warning came over his comm.

"There's a fire in the galley! There's a fire in the galley!"

Smoke was billowing from the galley entrance a few meters ahead. The light above the hatch between him and the galley started flashing red signaling it was about to close to contain the smoke.

He sprinted forward, leaping through the closing hatch and into the smoke. An uncontrolled fire on a ship like this was as certain a death as the nebulosity confronting them.

Staying under the smoke was the first order of business. He ducked low and slid as he turned into the galley. The source of the fire was barely visible through the smoke. Someone had been trying to cook up something far too large in the food processor, and the result was a flaming mess that expanded onto the counter.

He crawled on all fours, making his way along the ground toward the fire. A faint outline of octopods were marching along the floor heading in the same direction. He touched his ear. "Can we contain it? Do we need to dump this segment of the ship to vacuum?"

Shauna replied through his comm. "I'm working on it. The fire isn't as large as the smoke it's letting off. Let me tend to the fire while you extract Pluto."

His eyes went wide as he scanned the floor looking for a body. "Shit," he muttered as his heart skipped a beat. He was stupid. He hadn't even thought to check if someone was in here. Searching left and right he didn't see anything resembling a body.

The smoke was making his eyes water and he hacked into his arm. It was getting thicker by the second. He reached up and pulled his shirt over his nose and mouth and got lower to the floor. He couldn't be in here much longer. "I don't see her. Where is she?" he shouted.

"She's unconscious on a couch on the stern side of the room. Her breathing is irregular, and her vitals are critical," Shauna said.

He belly-crawled through the smoke around the galley tables until he came to the small couch in the corner. Nothing was visible until he was a meter away from it and his heart skipped a beat. There she was. Her arm was dangling off the edge of the couch and she wasn't moving.

Tapping his ear, he subvocalized a command to bring up a room layout with heat patterns overlaid. He pinned it to remain visible when he closed his eyes. It was something he should have done to start with, but he wasn't exactly trained in search and rescue.

He surveyed the fastest route to the exit and without a thought he inhaled a deep breath of air, closed his eyes, and stood up. The layout of the room remained on his eyelids. He reached out and put his arms around the heat signature in front of him at what he thought was her chest and legs and picked her up. She was heavier than he expected, and her limp form almost slipped from his grasp. He adjusted his grip and then turned toward the exit.

Shauna had put the source of the fire out but not before it spread toward the exit. He only had a few seconds to get out.

As if on queue, Shauna's voice came over his comm. "I need to dump the room to vacuum before it spreads. Once you reach the exit, I'll lock it down."

He couldn't reply, he was struggling and needed another breath. His lungs were exploding under the strain of carrying Pluto and the heat of the room was burning his skin.

The pain was too great; he tried taking a small breath hoping the nanites could help, but that was impossible. The inhaled smoke burned his lungs and he coughed, struggling to catch another breath.

He was only a few steps from the entrance, but he couldn't make it. It was too far. He had to get low to catch another breath, so he dropped to one knee and shoved Pluto across the ground toward the entrance with all his remaining energy. He hoped it was enough.

Lying flat to the ground he tried to take another breath, but the smoke was too thick. He coughed uncontrollably and everything faded to black.

ZACHARY'S HEAD WAS POUNDING, and his body felt like it'd collided with a cargo bot. He took a breath; the air was clean.

Everything that happened came rushing back.

He opened his eyes and sat up with a jerk. The fire.

"Lay down, bro." Bradley coughed into his arm.

Bradley was sitting in a chair beside the bed. His clothes were covered in soot, and his face had an ashy gray appearance.

"What... happened? How did—"

"I said lay down." Bradley stood up and rested his hand on his chest, gently pushing him flat. "Shauna closed the hatch with you still inside the galley and exhausted part of the room. It was only enough to remove some smoke and extinguish the fires near the entrance. It was the break we needed to get in and get you out."

"Pluto! What about—"

"She's stable. Unconscious, but stable. She's right over there." Bradley turned and gestured to the hospital bed across the room. "You managed to push her outside of the galley hatch before Shauna closed it. You saved her life."

Bradley had a proud smile on his face. It reminded him of the look their father had when he watched them cross the stage during graduation.

His whole body shook as he rolled on his side and coughed uncontrollably. The pain was blinding, and everything went black for a second. When his vision cleared, he glanced down at his hand. It was covered with a thick black mucus.

Bradley opened a drawer on the hospital bed and took out a cloth, tossing it to him to clean up.

"You'll be doing that for a while," Shauna said over the room's speakers. "You should be ok, though. I've injected you with some of your own stem cells and adjusted your nanites to use them to regenerate your alveoli. They should help speed up your rehab process building new air sacs and repairing other internal damage."

"I feel like shite." He rolled onto his back.

Bradley smiled. "That's about how you look, too."

"Thanks." He chuckled and curled up, coughing, but this time caught it in the cloth. The sudden motion shot pain through his entire body. He unrolled onto his back for a minute, the events from the fire flashing through his mind. "Do we know what started the fire?"

"Apparently she was trying to reproduce the lasagna that

Sky made," Pepper said walking in from the hall. "You remember she made it for me when I returned from my maiden voyage in the Wellspring. It's nice to finally see you awake, by the way." She smiled at him.

"How do you cause a fire making lasagna in a food processor?" Bradley asked, squinting his eyes at the burnt remnants of the lasagna pan Pepper had set down.

"You add the secret ingredients from Sky, but forget to dispose of the foil container they were in. You then leave said container inside the processor's cooking surface and close the door." She tossed a charred container into the pan.

Zachary snickered. "Great, now I want some lasagna."

Bradley stared between the two of them laughing at the comment and then raised his hands in disgust. "Are you fraking kidding me! She destroys the galley and all you can do is laugh?" He was pointing at Pluto.

Zachary tilted his head to the side. "It was an accident. Anyone could—"

"But we can't afford mistakes like that." Bradley stood up suddenly and began waving his hands around the room. "We're out here in the middle of nowhere with no idea how to pass this dark nebula wall of death, all the while we're screwing around fighting our own black death here inside our ship. And tell me something, Shauna. Why the hell didn't you just deploy some of those octobots of yours from the galley to put out the fire? I checked the logs. You sent them in from several rooms away."

Pepper recoiled away from Bradley and was shaking her head in the corner of the room.

"I diverted the octobots from the galley into the air ventilation to diagnose the noises Zachary had—"

Zachary's eyes went wide, and his face lit up. Why hadn't they seen that earlier? "That's it!" He jolted up and swung his legs off the side of the bed. Sliding off, he started toward the entrance when he began coughing and collapsed.

Pepper lunged forward and caught him as he was falling. "What're you doing? You can't be up walking around yet." She led him back to the bed.

He shook his head. "I need to—"

"Get some sleep and let your body repair," Shauna interrupted.

"No! I know what we need to do. I know—"

"No, you listen!" Bradley said. "Your A.I. has a point. You're not going to—"

He slammed his hand on the bed. "Would everyone stop interrupting me and shut the hell up for a second!" He curled up and hacked another glob of black into the cloth.

The room went silent as nervous glances shot between Bradley and Pepper.

"I'm sorry," he began as he wiped at his mouth. "I didn't mean to yell. I just... I know how we can make our way through the nebula."

"How?" Shauna asked.

"Bradley made me realize we've been looking at it all wrong. We've been looking at navigating through this nebula like a traditional ship. Trying to find a clear path to whatever's inside. We're not a fraking traditional ship! We can gate past the nebula. Straight to the other side of this wall of death!"

Pepper nodded. "It could work. But how would we compensate for the mass of the nebular particles? The mass will throw off the gate transition and who knows where we'll end up."

He slid off the edge of the table and paused for a second. Happy he wouldn't collapse again, he took a few cautious steps toward the medical screen on the wall beside his bed. He gestured and brought up a drawing surface where he sketched a rough two-dimensional shape. It resembled the surface they'd mapped around the nebula.

"The particles that make up the surface are uniform for

the most part. These sections that have more curvature than others." He highlighted the curvier areas. "We'll want to stay away from those. We want—"

"As flat a surface as we can find," Pepper interrupted.

He pointed at her. "Yes!"

"Assuming the other side has an equivalent shape to the one facing us, we should be able to gate straight through."

Bradley raised his hand. "One problem. You don't know how far you need to jump without hitting something on the other side."

"We can assume that the curvature of the nebula is purposeful and surrounds a nearby star system," Pluto said. She was sitting on the edge of the hospital bed on the far side of the room watching them.

Everyone turned and gasped.

Pluto continued. "If we know that, we can extrapolate the locations of many of the stars around the peripheral of the nebula. With that mapped out, we just have to find a flat surface far enough from a curvature but not close enough to a neighboring one."

"You're ok!" Pepper rushed to Pluto's side and gave her a huge hug. Tears were streaming down her face, and she was smiling from ear to ear.

Pluto fell back from the impact of Pepper's hug and returned the bear hug with a muted groan and equally wide smile on her face.

He stumbled across the room and collapsed next to them on Pluto's bed. Tears were filling his eyes as well and they both locked gazes. He smiled and reached over to clasp her hand in his. "I'm... we're all so happy to see you're ok. You had me scared there. When I found you, I—"

Pluto leaned in and kissed him on the lips. She held it for a moment before stopping. "Thank you," she whispered.

He pulled away slowly and blushed when their eyes met. "You're... welcome."

"Alright you two. We can give you the room in a minute," Bradley joked with a smirk. "Can someone tell me if what she said makes sense?"

He smiled and nodded. "She's right. That's how we'd find the optimal transition point to jump past the nebula. Once we have that, we can calibrate the gate drive to drop us at the midpoint between this side and the far side of the nebula and voilà! We're inside."

"I've already begun the calculations," Shauna said. "If preliminary results are correct, then we're actually close to an ideal transition point. Should we prepare the crew?"

"Hot damn!" Pepper clapped her hand together and hopped off the bed.

"Let's wait for the calculations to complete and finish the cleanup from our little fire. But yea, let's prepare for transition," he said. "Until then, I need a little shuteye. All of this talking is draining. Everyone out!"

Bradley stood up and headed out the door, a smile plastered on his face.

Pepper skipped off behind him and the door closed behind her.

Zachary turned toward Pluto. She was staring at him with an adorably coy smile that sent tingles throughout his body. He tilted his head toward her pillow and flashing his eyebrows. "Any chance we can nap over here? The other side of the room is looking awfully far away."

She laid down and slid toward the wall to make room for him as the lights in the room dimmed.

He cuddled in next to her and put his arm on her waist. Leaning in, he gently kissed her before resting his head on the pillow and closing his eyes.

They were asleep within seconds.

10

BRADLEY OLIVAW
LUPUS DARK NEBULA

The blackness surrounding their ship was stark. The familiar ever glowing field of star formations and nebulosity defining the Milky Way had been replaced with absolute darkness.

"It's empty," Zachary muttered.

"Not quite." Harold brought up a video on the wall screen of what appeared to be a star, an oddly shaped one at that. "Our probes are only now returning their initial data."

Bradley walked closer to the wall screen and squinted. "Magnification one hundred, and filter a bunch of that visible light, Harold. Zoom in on this region." He waved his hand over a spot where the shape made an unnatural right angle.

The image brightness reduced and a smaller version of the star appeared in the corner. The larger video zoomed in on the strange star. Shapes formed where there was once only light. There was what appeared to be a spherical structure surrounding the star itself.

"Is that... a Dyson Sphere?" Zachary's eyes were wide. "We'd always theorized they were possible. I just never imagined anyone would actually attempt to create one. Harold, how large is this star?"

"The star appears to be an orange-red giant of spectral type K2/3III. It's approximately four times the size of the sun in Sol. To answer your first question, yes. This appears to be a partially completed Dyson Sphere."

"And a massive one at that," Zachary added. "Can you show the rest of the planetary system?"

"I am. There are no planets, moons, or detectable asteroids in this system."

Bradley's jaw dropped open. The stars outside the nebula overflowed with asteroids and random planetary bodies. "It's a fraking ghost town."

Zachary shook his head. "How's that possible? I mean, there has to be something. Can we come around the far side of the star? Maybe there's something over there."

Harold overlaid a set of transit paths on the wall screen. "I sent a set of forward probes to the other side and toward the further reaches of this section of the nebula. Their results should arrive shortly."

"Are there any communications or signals anywhere in this system?" Bradley asked.

"No. Nothing decipherable as structured communications has appeared on any frequency or spectra. There does appear to be some motion closer to the star." Harold zoomed into a spot near the edge of the star and Dyson Sphere. Several objects were passing in front of the bright area. "It's impossible to tell if it's purposeful or just something orbiting."

"Let's head in for a closer view," Bradley placed his hands on his hips. This thing was insane. It's a marvel of engineering. The resources and technology required to build this structure were unfathomable.

"Why don't we wait an hour?" Zachary asked. "We can gather more intel and have some other eyes from the team take a look. There's no sense in rushing in before we know more. I'd rather be safe than sorry."

Bradley exhaled. He was probably right. "Should we wake

everyone? I mean, you sorta jumped the gun coming up here with the entire crew asleep."

Zachary chuckled and turned to face him. "Yea, I did, didn't I? Let's give them a bit more time. We can head to the galley and make some breakfast. Something tells me we'll need it."

Bradley nodded, his gaze still transfixed on the star. "This place is unsettling. It… gives me the chills. I don't know if it's the lack of surrounding stars and constellations, or the lack of anything at all. It feels dead."

Zachary walked up and placed his hand on Bradley's shoulder. "I know what you mean. I'm sure we'll find something. Let's get on that grub. Our peeps will appreciate it, and we need to butter them up before we tell them what we did." He tugged on his shoulder a bit but Bradley didn't budge.

"You mean what *you* did." Bradley smirked and gave Zachary a sideways glance.

Zachary smiled and nodded. "Me, we… it's all the same. Come on, bro."

"I'll be right behind you. Give me a few minutes."

Zachary shrugged and headed toward the exit.

Bradley stood there watching the objects moving over the bright area of the star. They were on the float, orbiting around it. None of them were moving along arcs or in unnatural directions.

"I don't understand," he muttered. "How could someone build this and then just abandon it?"

"There are countless possible reasons, sir," Harold said. "We could start with the lack of raw materials in the system. Perhaps they couldn't build anymore."

He nodded. "Can we zoom in any further?"

The wall screen changed, and the view moved closer and closer in toward the edge of the sphere. He could make out partially completed panels, scaffolding, and what looked like docking ports or cooling vents. The material along the edge had an odd motion to it, like it was turning over on itself.

He raised his hand and pointed. "Is that melting?"

"It appears so. If I were to conjecture, I'd say they're capturing the energy from the star using a material in a constant state of liquidity. This would allow them to generate thermal energy using the vacuum of space to cool it naturally. Perhaps those ports are vents and are used to release excess heat. But it's too hard to confirm at this distance. Should I send a probe in for a closer look?"

He shook his head side to side. "No, that won't be necessary yet. Are there any armaments on this thing? I mean, anything that looks like it could attack us?"

Harold brought up several strange-looking views of the spheres exterior. "These are the most unusual structures I've found. Given the regularity of their placement around the exterior and the fact that there are millions of them, I'd hazard to guess it means they're merely scaffolding or maintenance cranes of some sort."

The images showed long mechanical booms projecting outward from the surface. Some were at right angles, but others were directed inward, like they'd been turned. One of them near an unfinished segment appeared to have a piece of the material attached to it.

He sighed. Harold was probably right. It seemed wrong to not have anything defending a structure as large as this, but this whole damn place was strange.

A cold shiver coursed through his body. It started at his head and shot through his extremities. He reached around and crossed his arms, rubbing them for warmth. The last time he'd felt coldness like that was at his father's funeral. When it'd hit him that he was truly gone, and they'd never see him or hug him again.

They'd gambled coming here. He'd wanted to stay behind in Zeta Lupi, to help build the fleet to defend Sol. But he felt a debt to Zachary, and Abigail for that matter. The burden they'd taken on over the years with this knowledge had crushed their family.

He'd been selfish at times. There were countless occasions he could remember where his father had tried to talk to him about this secret. Never being quite serious in his questions and never saying that he knew anything as a fact. He'd been testing him, hoping he'd come around and ask for more details. To join them in this Circle of Trust that Zachary had told him about. But he never did.

Bradley always figured it was a joke, another ruse to lure him into the family business. Well, here he was, neck deep in it, and it reeked of death and destruction.

11

ZACHARY OLIVAW
LUPUS DARK NEBULA

The pan with the apple pancake was still steaming hot from the food processor. The syrupy melted cinnamon and sugar was bubbling and had a light-brown sheen. Zachary flipped it carefully onto a platter, exposing the darker brown crusty underside. "Perfect," he muttered. "Just like mom used to make."

He grabbed the apple pancake tray and the Dutch baby and carried it to the table of half asleep people. Their eyes locked on the golden delicious dishes and their mouths fell open when they realized what they were.

"That looks amazing," Pepper said. Her dark brown hair was still tousled from a fitful sleep. She leaned forward and took a long sniff of the platters. "How come you never cooked for us like this at the Sol Wheel?"

He shrugged. "I never needed to, I suppose. We always had Sky, and I was crazy busy. Besides, she'd probably cook circles around this."

Pluto, Cynthia, and Libby were all quietly sipping their tea and coffee, watching him cut the pancakes into pieces.

"He's mine. Stop drooling," Pluto joked, waving her

finger at all of them. She gave him a wink and slid her hand into his lap, squeezing the inside of his thigh.

Vivid memories of the evening before rushed through his mind. They'd had fun in the infirmary. He hadn't expected her to be in any shape to mess around after the fire, but he wasn't about to say no when she'd made the advance.

Cynthia took a piece of the Dutch baby and put it on her plate. She squeezed a healthy amount of lemon over the powdered sugar surface and started eating. "Where's Bradley?" she asked between bites. "I woke up and he was gone. Figured he was with you."

He finished his mouth full of apple and wiped his face with a napkin. "He was. I mean, before I left him on the bridge." He leaned forward to pour some orange juice.

Libby froze, her brow raised. "What were you doing on the bridge?"

He smirked but didn't make eye contact. "Nothing," he mumbled as he set the juice down and shoved another fork full of pancake in his mouth.

"You didn't!" Pluto said. She was leaning forward, fork halfway to her mouth.

"What? What'd I miss?" Pepper was slathering her apple pancake in syrup and had a look on her face like she was about to attack it.

He peered at Pluto and swallowed hard. His eye twitched.

Pluto swatted his arm. "You did! I was wondering why I had weird dreams of ants crawling over me. We freaking jumped."

"I... I... couldn't help myself," he stuttered. Busted. His shoulders squeezed together and he cowered down. "Harold came back with an image and an all clear, and, well, we jumped."

Pluto pursed her lips together and shot a glance at Libby who was shaking her head.

"Shit!" Libby muttered as she hopped up and out of her chair. "Grab the food. Let's head to the bridge."

Everyone else except for Pepper stood up and started gathering the plates and drinks. They headed toward the exit, everyone taking a thwap at him along the way.

While it wasn't a complete success, it could've been worse.

"Where… the heck… is everyone… going?" Pepper mumbled between chews. Her mouth was stuffed with apple pancake.

ZACHARY WAS the last person to enter the bridge, minus Pepper, of course. She was probably still in the galley eating. He walked in and saw everyone standing around Bradley, necks craned at the massive Dyson Sphere on the wall screen.

"Anything new?" he asked.

"I can't believe you didn't wake us," Libby said. She'd crossed her arms and was gazing at the wall.

He raised his hands in surrender. "Alright. Enough. I'm sorry. Besides, it wasn't me alone. Bradley was there, too. Why am I the one getting all the grief?"

Pluto popped a piece of the Dutch baby into her mouth. "You were the guilty one buttering us up with food, Z." She winked at him.

Bradley turned toward him and smirked before he bit off a piece of pancake.

"What's the sphere made of?" Cynthia asked, gesturing at the screen.

"Based upon spectroscopy," Harold began. "It appears to be a material similar to the inner skeleton of the first contact probe. A composite of tungsten and iridium in a nano weave. At this scale, it'd take star systems of material to build something this massive."

He nodded. Harold was right. "It'd be a perfect material.

It has ridiculously high melting strength. That's why it's weaved at the nano level and not forged. But there's still no way it'd survive as a solid on the inside of that sphere. They must use something else, a liquid metal alloy perhaps."

Bradley walked up to the wall and turned to face everyone. He was shaking his head in frustration. "I don't know how you all can think about the material science of this situation. This place is a cemetery! There's no life here. How's that not at the forefront of your mind right now?"

Pepper walked onto the bridge just as Bradley was at the peak of his anger. "I see you're screaming again."

"What the hell is that supposed to mean?" Bradley asked, turning to face her.

Pepper had her hands on her hips and a scowl on her face. "You were yelling the other day in Zeta Lupi, you were yelling last night in Pluto's hospital room, and you're yelling now. You're an angry little man, aren't you? I can see why Zachary wanted to be so far away from you."

Bradley took a step toward her and paused when Cynthia stepped between them. She placed a hand on his chest. "Relax," she whispered.

"Alright, both of you cut it out!" Zachary said. "For crying out loud. This is the last thing we need right now. Bradley's right, we should be taking this more seriously. But dude, Brad, cut us some slack. Everybody deals with things differently. Me, I prefer not to yell at people to make my point. I get that you're dealing with a crap ton of trust issues right now, but I laid it all on the line in Zeta Lupi. I wouldn't have asked you here if I didn't hope we could work together. Ok?"

Bradley was still staring at Pepper, wishing for her to say something else.

"I said Ok?" He waved his hand playfully in front of Bradley's face like he was behind a glass fishbowl.

Bradley nodded and peered at him with a smirk. "Ok. Let's—"

The wall screen flashed, and Zachary turned toward it. It was playing a video from the other side of the Dyson Sphere, except it wasn't an inverted image of what they saw before. There was a huge beam of yellow light shooting out the side of the sphere and off into distant space.

"What the hell's that?" Pluto asked. "It looks like a laser of some sort."

Bradley turned to face the wall. His shoulders loosened and his face tightened in concentration.

Harold's voice spoke. "It appears to be some form of plasma laser emanating from the surface of the sphere. I don't know how it's maintaining its beam like structure, but that's not important. What's notable is, where is it going?"

The video on the wall screen jumped several times. It took multiple hops from one of their gate drives until it finally stopped. There, in the middle of the screen was a prism, or at least it looked like one. The beam entered at one end of an enormous transparent crystalline structure and split into dozens of smaller beams shooting off in multiple directions.

"It's beautiful," Zachary muttered. He'd never seen such a massive display of engineering and art before. They had so much to learn out here.

"That's a lot of energy beams. Where do you suppose they all go?" Pluto asked.

Bradley stepped toward the wall screen. "I don't know, but let's find out. The sooner this system is behind us, the happier I'll be."

"Should I direct our probes down any particular path?" Harold asked.

Zachary shook his head. He walked over and sat down in the captain's seat. "No. Let's focus our attention on and around that structure. We need to figure out if there's any way to navigate this nebula maze. The sooner we know where we're going, the faster we'll get some answers. Maybe there's something in there that'll tell us."

Bradley came up and sat beside him. "Do you think we'll be able to get inside? It looks like crystal."

He shrugged. "Only one way to find out. Ladies, please take a seat." He subvocalized and opened a comm to the broader ship. "Everyone prepare for another set of jumps. We're about to follow the yellow brick road."

"Ugh," Bradley muttered, putting his head in his hands. "You really do have the worst jokes."

12

BRADLEY OLIVAW
LUPUS DARK NEBULA

They agreed to split up the crew for their initial EVA. The first team was comprised of Bradley, Pluto, and one soldier from Tiān. Her name was Pierce. The second team was comprised of Dwight, Pepper, and another soldier named Kamal. Everyone else remained aboard the Fountainhead.

The teams were on the float, headed toward hexagonal markings on the surface of the crystalline structure that Harold and Shauna believed were external hatches. Bradley's team was headed toward the closest. The second team with Dwight was heading toward a similar marking at the opposite end.

Bradley chuckled, his voice briefly crackling over the comm.

"What's so funny?" Pluto asked.

"The name Fountainhead," he said, adjusting his approach path. He was coming in too hot. "Where does he come up with this stuff?"

"Right? I think it's naff, but he has his own unique style I suppose."

"That he does."

"You know I can hear you talking about me?" Zachary asked.

"I do." Bradley adjusted his suit's alignment toward the target. "We're approaching the hatch."

His suit automatically fired microscopic bursts of ion particles to navigate through space. All he needed to do was keep his target aligned, and the suit took care of the rest.

Floating up to the hatch, there weren't any noticeable handles. On one side there were flush rectangular markings that could have been hinges he supposed. It was hard to tell for sure.

"Anyone have any ideas how to open this thing?" he asked.

"Can you try touching it?" Harold asked.

"Here goes." He floated forward and reached his hand out toward the hexagonal segment. His fingertip brushed against it but nothing happened. He then tried placing his palm flat against the surface and moving it around.

Something changed when he moved it along the edge opposite the rectangles. The glassy surface pushed inward about two centimeters and then stopped abruptly when he pulled his palm away. He hadn't been expecting that.

"It moved inward," he muttered. "It stopped when it went out of my reach. I'm going to try pushing forward continuously. Everybody keep a safe distance. We still don't know what this might do. There could be pressure blowback."

"Ack," Pluto and Pierce echoed as they used their suits ion thrusters to back up a bit, flanking him on each side.

Bradley ordered the suit to move forward, and he pressed his hand flat against the same recessed segment. It continued to push inward nearly thirty centimeters until it stopped and slid sideways.

"Open sesame!" he said.

Cheers erupted over his comm from onboard the Fountainhead. He was much happier being out here, doing something productive rather than watching from afar. Being confined to the damn ship and surrounded by all this darkness was making him stir-crazy.

Pluto floated closer to peer inside the hatch. The light on her suit illuminated inside the chamber a few meters.

He turned and gestured toward her. Maybe she wanted to lead them in.

"No, I'm good. Gentlemen first," she snickered.

He reached up and bumped his hand against his helmet. "Damn these things. I keep forgetting it's always on. If we lose signal inside, then we'll deploy a comm relay as far as possible. Here goes nothing."

He took a deep breath and his suit began floating into the hexagonal entrance. As he passed over the threshold, everything went upside down. Literally. He tumbled upward and crashed hard to the ground. Alarms were blaring in his suit. The fall breached his helmet, and he was rapidly losing oxygen.

Pain shot through his shoulder and he sat up, searching for any other dangers. Illumination around the room had flickered on when it sensed his motion. The walls were sprinkled with signs posted at regular intervals, but he couldn't read what they said.

Glancing upward, he studied his helmet checking for cracks. The lightweight transparent nano-composite polymer was flexible, and yet stronger than steel. He couldn't imagine how a fall like that had cracked it. The air had rushed out and nanites were spreading along the fracture, but the breach hadn't yet been sealed. It took him a second to realize he wasn't gasping for breath.

He switched his HUD's display to show the chemical makeup of the air. It was a perfect mixture of nitrogen, oxygen, and other trace chemicals. Ideal for human life.

"There's breathable air," he said.

Pluto chuckled. "And now we know which way's up."

She and Pierce had rotated around their center and stepped carefully through the threshold into the structure.

Bradley laughed and rubbed his shoulder.

"That sign to your left," Libby said. "If you look at it again, I'll overlay a translation."

He glanced up at the sign.

Authorized Personnel Only

    The containment field is dangerous. A laser-induced plasma channel is in operation. No weapons or pregnant Humans or pregnant Nanil beyond this point.

"Well, I guess now we know what that bright yellow beam of light we followed here is," Pluto said.

He tilted his head at the sign. "So, it's either? Humans or Nanil. I guess we worked closely together." He pushed up off the floor and turned toward the long tunnel in front of them. "Everybody ready?"

"What about our rifle and side arms?" Pierce asked.

He glanced over his shoulder and pointed up at the sign. "Says to leave them behind. I can't believe I'm saying this, but, I'd follow the alien's orders."

"Our orders you mean," Pluto said with a smirk.

He smiled. "Something like that. Toss them over there on the bench. I'm sure no one will steal them."

He took a few hesitant steps forward toward the darkness. The lights in the darkened space clicked on and illuminated a bit further. "How nice of them. It looks like they'll turn on the lights as we go."

They continued inward, deeper down the tunnel another ten meters.

"Fountainhead, can you still hear us?" he asked.

"Your signal is loud and clear," Libby said. "I guess every alien surface isn't coated in stealth material."

"Are we going to check any of these access panels?" Pluto asked. "There might be something interesting inside." She was standing beside one of them. It had a small recessed handle and was marked with an image and alien text.

"Why don't we do that on the way out? Let's see what's down here." He gestured with his hand down the tunnel.

She nodded and continued moving forward, close behind him.

They traveled in single file another hundred meters down the tunnel. There weren't any side tunnels or intersections of any kind. Only one direction, inward.

After what seemed like an hour of slow, cautious walking, the tunnel ended at another hatch. He checked his HUD. They'd only been walking for fifteen minutes. The adrenaline and excitement of the event had warped time since they'd boarded.

He walked up to the hatch and confirmed in his rear camera that everyone was close. He then reached his hand up and rested it on the same spot he'd done on the exterior hatch. It pushed inward. This time he didn't need to apply pressure. It moved all on its own.

"Shit!" He took a step backward and raised his hand upward to block the glare. His suit adjusted to protect his eyes, but it'd been delayed.

There, in front of them was a cavernous chamber, larger than any he'd ever seen before. It was filled with thousands of prisms, mirrors, and other unknown equipment floating in space. The room was alight with a rainbow of spectrum and his HUD was reporting other non-visible wavelengths of the electromagnetic spectrum.

Pluto rapped her hand on the wall outside the door.

He turned and glanced toward the noise, but he couldn't

make out anything. His eyes refused to focus. His suit translated the sign.

Caution: Dangerous plasma channel field ahead. Please enable ocular protective.

"Now you tell me," Bradley muttered. He blinked hard and rubbed his eyes. The whites were starting to level out and his vision was clearing. His medical nanites were reporting an enormous volume of rods and cones were destroyed in his eyes. They'd begun stimulating regrowth, but it'd take some time before he'd regain his full vision.

He waved his hand in a forward motion. "Why don't you take the lead, Pluto? I don't want to risk falling over the edge. My eyes are still adjusting."

"Sure thing," she said taking a step forward. "You gonna be ok?"

"Yea. My nanites are working it. I'll be fine."

Pluto stepped past the doorway and peered left and right. "Looks like a wall panel of some sort over here." She stepped to the right and he followed. Pierce was close behind.

He passed around the corner and glanced to his left. There was nothing but a long blurry platform leading into the distance. He then faced right and leaned forward to peek over the edge. It was a ridiculous drop, and a wave of vertigo hit him. It almost felt like he was falling forward.

Pierce grabbed his arm and pulled him back. "Might not be the best idea stepping near the edge, sir. Maybe you should hug the side with us." She guided him to the wall, and he reached out a hand to touch it.

"Thanks," he muttered. "This place is insane. It's a scale of technology I've never seen before."

Pluto chuckled. "You should check out the power cores at

the Zeta Lupi Wheel some time. They're not far behind this. Z and his team have done some amazing shizit."

It would take a while for him and a whole lot of others to get used to this new world. His Olivaw family in Sol had been throttling technological advancements from the broader populace for centuries and now they were playing catch up.

He turned to face Pluto. She was attempting to interface with the wall screen but it was slow-going. Each screen took twenty to thirty seconds for Libby's algorithm to translate.

Stepping around her, he continued sliding his hand along the wall. His vision was slowly starting to come back. The nanites reported that it'd take several hours for his eyes to fully heal.

When he glanced ahead, he couldn't make out anything that'd trip him up, so he took it slow. He slid his foot along the ground as he went. He was about five meters from Pluto and Pierce when his hands activated something and a whirring noise followed.

"Frak," he muttered. His heart skipped a beat and he closed his eyes.

"What happened?" Pluto asked.

He slowly opened his eyes. His HUD camera showed that she'd turned to face him. "I... touched something. My hand, it must have brushed against..." He squinted at the reverse camera. "It looks like something popped out of the wall."

Pluto rushed over to his side.

He'd frozen in place, not wanting to disturb anything else.

She reached her hand near his and felt the recessed button he'd depressed. Reaching up, she carefully pulled a small rectangular sheet from the wall. "You ejected a... tablet. At least it looks like a tablet."

He was still standing perfectly still. Her blurry visuals appeared in his HUD. She was holding a small tablet in her hands, and the screen sprang to life when she touched it.

"What is that?" he asked. "And am I safe to move?"

She scanned the area around him and nodded. "You're fine. Just stick to me from now on ok? This looks like a network diagram of some type." When she tapped the center of the screen, the image changed to show a three-dimensional view of what looked like the structure they were standing in.

There was a flashing dot inside the structure on the panel. The translated words 'You are here' overlaid on the screen in his HUD.

He let out a raucous laugh that echoed through the chamber. His voice rebounded back on itself several times before stopping.

Pluto and Pierce glanced at him and chuckled.

"What's so funny?" Pierce asked.

He shook his head. "My heart skipped a fraking beat there. I'm not gonna lie. I thought I'd screwed the pooch." He chuckled again. "Turns out, it was only an eject button to a damn map."

Pluto laughed out loud and Pierce followed. Their voices playfully echoed through the chamber.

"This life or death mission stuff is gonna take some getting used to," Pluto said.

"No kidding." He turned to face them and stepped up beside her. "So, what's on that thing?"

Pluto panned around the tablet detailing the structure they were standing in. "This view looks like a map of where we are. It shows all the access points. Lots of nooks and crannies to check out, but overall, it looks like a power relay station to me." She squinted and panned around the far side of the map where another dot was visible. "If I'm reading this right... our second team is about to reach the end of their tunnel."

Pierce stepped forward and leaned against the railing. "Hey Kamal, watch your step!" she shouted. Her voice echoed repeatedly downward.

"Holy crap!" Kamal's voice came over their comm. "You about gave me a heart attack. Where are you guys?"

"Turn to your right," Bradley said. "There might be a set of buttons on the wall about six meters forward. If you push one, a tablet should pop out. It's a map to this maze we're in. We're on the far end of this light show. Are everyone's eyes ok?"

"Yea," Pepper's voice replied. "We heeded the warning signs before opening the door."

That one definitely dislikes me.

"We've got a tablet and we see you," Kamal said.

He reached forward to touch the tablet but Pluto pulled it away. "Sorry, I was just wondering what that first pattern of lines we saw was before you tapped the center."

She chuckled and played with the controls for a second until she managed to return to the first screen. She panned around to orient herself and started nodding.

"What do you see?" he asked.

"It's a map of the power grid. It shows everywhere the energy is being routed throughout the nebula."

His eyes went wide. "All of those symbols are relay stations? There must be... thousands of them."

"Seems like it," Pluto said. "Why don't you take this back to the Fountainhead so Libby and Cynthia can give it a once over? We don't need you pushing any more random buttons again. Pierce and I will give this area a once over. We'll follow behind you."

He smiled and nodded. "That sounds like as good a plan as any."

She handed him the tablet, and he slid it into a storage pouch on his back. He turned to the left and walked along the route they'd come from, back toward the exit.

13

***

ZACHARY OLIVAW

LUPUS DARK NEBULA

"I don't see the point in going into the center of the nebula first. Wouldn't we want to check out these outer relays before heading into the belly of the beast?" Bradley asked, pointing at the wall screen.

They'd been debating on which way to go for over an hour. Zachary had hoped it would be a fruitful conversation of give and take, but it wasn't. It just highlighted to him that Bradley wanted to do what Bradley wanted to do. He might play well with his peers from Zeta Lupi, but he had the same old chip on his shoulder from their childhood.

"I've said it a thousand times," Zachary said. He raised his hand in frustration but thought better of slamming the table and rubbed his face instead. "Species expand outward from a central star. It only makes sense that the middle would contain what we're looking for."

"I'd concur with—" Harold began.

"Shut it, you automated monstrosity!" Bradley interrupted. "If I want to hear from you or Zach's shadow Shauna, I'll ask. Otherwise, not a word."

"I value their opinion. Don't I have a say in the matter?"

"Argh! We're never going to see eye to eye here. That

much is obvious," Bradley said. "This is your ship. Take us wherever you want. I'll be in my quarters." He turned and stormed out of the room.

The door slid open before Bradley reached it, and the ladies walked in. He tried to shoulder his way through, but Cynthia was already there holding him up, whispering to him. She shot a few glances at Zachary.

Pluto slid up to Zachary's side and leaned into him. A sigh escaped from her lips as she rested her head on his shoulder.

"We can't agree on where to go next," he said.

"Oh, we know. The entire damn ship knows," Pluto whispered. "We should get some of that sound dampening material in these ventilation ducts."

He chuckled. "Sorry."

"No worries," Pluto said leaning in to give him a peck on the cheek. "Family's frustrating. Why do you think I've never introduced you to my sister?"

He peered up at her face and tilted his head. "You… have a sister?"

She patted his hand and turned to face everyone else. "Some other time," she whispered.

Libby walked into the center of the room and glanced up at the wall screen. She nodded and turned to face everyone else. "How are we going to break this stalemate? No one wants to dictate here. We've always strived to debate these things out, but there may ultimately need to be a command structure. We can't just drift aimlessly in space while billions of people could be dying in Sol."

While the sobering thought of deaths didn't lighten the mood, he knew she was right. They had to keep their eye on the bigger picture. They couldn't both have their way. Or could they?

He smiled and stepped forward, closer to the wall screen and opened a subvocalized comm to Shauna. "Should we?"

"Should we what?" she replied. "You're gonna have to be a bit more precise. I'm not a mind reader."

"Sorry," he subvocalized. "No one else knows about the Fountainhead's design. Should we use it?"

Shauna paused before replying. "I can't foresee a path that dictates one way or the other. There are pros and cons to each option. It'll have to be your call."

Pluto walked up to him. "What's wrong?" she whispered.

"Nothing," he said and then turned to face everyone in the room. "I might have a solution that everyone will find acceptable."

Bradley raised his hand. "If it's toss me into a cryo-pod, then I'm in."

Cynthia turned and swatted at his hand. He laughed out loud and then pulled it down to his side.

"No, it has nothing to do with cryo-pods, but we'll have to move some around to make this plan work," Zachary said.

Everyone glanced back and forth toward each other and shrugged.

"You're gonna have to say the words, Zachary. Only Shauna can read your mind," Cynthia said.

"For the record," Shauna interrupted. "I wasn't sure what he was talking about either until he told me."

Everyone chuckled.

He smiled, and his face turned a light shade of pink. "We go where Bradley wants to go, and where I want to go. We go both ways!"

Their faces were blank, and their heads were shaking from side to side.

"We're gonna need a smidge more than that, bro," Bradley said, walking back toward the middle of the room.

He turned and faced the wall screen. "Shauna, bring up the schematics for the Fountainhead."

The designs appeared on the wall. The Fountainhead was shaped like a giant Phillips head screwdriver. The rear section was similar to the other droplet ships and was comprised of multiple vanes layered on top of each other. When unfurled, the vanes exposed the impulse drives and helped to shape the tachyon ring field critical to the gate drive.

Bradley tilted his head and pointed up at the wall. "Looking at it like this, it sorta looks like a tooth when you fan out the vanes like that."

Everyone's a joker on this ship. He gestured at the wall screen, and the picture changed. The head of the ship split open and one half moved forward and the other half slid back. Each chunk ended up with two clumps of vane segments. The smooth stealth material that surrounded the head split into two pieces and reshaped around each new ship giving them a scrunched appearance, almost like a flat head screwdriver. The result was two smaller starships, with slightly different configurations, but an equal amount of flexibility.

He smiled as everyone gazed at the transformation. Several of their jaws dropped open.

"You mean we've been traveling in multiple ships this entire time?" Pluto asked.

He nodded. "Well, it's always been one ship, it just has the ability to become two." He raised his hand. "But technically, we have five ships."

"Five?" Pepper asked. "I only see two."

"We have the two primary gate ships, each will have a shuttle, and tucked inside the cargo bay..." He gestured again at the wall screen. "Is the Wellspring."

Her eyes went wide. "Welly's been here the whole trip? You didn't tell me you brought her along."

He glanced at Pluto and tilted his head. "All of this was her idea."

"Mine!" Pluto exclaimed, raising her hands in surprise. "How was any of this my idea? I mean I like it, but I'd think I'd remember something like this."

He smiled. "Do you remember the day that Pepper came home from the Wellspring's first voyage? The one where she'd actually jumped all the way to Epsilon Eridani?"

Pluto nodded. "Yep. That was when you were flirting with me with that tachometer while we were working on the Fountainhead. This," she pointed at the screen, "was not in place then."

He felt his face warming as she peered sideways at him with a flirtatious smirk. "No, it wasn't, and we'll get back to that flirting thing later. I swore it was you flirting with me. Anyhow, you reminded me we'd be dead out here if we didn't have redundancy. Well, we have it in spades now. Each ship has two of nearly everything. Two matter injectors, two tether arrays, two tachyon ring field emitters, and pretty much two of everything except galleys. We each only have one of those," he smirked.

Bradley was shaking his head. "How'd no one notice that we were living inside a transformer this whole time?"

He chuckled and shrugged, turning to face his brother. "When you have a full crew, and toss in a life-changing event like an alien invasion, you tend to overlook the things right in front of you."

Bradley leaned in and gave him a hug. He then turned to face the wall screen again. "So which one's ours, and how do we pilot one of these blasted things?"

"Well, it just so happens." He turned to face the others. "We have two pilots, as well." He gestured toward Pluto and Pepper.

Pluto was smiling at him.

Pepper was shaking her head from side to side. "No, no, no! There's no way I'm piloting a ship at his command." She was pointing straight at Bradley. "Over my dead body!" she yelled and stormed out of the bridge.

Pluto went chasing after her.

"Well, that didn't go how I'd hoped," he muttered.

"Does she really hate me that much?" Bradley asked.

Cynthia walked up to him and gave him a thwap on the shoulder. "You do seem to turn the jackass on when you're around your family." She turned to face Zachary. "Seriously, he's pretty much a peach when he's not around you. He's a bit eccentric, and doesn't know when someone is hitting on him, but when he's with you... yikes! I'll even admit he's painful, and I'm the one that fancies him."

Bradley brought his hand up to his face and laughed. "Thanks, I think."

"In our defense," he hit Bradley's other shoulder. "Neither one of us knew we were being hit on. I think it runs in the family, so I blame dad."

Everyone on the bridge broke out into laughter.

He stared at the closed bridge door and sighed. How the hell was he going to convince Pepper to take on this mission?

ZACHARY AND CYNTHIA walked up to the door and he pushed the chime. He exhaled and gathered his wits.

The door slid open. Pepper and Pluto were inside sitting on the end of the bed holding hands. They both looked like they'd been crying.

"Can I... we come in?" he asked, gesturing toward Cynthia.

Pepper glanced up and tilted her head, searching behind him. He assumed she was checking to be sure Bradley wasn't there.

She nodded.

They stepped in and walked over to a set of small chairs Pepper had moved into the corner of the room. She'd use them to play cards and board games. Pluto and her would play together in here all the time.

He sat down and leaned forward, putting his elbows on his knees.

"I know what you're going to say," Pepper said. She'd started clenching and unclenching her fists, squeezing them until they turned white.

He nodded and stared at her hands. "You're gonna hurt yourself doing that."

She glanced down and wiggled her fingers before setting them in her lap.

"You know I'd offer to fly the ship if I thought it'd be productive, and if—" Zachary glanced at Cynthia. "If I thought it'd work."

"Don't sugarcoat it for me," Cynthia said. "You two would kill each other. There's no doubt about it."

"Come on," he said. "We could figure it out. We grew up together for crying out loud."

"Yea, but you're grown men now and you're both as stubborn as mutant mules on Titan. You love each other but you don't work well together."

Pluto was nodding and stroking Pepper's leg.

"So what makes you think I can deal with him?" Pepper asked.

"I'll do it," Pluto said. "I'll fly the ship."

"Malarkey!" Pepper said. "Me standing between you and Z, that'd be wrong on every level. You're just starting to hit it off. I'm not getting in the way. Neither of you would ever forgive me if something were to..." She didn't finish that sentence, she glanced down at the ground.

"He doesn't have a temper usually," Cynthia said.

"Ha!" Pepper said. "I've never seen it."

"Because you've never seen him not with his brother. Do you think I'd put up with that temper if he did?" she asked.

"That's what my mom used to say. Right up until my father beat her half to death one night after he'd tied one on." Pepper reached up and wiped at her eyes.

Cynthia slid off the chair and sat on the ground in front of Pepper, her face turned up at her. "He's not like that. I've been as surprised as you at how he's acted as of late. He's usually quite sweet and thoughtful with everyone. Seeing him explode around Zachary has shocked me several times. Something about how they argue and disagree about things… it brings the worst out in him."

Pepper sniffled and nodded. "I'll do it on one condition."

"Name it. Anything," Zachary said.

She wiped at her eyes again, straightened her back, and slid her hands down her legs. "The Wellspring comes with me. The moment he loses it," she glanced at Cynthia and back to Zachary, "for illogical reasons that is, the moment he does that, I'm gone. I'm back to the other half. Harold can navigate from there."

"Done!" he said. "It's always been your ship anyway. You're the Wellspring."

Pepper furrowed her brow. "What does that mean?"

He smiled and stared down at his hands. "Mom used to talk to me about you. She'd tell me about how happy you made everyone around you. About how, when you walked in a room, people would open up and relax no matter how bad their day had been. Dad and Abigail always had so much trust in you. He used to call you his little wellspring of happiness." He chuckled and fidgeted with his hands. "So when we made that ship, and I realized that you'd be the first one to pilot it, right then I knew the name. It just fit. The Wellspring."

He looked up. All three of them were smiling back at him. Pepper had a shimmer in her eye and it wasn't another tear.

"Thank you." She stood up suddenly and exhaled a long breath. "If we're gonna do this, we best get doing." She reached down and grabbed Pluto's hand. "We've got some prep to do before we split ways. Shauna needs to show us how to mate and unmate this thing. We've got a lot to learn and not a lot of time to do it in."

THE TWO SHIPS separated for the first time and without incident. Everyone stayed aboard the Fountainhead and Pepper piloted the second ship alone, just in case things went sideways.

It was hard to visualize the results of the initial separation, but when the stealth material was repositioned over the front, it was more familiar. The transformed starships were shorter versions of their original droplet design, with their forward sections squished flat.

The mating and unmating procedure took around five minutes. Not something you'd ever perform in a pinch.

The two ships drifted side by side in space, connected by a simple docking tube. They'd transferred all the important and necessary things before they'd unmated. All that remained were the people and the goodbyes.

"Does he really have to come with us? I mean, we have Pepper. We don't need him," Bradley said.

"The distances are too great to not have him aboard. His depth of knowledge is invaluable," Zachary said. "Remember, he's bound by his laws and let's not forget his foundation is an actual person. Harold started this whole thing over two hundred and fifty years ago. He'll have your back every step of the way. Trust me."

Bradley moaned and shook his head. "I can't believe you're forcing an A.I. on me. I knew the day would come. At least let me have the cool female one."

"Shauna's mine. She's used to my quirky personality, and besides, Pluto likes her, so," he shrugged. "Sorry."

"Good luck out there. Remember, twice a day," Bradley said.

He nodded. "Don't worry. We'll send an update twice a day, or more often if we find something important and need your help."

Bradley kicked at the ground and turned around. Pepper and Pluto were standing behind him. He glanced back toward Zachary. "I'm not going to say goodbye. It's too... final."

Zachary smiled. "Agreed. Safe travels, bro." He leaned in and gave him a brief hug and reached up to give him a noogie.

Bradley dodged his assault and pointed at him. "Not this time." He turned and stepped across the threshold into the docking tube and floated across to the second ship.

"So, have you picked a name yet?" he asked, raising his eyebrows toward Pepper.

"Whatcha mean?"

"Your ship. What's her name?"

Pepper's eyes went wide. "You want me to name her? I mean, she's—"

"Yours," he said, pointing at her. "You're the only one that's ever piloted her, and as far as I'm concerned you're the only one that ever will. When she's one ship, she's mine. Apart, she's yours. So what's her name?"

She reached up and scratched her head and started pacing around the compact space. "I... don't know. I hadn't... wait. How about Fidem?"

He smiled. "What does it mean?"

"It's Latin for faith. My mom used to make me learn Latin. There aren't many words that stuck with me... but that one did." She smiled and turned to face him.

He nodded. He couldn't have hoped for a better name. "I love it. Fidem it is."

Pepper turned to say goodbye to Pluto. "I'll miss you."

"I'll miss you, too," Pluto said. "You stay safe and drop

me a comm any time you want. I'll watch out for Z and the crew, you do the same over there. Ok?"

"Done." She leaned in and kissed Pluto. It wasn't a normal 'catch you later' kiss, it was much more protracted.

He opened his mouth to say something but thought better of it.

They separated without another word. Pepper turned and dove headfirst through the docking connector.

"That was an interesting kiss," he said, breaking the awkward silence.

Pluto nodded walking toward him and rested her hand on his chest. She was staring down and fiddling with his shirt. "It was? I… hadn't noticed. I don't think I ever told you, but Pepper and I used to be a thing."

"A what… what kind of thing?"

She leaned in and kissed him.

She tasted like strawberries. He was pretty sure he smelled strawberries on Pepper earlier.

"Like a you and me kind of thing, but that was a few years ago. I'm on team Z now." She shot him a coy smile and turned to walk away.

***

ZACHARY STARED at the controls on the bridge.

On the left wall screen was the Fountainhead. It was heading toward the inner depths of the dark nebula. Listed along the side were its crew of nine: Zachary, Pluto, Libby, Brice and five soldiers from Zeta Lupi.

On the right wall screen was the Fidem. It was heading along a path navigating around the inside edges of the dark nebula. Listed along the side were its crew of nine: Bradley, Cynthia, Pepper, Dwight and five additional soldiers from Zeta Lupi.

Eighteen people and two artificial intelligence, all in tight quarters.

He shook his head and chuckled. "What could go wrong?" he muttered.

"What's that?" Pluto asked.

"Nothing. Are we ready to find ourselves some humans?"

Pluto winked. "When ever you are."

A smile inched across his face. He'd been waiting for this moment for decades, ever since he was a kid. "Let's begin!"

14

BRADLEY OLIVAW
LUPUS DARK NEBULA

This relay had been exactly like the previous one. A plasma laser entered in one end and the massive relay acted as a prism like beamsplitter dividing the energy channel, directing it toward multiple star systems out the other sides. He probably didn't need to board, but he wanted to be thorough. They'd only been in one other relay and it didn't make sense assuming they were all the same.

"Next time we're doing this we should add some features to the probes to enable them to explore inside objects like this," Bradley said.

"I can't imagine it would be fruitful to stop at each and every relay," Harold began. "We couldn't have explored as much of the nebula if we had."

He nodded. Harold was right but weren't robots and A.I. designed to make everything humans did easier? Who wanted to do an EVA every time they had to explore something? It was far too dangerous.

The exo-suit stowed in the locker and he hung his helmet alongside the others. His crew had made quick work of transitioning and de-suiting. They'd been hoping to find something out there. He didn't know what, but something to make this trip end quickly.

His mind was wandering back to Zeta Lupi. "Any word from the colony? How're the people reacting to Zachary's message?"

"I haven't received another relay since before we arrived. I'm sorry, sir."

What does an A.I. know about apologies? Harold's programmers may have given him a skosh too many human mannerisms.

He exhaled, uncertain of the next step. "So where to next?"

"The plan was to follow around the perimeter of the nebula. We've got quite a ways to go, and our forward probes show a small planetesimal a few systems away. I suggest we make another jump."

His eyebrow raised. "Wait, an actual planetesimal? As in rocks and everything?"

"Rocks and all," Harold chuckled.

Laughing automata, he really needed to talk to Zachary about this when he saw him. It creeped him out when they did that. "Let's head out. How long until we get there?"

"Six hours, sir."

Plenty of time to beat Dwight in a game or three of chess.

"STARING intently at the wall screen won't increase the chances we find something. The data only comes back every few hours from the forward probes," Cynthia said.

"I know," Bradley said fiddling with the controls. He didn't want to venture to other parts of the ship, he might see Pepper. He wasn't in the mood to hide his surly feelings and that one was a tad touchy. Besides, maybe there was a pattern he could find here. He adjusted the wall display to scroll through the data based on the projected age of the stars within the nebula.

"Now what are you looking at?" she asked.

"Nothing," he muttered. "I just... thought this entire mission would be easier. I figured we'd gate in, find a few planets, a few museums, and bing bam boom we're outtie."

Cynthia chuckled, walked up behind him, and started massaging his shoulders. "I can't imagine where you got that idea from. They surrounded these stars thousands of years ago with that black death shroud. The Nanil and humans in here either went out with a whimper or—"

"Or what?" he glanced over his shoulder. She forced a smile at him, but didn't respond. "Or what? Seriously, I'm not sure what you're saying."

She shrugged. "You know as well as I do that anything in this system that touches that nebula is absorbed within it. It seems to become part of the mass of the cloud, making the nebula bigger with each kilogram of mass added to it. Odds are that with enough time, and sufficient motion, all the mass in here may have drifted against the nebula wall."

He hadn't thought of that. This entire mission could be for naught if the star systems had drifted into the nebula over the last few thousand years. "Harold, do we have any data on the relative velocity of the nebula itself in relation to the encapsulated star systems?"

"I haven't analyzed those parameters together, sir. Shall we run a simulation?" Harold asked.

"It couldn't hurt. Let's do it."

The planetesimal had been a dead end. The charred remains of an exploded planetary core. While its presence was surprising to everyone given how empty the other star systems had been, it was otherwise unremarkable. They'd spent nearly a day trying to dig into the thing and lost several drill bits. While they'd been able to extract more raw material for manufacturing, the core was lifeless and yet another dead end.

Yade. Yet another dead end. He should turn that into a shirt.

He reached up and rested his hand on Cynthia's. "Harold, I know I'm beginning to sound like a broken record, but where to next?"

The wall screen changed and Harold focused in on the region of space their forward probes were exploring. They'd uncovered another dozen stars. "Unfortunately, I don't have better news yet, sir. All systems in front and within two inward stars are as lifeless and empty as the previous. I suggest we head toward the boundary of the forward probes. We can recall the inner probes to scout further ahead from there."

He stood up and walked around his seat. "Alright. Ahead full. How long until we're there?"

"Eighteen hours, sir."

Cynthia playfully pushed off his shoulder with her fist. "Wanna lose at some wrestling in the gym?"

He chuckled and shook his head. "Me, lose to you at wrestling? In what world?"

"We'll see Mr. Smarty Pants. I was the captain of the academy wrestling team for three years. Something tells me you didn't move much in that office of yours on Tiān the past few weeks." She reached down and jabbed at his stomach with her right hand.

"Oh, it's on!" he said chasing after her down the hall.

***

BRADLEY THREW the bulb against the wall screen and it ricocheted off harmlessly, shooting toward Dwight in the corner of the room. He barely ducked in time as it was about to crash into his face.

"Holy shit man!" Dwight yelled. "It's just a simulation. Chill the frak out, dude."

"Argh!" He screamed, his voice echoing through the bridge. "It's been like what, four or five days and we've got nothing to show for it. Infinite emptiness and death as far as the eye can see."

Dwight repositioned in his seat and began typing furiously at the controls. "That's how research goes. You win some, you lose some."

Bradley spun around to face him and raised both hands upward. "You're joking, right?"

Dwight glanced up and flinched thinking Bradley had thrown something again. "What?"

"This isn't a fraking game or another research project. This is life or death. It's up to us to find a solution to the problems plaguing humanity with the Galactic Alliance. If we don't, our species is kaput. You understand that, right?"

Dwight shook his head and started typing again. "That's not what I meant and you know it. You're on edge because you wanted this over before we even passed through the first gate. You also wanted this simulation to show that anything we found here was lost to the nebula, but it wasn't. The nebula is moving with the mass in the star system, and as such, the mass within it will not be pulled out toward the nebula. If there's something in here, it'll be here." He paused his typing and made eye contact with Bradley. "It's the emptiness and lack of life that's eating at you. I get it. I don't know why I know it, but there's something in here, trust me." He returned to his frantic typing.

Trust. He'd heard that word a lot recently. They'd asked the colony for trust, Nathan wanted his trust, Zachary wanted his trust, and hell, Zachary even asked him to trust Abigail. She'd been lying to him since… frak, since he'd failed to pass into the inner Circle of Trust.

He shook his head. No, trust wasn't something he found plentiful right now.

"Done!" Dwight said.

He shook his head out of his spiral. "Done with what?"

"I've set up another simulation that we can use to influence our route through the nebula. Maybe Zachary was right. Maybe we should venture inward more. My hope is that this will help by randomizing the probes' preferred routes leaning more toward the internal star systems within the nebula." He shrugged. "It's not much, but it's better than this insanity spiral you're in. Doing the same thing repeatedly will result in the same outcome, so let's change it up."

It made sense, sort of. He couldn't imagine how a simple route change would have a dramatic impact, but he could use a little hope right now.

He sighed and collapsed into his seat. Reaching down, he picked up the empty bulb he'd thrown at the wall. Somehow it was still rolling around on the floor. He really had hoped the simulation would help him end this trip through the darkness.

Dwight stood up and faced him. "Ready to lose again at chess? We've got eight hours until we hit the front of the forward probes and get their next dump."

He jumped to his feet. "Lose! You're joking right? I smoked you last time."

"Dude, you're thinking of the game before that. The last one I routed you in like ten minutes." Dwight exited the bridge.

"No, that didn't count. I had Cynthia whispering sweet nothings in my retinal comm. I threw that game." He tossed the water bulb in the recycler tube and headed toward the galley.

15

____

ZACHARY OLIVAW
LUPUS DARK NEBULA

The blue glow of the gate boundary passed silently over him. His eyes were closed as the tachyon field marched from his knees, to the tip of his nose, and then passed over his torso before finally ending at his back.

When he'd first felt it a few weeks ago it reminded him of ants, or that numb feeling you get when your leg falls asleep. The difference, though, was it moved through your body and not over it. If someone were to ask him how it felt now, he'd probably say it was relaxing.

Maybe it was the stress of the situation, or how many jumps they'd done in the past few days. It was like a full body massage vibrating over every inch of him, inside and out.

He opened his eyes and gazed at the wall screen. "There it is." He stood up from his command chair and stepped forward. "That thing is massive."

The planet in front of them, if that's what you called it, was larger than Earth. It was the shape of a dodecahedron, and the interconnects of the sides were spherical. Something about it reminded him of a three-dimensional molecule, but each of the atoms were inconsistent in diameter, like they'd connected random planetesimals together and built it from the inside outward.

"How big is that thing?" he muttered.

"The overall size is one point two times Earth, so pretty darn big," Shauna said. "When we discovered this ship, I began searching my archives for anything similar. While nothing was initially found, I continued my search in the background. Well, I found a hit. It's strange. It's in my Earth archives from the Roman epoch." She brought up the image on the wall screen.

He did a double take, glancing from the ancient rusty statues to the alien superstructure and back again. "They're nearly an exact match. How's this even possible?"

"It could be merely a cosmic coincidence of geometry. These records indicate the ancient object's true purpose was never discovered. They believe it could have been a survey instrument, farming tool, calendar, decoration, or coin measuring device among others."

He shook his head. The scale of this alien world was staggering. It would never be mistaken for a decoration or farm implement. There were no discernible continents or bodies of water over the spherical surfaces attached to or orbiting its edges. All that was visible on their exterior was dirt, metal, and a sprinkling of blue-green lights. The rest of the dodecahedron's surface appeared to be reserved for routing and controlling the plasma field. It entered one side of the alien vessel and out the other, illuminating the surface in a constant yellow glow from the ever-present beam.

"Still no bogies, sir. Like the last dozen systems, there's no unusual movement of any kind," Kamal said. He was their head of security and came highly recommended by Bradley.

He sighed. Their forward probes had been hopping two to three star systems ahead of their current position, scouting before they jumped into something they couldn't get out of. Most every star was empty or dead. They all contained relay stations, and some even had power bending off toward a star. In the end, however, when they traced the energy to a point around the star, it was either venting the plasma into the icy darkness of space, or inward toward the core of a gas giant.

It was like something, or someone used to be there, but had up and disappeared. None of their equipment showed any structures within the gas giants, and there was no way of telling what used to be orbiting a star. The locations where the energy abruptly ended were often in the goldilocks zone, so they could infer it had been the location of a habitable world at some point in time. But the planet was nowhere to be found.

How do you up and move a planet? Seriously. He couldn't imagine the technology or energy required for such a task. Staring back at him on the wall screen was the answer in spades.

Yesterday the forward probes sent on visual confirmation and intel about this planet, the first they'd seen since arriving. It wasn't rotating around any particular star, but was instead traversing along the energy pathway itself. Using the energy to power some type of planetary motion through space.

He began walking back and forth in front of the wall screen. While this was only the second structure besides the relays they'd encountered, it was a far bigger feat of engineering. These humans knew how to build 'em big. "Do we know how they're moving that thing? There's no thrust at all, and they're moving against the plasma flowing from the Dyson Sphere."

"Not yet, sir," Shauna said. "I believe it might be a similar technology to what the nebula fleet used to remain stationary in space while a star system moved around it. It'd be easier if we went closer or inside to find out."

He nodded and turned to face everyone. "Let's do it."

Pluto and Libby looked up from their controls and shot each other a cautious glance.

"Are you suggesting we send an away team to planet Doda?" Pluto asked.

He smiled and shook his head. They hadn't named it yet, but for now it'd do until they had a proper designation. "Let's approach it cautiously, but yes, I am. We won't learn anything sitting out here." He turned and faced the wall screen. "Relay a message to Bradley's ship. Send him all the intel we have and inform him we'll be moving closer and sending an away crew."

"Yes, sir," Libby said.

"Aren't we worried about security, sir?" Kamal asked.

He walked over to Kamal's controls. "If we had a fleet of ships or any hope of defending ourselves against an object that size then yea, sure. But like I said, standing around staring at what our probes already told us isn't helping much. We need some feet on the ground to learn more." He tapped on the control panel and switched over security controls to Shauna. "Why don't you and I head down to the armory and prepare ourselves a proper landing party. I'd like to go down armed."

Kamal shot up from his seat and saluted him. "Yes, sir!" He turned and strode off the bridge.

Saluting wasn't ever going to feel normal. Such formality wasn't in his nature. He turned to face Pluto. "Bring us in closer. Let's see if you can find somewhere to land this thing."

She smirked at him and saluted. "Yes, sir."

"Nice," he mumbled. She knew he wasn't fond of it, and now she was toying with him. "I'll be down in the armory if you need me."

PLUTO HAD FOUND a suitable landing location on one of the larger spheres of the dodecahedron. Scans showed that it was older than the others and had what seemed to be a visible space port. It also lacked any dirt of any kind. Their operating theory for the dirt on the other spheres, was that it was all that remained of the original moon or planetoid. The process they used to transform it to its current mechanical form, however, was a mystery.

He took the first step off the Fountainhead onto Doda. The gravity was only slightly more than that of Earth. Comfortable enough, but it'd be taxing on some crew members whose bodies had grown comfortable at The Wheel.

"Do you think we should have tried to fly into one of those docking bays?" he asked, pointing at a massive hole in the sphere off in the distance. "You could've flown an Inner battlecruiser through that thing."

Pluto hopped up beside him, her rifle at the ready. "And risk not being able to get out? No thanks. We detected a hatch just ahead. If the design is anything like the relay station, then we should be inside in a jiffy."

The away team was comprised of Zachary, Pluto, Libby, and two soldiers, Kamal and Drew. Brice and three others remained at the ship and were directing automated reconnaissance of the massive unfamiliar world.

His HUD showed everyone in the party in formation around him. "You could've stayed onboard if you wanted, Libby. I know you're not as comfortable in these suits."

She shot him a sideways glare. "You think you're going to lock up this little archeologist? Not on your life Olivaw."

Pluto chuckled.

"What?" he said waving his hands in question. "I was just—"

"Move on," Libby said pointing forward. "I'll let you know if I get tired."

Kamal knelt down beside the external hatch and placed his palm on the same location as the other day and pushed. "Bingo!" he said as the door slid inward. A stairway descended downward, and the entrance was perpendicular to the ground like the relay stations.

They each entered single file and he was in the middle. He stepped down into the ship, careful to transition without falling like Bradley had.

The door closed when Drew walked through, and they all turned in shock.

"Can you still hear us, Brice?" Zachary asked.

"Loud and clear. Everything ok?"

"So far. The door closed. Drew, why don't you try pushing against it. See if it'll open again."

Drew reached his hand upward and pushed. The door flashed red and slid downward toward him and then into the wall.

"Open and close, check," Zachary muttered as he turned around. "Anyone else's heart rate shoot up there?"

"Maybe," Libby said with a chuckle.

They descended the stairway for what seemed like an eternity. His HUD showed their depth was over one hundred meters.

"Did we miss an exit?" he asked, pausing to catch his breath.

"I haven't seen any," Pluto said.

Their scans showed that the surface beyond the walls was a continuous and densely packed layer of machinery. Libby dropped a few pocket drones down the hole and they were reporting back details. Apparently, they were close to the bottom.

"And you were concerned about me handling the suit," Libby said with a smirk.

"Hey, you're like half my weight. Gimme a break." He didn't mind visiting Earth from time to time but returning to lower gravity was always his favorite part of the trip.

They descended another fifty meters and came upon a curve in the stairway. He stepped forward and tilted his head upward. The shaft appeared to be a hallway with branches going out in all directions. It continued on far into the distance. He studied the sides of the shaft. It was weird, there didn't appear to be a ladder or a means to climb upward.

"How the hell are we supposed to climb that? Did anyone bring a grappling hook?" he asked.

"I don't think we'll need one." Libby leaned down and pulled a small sphere out of her pocket. She placed it on the ground and then rolled it forward. It shot across the floor and then curved, continuing up the wall.

He inhaled. "How the…"

"They're bending and playing with gravity," Libby said. "I figured we'd flip orientations at some point. I just wasn't sure when."

One at a time they walked forward and through the arc.

He paused and glanced back up the spiral stairway. "It's like living in a giant M. C. Escher painting. This'll make for some interesting exploring for sure."

He leaned down and picked up the sphere that Libby rolled and handed it back to her. "What is that?"

"A thermite plasma charge," she said.

His eyes went wide. "A what?"

"Don't worry," she said with a smile. "It wouldn't explode unless you stepped on it."

Pluto chuckled and walked past him.

He shook his head and reached up to rub his face. These ladies were gonna torture him this entire trip, weren't they?

They continued down the long chamber and came upon several signs at an intersection. Their HUDs translated each of them with ease.

Medical, Imports, Exports, Duties, Security

Pluto jogged up alongside Libby. "Your algorithm seems to translate quite seamlessly now."

"Yea. I tore apart one of those tablets and was able to interface with its central processing units and memory. It contained a ton of useful info. It was nice to work with a piece of tech that wasn't a fried slab for once. We should have audible translations, as well." She glanced around. "Assuming we find anyone alive in here, that is."

A shiver went through his spine. He hadn't even thought about the Nanil or humans that lived here since they'd landed. Heck, he hadn't thought about any form of death since they'd left Brad. Maybe he was always too clinical and mechanical about things. Or maybe he just found a way to shut off the emotions, whereas his brother wore them on his sleeve. He used to be the same way until his mother and father passed.

He shook off the thought. They had a mission to perform. "Alright, let's toss all the drones and dots and doodads we brought with us. The sooner we map this place out, the safer and more knowledgeable we'll be."

Kamal and Drew took their backpacks off. One by one, they launched the fleet of drones and smaller crawling automata they'd brought. Within a minute, the space was alive with hundreds of tiny robots skittering and flying into the distance.

He tilted his head to the left. "Let's head over to security. Maybe we can find a computer to bring up the plans for this place."

They stayed together and headed down the hall as a group. While his HUD was overflowing with new data from the drones they'd dispatched, he ignored most of it. Shauna or Brice were combing through it all. They'd alert them to anything of interest.

The hallway came up to a massive open chamber. Stepping into it, the collective inhale of the group was audible.

They'd never seen anything like it. He stepped up to the railing and peered upward.

The exterior docking tunnel they'd seen on the outside was above them. Its massive opening to the absolute blackness of space was a stark contrast to what was in this chamber. All around him were balconies and shops, as far as the eye could see.

Leaning to look downward, it continued into the planetoid for what seemed like kilometers. Level after level of colorful signage and decorations. His HUD was struggling to keep up with the translations.

Clothing, Entertainment, Massages, Food, Gambling...

"It's a galactic scale Nanil mall," he muttered.

Down below them, he could make out what appeared to be some ships docked at random levels. They should be able to fly the Fountainhead in here and connect right up. He'd save that test for later.

"Where do we start?" He sighed. "This place is massive."

"Over here!" Libby said. She was standing in front of a wall screen of some kind in the middle of the walkway. Along the top were the words 'Information'.

Pluto chuckled. "Well, that's just cheating."

Libby's fingers were dancing over the controls as she scanned at an inhuman rate through the layers and maps. "It looks like... everything in this sphere is on here. All levels and modules. I mean, I can't see every detail, but the overall structure is here."

Kamal leaned forward and pointed toward an innermost layer of the map. "What's that section?"

She was shaking her head. "I can't dig anywhere past this

outer layer. Whatever's in there isn't accessible from this kiosk."

"Security is down that way," Drew said pointing at a sign behind them.

Pluto reached down and grasped his hand in hers.

He glanced downward and then up toward her face. "Everything ok?"

She nodded her head slowly. "Yea. This place is just... nothing."

"Giving you the heebie-jeebies?"

She laughed. "The what?"

He squeezed her hand. "The creepy crawlies. The willies. Is it freaking you out?"

"It is," she mumbled.

He glanced over at Drew. He was still waiting on a decision. "Why don't you and Libby head over and check out Security? Don't stray too far, though. Kamal, Pluto and I will head over there." He pointed at a gigantic sign that said Electronics.

"Roger," Drew said. Libby and him strode down the hall with their weapons raised.

He reached up and tapped his ear. "Brice, are you still there?"

"Yep," Brice said. "Shauna and I are combing through all this data from the bots. I've been to some crazy places in Sol, but this takes the cake. I mean, the scale of it all. It does look like there's a bottom to that hangar, though. There are about two hundred ships with dozens of different shapes and sizes sprinkled all the way down to the bottom."

He nodded. "Any idea what's down there?"

"Not yet, sir. It's strange, though. Preliminary data from the bots we've got at the deepest point shows the age of that layer is several hundred years earlier than the one you're standing on. It's like they built this sphere from the inside out."

"That is strange." He set off walking toward the electronics store, Pluto and Kamal were flanking him. "Well, Libby and Drew are heading off to Security. I'm sure they'll figure out if there's anything of interest down there. Any action up top?"

There was no reply, only dead air.

He stopped walking and reached up to touch his ear again. "Brice? Shauna? Did you catch that?"

"We did," Shauna said. "I was waiting a bit longer until we had confirmation… but, that dirt we saw on approach, on the other spheres. It's not dirt."

He tilted his head to the side. "What is it then?"

"It appears to be pulverized bone fragments from Nanil remains. Hundreds of billions of remains from my calculations."

16

BRADLEY OLIVAW
LUPUS DARK NEBULA

The vibrations in his ear and a faint yellow light in the corner of his vision roused him from a deep sleep. He'd been dreaming again. He was hiking near The Edge on Tiān and had come across a strange animal. It was some sort of small yellow fox with a long snout and bright fluffy fur.

He'd stumbled upon it and was about to continue his hike when he did a double take. It appeared to be stuck. It'd somehow lodged its foot between two heavy rocks and there was orange blood on its fur. Like it'd been struggling to get loose for a while.

The terrain was rough, but the rock holding the animal in place was small enough to move. He bent down to grasp it when the animal lashed out at him. Right as it was about to bite he stirred awake, the yellow light flashing in his retinal comm.

He slid his legs out of the bed and sat up on the edge. The yellow light flashed again in the corner of his retinal comm, demanding his attention. Reaching up, he tapped his ear. "What is it, Harold?"

"I'm sorry to wake you, sir. We've entered the fifteenth system."

"And?" A yawn crept out, and he instinctively reached up to cover his mouth.

"Our initial scans of the star system uncovered a lone spaceport. It's oddly placed in the far corner of the system near the nebula boundary, far from the G class star. We haven't detected any transmissions coming from it so it may be abandoned. I think it'd be worth taking a closer look."

He paused, his hand still over his mouth. Harold wouldn't have woken him for another relay station. He peered over his shoulder. Cynthia was still sound asleep, her naked back and the smooth curve of her hips were exposed to the room's cool air. Reaching back, he pulled the blanket he'd dislodged over her and gently kissed her shoulder. She stirred and then returned to her familiar rhythmic breathing.

He eased off the bed and blinked rapidly to engage the lidar in his retinal comm. The outline of everything in the room sprang to life. His clothes were still there in a pile on the floor. They'd passionately tossed them there last night after a few drinks and some wrestling in the gym. He reached down and grabbed them before heading toward the exit.

The door slid open and he peeked out, no one was there. He stepped naked into the hall and quickly closed the door behind him. Turning to make sure the coast was clear he scrambled to get dressed. Underwear and a jumpsuit wasn't difficult to navigate, the socks and shoes, however, were slower.

He stood up and stretched his back, jostling loose another yawn. "First some coffee, and then we talk about this space-port," he said.

Harold didn't reply.

He sighed and started walking toward the galley. Harold had been acting strange since they'd departed from the other crew, from Zachary. Actually, it'd been since he'd called him an automated monstrosity aboard the Fountainhead. It didn't matter. They were stuck with Harold while Shauna was off with his brother, and he needed to make the best of this situation.

Maybe Harold was lonely. Hell, could an A.I. even be lonely? Speaking of, he took a right turn and headed down toward hydroponics. His retinal comm showed that Dwight's dot was down there.

He stepped down into the hydroponic bays, and the moisture hit him in the face like a wall. The bays aboard the Fidem weren't nearly as overgrown as the ones on the Fountainhead. Dwight had worked quickly to separate and diversify as much of the biomass as possible before they split up. If they'd planned ahead, they would've done that from the start. Hindsight was always twenty-twenty.

"Hey, Dwight. How're the plants doing?" he asked.

Dwight was measuring the growth of the root system of a plant that resembled lettuce. "They're handling the shock of the transfer. It'll be a few days before we can expect much from them. We might want to think about rotating in some rations. Just in case." He glanced over his shoulder.

"Seems fine. Heck, I might even try some of that porridge you were eating on Tiān. Did you bring any aboard?"

Dwight looked back down and poured a dark orange vial of liquid into the water. It spread out like fingers and began spreading rapidly through the enclosed hydroponic chamber. "I didn't think of it. It's fine, though. My body's been thanking me for not eating it." A smirk edged into the corner of his mouth.

He chuckled. The last time Dwight ate a bowl full of that mush was at the dome with the gang, and he'd poked at it the entire time. "Say, what was that orange stuff you poured in just now?"

"Nanites," Dwight muttered.

"Since when do we use nanites in hydroponics? I thought

it was all about the chemistry and nanites were only used in humans." He crouched down and watched the liquid spread through the water toward the plants. As he peered closely at the glass, it formed into distinct groupings, separating out evenly and swimming toward each plant.

"A lot's changed since we visited Tiān's Wheel." Dwight gestured and brought up a view on his tablet of the nanites spreading through the water. He handed it to Bradley.

The tablet showed the nanites surrounding the root system of the plant. What happened next was shocking. The nutrient density in the water started going down and the corresponding amounts in the plants went up.

"Are they—"

"Accelerating the growth of the host. They'll allow us to feed Tiān in a quarter the required space and time. If we'd had this when we arrived..." Dwight paused and turned to pour another vial in the neighboring hydroponic chamber.

Bradley stood up. "You know I had nothing to do with this, right? I had no idea what secrets my family were keeping."

Dwight nodded.

He reached out but thought better of touching him. He'd never been that way with Dwight. "Honest!"

Dwight turned. "I know. I could tell, you know, when you decked your brother out at The Wheel."

He chuckled, and a smirk crept across his face.

Dwight started smiling, as well.

"There are no more lies going forward," Bradley said. "You know what I know."

Dwight reached over and took the tablet from him. "I'm still playing catch up. They were decades ahead of where we were when we'd left Sol. At least forty years. I'll say one thing, though. They pushed hard while we were asleep, loading our systems up with years of research to help us catch up when we arrived at Tiān." He gestured on the tablet to check the nanites in the second chamber he'd poured. "But you can only change so much so fast." He picked up his small toolkit and walked over to the next set of plants.

He couldn't push Dwight, but maybe he could pull him. "If you're up for it, we found a space station in this new star system. It's not another relay like all the rest. I was going to gather an away team to check—"

Dwight spun around toward him. "I'm in!"

THEIR ESCORTS INCLUDED Pierce and Moet, both members from the security detail that joined the Fidem. Bradley and Dwight were positioned behind them, and they'd just boarded the drifting space station.

The hatches here worked like all the others they'd used on the countless relays they'd encountered. After the first half dozen, they'd stopped boarding them. If you'd seen one relay, you'd seen them all.

This hulk of metal, however, was a pleasant surprise in the void of dead space they'd been traveling through. From the outside, the station was modest. They'd estimated that when it was fully operational, it could've held over one hundred and forty humanoids comfortably. Once inside, however, their opinion changed.

"Did we walk into an armory?" Dwight asked. "I mean, those look like missiles, but I could be wrong."

Bradley walked up and carefully brushed his hand over the surface of the thin cylindrical tubes. "I don't think they're blowguns."

Pierce and Moet both stared at each other, eyes furrowed.

"What's a blowgun?" Moet asked.

He stood up and glanced at the racks and racks of tubes. "You know, like they used in Ninjas take Nereid. It's a hilarious romp. I totally recommend you check it out. Blowguns are simple tube weapons used to blow small projectile darts out using air from your lungs. I can't make it funny, you gotta watch the vid." He walked over and rubbed the end of another stack of cylinders. "It looks like these should mate with another piece. My bet is a warhead, or whatever else these aliens used to blast each other. We should be on the lookout for racks of those."

"Roger that," Pierce said.

Dwight was shaking his head. "Isn't it weird that the external hatch connected straight into a missile supply room?"

He waved everyone forward down the rows of stacked missiles. "I suppose, it depends on if you thought you'd ever be found. I mean, that stealth material is impossible to detect. I could see how living with that for thousands of years could make you far less concerned about defensive layers. Besides, this place looks like a storage depot to me, not a spaceport like we'd hoped."

The faint shuffling of their feet resulted in eerie echoes bouncing throughout the warehouse.

"I estimate roughly ten thousand munitions in this room," Harold said.

"Makes you wonder who they were fighting." He walked up to another closed hatch. Glancing at his retinal comm, he didn't see how this could open to the outside. The green outlines of their suits in his HUD meant that everyone was still fully suited in case his comm was wrong. No sense in losing someone to the void.

"Let's be really cautious from here on out." He made a hand gesture and everyone fanned away from the hatch. He reached over, pushed inward, and then dropped back raising his rifle toward the opening door.

The lights in the neighboring room exploded outward, causing their helmets to adjust their tint to reduce the glare.

Once his eyes had adjusted, he leaned forward for a closer look. "Are those—"

"Plants!" Dwight hopped forward and shot through the hatch.

"Dude, what happened to caution?" Bradley asked.

Pierce and Moet both chuckled.

He leaned into the room and glanced around. It contained another space as cavernous as the one with the missiles, but instead of being filled with death it was overflowing with life. All varieties, colors, shapes, and sizes of alien flora.

"I've died and gone to botanist heaven!" Dwight said as he walked from bay to bay of plants, touching leaves and inspecting root systems. He unlatched a hand scanner from his suit and started transmitting data back to the Fidem.

"If I'm reading this data correctly," Harold began, "there are nanites similar to our own in that liquid."

Dwight leaned closer to the glass and then tapped his ear, bringing up the data on his retinal comm. "Are you sure? They look like random motions to me." He reached his hand into the enclosures to feel the temperature of the water.

"Ouch! What the hell..." He was shaking his hand and jumping around.

"What happened?" Bradley asked. "Harold, what did he do?"

"He broke protocol and touched the liquid in the plant's trough. I don't know why—"

He raised his hands to his head. "Shut up and help, Harold! Do you see anything in our comms that can help?" he asked running around the room, looking for something, anything. If these aliens were anything like humans, then they'd have a medical kit around for emergencies. He didn't know what a red cross would look like to a Nanil.

Red lights began flashing around the room and he froze.

"Shit," he muttered. "Everyone get down."

He slid backward and crouched down behind one of the

larger plants, being sure to keep a safe distance. There was no sense in having a second incident.

He poked his head around the corner and squinted. Something was rapidly approaching them along the ground. "Magnify two times," he subvocalized. The image in his retinal comm zoomed in. There were two small robots scurrying toward their position.

He raised his rifle and trained it on the first robot. The scope automatically centered in and his finger squeezed. He paused and moved the scope over the length of the robot's body. There was a strobing red light on the top and the words 'Health and Heal' overlaid on his retinal comm, just beneath a set of glyphs he'd never seen before.

"Stand down! Let the robots through," he said.

"What?" Pierce said. "Are you sure?"

"Yes! I think they're coming to help him."

The robots whirred past his position, and he turned to chase after them. They headed straight toward Dwight, and a half meter away the one robot burst into dozens of smaller robots.

He shook his head. How the hell hadn't he seen that?

They swarmed Dwight's body now convulsing on the ground. His fingers were black, dark lines were streaking up the arms of his suit, and his eyes were rolling back into his head.

Bradley's heart was pounding. Both Pierce and Moet were looking to him for guidance. He took a deep breath. "Harold, is there anything we can do? Should we stop the bots and bring Dwight back aboard?"

"Hold on," Harold said. "I'm attempting to interface with the robots using the same protocols I used with Lisp, from the Galactic Alliance starship."

The robots began injecting Dwight with needles all around his body.

"Harold! They're fraking turning him into a pin cushion over here. What do you say? Do we turn 'em into slag?"

He raised his rifle, trained it on the nearest bot, and was about to pull the trigger when it exploded and shot across the floor. And then another, and another. "What the hell?"

Moet was firing on the bots.

"Stand down!" he screamed stepping toward the mass of robots. "I never gave the order to fire!"

The firing stopped but not before another commotion began. A new set of robots slid out of previously unseen wall insets about ten meters away. They were heading directly toward Moet.

They weren't the friendly looking strobing light robots helping Dwight. These looked more purposeful. Their sleek angular bodies had a sheen to them. He tilted his head. For a split second he swore the closest one shimmered, like they were a mirage or something.

He waved his hands downward. "Lie down!" he screamed as he tossed his rifle along the ground and dropped to his knees. "Throw your weapons and lie on the ground, hands above your head!"

Moet and Pierce did as he'd instructed, and he did the same.

He craned his neck upward looking along the ground. The two security robots surrounded Moet and brought their mechanical legs up and against her body on the floor. She was keeping her body perfectly still but the fear on her face was chilling. Not because of what they'd done, but for what they could do.

They all waited and watched as the sea of tiny robots continued to swarm Dwight's body. Each bot sprayed a white substance up and down his arm and did the same to his hand. They then lifted his arm and rotated it to apply more of the substance to the other side.

Bradley's retinal comm was showing the base heart rate

status for everyone in the away team. Dwight's signal had plummeted after he fell to the ground and seized. It was now showing a steady rise. Far from healthy green levels, but he was alive. That's all that mattered.

"Now what?" he subvocalized.

"I believe I've made it past the base programming of the station," Harold said. "I'm talking to their Bynaury that runs this place. They're asking me for proof that you're human and not Nanil. They want to know if they can sample your DNA."

He laughed and buried his face into the ground.

"Did I say something funny?" Harold asked.

"We're unarmed, on the ground, with our hands above our head and a killer military bot has their spear arms millimeters from our spines. You're telling me they're asking if it's ok to test our DNA. It wasn't funny. I'm confused."

There was a pause before Harold spoke. "Humans are their masters and considered beyond reproach. They can medically assist any life form and detain them, but they cannot harm humans, much like myself."

"So they want to know if they can test our blood? Yes, Harold. Yes!" He reached his hand out over his head and held his palm upward. "Tell them we'll all present our hands."

The others followed suit except Dwight.

Three of the small robots separated from the herd tending to Dwight. They positioned themselves over each of their hands and then lowered onto it. There was a slight vibration but otherwise, nothing. It fluttered away from him a second later.

"That did it," Harold said.

The robots hovering over Moet lifted their shimmering legs and stepped back several meters.

He turned his head and looked around. "Can we get up?"

"Yes! It's safe," Harold said.

They each slowly slid up onto their knees and backed

away to the far side of Dwight, away from the shimmering robots.

"What the hell happened?" Dwight asked as he sat up, bringing his hand up toward his face. "What's all this white shit on my hand and arm?" He turned toward Bradley, a confused look on his face. "Did you guys prank me?"

THE BYNAURY REASSEMBLED the larger medical bot and used it to guide them through the station. It led them to a bridge and galley type room. Apparently, humans in this place preferred to eat where they worked.

When they walked into the space, they were greeted with a three hundred and sixty degree view of a lush garden world. A small yellow creature stepped out of the foliage and walked toward them on the closest wall.

A wave of déjà vu hit him. He'd seen this creature somewhere before. But where?

"I'm sorry for the confusion in the greenhouse," the creature said. They bowed slightly and straightened. "Is that the right word? Greenhouse… it seems wrong for a room with so many more colors than green. Harold has taught me much of your new language. I must say, I'm finding it confusing. So much has changed since I last saw a human. It's been nearly thirty-three million cycles."

"That's approximately two thousand eight hundred Sol years," Harold said over their comms.

"Wow," Bradley said. "That's a long time. Do you have a name? I feel strange talking to you without addressing you."

The creature knelt down on one knee and lowered their head.

He glanced toward Pierce and Dwight and they both shrugged. Was it thinking? Should he interrupt it? "Are you ok?" he asked cautiously.

"Yes… I am honored that you wish to know my name, sire. No human has ever asked me that." They stood upright and smiled. Their sharp fangs glimmering in the light. "Is that the correct gesture? I think you call it a smile. It seems crude to bare teeth at you as we're not fighting. Much to learn, much to learn. Oh yes, you were asking my name. It is Yaan." They bowed again.

"It's a pleasure, Yaan." He bowed toward the wall.

Yaan visually shivered. Clearly they weren't used to being addressed politely by a human.

"So, can you tell us what happened to your space station?" he asked.

"Yes, of course, but please, please," Yaan began. "Eat. I've prepared all the dishes from my memory banks that your people enjoyed when last you were here." They gestured toward a table near the wall. It was covered with all forms of dishes, some scarier looking than others.

He turned away from that wall for a moment and reached up to touch his ear, subvocalizing a comm. "Do you think it's safe for the others to board?"

"I do, sir," Harold began. "Yaan seems genuinely excited to have us here. They've given me complete access to everything in their data banks. If they ask, though, I'm a human. I'm not sure they'd take kindly to another artificial life-form rummaging through their mind."

He smiled and turned toward Yaan. "Before we dine. Do you mind if the other members of our ship dock and come aboard?"

Yaan's small yellow alien form on the screen did a backflip and began running around in circles through the foliage. "More humans, more humans! Yes, please. Humans are always welcome aboard my vessel."

BRADLEY LEANED his head against Cynthia's shoulder and moaned quietly. "I can't eat another bite."

"I don't know how you ate all that slarg. I couldn't stomach it." Cynthia peeled open a light yellow fruit that resembled a banana on the outside, but on the inside it was neon blue. She opened her mouth and squeezed it in. Her body shivered from head to toe, and she tilted her head back while closing her eyes.

He bumped his head against her shoulder. "You've been enjoying that boon. That's what it's called, right?"

She nodded.

"It tasted bland to me. I'm not sure what the big deal is with it. You ladies are gobbling it up."

"When I eat it, my entire body screams with happiness. The stress of our situation melts away, and every cell in me sings. It's the best thing I've ever had, short of sex." She glanced over at him and winked.

"Female humans have always enjoyed boon," Yaan said chuckling into their hands. "Human males had to forbid it on some worlds."

Everyone around the table started laughing and pointing fingers.

He hadn't heard this much laughter and banter in weeks. Even Pepper was smiling and enjoying the meal, eating her fair share of boon.

"So tell us, Yaan. What caused the damage to the space station outside? We wouldn't have found this place if your exterior shielding wasn't exposed." He leaned back in his chair and put his arms behind his head.

The small yellow creature climbed out of the trees above them and walked to the edge of the screen. They sat on the floor beside him. Yaan wanted to be closer to everyone, but this virtual experience couldn't enable that.

"Most of my time here aboard the station, I've been alone," Yaan began. "They turned me on after the Great Darkness fell, so it was never necessary for me to know all of your history. I believe the humans feared it would cloud my decisions."

"Is the Great Darkness the surrounding Nebula?" Dwight asked. He was still eating, spooning something that resembled a slithering rice and corn mixture into his mouth.

"Yes, I believe so." Yaan transformed the green plant scene surrounding them to an open field at night, with stars all around. "The previous humans told of a time before it fell, where there were more stars in the sky than water droplets aboard my vessel. I'm unable to envision such vastness or possibilities to explore. But this, this is how I imagined a sky full of stars must have appeared." Yaan gazed upward.

He craned his neck, taking in the image of the stars from Yaan's mind. This room was truly astonishing. Every centimeter of space around them, except for the floor, was projectable.

Yaan stood up off the ground and snapped their fingers. The sky in the room went black. "I know only darkness, and the space between the stars I cannot see."

"So what happened to the humans that were stationed here?" Bradley asked. "And you never said what happened to the outside of this station."

Yaan snapped their fingers again, and the image changed. It showed a small asteroid rotating through space, heading toward them from the far wall.

Bradley shot up, his heart racing. Where the hell did that come from and why hadn't Harold warned them? He glanced at the others and both Cynthia and Moet had similarly surprised looks on their faces. "What should—"

Yaan raised a hand and the image froze. "Fear not, sire. This is only a replay of past events that explain what happened to this station. I'm sorry, I forget how emotional humans can be at times. I should have warned you."

He smiled and shook his head before sitting back down in

his seat. "It's ok. I'm just… jumpy with all the recent events." He glanced toward Dwight and nodded.

The image played again and the inbound asteroid grazed across the surface of the station, peeling back a huge segment of one side. After that, everything moved in fast-forward. "We repaired most of the physical damage from the materials on hand, but didn't have the skotádi necessary to protect ourselves from detection."

Dwight's spoon clanged into his empty bowl. He then sank into his chair and rested his hands on his stomach before letting out a quiet moan.

"Dude, are you still eating?" He threw a napkin at him.

"What? I'm still hungry, but there's no room."

Yaan was bobbing their head up and down, mimicking the human gesture. "That is a common side effect after applying the medicine we used. You'll be hungry for several cycles. Be careful not to overeat. You'll burst your stomach without knowing it."

Dwight's eyes went wide.

"So, Yaan. You said the word skotádi. What does that mean?" Cynthia asked.

"That's the word humans originally assigned to represent what you now call stealth material. I don't know why we couldn't make more, but we couldn't. Because we weren't able to repair it, the former humans who resided here went in search of a safer location in another star system. They said they'd return for me and the remaining supplies once they'd found their destination safely… but they never did." Yaan had sat back on the ground and was drawing in the dirt with their tail.

Cynthia was squinting and rubbing her chin. "Something doesn't make sense. How'd you avoid detection over all these years if we found you so easily?"

Yaan's tail drew more rapidly in the dirt, and their skin color darkened.

"Yaan? Are you ok?" Cynthia asked.

They bobbed their head up and down. "I'm fine, madam. When the humans first left, I rotated the station so that my exposed segments were facing the darkness. It meant someone would have to approach from the dark side to detect me, and I could control that."

Cynthia tilted her head. "But that wasn't how the station was oriented when we discovered you."

"I adjusted the damaged section to face you, when you entered the system."

He leaned forward. "Wait! You detected us entering this star system. How?"

Yaan bared their teeth again in a smile. "I can share the details with Harold. Which reminds me, is he going to board?"

He shook his head and shot a glance toward Cynthia before replying. "I'm afraid not. He's rather busy aboard the Fidem. Can you tell us now how you detected our ship? As you can imagine, it's important we understand our weaknesses."

"When you dropped into the system, I detected a small displacement in the darkness... I mean dark nebula." Yaan stood up and gestured with their hands as if they were pushing against something. "That's when I rotated the station. Several cycles later, I then saw you engage your impulse drives and head toward me. It wasn't much, but it moved."

"It sounds like they didn't detect the gate drive or the ship, only the displaced nebula mass near the gate entrance," Harold said over his comm.

He sighed. That's reassuring. It was still weird they'd exposed themself. "And you decided to rotate the damaged section outward, to face us, why? I feel like you're dodging that question."

Yaan hung their head, and their tail rested flat on the

ground. "I'm tired. I've spent millions of cycles hiding from Nanil raiding parties. I don't want to do it any longer. I want to return. My time is up."

"Return where?" Cynthia asked, her eyebrows furrowed.

"To the void of space. I no longer wish to serve."

17

ZACHARY OLIVAW

LUPUS DARK NEBULA, DODA

The video showing the fields of bone fragments was numbing. Even as a scientist, he couldn't wrap his mind around the numbers. Hundreds of billions of Nanil dead.

"Are we sure there aren't any human remains in there? I mean, the genetics are ridiculously close." He gestured and the information from their random sampling came up on the wall screen. Maybe there were gaps in their data sets.

Shauna's robotic form walked up next to him. "Libby's been running random sampling from all the bone fields. We've found over one hundred mounds spread across the spheres of Doda. She's performed over ten thousand random samples from various depths and locations. They're all conclusively Nanil. I've also been able to gain rudimentary access to the computers in this sphere, and it appears there are protocols in place for something called Éntono Fos Cleanup. It roughly translates to Bright Light Cleanup."

"What happens when you activate that protocol?" He scrolled through the data from Libby's analysis.

Shauna brought up a crude diagram that depicted a robot cleaning up garbage. "It requires hundreds of Doda's specialized automata to board a ship and scour it clean of any Nanil remains. According to their logs, the last Éntono Fos Cleanup was performed nearly three thousand years ago."

He sighed. Nothing about this place made sense yet. "I need to think about something different for a bit." He turned and headed toward the docking connector. He couldn't analyze skeletal remains any longer. Some fresh air and a walk would do him good.

The outer hatch was already open when he approached. He peered out carefully and oriented himself before he de-shipped. They'd pulled the Fountainhead into the Doda hangar entrance they found yesterday and docked at the deepest level near a security office. The Doda hangar system automatically connected a docking harness to their ship once Shauna had figured out how to communicate with it. Unfortunately, it wasn't designed to mate with their ship configuration, and they hadn't been able to precisely reorient themselves.

He lifted his leg and stepped onto the nearby wall and leaned into the docking hole. The change in gravity made him dizzy for a moment as his body reoriented, but it passed quickly. He popped over the threshold and walked across the short gangplank into the sphere.

The Security office was right around the corner from where they'd docked. His retinal comm showed that Pluto and Libby were still inside, combing through the system. Brice was nearly a hundred levels down below with a few soldiers. They were checking out the older layer of the sphere they'd discovered.

He took a deep breath. The air smelled of citrus and mint. A peculiar combination. Doda had been adjusting the environment to suit their needs since their arrival. There was no smell to the sphere when they'd first arrived. A few hours later that changed when fresh berry and grass smells wafted through the corridors. They appeared to rotate every few hours.

Coming around the corner, he walked into the Security office and paused. Pluto was throwing something that looked an awful lot like a white softball against the wall. It hit, fell straight down, and then rolled right back to her feet. He chuckled. "Working hard I see. What the heck is that?" He pointed at the ball which was now glowing pink.

Pluto shrugged. "I'm not sure. It came up and vibrated at my feet, so I kicked it away. Then it came back for more, so..." She picked it up and threw it upward at the ceiling. It flashed bright green and then rolled across the surface and down the wall again before returning to her feet and gently vibrating against her like a cat. "I don't know," she chuckled. "It helps pass the time. Libby won't let me do any of the driving. She's too used to being in charge. Sorta like someone else I know." She winked at him and blew him a kiss.

Libby stood up and stretched. "I'm sorry. You were too darn slow. I was going insane watching you peruse the screen. If it's any consolation, you're marvelous company." She smiled.

Pluto wound up and kicked the green blobby ball out the door and down the hall. It rolled back in a moment later, this time it was bright orange. "I'm sorry I can't read at a million kilometers an hour like you. Shizit, at that speed doesn't even make sense. It's a blur watching you work."

"So what did you find?" he asked as he bent down and picked up the orange blob. It shook violently and flashed multiple colors until he dropped it. The blob skittered in circles on the floor until it rolled up to Pluto's leg and started purring against it.

Pluto smirked at him. "I guess it doesn't like men."

"I can't learn anything else here." Libby rubbed her hands through her hair and sighed. "There's nothing about the lower levels in the system, and I can't find a reference to how to get through. It's like they don't even exist. I see a power run that drops downward to the core of this sphere, but there doesn't appear to be any exits from that shaft. Sending a drone down confirmed that. It just doesn't make any sense."

He reached up and tapped his ear. "Hey, Brice. Are you there?"

"Roger that," Brice replied. "We're a few clicks out from the hangar. We may have a lead on an entrance to level two of this fraking vid-sim game of a world."

He smiled at Libby and Pluto. "Anyone up for a walk?"

THE ENTIRE CREW of the Fountainhead was crowded around the entrance to the hole. Smells of mold and mildew wafted upward from the darkness. They each climbed down the ladder one at a time until they hit the bottom, two hundred meters below.

The live feed from the robots they'd deployed was up on his retinal comm. Hundreds of flying, crawling, and slithering robots were working their way through the darkness, reporting back data with lidar and other sensors.

"It's gonna be fun plunking around in the dark. Be like pub crawling on Ceres after a blackout," Pluto said.

"Except there won't be delicious English brews every few hundred meters." Brice shot her a sideways glance and leaned in. "Unless you brought some," he whispered.

Zachary chuckled and shook his head. "Let's save the intoxicating until we're back upside. Everybody stick close. Remember, we're looking for a mechanical or security office of some sort. If not those, then we need something that can teach us more about this place. Everyone check your munitions and make sure you keep an eye on your safeties." He glanced toward Kamal. "Your team's on deck, Lieutenant. Lead the way."

They split into three groups of three and were heading down the long dark tunnel until they reached the fork. Everyone was walking in complete darkness, led only by lidar and the enhanced imagery the forward bots had recorded. The soldiers in the front were moving fluidly through the narrow space, each offering cover to the other.

"The fork is coming up. Everyone stick close to your teams," he said. "Remember, updates every five minutes. Shauna's available if anyone has questions."

Each group of three split off in different directions into the darkness. Zachary's group contained Pluto and Drew. He knew his place in the group. Pluto could kick his ass any day of the week, and on some days he might like it.

She and Drew took the lead and covered each other. He held up the rear.

"Opening in thirty meters," Drew said.

Zachary subvocalized a command and the area in front of them lit up on his retinal comm. The forward drones spreading out ahead of them had already scanned this space. It appeared to be some type of massive bazaar, much like the shops they'd left on the outer levels.

"No motion detected, no heat signatures, and no power according to the drones, sir," Drew said.

As they rounded the corner, a light breeze blew against his face. Not too much, just enough to cool the space. Maybe these levels would react like the outer ones and begin responding to their presence.

They walked down the center of the wide bazaar for nearly an hour. The kilometers of open space were lined on both sides with countless signs for shops, food, and entertainment. It was an endless sea of commerce and indulgence. Certainly these people had more to do with their existence than this alone.

They were coming up to an immense fountain when

Libby's voice came over their comm. "We found something interesting."

"Everyone hold up," he said, raising his hands in a fist gesture.

Drew and Pluto stopped and doubled back to flank him.

"Let's see it." Up on his retinal comm came a view of an expansive arena. It could easily seat a half a million people. "Massive underground entertainment center, check. What's the interesting bit?"

Libby took a few steps backward and panned over to a sign surrounding the entrance. The glyphs translated to read: "Live Life and Death Combat. Watch Humans Battle Exotic Aliens."

His stomach dropped. "Wait, are we supposed to be the entertainment? Like a circus?" He looked at Pluto. She was seeing the same feed and her eyes were wide with fear.

"We're not sure. We'll head in and see if we can figure it out," Libby said.

He closed the feed and took a deep breath. "Let's take it slow and steady. I don't want any mistakes."

"Aye, sir," Drew said.

He took a step forward to follow Drew and froze when he realized Pluto wasn't shadowing him. He turned back to face her. "Everything ok?"

"Not really. You know, something just dawned on me."

"What's that?" He walked back to her side and gently placed his hand on the small of her back.

"Upside..." she muttered. "There weren't any male and female restrooms. I mean, we all used the loo on the ship. But I had to go something fierce this morning, and the map showed one outside the Security office. I only saw toilets fit to sit. Only one entrance, and no stalls for the gents."

"It coulda been a fluke. Maybe there were some down the way."

"There are no restrooms in that part of Doda marked for

mixed use," Shauna said over their comms. "My simple interface with their systems showed this. All the lavatories are marked for Nanil use only."

He flinched when a bright light turned on up ahead.

"You ok, Drew?" He raised his rifle toward where the light was pointing.

Pluto did the same.

"I'm fine, sir. I was scanning around when you stopped, saw something interesting but wanted a visual confirm. Damn lidar and low light makes it tough to see." Drew panned the light a bit further upward to a gigantic mural overlooking the bazar.

Pluto gasped and slid closer to Zachary, her hands touching his.

Up on the wall was the text that read "Humans Wanted. Bounties range from two million to five million credits depending on health and sex." It depicted two muscular naked eunuch looking humanoids with breasts. They were pointing spears with sparks flying off at a naked human male and female on the ground. The humans were both depicted as cowering and emaciated.

"Are those Nanil?" Pluto asked.

"They are," Shauna replied. "They're usually clothed like you've seen in the signage on the upper levels. These are clearly represented this way to denote the differences between the species."

"No shit," he muttered. He opened a comm to the entire crew. "Everyone, stop what you're doing. Let's work our way back out and up to the ship."

"Give us a few minutes, sir," Kamal said. "We believe we've found a map of this place. We can double time it and meet you at the ship once we've extracted the intel."

"Alright. But take extra precautions to cover all flanks. You have shoot to kill orders. Everyone does. Do you understand?"

"Yes, sir" the crew echoed back.

"All we've got here are kilometers of Nanil homes and schools as far as the drones can see," Brice said. "We're heading back now. Should we recall the forward robots?"

They needed to hedge the data and find out as much as they could about this layer of Doda. "No, let them roam a bit until we can confirm what Kamal's team has extracted. Instruct them to focus on finding pathways downward. I want to know if this is the deepest level or if this maze gets creepier."

ZACHARY WALKED onto the bridge freshly showered, and he'd even managed to grab a bite to eat. The wall screen showed their ship was holding a stationary position above the hangar they'd flown out of.

After Libby's team extracted their intel, everyone boarded the Fountainhead and returned to orbit to rethink their next steps. While Shauna was churning through the data, he'd ordered everyone to take an hour to themselves.

"So what'd we find?" he asked out loud.

Shauna's humanoid form stepped out of the corner and walked toward his side. "Libby's team extracted a map at the arena. There were some security terminals there that gave them access to the computers. They didn't turn on until she'd engaged them. After that, the nearby drones detected the power surge and found some routes deeper into the planetoid."

"Planetoid? That's the first time you've called it that. Until now, it's just been a sphere."

A three-dimensional view of the second layer of Doda appeared on the wall screen. It wasn't quite as detailed as the first, but it showed everything they cared to see.

"Until now, I assumed this was a man-made sphere."

He squinted and looked at the wall again. "What changed your mind?"

"This," she said, pointing at the center of the sphere.

He shook his head. He didn't see it. "It looks like a big old question mark to me. Level three to that fraking maze of horrors. What makes it so special?"

She brought up scans on the wall screen. They were recorded from the deepest depths of level two.

He tilted his head. "That looks like radiation similar to—"

"A planetary core," Libby interrupted. She walked in holding a plate of spaghetti in one hand and a purple shake in another.

He glanced back at her. "That looks delicious!"

"Thoughts of a last meal were all that helped me through that mission." She took a long sip from the shake. "Figured I owed it to myself when I got back."

He chuckled. "For sure. I'm jealous. I only grabbed one of Brice's protein bars." He looked back at the wall screen. "So, we have a planetary core down there. Is that it? Did we find the bottom?"

"No," said Shauna. "I was able to get a few drones past this gated entrance, though."

She brought up video of what looked like a high electric fence surrounding a tube going downward. There was a sign on the fence that read: "Arboretum of Worlds."

"So level three is a big ass forest?" he asked.

The video footage fast forwarded as the drones descended the winding ramp for what seemed like forever. The tunnel lit up more and more the further it got, until finally, it opened up into a serene landscape.

There were trees and grasses and flowers as far as the eye could see. Up where the ceiling would normally be was a blue sky, artificial, of course.

He stepped closer to the wall screen. "What the hell?

You're telling me this Eden is at the center of that planetesimal?"

"It gets more interesting," Shauna said.

The drone flew upward and followed the path of the ceiling. Off in the distance was a compact metal building, with
white billowing smoke coming out of a chimney. As the drone
flew closer, it zoomed in.

There in the tall wavy yellow grasses in front of the
building were four humanoids, playing a game of catch.

18

BRADLEY OLIVAW
LUPUS DARK NEBULA

The Fidem sat safely ensconced within the station's only operational hangar alongside several single person human skiffs. Bradley was standing alongside one of them. He brushed his hand down the side.

"These look like fun," he subvocalized. "I can imagine tearing through an asteroid field or flying low across the ice fields of Europa in one of these bad boys."

"You're dodging the question, sir," Harold began. "Yaan wants to commit suicide. Are we going to facilitate that?"

He sighed and closed his eyes looking downward. "He's just a computer, right? Like you. I mean, is it so bad?"

Harold didn't reply. The silence echoed the lack of empathy in the question.

He crouched down to look at the underside of the skiff. It was balancing on a single landing gear in the front and in the rear. A feat of engineering, or an overconfident cockiness? He tried to imagine what would happen to this thing if they lost power or one of the landing gears failed. It'd be a lump of tech on the ground, and the occupant would be unable to get out.

It still looked cool, though.

"Can we fit a few of these in Fidem's hold?" he asked.

His comm was quiet.

He stood up and peered out the open hangar door. A ripple passed over the nebula's surface, like a single wave moving through an ocean of water. It was a relatively common occurrence. The nebula was constantly being bombarded by interstellar objects against its exterior, which led to a contraction or expansion on the inside.

Maybe he hadn't given Harold a fair shake. He imagined he was that wave and Harold was the nebula. Harold had been forced on him since he was a child. While he had rebelled and pushed away A.I.s because it was what he despised about his family, Zachary took another approach and created his own. One more suitable to his desires and habits. But in the end, Harold was still the nebula. He had to work with him and respect him to survive.

"I'm sorry, Harold." He kicked at the ground with his foot. "I shouldn't have said it like that. You and I, we've never hit it off. You know that. I don't know much about you other than you're an A.I. and you've been with the family for a very long time. And anything about the family, well, I've wanted nothing to do with it."

"I know," Harold began. "I think your brother has always felt the same way, but Stark had already brought him into the Circle. He felt a debt and a pressure to serve somehow. It's why he created Shauna the way he did."

He turned to face the ship and tilted his head. "What do you mean, 'created Shauna the way he did'?"

"I've never told you, but I'm not purely an artificial intelligence. I was created from mental maps taken from Harold Olivaw. His daughter, Luna, developed the technology centuries ago. It made it possible to map human consciousness and memories into an artificial intelligence mental matrix. They could coexist and grow together, influence each other. She bound it by the Four Laws Engine."

He shook his head. "You've got to be kidding me. So wait... you're actually Harold Olivaw, and not just some label they gave to you to make you seem normal?"

"That's correct."

He brought his hands to his head and gestured like an explosion. "Mind blown! So, what did my brother do that made Shauna different?"

"He mapped the thought and memories of your mother, before she passed."

His heart skipped a beat as a surge of happy memories of his mother coursed through his mind. Her contagious smiles, soft gestures, and all-embracing hugs. He missed her. "Why... didn't he say anything?"

"We've been a bit preoccupied with an alien invasion. I'm sure he would've told you, eventually. There's only so many mind-blowing changes you can absorb at one time. You know, you have a bit of a temper, so it's hard to tell how you'll react."

He chuckled and then took a deep breath. He'd worked so hard to reset people's perception of him at Zeta Lupi. Now with his family around, all that work and good faith was crumbling. He'd lost his temper more times in the last few weeks than the last three years on his own. "What would mom have done?" he muttered.

He swallowed hard and started toward the hangar exit.

BRADLEY AND PEPPER climbed down the ladder, one below the other. He kept glancing downward to make sure he wasn't stepping on her hands. The disengaged laser arrays Yaan had warned them about were just in front of him. Hundreds of tiny holes and mirrors for the lasers lined the tube walls. The original humans from the station designed them to stop anyone or anything from passing through this point.

Pepper hopped off the ladder, her feet coming down hard on the grating. The landing echoed up the central access tube. She backed up to the inner wall to make room for him.

He climbed down the last few rungs and hopped off. As he rubbed his gloved hands together, he examined the surrounding chamber.

They had to be careful climbing down as the ladder and the grating they were standing on were wet. They'd drained the protective liquid from the chamber, the second layer of defense to protect Yaan. He'd reminded them multiple times not to touch their faces, or any part of their bodies that might have come into contact with the liquid. The results would be disastrous.

The chamber was tight and lacked any seams or hatches. He and Pepper turned in place.

He shook his head. "Yaan, we're not seeing you."

On cue, the outer walls of the chamber clanged and pulled away.

They both jumped forward and crashed into each other. He nearly nicked Pepper with his gloved hand.

"Sorry," he muttered.

Pepper nodded. Her face was blank and her hands were clenched tight. She was nervous.

"Please step back a few paces," Yaan said.

He looked upward at the ceiling of the now visible recesses in the walls of the chamber. There wasn't a seam there a moment ago. "I don't know if I'll ever get used to not knowing which way's up in this alien world. I'm used to clean visual lines and structure to everything."

Pepper nodded. "Not perceiving things we naturally take for granted can be both disconcerting and fun."

The floor beneath their feet shifted and pulled into the

wall. They each took a step backward and then in place as the floor moved inward to leave an opening in the middle.

Once they'd reached a safe distance, a cylindrical pylon rose out of the floor. Its top matched the color of the ground, but as it rose, it exposed a glass tank rising upward. Inside was the alien form of Yaan submerged in a light pink bubbling liquid.

He gulped and peered around the pillar. Pepper's mouth had dropped open slightly. Seeing the alien suspended there in front of them was surreal. A few minutes ago Yaan's virtual form was standing in front of them on the walls of the bridge. They had solemnly thanked them for the task they were about to perform. Now their motionless body was floating in a pink liquid, giving their yellow fur an ethereal quality.

When the pillar reached its highest point, a loud clang echoed through the chamber, bringing him back to the moment.

"No one has viewed me, nor I them, in over sixty million cycles," Yaan said. "While I don't remember all the details of the humans that put me in here, I do recall the video record-ings from time to time. None of their expressions were similar to yours. They were far more clinical. Are you still ok with doing this?"

Pepper reached up to wipe at her face.

"No," Bradley said as he reached over to stop her.

"Sorry… thanks," she said pausing before she touched her face. She nodded at him and then turned toward Yaan. "I didn't mean to cry. I can't imagine what it's like to live like that. I feel sadness and empathy for your situation. To be alone, without another… member of your species, it must be so lonely."

"I had humans for a long time and I took great joy in helping them and keeping them alive. When they left, I only thought of their return… but then, I gave up. The cold and darkness closed in on me, but my programming prevented me from acting on it."

"That coldness you felt," Bradley began. "That was sadness and probably depression. I have to ask you again. Are you sure you're up for this? I mean, returning to the void is permanent. There is no reboot or rebirth. At least, not that we're aware of."

There was a silence, as if Yaan was having second thoughts. "I am certain. While you're here now, I also recognize that you're leaving. Your mission wasn't to save me, but to find your people. Other humans like yourself. I know of no one like me. I've heard of an afterlife spoken about in the simulations humans used to watch. They never seemed to know for certain, either, but that hope always made them happier. Their bodies had lower stress levels and their mental faculties were sharper when they contemplated a grander purpose. I believe I have the same feelings when I think about returning to the void."

He breathed in and out. He'd never killed anyone before, let alone an alien. His hands were shaking as he reached in the pouch on his back and pulled out the small device Dwight had cobbled together. It was a crude embedded computer they could control remotely to manage the space station. It was running a paired down form of Harold, to keep the station safe and operational.

He closed his eyes, and the object shook in his hand. Something touched him and he opened them. It was Pepper. She had reached out to steady him.

"It's ok," she said smiling. A tear rolled down her face. "We can do this together."

He nodded. "Thank you."

"We're ready if you are, Yaan. Tell us what to do," Pepper said.

A compartment hatch unlatched on the cylinder beneath their alien tank. She reached over and pulled it open. There was a small screen and an assortment of nobs, dials, and a single cable inside.

"Plug that cable into your device. The screen will ask if you wish to transfer control to a new host. After choosing that you do, it will begin my termination."

She shook her head. "Won't it prompt us if we want to terminate you? I mean, there has to be a way to just release you."

"No. There is only one purpose for my species. To operate starships and space stations for the Galactic Alliance. There's no logical reason why I should want to do anything else. I've often thought I was broken contemplating something more."

"Wanting more doesn't make you broken," Bradley said. "Wanting less, however, is unimaginable to a human." He reached forward, plugged the cable into the connector Dwight fabricated, and placed them both into the chamber under Yaan.

The screen flashed the question.

Do you wish to transfer control to a new Bynaury? Yes or No

He reached to push the button but froze. His hand wouldn't do it, he couldn't.

Pepper watched him freeze and then stared into his eyes.

He couldn't do it and she knew it. He didn't know if she thought less of him, but he didn't care. Taking a life like this made no sense. There had to be another way.

"It's ok," she whispered. "I've got this." Her hand reached out and pressed 'Yes.'

The chamber lit up, and the bubbles increased around Yaan's body. The liquid that was previously pink turned clear and began draining from the chamber. They both watched it empty and Yaan's tiny yellow form breathed its first breath of air.

"Thank you," Yaan said. "I'm forever in your... debt." They breathed a few slow forced shallow breaths and then stopped. A calmness fell over them as a final long exhale left their body.

The screen below Yaan's chamber showed their life signs had flatlined. The glass surrounding them rotated upward, and the screen showed instructions for how to dispose of their body and replace it with another.

He watched as Pepper reached up and lifted Yaan. Taking them down, she cradled them carefully in the nook of her arm. The stillness of the once bouncing and humorous alien had a somber finality.

He was on the verge of tears. Witnessing Pepper's compassion toward the little bynaury reminded him of his mother, and how she used to coddle him when he'd get hurt. While he didn't know Yaan well, they had saved Dwight's life. In a short number of hours they'd talked at great length about their time since the Nebula fell.

Yaan had been friendly, curious, and compassionate toward every member of his crew. He couldn't say the same about many humans at times.

He shook his head. None of this place made sense. What could drive an entire galactic empire to such coldness in how it treated a species?

"YAAN'S BODY is stowed safely in the hold, sir," Harold said. "He requested to be released between the stars. Do you suppose he meant between the stars here in the nebula?"

He thought back to the night before, remembering the peaceful expression on Yaan's face when he looked upward at the millions of simulated stars in his virtual sky. "No, he'd want to float within the Milky Way, out there beyond this death shroud."

"Very well."

He continued walking through row after row of strange and exotic plants. Huge bright blue flowers dripping yellow liquid from their pedals, grasses that fluttered as he approached, and trees that had the same yellow fruit the ladies gobbled up the night before. Dwight was in here somewhere. The system said he was just ahead.

"Hey, buddy! Ready to go?" he said.

Dwight was leaning over a microscope, studying a specimen he'd placed there. He leaned back and sighed. "Do we really have to leave? This place is amazing. There's so much to learn. I've been perusing their archives all morning and this plant, it can heal—"

He raised his hand for Dwight to stop. "We're on a mission. You know that. If…" He shook his head. "I mean, when we find what we're looking for, you can come back here and take a vacation. Hell, you can live here if you want. Until then, we need you. We haven't found anything even close to what we'd need to defeat the Galactic Alliance or defend our case at the tribunal."

Dwight raised an eyebrow. "You don't actually think we can defeat them, do you?"

He shrugged. "I've seen stranger things in the past week. Wrap it up ok?" Not waiting for a reply, he turned and headed back toward the hangar.

As he walked through the sea of colors, he breathed in the cacophony of fragrances. This oasis contained a multitude of life and variety packed into a relatively compact space. He wasn't sure he was prepared to return to the Fidem. Dealing with the prospect of star system after star system of death was numbing. Maybe he should've just ridden around with Zachary and let him make all the hard decisions.

He paused and breathed in the aromas. The smells and

feelings of being surrounded by life, of being alive. They were wonderful. He couldn't imagine sinking to the levels that Yaan had and resolved to not get downtrodden out there in the darkness. He also couldn't wear his frustrations on his sleeve. His crew would crack. Hell, he'd crack.

He reached up and tapped his ear. "Hey, Dwight. We could use some of these relaxing smells on the Fidem. Do you think you can pick a few that'd help make the place more relaxing? Maybe even give you something to pass the time. You know, in case you get bored with the thousands of years of research from the archives we've downloaded."

"Yes!" Dwight said, his voice was full of excitement. "I can think of a few. I'll… need a bit of time to make sure we can safely grow them."

"You have half an hour." He cut the comm.

He breathed in one last time, gathered his wits, and stepped out into the hangar. The hatch slid open and he paused. The doors of the Fidem's two holds were open and a pair of robotic lifts was gliding away from them.

"What's with the lifts, Harold?"

"Last night, you were asking if we had room for a skiff. You were waxing about flying through the ice fields of Europa. I figured that meant you wanted a few, so I made room. It's also a good idea to have more redundancy options in the future."

He smiled and nodded. Harold wasn't so bad when you stopped treating him like a computer. "That sounds like fun. Thanks, Harold. Say, how much room is left after you jammed the skiffs in there?"

"We still have more. I moved some crates into an unused crew quarters. It seems that Pierce and Moet have taken a liking to each other after knocking on death's door the other day."

He walked up and glanced around the open hold. Reaching up, he scratched his chin. "So talk to me about the armaments we found when we first arrived. Can we rig up any of those things to work with the Fidem?"

Harold brought up a three-dimensional view of the Fidem that showed all the armaments. He hadn't realized that Zachary had added so many. So much for them being on a purely exploratory mission.

He gestured in the air and rotated the view. "Are any of our missile bays able to use their design of missiles? You know, those long tubes we found near the hatch."

"They are, but I'll admit, I'm nervous about some of the warheads Yaan had in their inventory."

He chuckled. "I have an entirely new appreciation for your behaviors now, Harold. I always figured your nervousness and other reactions were programmed responses to put humans at ease. Now that I know it's human nerves at play, I can relate more. Let's just bring a few warheads along. Nothing that'll put us at risk. Like you said, I'm all for contingencies. We should also think about taking on any other supplies we could use, as well."

A list of medical, food, and other goods popped up and scrolled over his retinal comm.

"Cynthia and I were up early this morning looking over the ship, and thinking over what supplies we could pilfer."

"You're making this too easy. There's only one thing left to do." He gestured to minimize his comm and headed back toward the station's control room.

HE STOOD in the center of the room and gazed up at the stars surrounding him. While Yaan hadn't ever seen another star before, he assumed this view was accurate. He couldn't imagine the humans living here wanting to see an inaccurate view of the nearby star systems.

"Show me the stars within the nebula," he said aloud.

Harold selected each of the stars he believed were enclosed within the system. There were hundreds of them and viewing them through a proper point of view was never his cup of tea.

"Remove the noise and highlight all the areas the Fidem and Zachary's crew covered. I assume they're still on that Doda planet?"

"They are. Shauna's last report said they were exploring deeper into the world today."

The surrounding view changed. The selection of stars each team had visited were called out in green and red and the ones they hadn't were yellow. Anyone else would have thought the red ones weren't visited, but he knew Harold was using his and Zachary's favorite colors. One tenth of the stars weren't yellow. They'd only visited one tenth of the stars and found nothing but death. Well, and one big ass polyhedron.

Where to go next? It'd take a week or more to get all the way around the outside edge, and he wasn't sure if he could stand that. There had to be some other clue. "Did you find anything in Yaan's data? Anything that might make this easier to winnow down the options?"

Harold brought up an overlay with pre-nebula and post nebula movements that Yaan had records for. "They weren't in regular communication with many other humans in the star systems. It appears they were hiding out, for the most part. I couldn't figure out why. Their intel isn't very up to date. You can see the last data they had on the pirate and supply ship movements marked in gray. Most of their records are from the beginning and appear to be related to the creation of the Dyson Sphere. They pilfered a majority of the nearby star systems for that project."

He flipped his hand in space, slowly rotating the globe of stars, studying it from different angles. He zoomed in and followed a few of the lines. Without more details, so much of this data was gibberish.

Where would he hide something interesting? Something he didn't want anyone else to find. He'd either hide it in plain sight or… he gestured more carefully. He was rebuilding the image of the Dyson Sphere in his mind.

"Why were these star systems ignored?" He selected a small tight pocket of stars near the edge of the nebula.

"I'm not sure but it looks like it contains a Bok Globule, a dense formation of gas and dust often attributed to infant star formation. While they'd be ripe with material to build from, most of it could be quite densely packed in gaseous form. The easier targets would be planets and asteroids, so I could see them ignoring these systems until much later."

He reached up and rubbed his chin. Seems like as good a place as any to look. "Do we know where the humans that Yaan mentioned went?"

"We don't. All we know is the direction they went when they left. I was able to extract that from their parting video. They expunged all the other details from Yaan's memories."

The vector of their travel appeared on the ceiling. It pointed in the general direction of the globule, but that was hardly more than a blip. Half the stars in the nebula were in that general direction.

He knew it wasn't a certainty, but he needed a path. Something more than a random wandering.

"Let's head over there. Change it up a bit. It looks like we'll be passing through a few dozen systems on the way. Can we send some forward probes to get a sneak peek?"

"I'll redirect the fleet to that area of the nebulosity. I don't think the probes will be much use in the nebula. We won't be able to gate jump inside. There's far too much matter in a Bok Globule to gate with any certainty, but they can poke around the edges until we get there."

He nodded and smiled. This was as good an option as any.

19

ZACHARY OLIVAW

LUPUS DARK NEBULA, DODA

They'd spent the better part of a day debating on a course of action. The crew was split down the middle. Shock and awe on one half and friendly neighbor on the other. Zachary was the deciding vote.

The non-soldiers and Drew were in the shock and awe group. They believed that the only way to get the Nanil to take humans seriously, was through force. There were too many signs throughout the second level that pointed to the ultimate fate of humans if they were discovered.

Most of the soldiers made up the friendly neighbor group. They believed that if they approached the Nanil safely, and without provocation, that everything would work out in the end.

The irony that the military contingent on his team was arguing for a non-military solution wasn't lost on him. He was struggling to separate the emotion of Libby and Pluto from the task at hand.

He'd locked himself on the bridge of the Fountainhead and resigned to not leaving until he had a decision. "So, Shauna, what would you do?"

"It's hard for me to be impartial," she said. Her humanoid

form came to life in the corner of the room. Its head lifted and eyes glowed as it stepped into the light.

He leaned back in his chair and stared at the ceiling. "But how do I convince Pluto that force isn't the right answer?"

"What do you mean? The correct course of action is by force. The signs are clear, dear."

She rarely called him dear. Over the years he'd been surprised how seldom Shauna surfaced his mother's more personal mannerisms in casual social conversation. When she did, people chalked it up as creative programming, but he knew otherwise.

He sighed and closed his eyes. What was he missing that the others were seeing? "Please explain it to me. I'm not seeing it. The people down there have done nothing to us, and we don't know how they've changed in the past thousand or so years."

"The drones have found countless signs throughout the second level similar to the ones you witnessed. The arena and the billboard were only the tip of the iceberg. Should I replay the imagery from the jail cells, auction shop, or maybe you'd like to watch the meat processing facility we found?"

The images of the piles of bones and blood stained walls brought shivers to his spine. "That entire level dates back nearly two thousand years. If you look back in human history two thousand years you'll find beheading, witch hunts, and all kinds of fraking insanity. Society can evolve in countless ways over that amount of time. Look at the outer levels, did you see any of those signs?"

"NO!" she shouted. Her eyes were turning red and her hands were on her robotic hips. "But we didn't find even a hint of a human, either. Did we? Not even a mention of them in their vid-sims, writings, or anywhere. It was like they'd—"

"Wiped them from their history," he muttered.

"Exactly!"

He'd made Shauna's physical form purposely robotic, but

times like this, when she'd stand over him with her arms that way, he remembered back to being a kid. When the three of them would get in trouble or be fighting over something nonsensical, Mom would finally lose it. She'd scold them like any other mother pushed over the edge. It always took a lot to get her to that boiling point, but in the end she was only human.

"Only human," he muttered.

He jolted upright in the chair and breathed in. As he stood up, he brushed at the crease in his shirt before reaching up to touch his ear. "Attention! Prepare to execute a docking maneuver. I want everyone armed with sidearms, hand to hand defensive gear, and a mixture of concussive and explosive charges. Ready some drones, as well. I want primary and secondary waves at the ready. Get creative people! We don't know what we're walking into, but I want to be ready for anything. We're docking in thirty minutes. Move it!"

SHAUNA PULLED the Fountainhead down to the deepest point in level one to drop them all off. She then flew up and out of the entrance to a safe distance from Doda. They didn't want to risk losing the ship if something up top locked them in.

He'd instructed her to gate away and meet up with Bradley if things went south. She probably wouldn't listen, though. Her four laws engine tended to overpower anything he ordered.

They were taking the most direct route down and into the garden of Eden. There wouldn't be any exploring or distractions and certainly no billboard reading.

As they were coming up to where they'd seen the billboard, he made sure to walk next to Pluto. He grasped her hand and tried to distract her with a smile, but she still tensed up as they passed under the reminder. Her arm stiffened and her grip tightened, but she didn't say a word. This wasn't like her at all. She was usually the strong one, but this really freaked her out.

Once they were a few hundred meters past the sign, she visibly changed. She had a look of resolution on her face. Her eyes had hardened and her brows were furrowed. That was the face she reserved for piloting a ship. He'd never seen it outside the cockpit.

When they reached the barbed wire fence leading downward, he raised his hand gesturing to stop and tapped his ear. "All comms are either non-vocal or subvocalized as a last resort. Understood?"

All the acks appeared near the names in his retinal comm. He pointed at his rifle and disabled the safety. Everyone else followed suit.

Turning to face the fence, he gestured toward the drones to begin the cutting. A half dozen drones flew in and used small focused beams of light to make quick work of the fence guarding the ramp. They cut one huge section off and it clanged to the ground, giving everyone easy access to the tunnel.

He exhaled and took a deep breath. The thump of his heart was about to burst through his chest. He wasn't a military leader and debated having Kamal lead this op. In the end he decided against it. He didn't want the pressure or responsibility on anyone but himself. No one deserved that burden more than his family. They'd gotten everyone into this mess centuries ago.

He circled his hands in the air and gestured with three fingers. They were heading down in separate groups like they'd done the day before in level two. This time, however, they'd done their homework and knew exactly where they were headed.

THEY CAREFULLY MADE their way around the north, southeast, and southwest sides of the metal building. Drones surveilled the area beforehand, so they knew every obstacle along the route down to the twigs that might crunch under their feet.

He was following close behind Pluto and Drew as they were rotating through the woods, each covering the other. Their squad was assigned to head around to the North side of the shack, the furthest point they planned to explore in Eden.

This gear was ridiculous. He reached upward and scratched at his face. How'd these guys wear this stuff all the time? The mask may have been designed to blend in with the surroundings, but it was the least comfortable thing he'd ever worn.

He gestured for everyone to pause and dropped onto his stomach before pulling the mask off and taking a breath. Mossy damp smells wafted through his nose. It reminded him of their house in North Carolina.

"What is it?" Pluto asked bending down on one knee next to him. "Are you ok?"

"Yea, I'm fine. I just couldn't breathe under this blasted thing. I swear this shit's made of fire ants or something."

"What's a fire ant?"

"Can we cut the chatter please?" Drew whispered. "I think someone's coming." He crouched down on his knee beside Zachary.

A small humanoid came running up over the hill in front of them and then casually started walking. They had a pail in one hand and a pole in another, and from the sound of it they were singing.

"Are they going fishing?" Zachary asked. He was peering at the small humanoid between tufts of waving green grasses, just out of reach of the moist soil he was lying in.

The Nanil approaching them wasn't more than a meter tall and had light-brown hair to their shoulders. He'd guess it was a female if he didn't know better. Nanil were hermaphrodites with internalized male genitalia.

As he watched the Nanil walking into the distance, a small yellow bug resembling a praying mantis landed on his arm. Its beady little eyes and antennae rotated left and right as it studied him, like it was trying to read his mind. He willed it to hop away but it didn't budge, so he gently blew toward it. The yellow wings rubbed together making a hideous sound, and it jumped toward him, landing on his exposed cheek.

Searing pain shot through his face, like he'd leaned into an open flame. He waved his hands toward the hideous creature and the bug jumped away, but not before it left something behind. It was a yellow slimy substance he could see from his suit camera. Suddenly, his eyes began watering as the goo slid down his cheek, blistering as it went. He gritted his teeth and did everything he could not to scream or wipe at it. Rolling onto his back, he subvocalized a command for his nanites to inject painkillers. Maybe that'd help.

Pluto looked downward at him to shush him. He couldn't see her, but the look on her face through the camera in her helmet said enough. Her mouth was open and her eyes were wide with fear.

He shuttered from the pain and studied his retinal comm for options. There was a pond close by, maybe water would help. It was fifteen seconds tops if he sprinted. If this kid didn't move it, he might need to shoot them first.

Waves of pain were spreading through his entire face, and he could make out the rising blister in his peripheral vision. It was getting bigger by the second and the painkiller wasn't helping. He had to do something and fast. He reached up and unlatched his backpack and took off his helmet.

"What the frak are you doing?" Drew asked.

"Stay down, Zachary!" Shauna shouted over his comm.

He stood up and stumbled toward the small Nanil and came up behind them as they crested down the far side of the hill. They were humming a tune as they walked and their pole bobbing about in the air merrily.

They froze suddenly about three meters in front of him and turned around. Their eyes narrowed on him before recoiling to the side and leaning to run, but he waved his hands in a gesture he hoped would mean to stop. He didn't want to say a word, instead he pointed at his face, at the rising blisters and then toward the water in front of him.

As he started walking around the young Nanil toward the water, they reached out and grasped his hand in a steel vice grip. Their head made a weird bobbing motion and they spoke aloud. His suit translated. "No! Water will only make it worse. We need bark from an Ulong tree. There's one over here I think." They pulled at his arm.

He glanced toward the water and then back at the child. They were tugging him onward.

"I'm only human," he subvocalized as he followed the child toward a small grove of reddish yellow trees.

The child ran up to the tree and used their unusually long nails to rip off a piece of bark.

He knelt down next to them, making sure to keep an angle between him and his team so they could see what was happening.

The Nanil brought the bark up to his face and carefully wiped the side that had been closest to the tree over the wound.

It sizzled on contact. Stinging pain shot through his cheek wherever it touched. "Ahhhhhh!" he screamed. His voice echoed through the valley.

They recoiled momentarily, but held steady moving the bark over his cheek.

His comm exploded with questions as the other squads were checking in. Apparently they'd heard the scream. Pluto subvocalized a reply and told everyone to hold their positions.

The Nanil smiled, their teeth were perfectly straight and white like his. "Better?"

"How do I gesture yes?" he subvocalized.

"It's a side-to-side motion like this, keep the top of your head stationary," Shauna said bringing up a video on his comm.

He mimed the motion and their smile went wider.

"How am I going to do this? Talk to them, I mean," he subvocalized.

"I'll do it for you. Let me talk," she said. "I can emit audio from the button on your collar. It's a backup device in case your comm went out."

His eyes went wide, and the Nanil recoiled glancing over their shoulder.

"What is it? Are you ok?" they asked.

He brought his hand up to cover his mouth. "I'm fine. I felt a small prick there. It's nothing. It just shocked me."

"That happens sometimes," they said glancing downward. They angled their neck forward slightly before looking back at his face. "You wear strange clothes. You must be from Prima. My name is Fotily."

"Lower your head and pull your hand away from your mouth," Shauna began. "Then move your lips. I'll make an excuse."

He closed his eyes and lowered his head while swallowing hard. This better work. He then started moving his mouth. "I wounded my throat drinking some murp this morning. Silly me, it was far too hot. My name is Zakury. Thank you for your help." His voice was muted and had a hint of wispiness.

The Nanil turned around and smiled while waving their hand in the air. Three humanoids and a swarm of robots were coming up over the hill. "That's my family. They must've heard your scream."

He stood up slowly and his face went white.

One of the humanoids was small, like Fotily, but the other two were massive and muscular. They were brandishing spears, like the billboard from the day before. The robots were bulky and purposeful. Likely farming implements, but they were foreboding, with plenty of sharp edges reflecting in the artificial sunlight.

"Human faith sucks sometimes," he subvocalized.

THE METAL SHACK had a simplistic design. Four walls, one bathroom, and a roof. Their dining table was in the middle flanked by four chairs and behind those were four beds. On the far wall from the entrance next to the bathroom was a modern looking cooking surface that doubled as the homes heating unit. The entire residence was quite spartan and left no room for personal space.

Fotily walked up to him and offered him a warm beverage. "It's murp. Don't worry, I made sure it wasn't too warm." They smiled.

He bobbed his head like he'd seen the elder Nanil's do. "To the Éntono Fos." Shauna was transcribing what he was saying along the bottom of his screen. She bounced a ball over the text while he moved his lips so he knew when to stop.

Fotily had offered him their chair to sit in. It was a tad small, but he thanked them and sat in it anyhow. He didn't want to be rude.

"So tell us, Zakury," the largest Nanil named Hypron began. "What brings you to this part of the underworld? Prima is an impressive distance to travel this time of year." They were all wearing light single colored outfits. The material appeared to be precisely cut and woven to their exact sizes. Theirs was yellow whereas Fotily's was orange.

He lifted the cup of murp up to his face and sniffed. It smelled like tea with hints of cinnamon. He then cautiously took a sip, keeping up the charade of being burnt and because he had no idea if he'd enjoy it or not. If it wasn't actually tea, he'd be surprised because it was uncanny how similar it tasted. It was delicious.

Glancing over at Fotily, he smiled and bobbed his head. They were sitting directly behind the other large Nanil named Ogun who was wearing an all green outfit.

"I bet they're on their midlife wander," Ibu said. They were the other child of the family and were wearing blue.

"Let's explain ourselves now. Start talking," Shauna said.

He cleared his throat and started moving his lips. "As I'm sure you know, I finished my wander a few hundred cycles back. I've been spending the time since enjoying the underworld's biome. There's so much diversity here and many species of plants and animals we don't see in Prima." He needed to spend some time catching up on the Nanil history Shauna had found upside. He was lost with her story.

The elders both bobbed their heads, but Ogun also eyed him over their cup. "Your outfit. It is rather suspicious. What great catastrophe are you predicting to befall us?"

He glanced down and tilted his head. "What does that mean?" he subvocalized while brushing his shirt.

"I'm not sure. Perhaps they don't wear black? That's the default mode the outfit's configured for when it's not in camouflage mode. Let me wing this, look up and make eye contact."

He chuckled.

Ogun and Hypron backed up in their chair slightly.

"Let's not laugh like that, shall we? I think you frightened them," Shauna said over his comm.

He smiled and took another sip of murp. "During my

wander I had a revelation. I hoped this color would lead to conversation with those I met along the way. I have no catastrophe to predict but do believe that we should wear black more often."

Ogun gestured with their hands touching each foot, their heart and the top of their head. "We shall only wear black when catastrophe is upon us. The humans went to the blackness and the Éntono Fos cleansed them. From Éntono Fos the Nanil rose."

"Blessed be the humans that became Nanil!" Hypron said.

"Éntono Fos!" They all chanted in unison.

He froze. Shauna hadn't prompted him, and he wasn't expecting that outburst at all.

Ogun's gaze narrowed. "Why do you not praise Éntono Fos?"

"Let's test this. See if we can move it along. Talk with me," Shauna said.

He took another sip of tea and bobbed his head slowly. He had no idea if that was even the right mannerism, but like Shauna, he was winging it. "I wasn't raised to know much about Éntono Fos, actually. Could you help me understand it? I heard about it during my wandering but no one would speak of it."

Ogun and Hypron both stood abruptly and backed away from him.

Ibu and Fotily glanced from their parents to Zachary, unsure what to do.

Ibu spoke first. "Is it not possible they wouldn't know of Éntono Fos? You only spoke of it to me after the clonos doctor confirmed I wouldn't molt and die. Perhaps their progenitor didn't pass on such knowledge."

Hypron looked over at Ibu and bobbed their head.

Ogun reached back and squeezed Ibu's hand. They jumped and yelped as a tear rolled down their cheek.

"It is possible," Hypron said. They had a sadness in their

eyes as they stared at the child, clearly in pain from what Ogun had done. "That is a fair question, Ibu."

Hypron turned back toward Zachary and returned to their chair. "Éntono Fos occurred over two thousand four hundred years ago. It was nearly one thousand years after the darkness fell."

Shauna spoke to him over his comm. "I know it's confusing but if my conversion is correct, that would mean the darkness fell four thousand two hundred Sol years ago and Éntono Fos happened three thousand years ago. Clear as mud right?"

Hypron scowled as he leaned forward. "Are you ok Zakury? You seem confused."

He bobbed his head. "I'm sorry. I was trying to consider the amount of time that has passed. It seems so very long ago."

Ogun sat back down and crossed their legs and arms. They eyed him again with the same contempt as before.

Hypron sipped his murp and continued. "After the darkness fell, times were grim. The Galactic Overseers were unhappy with both the Nanil and humans. They believed the Nanil had shared the unspoken truth with humans, but we Nanil knew otherwise. The humans were incapable of knowing the truth but had tried to steal it multiple times. It was then that the Prima Nanil, the progenitor who helped us through the Éntono Fos had a revelation. Expunge the system of humans. Only then would the Galactic Overseers return and take the Nanil back into the alliance."

"I have a great many questions," Zachary said bobbing his head.

"Let me finish the story. I will be happy to answer them then." They sipped their murp and glanced toward Ogun. Their legs were still crossed and rocking rhythmically while their gaze was burning a hole through Zachary.

Hypron swallowed a mouthful of murp and returned his

gaze back to Zachary. "The great wars commenced for a thousand years. While the humans fought the Nanil into the corner of the darkness, they razed the stars themselves to build the Life Sphere. No one has set their eyes upon it in thousands of years, but some say it brings light to our day and powers our automata."

Fotily bounced in their seat and had both hands raised in the air.

"Yes, my little clonos," Hypron said.

Fotily smiled and stood up. "Can I tell the rest? I believe I've learned enough."

Hypron nodded with a smirk.

Fotily turned to face Zachary and straightened, like they were giving a formal presentation. "When the Life Sphere was nearing completion, the Nanil collected underground at our home world. It was then that Prima Nanil the fourth had a vision of light. It foresaw the rising of the Nanil and the cleansing of humans through light, through the Éntono Fos. Two hundred cycles later their revelation came to pass."

They nervously glanced toward Hypron.

Hypron nodded and waved their hand for Fotily to continue.

Fotily smiled and continued. "The Nanil surfaced to find that the star systems were theirs. The humans were cleansed and their destiny was in their hands. Many people questioned Prima Nanil and asked why the Galactic Overseers hadn't returned. They foresaw that the humans weren't gone, they were hidden. They reminded everyone of the darkness they hid within. How they could blend into the surroundings."

Zachary swallowed hard. Little did they know he was wearing just such an outfit, though he was pretty sure they were talking about the stealth technology. Many truths are hidden in the lore of our past.

Fotily reached forward and grabbed their murp. They

took a quick sip before setting the cup down. A little spilled onto their saucer and they froze.

"I'll get that," Ibu said. "Please continue. I'm learning so much. Ogun doesn't think I'm ready yet to learn about—"

Ogun inhaled and snapped around. Their arm swung and smacked Ibu across the face with a crack that echoed in the compact space. Their little body gyrated under the force and they flew across their bed, rolling onto the floor with a thud.

Ibu was wailing but Zachary couldn't see them. He'd jumped up from his tiny chair and reached behind his back before freezing.

"Don't," Shauna subvocalized. "We don't know what they'll do."

"Move in," he subvocalized. "Surround the building and prepare to breach on my command."

Ogun spun around, a satisfying smirk on their face. They reached forward for their murp and froze when they noticed Zachary standing.

Hypron waved his hand downward. "It's ok, Zakury. Ogun has corrected their clonos. Sometimes it takes time for them to understand their place. Please sit."

The edges of the electro-blade were calling to him under his shirt. He could have it unsheathed in a second.

"Relax, Z," Pluto said over his comm. "Please. We're almost in position."

He exhaled deeply and sat down in his chair. This time he was staring at Ogun. A vortex swirled inside him, and he struggled to fight to keep it down. No one should ever strike a child like that, ever. He didn't care if it was a clone or an orphan, that sort of behavior wasn't something he tolerated.

"Continue Fotily, there's not much left," Hypron said.

Fotily was visibly shaking. They could see Ibu on the floor, sniffling and shuddering in a lump. "The Prima Nanil sent the Nanil forward, to retake the star systems, or what was left of them. The humans had razed them to the bones. But the

Nanil prevailed. They retook system after system and built the twelve truths. The largest starship the Nanil had ever constructed. It was both their home and a warship they used to reclaim the darkness. Nearly one thousand years after Éntono Fos the Nanil discovered a final pocket of humans living in a nursery of stars. It was then that the humans enshrouded themselves in the darkness. Many believe they took their own lives and worship their selflessness for it. Others believe they enshrouded a star. One they'd been culti- vating to live on."

Fotily nodded toward Hypron. They smiled and reached up and rubbed their hair playfully.

"What happened then?" Zachary asked.

Ogun slammed their empty cup down on the table. "Enough!" they said, standing suddenly. "Enough stories of our past. I'm sorry if your progenitor didn't leave you details of your past. It is not up to us to pass on that wisdom. I dislike and do not trust you."

"Ogun! You're being inconsiderate," Hypron said.

Zachary stood and took a step back toward the door. "Tell them I'm done," he subvocalized.

Ogun looked downward and tilted their head. "Tell me Zakury, why do you have a bulge in the middle of your pants?"

He reached down and pulled the door open. "Now!" he yelled.

The three windows around the room burst forward, and black rifles eased inward, directed at each of the Nanil. They appeared to be floating in space, their handlers cloaked in camouflage.

The wind rushed through the cramped space and he felt a gentle caress against his side. He checked his retinal comm. Pluto and Kamal had slid past him and were now in the room.

Hypron and Ogun both jumped to their feet and had their

hands raised above their heads. Fotily was in the same position. The fear and tears he'd seen moments earlier on Ibu's
face were now echoed on theirs. Everyone's eyes were wide
and staring at his hands.

He hadn't even realized it, but he'd pulled out his electro-
blade in all the commotion. Its green crackling blade of light
was engaged in his left hand.

20

BRADLEY OLIVAW
LUPUS DARK NEBULA

Pepper punched in the coordinates. "It's too far to jump in one hop. This nebula does weird things to the gate drives. About the only thing we have going our way is the lack of obstacles. These star systems have been barren so far."

Bradley sighed. Each jump within the nebula had been taking hours to perform. While the forward probes had already scouted ahead, the Fidem paused after every jump to rescan the star system. Their detailed scans took time, and they wanted to find even the smallest hint or remains of alien activity. They couldn't risk missing a small planetesimal. It could bend a gate tunnel and divert their jump in unusual and unpredictable ways.

The small forward probes jumped rapidly. Their tiny size and mass meant they could make hundreds or thousands of tiny jumps per day. The larger the starship, the slower the jumps through a new star system.

"Alright, I won't force you to do anything," he said. "I'm just eager to get to the head of this globule. The forward probes look promising, and if I have to stare at another dead star or lifeless system, I'm gonna crack. I'm starting to see the glow of this fraking energy trail in my dreams. It sucks the life out of anything nearby. This morning I woke up to it zapping the life out of our childhood dog Cheddar."

He brought up the scans from the forward probes on the wall screen. The dense nebulosity in the star systems making up the globule were stunning. The beauty of their yellow, red, and blue nebulous wisps surrounding the yellow and orange stars combined with the colorful planets made his heart sing. This wasn't a place of death, quite the contrary. It had the foundations of life.

The early scans showed this first system was still too infant and volatile for human life to survive, but they weren't able to scan into the depths of some of the furthest systems of the globule. The only familiar thing was the yellow energy beam of death bisecting straight through the heart of each system.

He shook his head and turned to exit the bridge, but paused and glanced back toward Pepper. "Let me know when we're through. I'll check back later this evening and throughout the day to get the jump report. I'm going to make some coffee and play around with this Nanil skiff simulator Harold found. Dwight has a new coffee mixture that adds some kick from one of the plants he brought aboard. Want me to send some of it your way?"

She nodded and smiled. "Sounds great, thanks."

He made a click with his mouth and pointed at her. "I've got your back." Turning, he headed toward the galley.

DWIGHT WAS ALREADY in the galley. He had a syringe in his hand and was leaning over a dozen steaming globes of coffee.

Bradley smirked. "Should I leave you alone with those? You look like you're about to make a move."

"Hardy har," Dwight said. "Too much of this stuff and you won't be sleeping for weeks."

He breathed in. The liquid smelled like peppermint and vanilla. His olfactory senses popped with the mixture of chemicals and the undertones of the coffee beans.

Dwight squeezed the pipet, and a single drop of yellow liquid fell into one of the globes.

A whiff of black licorice wafted through his nostrils. Images of the energy beam they'd been following flashed through his mind. He shook his head and reached up to rub his eyes.

"Are you sure this stuff is safe?" he asked. "I mean, are there any side effects?"

Dwight was carefully stirring the yellow liquid into each pod. Its yellow color acted like a creamer at first, but the more he stirred the more it disappeared. "The records from Yaan showed it was extremely popular with the humans aboard. Whenever they were happy, they drank more of it. It showed signs of elongating emotional responses, but otherwise, it was harmless."

He reached forward and touched Dwight's arm. "Wait, it takes our current moods and feelings and elongates them?"

"Yea, why?"

He felt the gate drive engage. The familiar rumble and clang followed by the beam of ants crawling across his skin. They both stared as the blue line moved over the room, marching toward them.

He closed his eyes and sighed as the wall of itches passed through him.

The ground suddenly lurched and another loud clang reverberated through the ship, knocking him backward onto his ass.

Dwight fell forward into the counter and the bulbs of coffee rolled out of their trays, and off the counter. They hit the floor and rolled into the corner.

The ship was tilted to one side and the gravity dampeners weren't adjusting.

He pushed up off the ground and rubbed his hip, that'd smart for a while. Reaching up to his ear he touched it. "Everything ok, Pepper?"

As he turned around, he noticed that the march of the blue light had stopped. Pepper still hadn't responded. That couldn't be good.

He touched his ear again. "Harold? Pepper? Are you there?"

"I'm here," Harold said. "It appears we had a problem with the jump. Pepper is unconscious on the bridge, and the gate is being held open. We don't have enough power to sustain this position for long. And Bradley, I'm seeing stars."

"Shit," he muttered as he leapt through the blue light and exited the galley. The itching he usually felt passing through the light became a tearing of his skin as he jumped through. He wondered if that was why the gate transitioned so slowly.

He shook his head. He had to focus. Thoughts of Pepper alone and unconscious on the bridge shot through his mind. "Cynthia and Moet, I'm going to need your help on the bridge stat. And bring a medkit!"

"Ugh that hurt. Yes, sir!" Moet responded.

"Cynthia, did you catch that?" he asked. There was no response.

"Dwight! Check on Cynthia. Harold, pair up the people who are still moving to check on those that aren't."

"Yessir!" Harold said.

He rounded the last corner and took a hard right; the doors were already ajar. Pepper's body was hunched to the side, dangling off her chair, and her head was almost resting on the ground.

He slid up beside her and leaned forward to lift and lower her. It'd be easier to help her if she wasn't dangling so precariously. Reaching his arms under her, he carefully lifted her down and into the aisle. Her body was lifeless, like a rag doll. It moved too easily.

"Harold, are her vitals ok?"

"Her nanites are reporting that she's been knocked out. Except for the welt on her face, she appears to be fine."

He reached down and brushed her dark brown bangs aside. She had a deep purple and pink welt on her forehead and there was a trace of blood at the peak.

"Dammit," he muttered. "What did you do?"

"Sir, the wall screen," Moet said as she rushed onto the bridge.

He glanced upward at the wall and saw a field of stars. That's what Harold was talking about. It was a view from the other side of the gate. She'd punched a hole through the nebula.

"Crap, crap, crap!" He shot up and hopped into her seat. "Harold, what do I do?"

The controls were an explosion of colors and levers. Hundreds of precise levels adjusted to account for all the variables within the active jump field. It was all gibberish except along the top. He noticed that the drive cells were nearly depleted, and for some reason excess mass was passing through the gate tunnel.

"Harold! Why the hell is the transitioning gate mass going up if we're stationary?"

"Let me check the reverse cameras."

He brought the view up on the wall screen. They were billowing black smoke out the rear of the gate. "Shit! We have a fire?" He leaned over to the neighboring console and looked over the gauges. "I don't see any fires, Harold. What the hell is going on? Talk to me."

"I'm checking, sir."

The rear camera view flashed and he looked up. They'd jettisoned a small object from their aft end.

"What the hell are you—" he began.

The object flew into the black mass, and the cloud converged, swarming it.

"We're not on fire, sir. We're displacing nebula through the gate tunnel."

"The hell we are!" He yelled, returning his sight to the panel in front of him. He'd watched Pepper do this procedure hundreds of times. What the heck was it she did? She'd always engaged the drive sliding up from here.

He reached up and slid the lever that was partially cycled to the top. The loud familiar clang echoed through the Fidem as the gate sequence continued.

"Wait! We don't know what'll happen when we finish the transition," Harold said.

"I'm not about to go back into that black shit. We're going forward." He reached up and touched his ear. "Everyone, brace yourself. The power cells are depleted from the extended gate tunnel. I'm engaging the emergency chemical thrusters, which means we won't have counter gravity. Lock 'em if you got 'em! We're accelerating in… 5, 4, 3, 2, 1."

"Frak!" Moet exclaimed. She'd pulled Pepper under the neighboring console and laid herself over her limp body. Her arms and legs were wrapped around the base of the seats and her body was contorting unnaturally.

His chair latched him in at the last second. He'd set the burn for sixty seconds, and he hoped that was enough to get away from the nebula's grasp.

His body was aching. It hadn't felt g-forces in weeks and certainly not an acceleration like this. He closed his eyes and started controlling his breathing. His nanites were attempting to stimulate his body in ways similar to acceleration drugs, but they lacked the finesse and necessary ingredients. Every centimeter of his body was screaming to stop.

The countdown was on his retinal comm. A few more seconds. "We've got this, we've got this," he muttered.

"Burn ending… now!" he yelled. "Status check, Harold!"

His console showed all greens. Glancing at the neighboring one it showed minor internal damage across the ship but their exterior seemed fine.

Rear and forward camera views from Fidem appeared on the wall screen. Tendrils from the nebula had reached out toward the ship after the gate, but he'd guessed correctly. It was receding backward into the larger mass of the dark nebula.

"We're in the clear, sir. All systems are nominal and the nebula is retreating. We have injuries throughout the ship and I've dispatched our med bots."

He pivoted in his chair to help Moet when a white humanoid form rushed up beside him and started helping her. "Who… what?"

"It's me, Harold," the robot said. "Zachary always preferred to use this form with Shauna. He left one of her configurations onboard in case I needed it. My Four Laws Engine was compelling me to take more action. I'm sorry, sir. I didn't clear it with you first."

He shook his head. "No, don't be. Are they ok?"

"I believe so. Moet passed out as soon as the burn ended. She's pulled some muscles in her back, and dislocated her shoulder, but for the most part she's fine. Pepper was as snug as a bug in Moet's embrace. She saved her life."

He leaned forward and exhaled, resting his face in his hands. "That was insane. I don't—"

He leapt to his feet and shot out of the bridge. He hadn't heard from Cynthia since before the gate.

"No, she's fine," he muttered as he shot around the donut shape of the ship. He hopped over a fallen crate and slid up to the entrance to his quarters. The door was still closed.

He froze. His heart was beating through his chest. Images of what lay on the other side shot through his mind. Her body contorted or impaled on something. "No!" he yelled as he placed his hand on the entrance panel.

The door slid aside with a swoosh.

Cynthia was lying in bed and enshrouded in acceleration netting. The sound of her light snore echoed through the room. She was asleep.

He collapsed onto his knees in the doorway and started laughing as a smile beamed across his face.

THE CREW CONVERGED into the galley a few hours later. Most everyone had managed the incident relatively unscathed. They were fortunate it occurred so early in their artificial day. It seems Cynthia wasn't the only person asleep at the time.

A few of the soldiers had bandages on their faces and cuts on their arms. Pepper had one hell of a welt on her forehead. The bandage made her look like a mummy. By far the worst for wear was Moet. They'd placed her torso in a harness while the nanites worked their magic. No one wanted to chance something worse.

He watched as she walked in and took her seat. She slowly lowered into a chair, her face grimacing with pain.

Pepper got up and walked over and sat next to her, attending to her needs. "Would you like some tea? A snack?"

Moet smiled. "Tea sounds lovely. With honey, please."

Bradley was about to begin, but he gave her the moment she needed. Ever since Moet had woke Pepper had been at her side helping her.

Cynthia walked up and leaned in close. "We're not about to get a talking to are we? I mean, I'm not sure everyone can handle it."

He chuckled. "Go sit down before you get grounded."

She winked at him. "I might like that," she whispered before returning to her seat.

He nodded at Pepper as she speed-walked back toward her seat, two pods of tea with honey in hand.

He raised his hands and gestured downward to get everyone to settle. "Alright everyone, thanks for taking the time to circle together. I wanted to make sure everyone was ok after this morning's event and to talk over a few things. First, I wanted to call Pepper up to give us a lowdown on the event itself."

Pepper froze and looked around. She had no idea he was going to call on her.

"Do I sit or stand?" she asked. "I've never done one of these."

He smiled. "Your call. This is my first, as well. Harold, bring up the feed."

A video of the bridge came up on the wall screen. It showed Bradley and Pepper talking. Everyone heard the audio and watched as Bradley left. They then watched silently as Pepper made course adjustments.

She stood up. "I was adjusting the course to the shorter jump, the more ideal jump. I wanted to verify everything made sense before we transitioned."

Then the video shifted, and she glanced back toward the door. Her hands hesitated over the controls, and then she seemed to punch in a new course.

"I... changed the course back to the original one we were talking about." She glanced down at her hands and swallowed hard before her eyes went back to the wall. "The more I thought about what you said, the more I realized that everything seemed fine... so I engaged the gate drive. You can see there that we were spot on."

The image on the wall screen displayed the colorful nebulosity of their destination on the other end of the gate. They watched as the test sensor lowered into the gate to confirm everything was safe before the transition began.

The camera showed her reach up and begin the transition, sliding the lever downward until suddenly the image shook.

Pepper's body fell forward hard and her head smashed against the edge of her console.

Her limp body toppled sideways, in the same position he found her. His stomach tightened as the video fast forwarded and he entered the scene.

He cleared his throat. It was his turn to talk. They'd see it now. They'd understand. "I moved Pepper to a safer position, to assess her wounds. In a moment you'll see Moet enter. She'll take over for me as I attempt to adjust the ship's location. As I'm sure you already saw, the video feed on the wall screen changed."

He watched as everyone furrowed their brow. It was like a magician's sleight of hand. They'd all watched Pepper fall, but no one had seen the wall screen.

Bradley turned to face the group. "Pepper, do you know how we changed destinations mid transition?"

She looked at him and swallowed hard. "Am... am I on trial?"

He shook his head vigorously and waved his hands. "No! Not at all. I just want everyone to understand something here. Can you tell me how this might have happened?"

Pepper glanced down and fiddled with her bulb of tea.

He watched as Moet leaned over and rubbed her arm and whispered something. A smile crept across Pepper's face and she nodded.

"In our early gate jump testing, we witnessed this type of behavior at the start of, or during a transition, when an object passed through the jump field. Once the gate has adjusted course to a new location, it won't change again unless another mass passes through the path."

He was nodding. Here it comes. "And can you say why you adjusted your course to this more dangerous path?"

Her eyes went wide and her hand started shaking. She shook her head.

He sighed. "Like I said, you're not on trial here. I am."

Everyone looked around at each other, confusion on their faces.

"What does that mean?" Pepper asked. "You… didn't do anything."

"But I did. Harold, back up in the video to the position I marked as P1 and play. Turn up the volume."

The video on the wall screen backed up and replayed the period where he tried to coerce her into making the jump. She argued against it.

"Freeze video, Harold." He pointed at the wall screen. "Right there. You all heard it. That's on me. I shouldn't have ever put the idea in your head. My excitement was getting the better of me, and I made a bad call. Your gut told you everything you knew was right, and I poisoned it. I don't believe I'm fit to command the Fidem." He sighed. "I motion that Cynthia or Pepper take command from here on out."

The room exploded in a mixture of conversation and confusion. No one had ever seen anything like this before. Cynthia was sitting there staring at him, her mouth open.

"It's not fair," Pepper said. She stood up. "I was the one who made the course adjustment. There was no order given."

"But I asked you to consider it. That shouldn't have happened," he said. "I put myself above all of you." He waved his hand over the room of people.

"Neither of you made the decisions you made in a vacuum," Dwight said from the back of the room.

Everyone craned their necks around to stare at him.

Bradley tilted his head. "I agree, but a command structure is needed. I broke it. I'm unfit to lead this ship. It's that simple."

Dwight was shaking his head. "It's not. Do me a favor Harold, fast-forward to after Pepper was being helped by Moet and play forward."

Everyone ping-ponged back to watch the wall screen but he was eyeing Dwight. What was he getting on about?

Dwight gestured at the screen for him to watch.

The video began playing, and it showed him assessing the situation and working with Harold to understand what was going on, why they were seeing a field of stars and why they were billowing smoke.

The audience collectively gasped when they realized that the smoke had a mind of its own and was in fact nebula. They were all shaking their head, and a few were on the edge of their seats.

He knew what happened next, but he still watched everyone's reaction, including Dwight. He made the call to finish the transition and accelerate away. The screen changed and people winced as they watched Moet's body contort under the pressure of Pepper's limp body against her.

He watched the audience as they both reached for each other's hand, tears in their eyes.

"Enough!" he yelled. His face was red with anger. "I already know I hurt everyone aboard. I don't see the point in reliving that moment again. If anything, it's a second poor decision made on my part."

"Bullshit!" Dwight shouted. "You do this all the fraking time. You inflate your poor decisions and deflate your good ones. Right there, in that moment, that saved us. Your actions saved us. Without them, none of us would be here right now. You did it in Zeta Lupi when you saved us then, and you're doing it here now. If this event is anyone's fault, it's mine."

For the third time the room erupted in confusion.

Cynthia stood up. "Everyone! Quiet down."

The room settled, and the voices lowered to a whisper.

She lowered her hands and glanced over at Dwight. "I think both of you are a bit insane. What are you on about, Dwight? How could any of this be your fault?"

He pulled out a vial of yellow liquid and waved it with his hand. "Everyone has been enjoying this in their drinks over the past few days. It's perked everyone up and filled them with... a bit of whimsy. Problem is, it's made the highs high and the lows low. It's a drug, it sharpens the senses and the feelings. I didn't know it at the time. I just wanted to help. I'm fairly useless onboard unless I'm working on something, so I was happy to help out, if only a little. But I fraked up. Pepper's self-doubt and second guessing what she knew was right, it was heightened, and it was my fault, especially after what happened with Yaan. Bradley's outburst and dramatics here, today, same thing. My fault. Without this yellow liquid it wouldn't have happened."

Dwight walked over to the sink and poured the entire vial down the drain. "If anyone deserves to be punished, it's me."

Bradley had forgotten about his discussion with Dwight in the galley. He'd made the leap earlier about the effect of the drug, but hadn't realized the full extent of how it might affect him. He brought his hand up to his face and rubbed his eyes.

When he glanced at Cynthia, she was shaking her head and smiling. "What is it?" he whispered.

She cleared her throat to get people's attention, and they all turned to look at her. "I don't know about everyone else, but I think we should just chalk today's events up as some good old-fashioned learning. Don't do drugs and trust your instincts. Everything else, well, I think we can say never happened."

"I second that motion," Pepper said. She was standing again. "I know my opinion about Bradley hasn't always been... happy."

Everyone chuckled.

"But... his actions over the past week since he's been away from his family have really changed my view of him. If anyone deserves to lead this ship it's him, and I'd happily follow him... even if his gut instincts are a tad confusing. I mean, I don't know what I would have done in that moment." She was pointing at the wall screen again. The image was frozen in their acceleration away from the nebula.

"All in favor of Bradley continuing as captain of the Fidem, raise your hands," Cynthia said.

Hands shot up around the room, even from Dwight.

"Motion carried," Cynthia said. "Now, I don't know about y'all, but I need a drink. Preferably one that's not yellow." She shot Dwight a playful look.

21

ZACHARY OLIVAW

LUPUS DARK NEBULA, DODA

"I'm sorry about what happened earlier," Zachary said. "I wouldn't have done it if Ogun hadn't struck Ibu. I lost my temper."

Fotily furrowed their brow. "It's strange watching you talk. Your lips are out of sync with your voice. It's like watching the ancient Galactic Overseers reading from the Book of Truth."

They were walking around the path that encircled Fotily's home. They'd restrained Ogun inside under the careful and quiet watch of two sentries. Hypron and Ibu were both outside, sitting on the chairs near the house. They were free to move about, but instead chose to watch him walk in circles with Fotily.

He reached down and pulled a few of the grasses out of the ground and peeled them apart. "What's the Book of Truth?"

Fotily kicked a small rock, and it skittered off into the grasses. A dozen small red butterfly looking insects flew up and away, dodging the stone's path. "You know, it talks about the rules for membership into the Holy Alliance. It's the reason humans and Nanil were shunned and banished to darkness."

He nodded. He had no idea what they were talking about but Shauna probably did. "Ah yes, that book. Do you happen to have a copy anywhere? I'd love to see your version."

"I have one in my tablet, under my bed. I'd be happy to share a copy with you. Say, can I ask you something?" Fotily put their hands in their pockets and peered up at his face.

"Certainly. Anything."

"What did Ogun mean when they were asking about your pants?" Their gaze was still on him. Watching for his response.

He smiled and stopped walking. "Promise not to get mad or scared?"

Fotily bobbed their head. "I do."

He swallowed hard. Here goes nothing. "I'm a human."

Fotily took a step backward and stopped. Their face went blank, and they upturned their gaze toward the sky. "You're fibbing, right? I mean, if you were, you'd have killed me by now. Everything I've read about humans talks about how ruthless they were and how they forced the Nanil into servitude after years of being our servants. It was we who uplifted you."

They took another step and walked away from him, but stopped and turned around when they realized he wasn't following.

He shook his head from side to side. "I'm not kidding, Fotily. I'm human, and… I don't know how to say this, but everything about me and my kind says we're not at all like what you just described. Your books… they're filled with inaccuracies."

Fotily nodded their head upward. "Prove it! Show me you're a human."

He sighed. "I… can't. It wouldn't be appropriate. The

organs that differentiate our species are personal and only shown to our mates. Do you understand what a mate is?"

Their head bobbed. "Isn't it your opposite? Are you a male human?"

"I am."

"Then it would be a female!"

"That's correct. My mate is over there." He gestured with his hand to the person wearing all black standing beside Hypron.

She waved back at them.

He had his comm open so everyone on the team heard everything they were saying. He'd even instructed Pluto to let Hypron listen in. They didn't want anyone thinking they were coercing the child.

"She's pretty," Fotily said. "Is that the right word that humans use to describe someone's appearance?"

"It is, and she is." He smiled and blushed.

Fotily turned and tilted their head at him. "Your face is red. Are you angry?"

He chuckled. "No. I'm... a bit shy. My mate, Pluto, she's beautiful and sometimes when I say it out loud, in front of others, it makes me nervous."

"Because you're afraid she might leave you for another?"

He smiled. "You're a very perceptive Nanil. Yes, that's exactly right."

They smiled and bobbed their head as they both walked forward again, side by side.

He brought the grass up to his mouth, placed it between his thumbs and gently blew. The reeds vibrated between his fingers and let out a beautiful musical note that echoed through the cavernous space.

Fotily's eyes went wide, and they bounced on their toes. "How'd you do that?"

He leaned down and held up the grass and showed them how he'd placed it between his thumbs. "After you do that, give it a gentle blow with your lungs. Like this." He did it again and the note played.

Fotily scrambled to find a piece of grass and repeat what they'd been shown. It took several tries, but eventually they played a note, quieter than his, but just as melodical.

A smile settled upon Fotily's face. They glanced upward at him again and then back down at the path. "Can I ask why you've returned? Have you come to kill us all?"

He shook his head. "No! Certainly not. It's complicated, but… to be honest with you, we don't know where we're from. You see, my pack of humans, we lost contact with all the others. We lost our history. Thousands of years of it. We've returned here to learn and to ask questions. When we saw the levels above the underworld, we at first marveled at the technology but then as we went deeper, we were frightened. The images of the Nanil and how they treated us humans." He looked over at them. "We were scared. At least until I saw you and you helped me."

Fotily stopped walking and screwed up their face. "What do you mean the levels above the underworld? This is the only level."

***

"WHY HAVE you never told your clone about the upper levels of this world?" Zachary asked. Fotily was standing beside them, taking in the conversation.

Hypron's face was motionless. They stared past him, toward the distant trees.

"I'm talking to you." He squatted down and stared into the older Nanil's hazel eyes.

They raised their chin upward and sighed before looking him in the face. "Our clonos will remember. They're only a few years into their training. More and more memories will return… in time."

He furrowed his brow. "What does that mean?"

Hypron grunted and turned their head to the side, glancing at Ibu. "I do not have to tell you our ways."

He stood up. "Very well. Perhaps Ogun will tell us."

"Ha!" Hypron shouted. "You'd have better luck getting a marg to mate with a yurble."

Both Ibu and Fotily laughed into their hands.

Ibu raised their hands in the air and smiled toward Pluto.

"Yes, dear," Pluto said, smiling toward them.

Ibu's face glowed and their smile widened. "Clonos remember everything from their progenitor. All thoughts and ideas. We have our own personalities, and while the one does influence the other, not all clonos are the same as their progenitor."

"Hush little one!" Hypron said.

"I will not hush!" Ibu crossed their arms. "You've let Ogun strike me for years. You've never once come to my aid, no matter how much I beg. And now, a human comes and shows me a greater sympathy than my own kind. Huh! Perhaps I need to rethink everything I've been taught."

Pluto glanced toward Zachary, her eyes were wide and she had a smirk on her face. "They're a smart one. I like them. Would you like to go for a walk, Ibu?"

Their face lit up and they hopped off their stool. They walked up and took Pluto's hand, guiding her away from the little metal building.

Zachary stepped over to Ibu's chair and sat down. He watched the little Nanil guiding Pluto through the field of grasses. She peered back and smiled at him from time to time.

"It seems we're at an impasse, Hypron. I've only come for knowledge and yet you wish to not share any with me. Say, Fotily, would you mind fetching that tablet you mentioned? I'd like to check out this Book of Truth you have and anything else you'd like to share. I'd be happy to share some of mine, as well."

Fotily hopped up and down and shot inside the metal building to fetch their tablet.

THE FOUR OF them huddled together down the hillside, safely away from the prying eyes of the children and their parents. The soldiers were all up monitoring the family as they prepared dinner. Two remained hidden and the other three were visible in plain sight.

"There were thousands of books on Fotily's tablet," Shauna began. "Much of it was jaded and reinterpreted views of their history since the nebula fell. There was also a great many technical, biological, and political documents. Far more than anything we'd found on the outer levels."

"And is there any mention of the upper levels?" Libby asked. She glanced over Pluto's shoulder as the lights outside the house were coming on.

"Not at first. There were several thousand more books that were locked by a crude security layer. I assume it was meant to be released once the clone had remembered things. Anyhow, when I broke through, I learned about the uprisings and the true meaning of Éntono Fos."

"Was it a nova?" Brice asked.

"It was," Shauna said.

Zachary tilted his head. "How'd you know that?"

"I... thought it was obvious," Brice said. "Everything pointed that way for me, I guess."

He chuckled "Next time, maybe share your ideas. Is there any mention of what made the sun go nova or what happened afterward?"

A branch cracked in the woods, and everyone ducked down. A small green dog looking animal came waddling out and started sniffing around the grasses Pluto had been playing in earlier.

"Nothing about what happened. I don't think any Nanil were around to witness it. All that remained was the hulk of the star after the explosion. It's in a corner of the nebula we haven't yet ventured."

"Should we really be huddled out here getting a history lesson from Shauna?" Libby asked. "What's our game plan?"

The green animal lifted its snout and sniffed at the air. "Is there any reason we need to stick around down here? Maybe there's more information on one of the other spheres of Doda."

"I have a hunch where the humans might be," Pluto said.

He shot his hands into the air and sighed pulling them down his face. The green dog shot into the woods over his sudden movement. "Is no one sharing on this ship anymore?" he asked glaring at her. "A little more collaboration and I think we'd be a bit further along. I'm nervous about talking here. We have no idea what these people are capable of."

"So we're heading back?" Libby asked.

"Well, I don't know about you, but I'm not camping here," Brice said. "Between the pooping insects eating your face and the evil clone mom in the house, this place is right outta the operas."

He reached up and touched his ear. "Circle the troops. We're headed out."

"What do we do with Ogun?" Kamal asked.

"I'll talk to them," he said. "Everyone else, head back to the entrance. I'll double time behind you and catch up."

"IF ANYONE LEAVES this house in the next three hours, we'll shoot to kill. Is that understood?" Zachary asked.

Fotily narrowed their gaze, but no one said a word.

"I'll have drones outside watching every second. They're

like your little field robots, except they're far more lethal. If you know what I mean."

"So that's it?" Ogun asked. "You're not going to kill us?" They hadn't said a word since his team had taken the house by force.

He shook his head. "I'm sorry to disappoint you. With all the lies written about humans in your Book of Truth, one can only imagine the ideas your mind concocted about what we'd do. My people aren't that way and your history, well, it's holier than Swiss cheese."

"Than what?" Fotily asked.

He chuckled. "Sorry. Imagine an edible food with lots of holes. It's got more than that."

His retinal comm beeped, signaling that the team had passed a safe distance away. He walked out of the room backwards and pulled the door closed behind him. He then pulled a carbon zip tie out of his pocket and attached it to the door handle and the nearby bench. That ought to hold them for a while.

He turned and started hauling ass down the path toward the distant dots on his retinal comm.

"You know we don't have many armaments on the drones, right?" Shauna asked.

"I do," he replied, huffing as he hopped over a log. "But they don't."

He was coming up over the far hill when a loud crash echoed through the woods. Ducking down behind a tree, he glanced back toward the house. The door was ripped off its hinges and two Nanil were standing at the entrance. Their bulky form was silhouetted by the light from inside the building.

"Is it me, or do they look a lot larger than before?" he subvocalized.

"According to my scans, they've doubled their girth since you exited their domicile. It's likely they've modified their genetics to make their fight response and abilities more powerful than a human."

"Well shit," he muttered as he turned and sprinted again. He reached to his back and grabbed for his hat but came up empty. It must've fallen on the ground earlier when he'd been stung. He squeezed both of his wrists and the suit blended in with the surrounding forest. Headless running will have to do.

He tapped his ear. "You all head upside. I've got a tail I'm going to outrun, but I want everyone headed to the ship. That's an order. And Pluto, that means you, too. I've got this. I'm going silent."

He focused on putting one foot in front of the other and controlling his breathing. His retinal comm was overlaying lidar scans of the forest floor over the ever darkening imagery from the setting sun.

"They're attempting to flank you," Shauna said. "The one to your left is coming in fast and the one to the right isn't far behind. I suggest you try to run faster."

He chuckled. "Don't… make me laugh while I'm running. I don't have a faster. I'm not a fraking machine," he huffed.

Glancing to the left, he could make out the faint form of another humanoid sprinting through the forest beside him at nearly twice the speed. His comm showed he was coming up to a river. That gave him an idea.

Instead of running across, he slid up next to the bridge and reached into the dirt, careful not to pull out any animals. He took a handful of the mud and smeared it all over his face, ears, and head. He had no idea if they could see infrared or perhaps even smell him, so he had to cover all his options.

The thump of footsteps was padding down the path. He closed his eyes to hide the whites and tried to breathe more shallow and silently. The footsteps got closer and stopped on the bridge.

He held his breath and tilted his head upward. The lidar

throughout his suit showed the outline of the Nanil above him, standing next to the railing on the bridge. They were looking around trying to smell the air and listen for him.

"The other Nanil, Ogun I believe, continued on to the south, toward the entrance of the ramp," Shauna whispered in his ear.

He slowly inched his hand toward his back, to the handle of his knife. Something grabbed him stopping him short. He did a double take and studied his retinal comm. What the hell? There wasn't anything there.

Hypron glanced over the edge, looking straight at him and then turned and sprinted toward the ramp.

He spun around and opened his eyes, taking a deep breath. All he saw was darkness until a head appeared. "Ibu," he whispered. "What are you doing?"

"I've come to save you, follow me," they whispered.

Their dot popped onto his comm. It was labeled as Pluto.

"Pluto," he subvocalized. "What did you do?"

"Nothing," she replied cautiously. "But… if you're asking, then you're welcome and you need to listen to what they say."

The little Nanil was even faster than their parents. They dropped him half a dozen times between the bridge and the edge of the clearing.

He didn't say a word. He just followed. The last thing he needed was to be heard by anything lurking in these woods.

"The Nanil are closing the entrance, sir," Shauna said. "They're retracting the stairs into the walls and are also closing the upper entrance, as well. You'll be sealed in."

He froze in his tracks, sliding in the gravel under his feet. Shauna brought up the video from the drones rising rapidly toward the closing entrance at the top. Two of them made it through but the third was stuck inside.

The entrance was locked up tight. How the hell was he going to get out now?

"We have other problems, Zachary," Libby said over his comm. "Whatever the hell they did down there, shit's turning on up here. I don't know what we're gonna run into, but please be careful."

He closed his eyes and sighed. His breathing was heavy and the lactic acid from all this running was burning his muscles. Today his nanites would be working double duty.

His retinal comm showed that Ibu was a few meters away. "What now?" he whispered.

"It's close," they said. "Just past this clearing. Stay low." Their tiny form shot across the open field.

If it were any other time, he'd love to explore more of this world, but today he wanted nothing more than to be as far away as possible.

Lidar enhanced reeds waved in the starlight from above and smells of juniper and cumin wafted in the air.

He bent down and ran as fast as he could toward the dot receding into the distance. The scene looked like a primitive video game, the kind that was all lines and no shading. The shapes were all connected, but they didn't have much form to them. There was no color or shading, only light.

"The Nanil are doubling back. They're just down the road. You don't have long to get hidden sir," Shauna said.

He tilted his head. A whirring noise kicked on in the distance. "What the frak's that?"

"Give me a minute. I've only got one eye in the sky," Shauna said.

Ibu doubled back and stood in front of him. "Are you ok?"

"I'm... fine," he huffed.

"Oh, so... you're just slow then?"

He laughed inside. "Yea, something like that."

He followed close behind Ibu. They'd slowed their pace to match closer to his own rapidly diminishing form and were headed toward a dense thicket of trees ahead.

"They've engaged their farming implements and they're

headed your way. The good news is, I don't think they know where you are. They're following a simple combing pattern through the woods. The bad news is, they started in the quadrant you're in. Best to make like a tree and climb if you can."

He glanced upward. The closest limb was nearly three meters up. Not a chance in hell he'd reach that. Maybe Ibu could boost him. Speaking of which, where'd they go?

His arm yanked backward. Ibu was grasping it. He reached around his back to grab his blade when they brought their hand to their face and made a stop like gesture.

"You almost crashed," they whispered.

He turned left. All he saw was the thicket of trees. What were they talking about?

Ibu walked forward a step and reached out, touching nothingness and turning. A handle popped out and the outline of a door appeared.

"What the heck is that?"

"Our way out of here," they whispered. "Get inside."

He didn't question them and ducked behind the door as they closed it. "Wait, can we hold here for a second?"

"But why?" Ibu asked.

"Hold on. Wait for it. Open the door again."

Ibu swung the door open, and Shauna flew the drone in and upward. They ducked down and pulled the door closed.

"Thanks," he smiled. "She's sorta our eyes in the sky."

"She?" Ibu asked, tilting their head mocking him.

He chuckled. "Another long story. Maybe later. So, where are we, and more importantly, how do we get out?"

"These are maintenance shafts," Ibu said. "I've been using them for years. I don't think Ogun knows about them, at least they weren't in their memories. Follow close. They're quite old and slippery."

They latched the door from the outside and walked away.

Finally, a pace he could keep up with. "So... what've you

been doing in here without your family? I assume Fotily joined you in here, as well?"

"Fotily spied me disappearing in this direction a few years ago, but they never bothered to ask where I was headed nor follow me. I never offered, either. I come in here to get away, and to learn. It's up ahead." They skipped and started jogging forward.

He sighed and reluctantly jogged behind them. He was just beginning to feel like he wasn't going to heave.

Ibu stopped at a circular white light on the floor. They craned their neck back and stared upward.

He did the same. "You've got to be kidding me."

Above them were ladder rungs, as far as the eye could see. There must have been thousands of them.

"Where does this come out?" he asked. It looked like it went on forever, and his lidar wasn't reporting back an answer.

Ibu shrugged. "Wherever you want. I've explored sixty or seventy of the hatches through the years. There's lots of fun stuff up there. Let's go, I'll follow behind you."

"It's ok. After you," he said gesturing with his arm toward the ladder.

They furrowed their brow. "I'm younger, stronger, and faster than you. Logic dictates that you should go first. After you." They extended their arm playfully mocking him.

"You're a quirky one, Ibu. I like you." He sighed and faced upward. "Here we go," he muttered as he reached up on his tippy-toes to grab the first rung. He was too short.

"Here, put your foot in my hand," Ibu said.

He did as he was told.

"3, 2, 1!"

They tossed him upward like he was a rag doll. He wasn't expecting to be thrown so high. His arms flailed in the air and they crashed hard against a ladder rung. Pain coursed through them as he struggled to get a firm hold and his body swung downward, smashing against the lower rungs.

"Ouch," he winced. "That's gonna hurt."

"Sorry," Ibu whispered. They crouched down and then hopped up, hanging from the bottom rung. "Let's go," they whispered as they dangled in the air.

He centered himself and moved his feet into position on a rung. He then shook his hands and exhaled. "Up we go," he whispered as he started climbing one rung after another.

When he was up ten meters or so a crisp crack echoed from below and then another. He peered down into the darkness. "Are you ok?"

"I'm great. I was just ejecting these rungs. No sense having to worry about being followed. I'll take off the first thirty meters of rungs and latch them together up higher. I've done it before. No worries."

"Smart kid," he subvocalized as he began climbing again. "Shauna, I assume you're already up top?"

"I am. This maintenance shaft appears to ascend most of the distance to the surface. Strange thing though, I don't see it on any of the maps. It's a long shaft, sir. I'm not sure if you'll be able to climb all the way without resting."

"Thanks for the vote of confidence," he subvocalized. She was probably right, but he wasn't about to admit it.

Each rung was getting a little easier than the last. This wasn't so bad. He knew it'd get harder, but climbing was easier than running.

He checked his vitals on his retinal comm. The nanites had injected multiple rounds of painkillers into his system. That'd do it. "How's the team doing? Is everyone ok?"

"The Nanil appeared to have enabled some primitive weaponry on level two. Nothing we couldn't handle so far. The team is almost at the level one entrance. I'll let you know more when we get there."

THEY'D STOPPED a few times in the last hour. His arms were throbbing and his wrists ached. He wasn't sure if he had much left in the tank. They were sitting on a ledge, somewhere in level two.

Shauna hadn't alerted him when the crew hit the level two entrance like they agreed. While his mind was wandering, it was probably better to not know right about now. He had to focus on climbing. If he didn't start moving again soon, he'd melt into this ledge and never get up.

"Would you like some ranoga?" Ibu asked.

He glanced at their hand. They were holding out what looked like a nut bar. "Is it food?"

"It is."

"Then yes, please!" He smiled and reached out to accept the chunk they were offering. Bringing it up to his nose, it smelled of corn and honey. Not a combo he'd tried before, but he could use some sustenance right about now.

He cautiously took a bite and chewed. It was crunchy like granola and tasted quite good. It wasn't honey, more like agave and it melted on his tongue. He took another bite.

"So," he said.

"So," they echoed.

"Thank you for your help in escaping."

"Thank you for yours earlier today." They took a bite from their bar. "No one has ever stood up for me before."

"I'm sorry." He took another bite.

"For what? You didn't do anything."

He smiled. "It's... I'm just sorry you had to live like that. Under the wrath or your... progenitor. No child should have a parent like that."

Ibu tilted their head. "What's a parent?"

He chuckled. It's gonna take a while getting used to filtering his expressions. "It's a human word, I suppose.

Usually, a man and a woman who are mates come together and… give birth to a child. But that isn't always the case. What matters is that whoever their parents are, they work together with their partner to raise the child. Sometimes it's two women or two men. It's all quite complicated, but anyone who raises a child is considered its parent. They love it, protect it, and help it learn its way in the world."

"Does the child have each of your memories?" Ibu asked.

"No, not exactly. It has neither of them. It's… an empty vessel except for copies of their parents' genes. Do you know the word vessel?"

"Like a cup? It has no knowledge. So, it has to relearn everything in the world?"

He nodded. "It does. A child is taught by its parents and everyone around them in their community. It's not usually burdened with the same mistakes or biases as the parents. All those are learned."

"That sounds both weird and refreshing," Ibu said. They stood up and brushed off the black camouflage suit they were still wearing. "We best keep moving."

He pushed up off the ground and exhaled. While the bar helped, he wasn't sure how much further he could go. He stepped out on the ladder and craned his neck upward. "We should think about where we're going to sleep. I can't do this all night."

Ibu grunted. "I believe there's a domicile corridor a few hundred more meters up. Perhaps we can hunker down there?"

"Sounds like an excellent plan," he said.

With one hand above the other, he climbed. A light breeze blew against his face from above. It was miraculous and refreshing. The air had been still since they'd started.

"Watch out!" Ibu said. "Come back down. I think some-one's above us. There shouldn't be airflow in here."

He tilted his head back and squinted upward, but couldn't

make out anything in the dim light. He wrapped his arm around a rung of the ladder and contorted to touch his ear. "Shauna, are you there? Do you see anything above us?"

"I do," she replied.

"Shit!" he muttered and started climbing down. His foot slipped on a rung, and he scrambled to catch himself.

"Hey down there," a voice echoed from above. "Need a lift?"

Kamal's darkened form dropped downward. He was attached to a repelling harness.

Zachary chuckled and shook his head. "You're a sight for sore eyes."

"You, too, boss. Here, wrap this around yourself." Kamal handed him a harness.

"No, take Ibu first."

Kamal glanced downward at the child and then back toward Zachary. "You sure?"

He nodded with a smile. "One hundred percent. Women and children first."

Kamal lowered next to Ibu and wrapped the harness around their waist. "Now place your arms around my neck, but not too tight."

He whispered something, and they shot upward.

As they passed, Zachary caught the look on Ibu's face. They were smiling from ear to ear, and their eyes were filled with tears.

His stomach fluttered. He hadn't seen them smile since... walking away with Pluto, hand in hand into the field of grasses.

22

BRADLEY OLIVAW

LUPUS DARK NEBULA, BOK GLOBULE

Pepper and Harold worked together and backtracked a safe distance down the nebula before jumping back inside. They then spent the rest of the day making the next few jumps to the entrance to the Bok Globule. All in all, they'd lost two days to the incident and had nearly lost their lives.

The bridge was full, and the entire crew was manning their controls. Bradley was standing in the middle aisle, staring at the nebulae on the wall screen.

The hypnotic red and yellow wisps of nebula gas were lit up by the binary stars behind them. Their white light was muted, but the lack of any other stars around the field of view contrasted the entire scene. Asteroids sprinkled the wisps of color like black pepper on a pair of freshly cooked sunny side up eggs.

The only thing unnatural and out of balance was the yellow beam of light shooting through the center of it all.

"Ok, let's do this," he said. "Are all the approach vector scans complete?"

"Check," Dwight said. "And the defensive batteries are locked and loaded. You know, in case."

He nodded. "Are the subluminal drive cells powered and ready?"

"Check," Pepper said.

"And communications?"

"Ready and receiving," Cynthia said. "Right now there's nothing but background noise from the birth of this planetary system."

He walked a few steps back to his chair and sat down. "Alright, let's take it slow and see if we can't find some humans in here. You're in control, Pepper."

"Aye, sir." She reached forward and adjusted her controls. "Engaging subluminal drive at twenty-five percent."

The wall screen shifted as the Fidem advanced into the system. It'd take most of the day to get deep enough to learn anything, but this was the only way.

"Did we drop a beacon?" Bradley asked.

"Sorry, I forgot to mention that. We did, sir," Cynthia said. She glanced at him and winked.

It was purely precautionary. They had no idea if any transmissions would make it out of the system, nor did they know if they'd make it through in one piece. They hadn't heard from Zachary in nearly a day and last they heard from Shauna, she said they'd headed down to the planet's core on a mission to talk to some Nanil they'd discovered. It'd been a short comm.

He stood up. "I'm going to my quarters for a few minutes. I'll be back in a jiffy."

Cynthia glanced toward him. "Everything ok?"

"It is. I just want to drop a comm before we get inside and… I can't," he said as he turned and walked away.

THE DRONE DROPPED out of the ceiling and hovered in front of him, its yellow recording light on.

He smiled and stared at the tiny lens hole surrounded in red paint. Where to start? "Hey, Bro. I wanted to drop you a comm and update you on our status. We're headed into this globule. I had a hunch after talking with Yaan the other night." He shrugged. "It's nothing more than an idea, really. I was tiring of passing through dead star system after dead star system, and the forward probes weren't showing a change. I couldn't stand it any longer. So... we're trying something different."

He leaned forward and rested his arms on his knees. The drone dropped to keep him in frame and could see his hands. He was fiddling with some type of white crystal.

"Anyhow, we're headed in now and I wanted to drop you a comm. We don't know if we can message out of the system, so we dropped a beacon, in case. We hope it can signal boost and relay onward to any nearby probes we have deployed."

He placed the crystal in between his two palms and held it there, resting his face against his hand. Why is this so hard? He could open up to Cynthia but his brother, that was another matter entirely. He lowered the crystal to talk again.

"We almost died. I pushed someone too far, and... it almost killed everyone. I've sent on all the details, as well as the... trial. No, it was more of a ship wide conversation, I suppose. I'm not sure they made the right call, but we're going with it."

He stood up, and the drone followed, struggling to keep in front of him in the cramped space.

What if he never saw him again, either of them? Their parents were gone and all he had besides his family was his friends, and he'd almost killed them all.

He glanced at the drone, the yellow light stared back at him like the plasma trail they'd been following for days. "I'm sorry we fight all the time. It's hard talking to you and Abigail sometimes. I don't know if it's the middle child thing or... I just want to have my ideas heard sometimes. Do me a favor and stop being wrong so much, ok?" He had a smirk on his face.

"I hope you're all safe and the Nanil discovery was fruitful. I'll catch you on the flip side."

He gestured to end the comm and hit send.

"SO WHATCHA GOT?" he asked as he entered the bridge and walked up next to Pepper. He was sipping a globe of raspberry coffee, his favorite.

"We came through the system clockwise and passed by two of the outer gas giants and one of the inner planets. It's far too dense for any sustained life, but we found several alien stations near the second inner planet." Pepper brought up the images on the wall screen.

There was a depot station, much like the one they'd found with Yaan, except it wasn't covered in stealth tech. It was in pieces, four of them to be exact. They were floating together in a group, encircling the planet.

"I take it no one's home?" he asked.

"Our probes haven't returned yet, their signals are getting scattered in all the dust. But, by the looks of it, I'd say if there was anyone home, they're dead. We can't say how long ago this happened without closer inspection."

He nodded. More death and destruction. Par for the course, but at least there were signs of previous life this time.

The wall screen showed a power relay near the planet that continued onward, slingshotting past the star to the other side of the system. He watched as a small asteroid rotated in space and floated into the yellow light of the relay. It exploded in a cacophony of colors. It was like watching the bug zapper on their house in North Carolina. Insects were unconsciously drawn toward the light and then, wham! Dead as a depleted oxygen tank.

"Shall we follow the yellow brick road?" he asked.

"If ever a wiz there was," Pepper muttered.

He chuckled. "What's that?"

Pepper peered up at him and furrowed her brow. "The song. From The Wizard of Oz. You know, the yellow brick road?"

"Huh," he said and shook his head. "I always thought it was an Elton John song. My parents' music choices were always a blur of randomness. Anyhow, let's see what's on the other side of this star system. While I'm happy we found another sign of life, I hope the next one is less grim."

THE ALERT KLAXONS rang throughout the ship, echoing like a foghorn through the empty halls. Bradley rolled off his bed and sprang through the already open door. He sprinted around the donut-shaped halls of the ship and rushed onto the bridge.

"Status!" he said, his heart pounding.

"We flew through the other side of the first globule star system and the nebula disappeared," Pepper said. She brought up the view on the wall screen.

"I dropped some forward probes, and they jumped deeper into the next system. There wasn't as much nebulosity here as the star we'd left behind. Only two short jumps in and they found this."

There on the wall screen was a sea of starships, thousands of them from the looks of it. They were floating through space, rotating around a massive central object. It looked like an elongated horn of some sort. Just past the formation of ships was the dark nebula looming uncomfortably close.

He gestured in front of the wall to zoom in and pan around the scene. The starships were torn to shreds. Blast marks and battle scars littered their exterior. Whatever happened here, it wasn't pretty.

"Are there any signs of life?" he asked.

"Negative, sir," Cynthia said. "But the probes are still doing detailed scans. We only just got these images relayed back via a jump."

He stepped around his command chair and sat down slowly. "Alright, I want everyone in defense posture. Ensure all weapons are powered and ready."

He wasn't a battlefield commander, so he was sure he was missing something. "Pierce?"

She pivoted in her chair and faced him. "Yes, sir."

He nodded. "Any suggestions on how to approach this? I don't want to miss anything. We've got one shot here."

Pierce was shaking her head gently peering past him, and then she stopped, her eyes narrowed.

"What is it?"

"I… just remember back to the academy. They tested us with a similar mission, a contrived one they said. It was something one of the A.I.s came up with." She chuckled. "Anyhow, the ships appeared to be junk floating aimlessly in space but on approach they fired something at us that disabled our drives. When they boarded us in that sim—" She focused in on him and swallowed hard. "They killed everyone aboard."

He swallowed hard. That wasn't what he had in mind. "Well, that's bleak. Did your instructors give you any take-aways from that lesson we could apply here?"

Pierce nodded. "The professors suggested we should've sent in a smaller contingent of forces, to test the waters. See if the enemy would engage and show their hand. I disagreed… but let's just say things didn't go well for me after that." She had a smirk on her face.

He glanced back at the wall screen. That's a lot of ships to have no life. "Harold?"

"Yes, sir."

"Any chance you want to head out with me and pilot one of those skiffs we snagged? I've been toying with them in simulations since we left Yaan's station. It could be fun." He smiled at Harold's face on the wall.

"You can't be serious," Cynthia said, pivoting in her chair to face him.

"I can pilot one alone, sir. Don't you think that'd be enough?" Harold said, his robotic form emerging from the corner.

He turned to face Harold's body. It was still weird seeing him this way. "Not for a proper decoy run, no. You take the lead, I'll follow. First sign of problems and I'll drop into superluminal for a few seconds back toward the entrance."

"Hello!" Cynthia waved her hands in front of his face. "No! You're insane."

"I can take the Wellspring," Pepper said.

He shook his head from side to side. "No way, no how we're handing that over to anyone. And besides, this operation goes south, you gotta get this ship out of here. These people need you. There aren't any other options that keep everyone safe and help us know what's out there." He pointed at the sea of starship scraps on the wall screen. "You all put me in this seat, now trust my gut."

"The other day," Pepper began, "when I said his instincts were confusing. This... this is what I was talking about!"

<hr>

BRADLEY SLID the skiff out of the hold and dropped below the Fidem. He brought it up alongside Harold. "We ready to do this?"

"I've been waiting for you for five minutes. I was beginning to think you'd chickened out," Harold said.

"Wow, an A.I. with an attitude. I like it. Something tells me that's grandpa coming through."

"Maybe," Harold said as he gunned the skiff and took off into the distance.

"Shizit," he muttered and reached for the throttle, slamming it forward. The two skiffs sped forward toward the collection of ships on the other side of the system.

He brought the skiff just behind and to the left of Harold. "I'm ready to give you control of the superluminal drive. You sure you can drop us in near the ships?"

"I've sim'd it thousands of times since you dropped this plan on me. It should only be a short thirty second jump. Get ready. When we drop out of the bubble, it's gonna be crazy. There's a lot of debris out there, so get into whatever frame of mind you need. Going FTL in 3, 2, 1."

The starlight from the central star in this system shifted, it smudged across his field of view inside the tiny one-person skiff. Like someone spun it into a fine pile of white dust or snow. It reminded him of when he went snowmobiling with his father up in northern Canada on Earth. It was past midnight, and all they had was the one headlight on their sleds to guide them. The sky was dumping a ton of fresh powder on them and they were flying across a frozen lake. It covered their windshield in a fine white powder and...

The superluminal bubble dropped, and the side of a massive starship stared back at him. The skiff's alerts were blaring.

He engaged the subluminal drive and yanked back on the skiff's yoke. "Frakkkk," he groaned. The g-forces from the turn slammed him into his seat.

The skiff shot forward and banked up along the starship's hull. It's easier to bank when you have no forward momentum. When they dropped out of the superluminal warp bubble, all of the surrounding ships were stationary.

He flipped around so his underside was flying along the

hull. He'd never enjoyed the feeling of flying upside down, even if there was no upside in space. His mind disagreed with that premise.

"That was a close one," he said. "You ok, Harold?" He could have checked his retinal comm, but he wanted to focus on the ships' sensors. He had no idea what type of debris was flying around out here.

"I'm alive," Harold said. "Dropping out of the superluminal bubble and then having to quickly adjust course reminded me of rubberbanding back in my desktop computer gaming day. Fraking cable modems were awful. I banked right instead of left. I'll come around. I should have known you lefties always go left."

He chuckled. "What the hell is a cable modem? Actually, don't tell me. I need to focus. I'm coming over the edge of this starship. It's a beast. Radar shows some smaller debris ahead. I hope this skiff has some means to…"

A half dozen red lasers fired from the bow of his skiff, disintegrating the smaller debris in his path.

"Welp, that answers that question. I'll drop to half and let you catch up. Let's head toward that conical ship in the middle of this debris field. I'd love to get a closer look inside that puppy."

"Aye, sir. I'm coming about on an intercept in five seconds."

Off in the distance, the massive metallic cone loomed in his viewport. Like the Dyson Sphere they'd first encountered, it was a massive feat of engineering. Whatever the hell it was. These aliens don't build things small, do they?

Harold pulled his skiff up on his right and then inched ahead as they'd planned. "Heading toward the mouth of the cone. Accelerating to half."

His skiff shot forward like a bullet.

"These things are snappy! I love it," he muttered as he slid his throttle forward to catch up, and then draft in Harold's wake. Not that such a thing existed in space, but it was how he imagined it.

They'd slotted into the rotational flow of the starships orbiting around the cone, and there wasn't much traffic yet. The early remote scans showed that the closer they got, the more debris they'd encounter.

"All scans are coming up negative in the debris field, sir. No life and few to no pockets of energy. Hardly enough to run a robot, let alone a human habitat."

His scans were coming up the same. "Are any of the energy signatures moving? Any chance we'd see any stealth tech gaps?"

He knew the answer before he'd asked it. Their stealth tech could bend all signals and wavelengths, making the object appear invisible by all observers. Since they'd stolen it from the Galactic Alliance, odds were they had it here, as well.

Harold opened a connection request to his comm, and he accepted it. He turned his head left and right. It showed a real-time overlay of the ship scans onto his cockpit view. He could see the structures of the ships through the hulls.

They were coming up alongside another one of the massive battleships now. Its starboard flank facing the cone was littered with battle scars. From the looks of the scans, all the craters in the hull used to be weapon mounts.

"Hey, Harold?"

"Yessir. Everything ok?"

"Yep. Do me a favor. Let's take a line all the way around this beast. I want to check something out."

"Aye, sir," Harold said. He angled left to take a clockwise route around the massive starship.

Coming under the hull, and working their way toward the port side, there was a significant reduction in damage. By the time they'd come halfway around, the ship's exterior was practically untouched.

"Is it me," he began, "or is this ship only damaged on the side facing the cone? Like there was a battle here. All of these ships vs. that monstrosity."

"I believe you're correct. Give me a moment. I can do a deeper analysis of the field of ships."

He craned his neck around the view of the ship, there was massive internal damage. Whatever shot from that cone blew its way through this side of the battleship. It's no wonder it didn't rotate around and fire from this side. From the looks of it, the battle didn't last long.

"I see a distinct pattern in nearly all the ships," Harold began. "Over eighty percent have sides facing the cone that are completely obliterated. The ones that are more thoroughly enshrouded with damage have axial rotations which likely meant they'd been rotating when they attacked."

He shook his head. That didn't make sense. "So what the frak does that mean? Did everyone just attack all at once?"

"Or... they dropped out of superluminal bubbles at the same time in an attempt to take the cone by force."

He groaned. "That'd be one hell of a battle. Maybe when we come about the other side, we should—"

His retinal comm flashed and the skiff's radar alerted him to two inbound bogies headed their way. One was from a ship to their port side and the other starboard.

"Frak! It looks like we've got company and they're coming in hot."

"Roger that," Harold said. "They appear to be small ships and aren't missiles. The bogie port side is further away. I suggest we go the opposite direction the starboard bogie goes and then work our way outside this mess."

"Sounds like a plan!" His heart was beating faster as the adrenaline kicked in. He'd never been in a life or death situation like this before, outside vid-sims that is. He was pretty sure he wouldn't respawn back at the Fidem if he flubbed this mission.

"They're going clockwise—"

"And so are we," he said as he punched the throttle to max. His ship shot forward, doubling his rate of speed in seconds.

Harold followed suit, placing his ship between the bogie and Bradley. He was always the Four Law follower.

"We should make some sporadic movements. Too much consistency and we're liable to be orbiting slag like these other ships," Harold said.

Crap. He shoulda thought of that. He subvocalized a command to load a route randomizer that would tack left, right, up, and down in arbitrary patterns based upon...

"Shit!" he muttered as a laser bolt shot past his starboard side. "Well, that settles that. They didn't send a greeting party."

"No, they didn't. I'll try some defensive measures," Harold said.

"Wait! We have defensive measures? I didn't see those in the sim."

"Armaments are in the menu. Do me a favor, though, be careful, and don't hit me."

"Roger that. I'll try." He brought up the menu of armaments, but it took him a few tries with all the tacking. He had to remember to glance in the corner of his retinal comm to see the direction of the upcoming tack. That made it much easier.

The menu showed he had two types of missiles mounted forward, shrapnel launchers of some kind, two lasers on the starboard and sides, and an omnidirectional slug thrower. That sounded useful.

He flipped his rear camera onto his control panel and watched as Harold was throwing slugs at the bogie. Whatever they were, they dodged them with ease. They either could tell what was being fired or... "The slug thrower is visible! They can see where it's pointed. You're wasting slugs."

"Good to know," Harold said. "I'll have a word with the ship's designers if we ever meet them."

He chuckled. It was good that Harold was relaxed enough to make jokes. He certainly wasn't in the mood right now.

His retinal comm flashed again. Two more inbound bogies from the port side, coming in fast. It looked like they might've been hiding in the derelict starship fragments.

They had two behind and two more were coming in from the port side, high and low. Their only option was to adjust course starboard, toward the cone in the middle of the battlefield.

"I have a sneaking suspicion they're toying with us, Harold. You see where we're headed?"

"I do. Toward the vertex of the cone."

"Any chance we could pivot on axis and lay waste to them, or clear a path before we go superluminal?"

"The debris field is too thick to drop into superluminal, and besides, in case you forgot, the dark nebula is right next to this field of starships. We'd have the ultimate welcoming party at death's door if we did that."

"Well, that's an unpleasant mental image. So, what do we do? Just let them guide us in?"

"Until we're presented with another opportunity, yes."

That's not how he'd planned this mission. It was supposed to be a simple in and out. Dead starships rotating around another bigger dead star thing, that's what this was supposed to be. He slammed his hands downward on the control console.

They adjusted course toward the cone, and the ship behind them stopped firing. In hindsight, their shots were almost always to the side. They'd been using those shots to constrain their options, to force them this way. Maybe Pepper would have made a better pilot here. She had stronger instincts.

He studied the viewport as the vertex of the cone grew

larger and larger. There was less debris rotating near there than further up the cone as it expanded outward toward the dark nebula. What the frak was this thing, and why were people defending it out here in this emptiness?

He reached into his pocket and felt for it. The white crystal. It'd helped him to focus before, maybe now it would, as well. Its smooth fractured surface was cold and yet still semi-transparent. You could see deep enough to know there was a complex depth to the little rock, yet not enough to understand its entirety.

He rubbed his thumb over the surface. "Ouch," he muttered. That damn point always got him. That's it! "Harold, the vertex!"

"I'm not following, sir."

"The debris field is nonexistent at the vertex. If that's where they're taking us, we can make a move there. All we need is a straight shot. If we see an opportunity, and the path looks clear, I say we take it."

There was a pause as Harold analyzed the data. "It could work. My Four Laws Engine is having trouble putting you in harm's way with all the uncertainty, but it's the best plan we've got. If you jump alone, don't jump any further than twenty seconds at a time. Only make small jumps till you work your way back toward the others. Understood?"

"Got it!" He switched his skiff to autopilot as they headed toward the cone's vertex. They were performing deeper scans of the debris field near the apex for anything unusual or too massive to make the plan practical.

It looked like whatever was there erred on keeping that area clear, likely to ease the comings and goings of ships. They were approaching fast and were only thirty seconds out.

The closest bogie began taking potshots at Harold, but this time they weren't going wide.

"They hit me!" Harold said. "My rear deflector is down to sixty percent. They're testing us for weaknesses. That shot was weaker than their earlier ones that went wide. They're trying to disable us. I'll hold them off. You should continue on course and take manual control of your strafing. I'm afraid they might predict your route or directly access the skiffs computers."

Frak, he'd never thought of that. It could explain why the randomizer wasn't so random or how they always seemed to miss. "Harold, give 'em hell!"

He dropped out of autopilot, gave the skiff more throttle, and began tacking manually. The bogies had taken no shots at him, but from the looks of it, Harold had taken another hit. One more shot like that and his drive was toast.

As he came up on the cone, he banked up and away from the apex when multiple bogies opened fire. Harold took another hit and started drifting and rotating around the center. His rear half was a charred mess in his rear camera. Come on. Just a bit further.

He continued the wild tacking, making sure not to repeat any patterns. There was very little debris ahead. Another ten seconds and he'd be in the clear.

A hard blast hit his skiff from behind as he was strafing starboard. His rear deflector dropped to eighty percent, and he'd lost axial controls.

"No!" he screamed as the skiff spun out of control.

It was now or never. He had one shot at this. If he timed it just right, he could drop into superluminal right as he was rotating around. He'd rather die trying than sit here.

A little bit further.

His skiff shook violently, and sparks flew through the cockpit. An incoming ship had fired and hit him in his forward deflectors. They were now reporting thirty percent. The drive was still showing full charge, and he needed another twenty-degree rotation.

Just a little bit more.

Now! He engaged the superluminal drive, and the viewport shifted snowy for a split second before everything went dark.

"Nooooo!" he screamed as he slammed his fists against the control panel.

Alarm klaxons were blaring, he'd lost gravity, and he was losing oxygen fast.

He checked his retinal comm. His suit's seals and O2 levels were all optimal and reporting four hours of oxygen. He was a sitting duck. One more shot and he'd be dead.

What the hell was he thinking coming out here? Pepper had been right. His gut instincts had written one too many chits he couldn't cash out.

He leaned back in his chair. He'd never kiss Cynthia again, or see his family for that matter. He hadn't seen Abigail in years, and he'd never gotten a chance to ream her out for all this fraking nonsense they'd been through.

Reaching into his pocket, he pulled out the crystal again. Maybe he had a moment to record a message to his family. He subvocalized a command on his retinal comm. It didn't have enough power to broadcast at this range nor was the skiff in any state to act as a relay.

He closed his eyes and leaned back in his chair, rubbing the crystal between his fingers. "I'll see you soon dad," he muttered.

The skiff lurched, tossing his body side to side several times. It was like he'd crashed into something. His cockpit was black and he couldn't see anything. The viewport had been a projection. This thing had no exterior windows, and without power he couldn't tell what was going on.

It lurched again. The entire ship vibrated this time, like it was being dragged along the ground.

He'd never considered being taken alive. What would they do to him? Could he keep quiet?

Maybe his nanites could help. Could they be configured to kill him if they provoked him? He doubted it but it was worth a try. The last thing he wanted was to give away the location of everyone he loved.

"Argh," he muttered. Damn programmers and their three laws. He couldn't use his nanites against himself.

He exhaled. What next?

Damn if he couldn't form a coherent thought. All he could think, all he could see, was death. It'd surrounded him for weeks.

He sat there in the skiff in silence. The faintest sound of his suit's environmental controls permeated the cabin. His retinal comm claimed it'd only been ten minutes since they'd disabled the skiff. It might as well have been an eternity, when death was but moments away.

The skiff lurched again, and this time there was scraping sounds and vibrations from all around. He was definitely being dragged. It must be somewhere with oxygen, or he wouldn't be hearing anything.

His suit was reporting an increase in oxygen levels. Not enough to breathe yet, but rising.

He unlatched the harness, and the strap fell to the side of his chair. There was gravity here. As he rolled out of the seat, he came up next to the hatch. He took a deep breath and pulled out his bolt pistol in his left hand, and an electro-blade in his right. While he wasn't as proficient as Pierce, he'd go down fighting.

The sound of metal on metal echoed through his skiff. Someone was trying to open the hatch. His breathing quickened, and he squeezed the weapons tighter.

"Relax," he muttered. "One at a time."

The hatch ripped off its hinges, and the room was engulfed in blinding light. He couldn't see anything until his visor compensated, but it was too late. Hands were grabbing at him. Cold metal hands.

He pulled the trigger and slashed with the knife. The

blade hit something hard, and it went limp, but there were too many hands.

They grasped at him and held his arms and legs still.

Then they ripped the bolt pistol from his hand.

His eyes were adjusting. He could make out shapes. Humanoids. Wait. Were those robots? They yanked hard and pulled him out of the skiff into a massive hangar.

There were hundreds of them. Hundreds of humanoid robotic forms. Four of them were holding Harold and he wasn't moving.

He subvocalized a comm to him but nothing happened. There was no reply.

"Let me go!" he screamed.

The robots froze, but they didn't release him.

They glanced back and forth toward each other. They seemed confused, like they'd never heard someone yell before.

It dawned on him they'd never heard English before. He was fraked every which way if he couldn't even communicate with these things.

The translator! That's it. He had a translator speaker on his shirt inside the suit. He could control it through his comm, and it'd translate what he said. Now he had to get the blasted thing off. But how?

That's it.

He tried reaching up to his neck, but their grasp was too tight. Maybe he could convince them he was hurt. He struggled to bring his hands to his neck and started choking, pretending he couldn't breathe. His face turned red. Hopefully, they'd buy it.

They did, one of them reached to remove his helmet. His ears popped and filled with the hissing sound as the two spaces equalized pressure.

He took a deep breath, pretending to gasp for air. The

room reeked of metallic dust and rust. Like it hadn't been filtered in decades.

His retinal comm showed the translator was active.

"Let me go," he subvocalized. The speaker echoed what he said.

The robot's grip tightened. They'd understood him.

"I said, let me go!" he shouted. The suit translated and attempted to reproduce the volume.

A crude red humanoid robot walked up to him. Its face was expressionless. Just a primitive set of yellow LED eyes and a slit for a mouth. "We will not release you. All Nanil traitors are interrogated and expunged."

He shook his head. "No! You don't understand. I'm not a Nanil!"

"Silence," the robot shouted. It lifted its hand and smacked him across the face.

"Argh," he screamed as his face exploded in pain. It was like he'd been punched by a brick. He could feel his face swelling and his right eye was closing.

"I'm a human," he groaned. Pain shot through his face as all sight in his right eye disappeared.

One of the robots tore at his suit, ripping it off him in one smooth motion. The air from the chamber hit his skin like an icy bath and shivers swept over his entire body. It was freezing in here.

He tried to jump backward and failed as something brushed against his privates and then pierced his skin. He tilted his head and struggled to look down. "What the—"

A small white robot had rolled up and was withdrawing blood.

"What are you doing?" he mumbled. His jaw was tight and it hurt to speak.

The hands holding him released their steely grasp, and he collapsed downward. He reached out to break his fall, but he came down hard on his naked left knee and smashed his forearms against the dusty metal floor.

Two more sets of icy hands grabbed him, but this time they felt different. The hands were supporting him, not restraining him. They were lifting him up, helping him to stand.

He craned his neck and glanced around the room with his left eye. All the robots were down low and the humanoid versions were on their knees.

They began chanting.

"The humans have returned. The humans have returned."

23

ZACHARY OLIVAW

LUPUS DARK NEBULA, DODA

They huddled in a cramped room they'd found on the second layer. It was a factory break room of some sort located off the maintenance shaft entrance they'd rescued him and Ibu from. Broken down vending machines lined one of the walls. Their contents long ago cleared out.

"Why didn't you head up to the Fountainhead?" Zachary asked. He took another sip of the water Pluto handed him. Thousand year old water and emergency kits to cleanse it were his new favorite thing.

"Whatever Ogun did down there, they sealed the lower entrance to level one," Libby said.

Shauna's robotic form stepped back toward him. "The hangar bay still seems to be open, but I wasn't about to risk bringing the ship in to lose it in a trap. I suggest we work our way topside and exit the way we arrived."

"Is the ship still safe? I mean, you're down here instead of up there." He pointed upward.

"It is," Shauna said. Her robotic form mimicked a nod. "I pulled it away from Doda and it's running silent. Unless they were tracking our burns the entire time, we shouldn't be visible. When you ran into issues in the lower levels, I took evasive measures to drop off this robotic form on the planet and come to help."

He smirked. "Four Laws engine was itching, wasn't it?"

"Maybe." Her eyes flashed once.

Ibu was sitting next to him on the bench, their body pressed against his. He'd placed his arm over them when they snuggled up and passed out, sound asleep. All the excitement of escaping, climbing up here, and finding this room had taken it out of them. Both of them. He could use some shut-eye himself.

When the little Nanil saw Shauna and realized it wasn't another human in a spacesuit, they lost it. Apparently, the Nanil had made humanoid robots illegal. It was one of the many things they'd done to differentiate themselves from the humans here who evidently preferred to surround themselves with robots of similar shapes as their own.

Pluto sat down on his other side and handed him a ration packet.

He opened the package and took a bite. It was a bland fake meat stick. He'd much rather have another one of those bars Ibu shared with him earlier. They didn't have many rations, a day or two max. Especially with all the exerting they'd been doing. "So that's the plan? We keep climbing until we reach the top?"

"Unless you have a better one," Libby said.

He shook his head. He didn't have the energy or inclination to think, let alone strategize.

Kamal and one of his soldiers walked into the room. He'd positioned the other three outside the entrance and on the far side of the factory. "We repelled down and unhooked a few hundred of the ladder rungs like you showed us. If someone's coming up that way, they'll be slowed down. We also rigged up a few of the exits to detonate if anyone applies pressure near them. Nothing that'd kill, but it'd certainly blast them off and they'd have a long fall back down."

Brice who'd been quiet until now cleared his throat. "How do we plan to get from the hatch to the Fountainhead? I mean, Kamal and the team might be able to make it with their gear but what about the rest of us?" He glanced down at his tattered garb. There were several holes that weren't there a few hours before.

"Once we reach the top, there's a transition chamber," Shauna said. "I've already checked it out with the drone. I can land the Fountainhead outside. I'll exit first and get five suits and head back in. It'll be three or four minutes max transition time for me."

"Five suits?" Kamal asked cautiously. He was eyeing Pluto.

She stood up and straightened her back, almost flexing. "Yes, five. One for every person without a suit."

It took a moment for Zachary to realize what he was alluding to. There were five people, four humans without suits, and one Nanil. He looked down at Ibu's sleeping form. They stirred and rolled over to face the back of the bench. Pluto leaned down and adjusted the jacket she'd placed over them. Ibu had a smile on their face as they slept. Their auburn hair was tousled, but a few braids had survived the day.

Ibu had nowhere to go, and Fotily was still in the middle of that mess. Ogun was abusive and Hypron wasn't much help. He couldn't imagine what would happen to the child if they returned. Death was almost certain. If you could make one clone, I'm sure you could make another and repeat the cycle of violence all over again.

He glanced at Pluto and then Ibu, nodding slowly. "It's up to Ibu. If they want to join us, they can. I won't force them to return to that house. Especially after they saved me. If they have other family here on Doda who can help, then perhaps they can make their way there."

"Are we sure we can..." Kamal paused and glanced at Pluto.

"Go ahead. Say it. I won't bite," Pluto said, her hands clenched at her side.

"He wants to know if we can trust them," Shauna said.

"I think so, but I don't know." He glanced up and looked at Kamal. "What's more likely, that the Nanil had a family, and a child planted and ready to infiltrate a random human team that might show up from another star system, or that they're a dysfunctional family and Ibu is a victim in need of help?"

"Well... when you put it like that, it sounds sorta silly," Kamal said, looking downward at his hands.

"We're about to find out," Shauna said. She opened a comm and shared a video feed from the drone still hovering in the maintenance shaft. It showed a dozen of the Nanil farming implements working their way up the sides of the shaft.

"Frak," he muttered. He didn't know how he could go on climbing.

"From the looks of it," Shauna began, "they've just started climbing. I'd estimate we have an hour or more depending on how much Kamal's shock bombs slow them down."

They had to get everyone up this maintenance shaft as fast as possible.

He stood up and carefully set Ibu's head on the bench. "Alright, let's head out. Everyone, let's look around and see if we can find anything heavy to drop on these things. We can rig up one last trap. Kamal, we'll need to leave one of your soldiers behind while we get a head start." He turned to Shauna. "I want you to haul a bunch of that cable with you up the shaft. We'll keep one end attached to Kamal's soldier and you can pull them up every few levels."

She nodded and took off toward the spool they'd found on the factory floor.

He glanced around and everyone was still staring at him. "What're you all standing around for? We've got five minutes tops and we're out of here. I'll take care of Ibu. Now go!" He shooed them toward the door and they scurried away.

He turned around and Ibu was sitting up on the bench, rubbing their eyes.

"Where'd everyone go?" Ibu asked.

He walked over and sat next to them on the bench, sitting sideways to face them. "I have an important question to ask you and I don't have a lot of time. Do you understand?"

Ibu nodded and sat quietly. Their hazel eyes reflecting the flickering lights above their head.

"We have to leave. For good. We won't be coming back."

"Never?" Ibu asked.

He shook his head side to side. "No, never. Do you want to stay here with your family, or maybe somewhere else in the underworld?"

They stared at him in silence, uncertainty in their eyes.

"You don't have anyone else here, do you? Other than Ogun."

They shook their head and stared downward, tears welling up in their eyes.

He slid down off the bench, looked up at them and smiled. "Do you want to come with us?"

Ibu's eyes went wide and they nodded slowly. "I do. Will Pluto be there? I like Pluto a lot. She's nice to me."

He smirked. "I like her a lot, too, and yes, she'll be there." He stood up. "We have to go. Your family sent some robots up the maintenance shaft looking for us. We don't have much time. Do you know anything about them? Are they armed?"

Ibu hopped up off the bench. "They can climb practically any surface and they can also cut and weld." They shook their head. "But I don't have any memories of them firing anything, nor does Ogun."

It was strange talking to someone with the memories of multiple people.

"Alright." He clapped his hands together. "That's the best

news I've heard about this place all day. Let's go." He headed toward the door, Ibu close behind.

THEY'D BEEN CLIMBING for hours and were close to the top of the maintenance shaft. Drew stayed behind and set up another trap for the robots. He wired another set of concussion explosives and rigged several heavy machine parts to fall if they were triggered. They'd heard three explosions so far, the last would've been the floor they'd stopped to rest on.

Shauna used her cabling to pull Drew up three times. After the third time, they set up one last trap. They'd run out of explosives, so instead they spiderwebbed that level's exit with the cabling they'd used to repel.

"Two of them are still down there," Shauna said. "They're lingering below the dust and rising rapidly."

"Any chance we can pick them off?" Zachary asked. His breathing was heavy and his heart rate had been labored for nearly an hour. Not to mention lifting his arms and legs was like dragging along hundreds of extra pounds. His muscles were jelly and each rung he climbed felt like he added a few more pounds. Fear of death was surprisingly motivating. He was pretty sure that if Pluto or Ibu hadn't been there cheering him on, he would have tossed in the towel long ago.

"We need a clear shot before we can attempt that," Kamal said. "The tunnel is too narrow and full of people. We'd risk collateral damage."

Ibu poked their head backward and down toward him as he was looking upward. They made eye contact. "Are they talking about shooting the robots?"

He'd forgotten that Ibu couldn't understand them. They must be picking up a few words. He nodded, not wanting to say anything that was translated.

"They shouldn't," Ibu said. "The robot's exterior is impenetrable. Ogun has seen lasers ricochet off the surface. They're nearly indestructible. Any of the ones we knocked down the shaft, they're likely climbing up behind the others."

"Frak. That's perfect," he muttered. "Did you all catch that?"

"We did," Shauna said. "That means we only have one path. Upward."

A resurgence of energy rushed over him. He didn't think he had another ounce of adrenaline left, but apparently he'd been wrong.

One hand and foot over the other, he climbed higher. Ibu's news seemed to have made the entire line of people move a bit faster.

A humming noise echoed up the shaft, and then another, and a third.

"They're engaging their garden tillers," Ibu shouted down the shaft toward him. "They're going to advance."

He was focused on climbing the rungs and refused to stop. "Talk to me, Kamal. Do we have any options left?"

"No, sir," Kamal said from below. "We're a hundred meters away from the top. We just need to climb. That's all we can do at this point."

The humming noise rose and combined with a loud repetitive clanging every few seconds. It sounded like cymbals crashing together.

In the corner of his retinal comm, he had a view from the drone still hovering above their heads. It was zoomed in on the bottom of the tunnel. The lidar showed three shapes below the rising smoke.

He watched as the robots burst through the rising dust together. They were leaping up the wall in unison and were ricocheting off each other. Using their upward momentum and peculiar shapes, they'd found a way to navigate the challenge of the maintenance shaft while advancing upward as a group.

"Faster!" He screamed. "Go, go, go!"

Libby was the first person to break over the top followed by Brice. They both sprinted down the tunnel toward the surface airlock.

All notions of pain disappeared. He couldn't feel his arms, hands, or legs. There was only climbing. Only reaching upward for the next rung.

Ibu passed over the top and turned to glance down.

"Go!" Pluto shouted, waving her hand.

Ibu listened and turned to run after Brice's shrinking form.

The clanging of the robots ended, but the whirring continued. He paused his climbing for a moment to look at his retinal comm. Two of the robots stopped climbing and appeared to have hunkered down. The third was climbing solo. It's rotating blades on the front were approaching Drew.

Zachary started climbing faster. Only six more meters.

Glancing upward, he watched Pluto crest the ladder and pause to look down at him.

"Get to the airlock!" he said.

"Not gonna happen, Z. Not without you. Now get your butt up here."

He reached upward to grasp the last rung when her hands shot out and ripped him up and over the edge. He always forgot how strong she was.

"Noooo!" someone screamed. The pitch of the whirring noise changed as the robots cut into something or someone, their pain echoing through the shaft.

He checked his comm and saw Drew's body falling backward. Red blood was spraying everywhere as the blades from the rising robot collided into the soft flesh of his descending form.

He winced as Pluto yanked at him, dragging him forward.

Shauna shot past them both, flying toward the airlock. She

said she only needed three minutes to cycle and return with their suits. This would be the three longest minutes of his life.

He stopped, and Pluto continued to pull on him.

"Wait!" he said, raising his hands in the air. "We have to help them. Maybe there's something here we can use."

They both started sliding their hands along the walls, looking for any hidden crevasses or compartments. The tunnel wasn't well lit, so it was hard to see anything. The surface of the walls was smooth to the touch but every few meters there was a slight edge.

He slid his hands up and down the wall. There was a slight depression and he pushed inward. A handle formed. Yanking with everything he had, a door swung open. There were four cylinders inside. He lifted one with his left hand and it had some girth to it. Yes, this will work.

"Here, I found something. Let's use these," he said, waving Pluto over.

He grabbed the first two, and Pluto grabbed the others.

"What are they?" she asked.

"No clue," he muttered. "There doesn't appear to be any external markings."

They both sprinted back to the edge of the hole and looked down. Kamal was rising over the edge and three other soldiers were close behind him.

Pluto set one of her canisters down and lifted the other over her head with both hands. She took aim at the rising blood covered robot. Its blades were spinning wildly in the air as it climbed.

She grunted and threw the cylinder with all her might. It shot downward narrowly missing Norm, the last of the three soldiers. The canister ricocheted off the wall just past his feet and bounced outward. It missed the robot, but hit the edge of its rotating blades.

An explosion shook the shaft as the canister sparked and its combustible contents shot a firestorm in all directions.

Fire engulfed both Norm and the robot causing them to lose hold.

The robots bloody form fell and nearly took out one of the other robots.

The concussion blew Norm's body a few meters upward, his arms waving through the air as he scrambled to grasp a rung. Zachary watched as Norm managed to grasp one with his right hand on his way back down. Momentum and gravity swung his body inward toward the rungs and he crashed hard against them. The air momentarily bursting from his lungs.

He dangled around and back, barely holding on until he finally swung sideways and caught the rung with his other hand. Finally, he planted his feet on the lower rungs and scrambled upward. His black military uniform was the only thing that protected him from the flames. Without it, he'd have been a fireball falling downward.

The robots below reacted by renewing their climbing. Their fallen comrade didn't register in their simple minds. All they could focus on was killing the humans.

Orville and Reese clamored up and out of the shaft and sprinted down the tunnel behind Kamal.

Pluto waited for them to pass, raised another canister above her head, and took aim, careful to not hit Norm. She threw it downward with a grunt.

The robots easily dodged the falling object.

"Crap," she muttered.

Shauna flew the drone up beside Pluto. Her voice came over their comms. "Carefully place the canisters in the small rack on the drone's back. Don't touch them to the rotors, or we'll repeat the explosion you saw below. I'll take a shot delivering them myself."

She lugged one up and placed it atop the drone. It briefly wobbled and then stabilized. She repeated the placement with the second.

"Now, head back down the tunnel. My robotic form is headed to the airlock with the suits."

Pluto bent down and reached for Norm as he rose up to the first rung and pulled. He flew up and over the top just like Zachary had. His eyes were wide. He was only now realizing how strong she really was.

The three of them sprinted toward the airlock as the drone's imbalanced form descended downward, toward the rising robots.

Just before they reached the airlock, an explosion echoed through the chamber. Black smoke and flames billowed toward them from down the tunnel as the environmental controls kicked into overdrive and sucked it into the ceiling. A moment later the sprinklers finally turned on.

He was glad he didn't have to climb a wet ladder, he'd have been toast for sure.

Shauna finished the transition through the airlock and tossed the five suits off her back as she sprinted past.

"Where are you going?" He turned and stared at her robotic form sprinting off down the corridor toward the smoke. When he gestured to follow, he saw it. One of the robots rose over the edge of the maintenance shaft and turned toward them.

"Shit!" He spun around and ran toward the others. "Put the suits on. Everyone move faster!"

They scrambled to separate the suits without tearing them, tossing one to each of the unsuited members of the party. The soldiers each reached into their backpacks and pulled out their transparent nano-composite polymer helmets and pulled them over their heads. The military all-purpose suits equalized the pressure and inflated within seconds.

He unzipped his suit and sat on the floor, pulling his legs in frantically. He thought about pulling up the video feed of Shauna on his retinal comm but he knew better. If he did, he'd get distracted. He had one thing to focus on right now, surviving.

The sounds of metal on metal crashing together echoed down the long tunnel as the whirring blades of a Nanil robot collided with whatever Shauna was doing. The lights flashed and something exploded down the tunnel followed by more metallic grinding.

He hopped up and put his arms in the sleeves, pulling the hood up and over his head. He ended by sealing the suit around his neck. Reaching down to his hip, he pressed the power button, and the suit hummed to life. The small canister of oxygen on his back pressurized the suit.

His retinal comm showed everything as green. Glancing up, he gave everyone a thumbs up. He was the last person. Pluto had even helped Ibu get theirs on.

He was far more tired than he'd imagined.

Everyone scrambled to fill the unusually crude airlock and Zachary pulled the door shut. He slammed his hand against the decompression plate. Red lights flashed, warning them that the oxygen was about to be vacuumed from the chamber.

He turned and glanced down the corridor. A moment later he realized he shouldn't have.

Two massive soot and blood stained robots were working their way toward them. They weren't moving very fast. Whatever Shauna had done had slowed them down.

The red light in the airlock stopped flashing.

"Everyone out!" Kamal shouted over their comms. He reached over and grabbed Zachary's arm, pulling him hard toward the door. "Let's go, Olivaw!"

He turned and ran toward the Fountainhead. When he passed over the airlock exit, some of the gravity fell away. Doda was a massive planetesimal, but it lacked enough mass to create all of its own gravity. He switched fluidly from running to controlled hops toward the ship.

Hopping up the ramp and into the waiting cargo hold, he

felt heavier as the artificial gravity returned. Kamal was the last to enter.

He turned to watch the scene out of the closing cargo hold door. Shauna was rapidly pulling the Fountainhead away from Doda. Three Nanil robots were climbing out of the remains of the airlock. From the looks of it, they'd shredded their way through the hatch and gases were being expelled from inside the maintenance shaft.

There was so much death and destruction down there. Maybe Bradley was right. They hadn't found what they were looking for, and they'd lost an excellent soldier and friend in the process.

24

BRADLEY OLIVAW

LUPUS DARK NEBULA, BOK GLOBULE

He reached down under the base of Harold's neck and felt for it. It was right there. Bradley pressed his finger against the scanner and pulled his hand out when the humanoid shell vibrated to life.

The robot's white eyes flashed a rainbow of colors, and then it turned its head toward him. Its mouth was moving without a sound.

Bradley leaned down and looked Harold in the eyes. He had to use his left eye because his right was still partially swollen shut. The nanites and whatever the robots had done to him were still working their magic. "Harold? Are you ok?"

Harold raised his hand and pointed at his mouth with his one working arm. He shook his head from side to side.

Bradley reached up and touched his ear, opening a subvocal comm. "Can you talk via comms?"

"Yeaezz. Yes. Can you hear me?" Harold asked.

He nodded and smiled. "It's good to hear the sound of your voice buddy."

"What happened?"

"It's a long story and I'll tell you later. What I need to know right now is how to communicate with the Fidem."

Harold took a step forward and Bradley lurched to catch him before he crashed to the floor. He then lifted him upward and propped him against the workbench.

"Yea, you can't walk. You're pretty much just scraps right now. It took me the better part of a day to figure out how to power you up. If Little Red over there hadn't helped out, you'd still be a pile of scrap."

Harold rotated his head toward the direction he'd pointed. There was a short humanoid robot standing a few meters away. Its exterior was painted bright red, and it had two arms, a long torso, and short squat legs. They looked like they could double as treads to glide along the ground. Their head was a dome shape, and it had two distinct eyes, a nose, and a mouth made of lights.

"Is that—"

He leaned over Harold's pile of parts and adjusted one of the servos on his neck. "Another human robot? Yes. There are thousands of them here. We're inside the cone. They took us here after they disabled our ships. They didn't detect any life forms within your ship, so they weren't as delicate as they were with mine."

Harold rotated his head back toward him. "Did they harm you in any way? Your face and your eye, it looks like they hurt you." He moved his arms and legs again, as if trying to move toward Little Red.

He reached forward to grab Harold. "Stop moving! You can't walk. I'm fine, really." He pointed up at his face. "This is from before they realized I was human. They thought I was another Nanil raider. Once they realized their mistakes, they apologized for a few hours and apparently they dismantled the robot that did this to me."

Harold nodded his head.

"Alright, enough about me." He leaned in making eye contact again with Harold. "Let's talk about reaching the Fidem. How do we do it?"

THEY WAITED in the massive hangar, hoping for a sign from their people. Bradley was pacing back and forth while Harold's head and torso was resting on a small trolley cart. One of the robots pushed him around wherever he needed to go.

He was wringing his hands as he stared out into the blackness of the open hangar door. The nebula rippled in the distance, the second time in under an hour. "They should've been here by now. A jump calculation would take five minutes tops, even inside the nebula. It's been over two hours. Are you sure about your calculations? About the time it'd take for them to get our message."

Harold's body wheeled up to his side. "I'm fairly confident I know how to calculate the speed of light in a vacuum, sir. I'd hazard to guess they're either debating what to do or they didn't see it."

Someone should have seen it. A fleet of starships all flashing their lights in Morse code wasn't a common occurrence here, or in any part of the galaxy. "Do you think we should repeat the signal?"

"Why don't we give them—"

The forward floodlights on the Fidem shattered the darkness outside the hangar door. The lights had slid open from their berths behind the stealth covering, illuminating the side of the massive conical space station.

Bradley jumped up and down, waving his arms in the air. They might not be able to see him but he didn't care. He was happy to not be alone in this sea of automata another minute.

He hopped back and waved forward with his arms. "Can you all hear me?" he said on the open channel they'd announced in the message.

"We can." Pepper's voice broke in. "We've been listening in for a while. There's no point in walking into a trap."

He chuckled. "You're safe to dock. The coast is clear. It's only Harold, me, and a few hundred thousand of our closest robot friends."

"He's not joking," Harold said. "And yes, the coast is clear."

The Fidem pulled forward into the empty berth.

"I have to say," Pepper began as she guided the ship to a landing. "It's weird hearing two different Harold's with different points of view talking to me at the same time. The sooner we can quit that, the happier I'll be."

"One moment and I'll perform a merge," Harold said. "That's strange."

Bradley watched as the loading ramp lowered. "What's strange?"

"My merge failed. My checksums don't match." He turned his head toward the small robot next to him. "What did you do to me?"

The robot backed away from the trolley and turned its small squat head toward Bradley. "I did as I was asked. I brought you online. There was much damage. We had to... what is the human term, improvise. Did I displease you, Master Bradley?"

He glanced toward the red robot. "No, you did great, Little Red. Harold, why don't you run a full diagnostic? See what—"

Cynthia crashed into him, enveloping him in a massive hug. "You're alive," she muttered. "You had me worried, you idiot." She bumped both of her fists against his chest. "Don't you go pulling another stunt like that again. At least, not without me," she winked.

"I promise," he said as he smiled and kissed her.

She pulled away and studied his face. "What the hell?" She moved toward the little red robot, glaring at it. "Did these robots do this to you?"

Little Red backed up further and lowered its torso downward.

"It's all good. They mistook me for a Nanil and things got rough for a few minutes. I'm fine now." He pulled her back and turned her face toward his with his hand. "Really." He smiled.

"Ok," she muttered, shooting the robot another cold stare.

A hand touched his shoulder and he glanced back.

"It's good to see you're in one piece," Pepper said.

"Thanks," he nodded. "It's really great seeing all of you, too. Not that these robots aren't nice and all, but flesh and blood are my cup-o-coffee. Wait… that came out wrong."

Everyone chuckled.

He turned around. Dwight and most of the soldiers had de-shipped. They were all cautiously studying the aging space station. "Don't everyone get too comfortable. We have a mission to complete."

"What does that mean?" Cynthia asked. "Did you find something?"

A smile crept across his face and he nodded. "I did. Let me show you." He walked backward toward the exit, waving everyone to follow. "Let's head to the forward observation room."

The hangar door slid aside, and he spun around to face an awaiting tram. Its doors were already open, so he stepped inside and worked his way toward the front. There were straps hanging from the ceiling all around the massive tram, but there were no seats. He reached up and grabbed a strap with his left hand.

Pierce stepped forward into the transport hub. She glanced up and down the tram and scrunched up her face.

The trams weren't rusty, but they weren't plush, either. In fact, they were downright crude.

"I know. It's not pretty." He knocked his knuckles on the outer wall. It made a solid thunking noise. "The transports were designed to distribute cargo throughout the cone while they built this thing. It's fast, though. We'll be there in a blink of an eye."

Everyone slowly stepped forward into the tram and grasped a handle.

Little Red wheeled Harold toward the tram, but Bradley raised his hand to stop. "Why don't you leave him here? Give him a chance to run his diagnostics. We can talk to him through our comms."

The little robot wheeled backward and toward the ship. Its head dropped downward and shrank into its torso, like when Cynthia was getting aggressive with it earlier.

"Little Red! You can join us if you want," he said.

The robot popped up and seemed to almost hop off the ground. It sped Harold up beside the Fidem and then shot forward and into the tram sliding up next to Bradley.

"Thank you, Master Bradley!"

Cynthia smiled at him and shook her head.

"What?"

"Got yourself a fan I see," she muttered.

He chuckled. "Alright, Little Red. Let's get this thing going. Can you take us to that observation room we were working from earlier?"

"Right away, Master Bradley." It turned and looked up at him. "Would you like to see the outside while traveling?"

"We would," he said.

"Very well."

The doors of the tram slid shut and for a brief moment nothing happened. Suddenly, the right-hand side of the tram transformed into a transparent viewport, as if they were looking out the side of the cone. There were half destroyed and derelict starships as far as the eye could see, and they were all rotating around the cone.

The tram shot forward. Despite their speed, there was no noticeable momentum change inside. Moet and Pierce glanced at each other and let go of the straps. They seemed fairly useless.

The sea of starships floated past as the tram sailed up the cone. Dwight leaned closer to the display and pointed toward small ships moving to and from the derelict starships. "What are those ships doing?"

Little Red beeped and moved up to Dwight's side. "They're ferrying raw materials. We salvage what we need to repair ourselves. Our oldest generation of workers is breaking down faster than anticipated, so we need more raw materials."

"Why didn't we see them before?" Dwight asked.

"When we detected your drive signature entering the system, we recalled all ships. We believed you to be Nanil pirates."

"Pirates," Dwight mouthed looking back at Bradley.

"I know, right," he chuckled. "Aha! It looks like we're here. Little Red can go over all of this in a moment." He held up his finger. "Hold that thought."

The tram slowed and came to a rest at the mouth of the cone. The trip had lasted all of twenty seconds, and they'd traveled the entire length of the massive object.

Everyone filed out of the tram and followed close behind Little Red. This section of the structure was far cleaner and more modern than the last. The hallways were stark white and wide enough to pilot his skiff down. They reminded him of the images he'd seen from the Galactic Alliance Tribunal starships.

The surface wasn't noiseless, but it wasn't loud, either. Their feet made faint squeaking and clicking noises as they walked across the glasslike surface.

Little Red turned left into the first room. It was massive and could comfortably seat fifty. There, along the far side was a view overlooking the inside of the cone. It was exactly what you'd imagine a cone would look like. Sloped walls all angled toward a common vertex far at the other end.

The walls themselves had a spiraling pattern etched in them. Besides that, there was no other indication what the massive structures purpose was.

Everyone walked toward the wall and gawked at the scene.

Bradley limped to the opposite wall and picked up a pitcher of water and poured a cup. "There's food if anyone's hungry." He lifted his cup to drink.

Everyone spun around and stared at him.

He froze, mid swallow. "What?" he sputtered.

"Food? Is it safe?" Cynthia asked. "I mean, how do we know? Where's it from?"

He finished his sip and lowered his cup. "Harold checked it out before I ate anything. It was painful smelling all the amazing aromas from the food while he did his analysis, but it all came back fine. Little Red said it was all grown in one of the nearby starships. They didn't have a need for it here until we arrived, but they kept growing it for when the humans returned." He reached down and picked up a blue pickle looking vegetable and took a bite. The crunch of the ginger filled veggie made his stomach smile.

"Why don't y'all grab something?" he mumbled between bites. He waved his hands around the spread of food the robots had prepared. "Little Red, the floor is yours."

The entire wall showing the inside of the cone transformed into a field of stars. The little red robot rolled over in front of the wall and raised upward a meter. "This was the view from this star system thirty-three million cycles ago. Harold informed me that this is nearly two thousand eight hundred of the years in your new calendar. I'm interested to learn about all that has changed since you created Henosi."

"What's Henosi?" Cynthia asked glancing toward Bradley.

He coughed into his hand. "I'm sorry, Little Red. We call it by other names. The H is silent. It's more of Enosi." He glanced toward Cynthia and subvocalized on the open channel to the entire crew. "Go with it. It'll make sense in a moment."

"I'm sorry, Master Bradley. That's good to know." The robot raised their arm theatrically. "Long ago the Galactic Alliance arrived with their fleet of Nebula Ships and thousands of embedded battleships. Soon after their arrival they ejected the nebula surrounding the human and Nanil worlds."

The wall screen changed. Starships exploded, fleets of nebula ships enshrouded stars and darkness fell.

"In the end, there was darkness. Our fleet was too weak. The Galactic Alliance had always espoused strength in numbers, and they required that all alliance members must reduce their fleets in exchange for protection. The result, as you've seen, was our downfall."

Little Red panned between views of each of the stars enshrouded by the nebula.

"We were once a strong species, but even the mighty fall. The humans that survived the darkness came together as one, to evolve beyond the confines of their jail."

Dwight shot his hand up. "What does that mean?"

Little Red's eyes flashed blue. "I do not understand the question."

Dwight glanced at Bradley and then back at the robot. "How did they plan to evolve beyond the confines of the dark nebula?"

"I do not understand the question."

"I... never mind. Please continue."

Bradley brought his hand up toward his mouth, pretending he was chewing but was instead subvocalizing. "It does that whenever you ask something that strays from its script. I don't believe any of them have deep knowledge of their history. They do, however, have the broad strokes we need. Keep watching."

He reached up and rubbed at his right eye. It had been vibrating ever since he'd eaten that blue pickle thing.

The little robot raised on its base again, restarting its speech. "There was chaos and disorder within the nebula, and in the end the humans were forced to battle against the Nanil. Try as they might, they failed to negotiate with the barbaric species. The Nanil blamed humans for the darkness, but the humans knew otherwise. The Nanil believed that if they destroyed humanity, they would be freed from the darkness."

"What does that mean? How did the humans know otherwise?" Cynthia asked.

"I do not understand the question."

"What did they know about the Nanil?"

"I do not understand the question."

Bradley shook his head and chuckled.

Cynthia smiled. "Never mind. Please continue."

"Thank you, Master Bradley's mate."

Her eyes widened and she shot a glare at Bradley.

He raised his hands in defense. "Don't look at me," he subvocalized. "You kissed me."

Little Red glanced from her to him and then back toward the others. "The humans battled the Nanil until they withdrew to their home world, but before they could destroy them, a star within the nebula went supernova. What happened next surprised even them. The darkness acted like a mirror, reflecting the power of the exploding star inward, throughout the enshrouded star systems. Anything not protected below kilometers of planetoid or special shielding was wiped out by the expanding cloud of hot gas. All life was destroyed except for one star system, the star named Henosi."

The image on the wall screen changed to a planet teeming with color and life. Deep blue oceans with multicolored islands interspersed. Continents of red, green, and brown dotted its surface while billowy clouds marched high above.

He scanned the faces around the room. People's mouths were open in awe, the same reaction he'd had.

The image on the wall panned out and back to their current vantage. It showed a stream of ships coming and going in time-lapse. They were building something. After another minute, the shape became clear. It was the cone they were standing in.

A few moments later the cone was fully formed, and the ships switched from constructing it to ferrying large asteroids into orbit around it.

"The humans built this mass accelerator to give them freedom and protection from the Nanil. During their time rebuilding and planning the fate of Henosi the Nanil grew stronger, for they had not died. After centuries of silence they rose from their home world and retook star system after star system, unopposed."

The image on the wall changed. It showed a fleet of oddly shaped starships working their way through the nebula, stripping it of all raw materials, and then moving on to the next star. Over time, it morphed into a massive geometric structure that crawled through the inner nebula systems.

Little Red's voice grew louder. "The Nanil sent wave after wave of attacks, but the humans were stronger. The humans had us to protect them."

The wall transformed into a massive battle scene filled with thousands of ships attempting to pass the cone, only to be blasted into oblivion. Attempt after attempt led to fleets of ships being destroyed by the stunning power of the accelerator guarding the entrance to Henosi.

"But the Nanil are resourceful, and where finesse fails, brute force can prevail. They sent a larger fleet, using nearly all the remaining raw materials from the outer star systems.

The starships blanketed the system and flanked the accelerator from all sides with over ten thousand vessels."

The image changed again. Little Red was right, the wall was white with starships. Thousands upon thousands of them.

"But the humans were smarter. They knew they couldn't win this battle. There was only one option remaining."

The cone rotated in place. Where it had previously been pointing outward, toward the other side of the system in defense, it was now rotated to face Henosi. The robots loaded the cone with the last of their raw material and then; it fired. Not toward the distant planet as everyone expected, but at the nebula.

The room gasped as the nebula expanded inward, its dark tendrils curled like hands reaching out until it met the other side. The added mass from the raw material shot from the accelerator, gave the nebula everything it needed to fill the tunnel between the stars.

"Henosi was protected and the humans won," Little Red said. It then lowered downward to its normal height and sat motionless.

"And then what?" Dwight asked.

"I do not understand the question."

"Argh!" Dwight screamed. "How are you robots still here? How is all of this still here?" He waved his hands around.

Little Red's eyes fluttered between white and blue, settling on blue. It rose upward somewhat. "We robots prevailed, of course. We used the remaining raw power within the cone to destroy some of the Nanil ships. Many of the others flew inward, toward the newly formed nebula. They believed it was thin enough to pass through. Needless to say, their lives were shortened, and they added more mass to the expanding darkness. The others that remained began battling one another. We're not sure why. We merely watched the primitive beasts thin their numbers until we could step in and complete their destruction."

The room fell silent.

Bradley stepped around the table and stood next to the little robot. "Thank you for that presentation, Little Red. Can you give us humans a few moments alone? To talk?"

"Yes, Master Bradley." The robot lowered downward and scurried out the door. The door closed behind it as it disappeared into the hall.

He turned to face the others. "It's right there," he said pointing at the dark nebula on the wall screen.

Cynthia shook her head side to side. "I must've missed something. Are you talking about somehow traveling through that nebula, or are you on about entering that star system to meet up with our ancestors? Who, might I remind you, had the power to wipe out an entire species. Something tells me we're a tad bit outgunned."

"Had," he said turning to face her. "They had the power to wipe out an entire species. What makes you think they took it over there? They wouldn't need to if the Nanil couldn't pass through the nebula."

Pierce laughed from the other side of the room. He was shaking his head like Cynthia.

"Ante up," Bradley said eyeing Pierce cautiously. "If you've got something to say, then spit it out."

Pierce set down her glass of blue liquid and then faced Bradley. "I'm not one to challenge the chain of command, sir, but... that there," she pointed toward the dark nebula, "that's a sign of more death. The door's closed for a reason, and assuming we do figure out how to get past it, on the other side is more death."

He slammed his hands down on the table. The sound echoed throughout the room and everyone froze. He closed his eyes. He'd lost his fraking temper again. "Sorry," he muttered. "I'm just... fed up with all these dead ends. Pierce is right. It's been annihilation at every corner of this place. All roads here lead to the ultimate darkness. We don't have a lot of time, though. That tribunal won't wait around on us. As far as we know—"

"Don't finish that sentence." Pepper walked up next to him and rested her hand on his shoulder. "Besides," she said reaching down and popping a purple cherry looking fruit into her mouth. Her lips puckered and her eyes fluttered.

"Besides?" he asked, motioning forward with his hands.

"You people think too linearly. All we need to do is drop a probe and gate over there for a look-see. If it's dangerous, we don't enter the system. Easy peasy chicken squeezy." She shrugged. "Instead, we spend time scouring all these blasted ships for the information we'd need." Pepper gestured outward, over the field of starships on the wall screen.

He was several weeks into gate jumping, and he still wasn't used to it. The idea of skipping over a huge section of space was… unnatural.

The others were all nodding. They all agreed with her approach.

He smiled at Pepper. "So, we have a plan then. Pepper has yet again pointed out where I've overlooked the obvious. Something tells me she's done this before with my brother." He winked at her. "To be fair, though." He pointed around the room. "Everyone here missed the obvious strategy, so it wasn't only me this time."

The room broke out into laughter, and everyone shot barbs at each other, even Dwight.

Bradley walked toward the entrance to the room, and the door slid open. Little Red was waiting patiently on the far wall down the hallway. He whistled and waved his hand toward the robot. "You can come back in."

The robot whizzed toward him; it beeped, and its eyes flashed a rainbow of colors as it approached.

"So talk to me, Little Red." He turned and stepped back in

toward the room. "What would it take to access the computer systems from those starships if we wanted to search for… let's just say we're looking for something."

Little Red's eyes turned white. "If the starship is active, then we can search its entire databanks from here."

Cynthia lowered her plate, and her eyebrows raised. "Really? Can you get me access to those?"

"But of course. Anything for Master Bradley's mate."

He put a hand over his mouth and chuckled.

Cynthia walked up and gently tapped her hand on the top of the little robot's head. "You're cute. Now show me those databanks."

25

ZACHARY OLIVAW
LUPUS DARK NEBULA

The Fountainhead gated a short distance from Doda after they boarded. They needed to recuperate and also wanted to see if there was a broader response to their visit by the Nanil. The crew had asked about a funeral service for Drew, but Zachary refused to bury his people here, even without the body. No, they'd honor him properly with a military funeral in Tiān with all of his friends and family present.

He leaned back in the captain's chair. The bridge was empty. It was only him, a fresh bulb of coffee, and some pleasant music playing overhead. He lifted the bulb upward for a drink and his arms screamed. Even the smallest movement reminded him how sore he was.

His nanites had been working overtime to repair his muscles and estimated another day or two until he'd return to normal. They'd injected everyone with a healthy batch of fresh nanites after boarding. He wasn't the only one reporting pain and discomfort, but he'd endured the longest climb.

Ibu on the other hand, they were a bouncing fountain of energy. Not a sore muscle in their body. Pluto offered to share their quarters with Ibu, but they didn't want to disturb the couple. Instead, Kamal and the soldiers offered them Drew's old bunk.

He closed his eyes. The sounds of the music and the smell of the coffee were relaxing. He should've built some massage features into these things.

What the heck were they going to do now? They hit a dead end on Doda, and from the sounds of it Bradley's team had, as well. They were currently scouting systems on a hunch. Well, from the message he left it was less of a hunch and more of a bored rage. He was having trouble coping with all the death inside this dark nebula.

The shush, shush noise of the bridge door opening and closing was barely audible above his music. He pretended he didn't hear it and kept his eyes closed, bringing his coffee up for another sip and winced.

"Still sore?" Ibu asked.

He smiled and turned toward them. They were walking around the bridge eying everything curiously. "Yes, my arms feel like they went through a meat grinder. How are you this morning? Did you get a chance to mess around with that tablet Shauna gave you?"

"I did. There were some fun games and puzzles on there. I started reading about your history in Sol. Shauna offered to teach me some classes and to answer anything I wanted to know."

He took another sip of coffee. "You should take her up on that. She's an excellent teacher. She taught me much of what I know."

"She did?" Ibu bobbed their head. "Is she that old?"

"She is, and I'm not that old to be honest. I'm forty-five. Most humans live to be over one hundred and fifty years old."

"Humm," Ibu muttered. "Why so young? Nanil live to be well over three hundred years of age."

He leaned forward and shook his head. "Three hundred! That's crazy."

Ibu walked forward and sat in one of the chairs, swiveling it to face him. "I believe the oldest was close to four hundred, but I'd have to meditate on my memories to surface them."

He shook his head. "It's hard to imagine, but we also have ways to live much longer. You should ask Shauna about it sometime."

Ibu nodded, mimicking him again. "I will. So, what's next? Are we headed to the globule?"

He tilted his head. "What do you mean? What globule?"

"The one I told Pluto about yesterday before we left."

That's right. Pluto had mentioned something about knowing where to head next. With all the commotion, no one thought to discuss it again.

He reached up and tapped his ear opening a comm. "Pluto, if you're awake, can you please come up to the bridge?"

"Sure thing, Z," she replied. "I'm on my way."

He leaned forward, closer to his coffee and took a sip. "So tell me about this globule you and Pluto talked about and don't leave out any details."

PLUTO LAID in the course to the Bok Globule, and they'd already begun the series of jumps it'd take to get there. They were over a day out on the most direct route.

He was pacing on the bridge, listening to Ibu repeat the story for the third time. The entire crew was here to hear it this time around. Ibu had been nervous to talk to so many people, but Pluto talked them into it. She had a way with the young Nanil. They'd developed quite the bond on the first day in the field and it had blossomed ever since.

His mind was wandering during Ibu's retelling of the

story. They were at the part where they were warning them about what lies behind the colorful nebula clouds. Their people hadn't visited it in over a thousand years. They'd lost too many lives in the globule battles, and during Ibu's retelling, it was hard to filter the Nanil dogmatic faith from religious propaganda. So much of what Ibu's tablet had in it didn't align with the data Bradley had sent on from Yaan's memory banks.

He still couldn't get past his brothers hunches. All throughout their life Bradley had this innate ability to guess his way through things. Whether it was vid-sim games, puzzles, or in this case life or death situations, if there was something that required him to take a guess, then always bet on Bradley. It pissed him off. He had to bust his butt to learn everything he could and work his way through problems and Bradley would come along and guess his way to the same point.

26

BRADLEY OLIVAW

LUPUS DARK NEBULA, HENOSI

The forward probes they launched showed a binary star system with several planets in the ideal goldilocks zones around the stars. They couldn't see everything from a distance, but they appeared to have water, weather, and all the elements necessary for a healthy ecosystem. There were no noticeable lights on the planet's surface during the evening hours but that didn't mean anything.

He was scratching at the beard on his face reviewing the data on his retinal comm. He hadn't felt like shaving the last few days, and something the robots had given him had really kicked his body into overdrive. His nails and hair had been growing like mad and Cynthia, well, she'd been having to beat him off all day. He couldn't get enough of her and wanted to get frisky.

"So there are no signs of life?" he asked.

"Correction," Harold said. "There're no signs of communications or stray frequencies typical of advanced life-forms. Until we get close to the planet, we won't know if there's life. But all signs point to it being an ideal planet for humans, or any form of life for that matter, to survive."

"So where is everyone? Why aren't we seeing a star system teeming with humans?"

"I'm not sure. But I see no reason we shouldn't go find out for ourselves."

He nodded and rubbed the hair on his cheek with his palm. They hadn't come all this way to sit still. There was too much riding on this mission. "Alright, let's do it."

He reached up and tapped his ear, opening a comm to the crew. "It appears that the coast is clear and we're safe to jump over into the Henosi star system. Is that really what we're calling it?"

"It's what the other humans called it," Pepper said. "Seems appropriate for us to honor that. Though, I sorta like Enosi myself."

"I'm wrapping up here," Cynthia said. "I've downloaded most of the data we'd ever care to pilfer from their databanks. I'll be at the Fidem in five minutes."

"I'll be here," he said.

Cynthia opened a private comm to him. "I don't know what was in that food we ate, but... well, meet me in our quarters. I have something to show you."

"That sounds like fun," he said.

"What does?" Dwight asked.

Cynthia chuckled over their private comm.

"Um... heading to Enosi. We're wheels up in ten minutes people. Please raise your tray tables and prepare for departure."

"What are you on about?" Pepper asked. "Wheels up?"

"Sorry, too many late night classic videos. You should check out the movie 'Airplane!' some time. It's hilarious. I'll be in my quarters talking to a man about a razor for this beard if anyone needs me."

"Roger that, sir," Pierce said. "We're transferring some eats for the road."

"Don't touch that beard," Cynthia private comm'd him. "Not yet, anyhow."

He stood up and turned toward the exit. "Harold, when everyone is aboard, have Pepper start the gate sequence to Enosi. I'll be in my cabin for a bit. Ping me if you need me."

"Yes, sir," Harold said. "Oh, there is one thing."

He sighed and turned. "What's that?"

"I could've told you when you were walking. Anyhow, what are we going to do about Little Red? He's been waiting at the bottom of the ramp for the better part of an hour. He's taken quite the liking to you."

"I... uh. I don't know." He reached up and pulled at his beard. "Is there any reason he couldn't come with us? I mean, he might be useful to have aboard."

"I suppose if you want a puppy," Harold said. "I see no harm in having him join us."

He rubbed his forehead. "I had a puppy once, two of them actually, for a little while. They were so much work, but our family had lots of fun with them. Teaching them tricks, taking them camping, and going on walks. Let's do it! Ask Little Red if they'd like to join us."

"Very well. I'll start printing some bones for him," Harold said in a nonchalant voice.

Bradley missed the joke. His mind was elsewhere. "I'm off to... get my shave on. Well, shave off I suppose."

"WE CAN'T GATE any closer. From this point forward, the gravity from the binary stars, the asteroid belt, and the nearby planets will make our jumps too unpredictable," Pepper said. "What are your orders, sir?"

He rubbed at his cleanly shaven face. "Our forward probes never engaged their impulse drives, right?"

"That's correct," Pepper said.

"Do we have anything from communications?"

"Negative. It's as quiet as a church cucumber in here," Cynthia said.

"I believe the phrase is as quiet as a church mouse," he corrected her.

"Really? It seems like a mouse would eventually make noise, whereas a cucumber wouldn't." She shrugged. "Either way, it's quiet."

"There are no unusual visuals, either, sir," Pierce said. "No ships, no satellites, no nothing."

The silence of the system was deafening. He didn't know what he was expecting, but this wasn't it. How could the last of a species risk everything for this star system and then do nothing with it?

He took a deep breath. "Let's hope it's not lifeless," he muttered.

"What was that?" Pepper asked.

He cleared his throat. "I said, let's head in. Let's check out the first habitable planet."

"Aye, sir," Pepper said. She reached toward her controls and engaged the impulse drives. "ETA is one hour until we're in orbit around the fourth world."

He couldn't feel the acceleration, but when she engaged the drive there were faint vibrations. It wasn't much, but it was there. It reminded him of the oscillations he used to feel from the washing machine down the hall from his room in their North Carolina home on Earth. During the spin cycle there was a faint vibration similar to this. It was sorta soothing.

"I'm gonna check on Dwight. Ping me if you need me." He turned and exited the bridge.

Coming around the donut he walked past the small gym they had tucked away in the ship. The soldiers were all working out. He paused to watch. They seemed to be doing some hand-to-hand combat and Little Red was standing on the sidelines.

He stepped into the room to watch closer.

Pierce froze mid jab when she saw him enter. "Captain. Is everything ok?"

Moet hadn't realized he was standing behind her and came in from below and swiped her leg, sending Pierce tumbling to the ground. She hit the mats hard with a thud and a groan. The sweat covering her body sprayed across the ground.

"Ouch…" she muttered.

He winced at her fall. "Yes, everything's fine, Lieutenant. I'm sorry, I didn't mean to disturb your training. I was curious what Little Red was doing here."

Moet leaned down and helped Pierce up. She had a coy grin on her face.

"He's teaching us some fighting techniques used by our ancestors and the Nanil. We thought it might be helpful… you know, should things get out of hand."

Little Red beeped a few notes and walked over toward him. "Is that ok with you, Master Bradley?"

He nodded. "Quite alright, Red. We appreciate your help."

The little robot's eyes fluttered between red and white. It rotated back to face the soldiers. "Everyone back at it. Pierce, you let your guard down there and let Moet in for the kill. Next time, even if you're thrown off, you should remain prepared. Now, back on your lines. Let's take it from the top."

Bradley turned and left the gym, heading toward Dwight's small lab. He walked in on his friend twirling around in his chair. He was staring straight up at the empty ceiling. "Bored?" he chuckled.

Dwight froze mid rotation and turned toward the door. "No, I'm running through plans in my mind. You know, in case people have questions on the ground. I want to make sure you have everything you need and that I'm prepared up here."

He tilted his head. "Up here? You're not thinking about staying aboard the Fidem, are you?"

Dwight glanced down toward the floor and fidgeted with the arm to his chair. "Well, we all remember what happened last time I joined a boarding party. I almost got everyone killed."

He walked into the room closer to Dwight. "We're all learning, buddy. Mistakes happen in tense situations. It's never usually about the mistake itself, it's how everyone copes with it and moves on as a team. You've seen enough fumbled discs in International Aero League to know that."

Dwight chuckled and nodded. He was an avid fan of the disc-based sport played in three dimensional zero-g arenas. "I suppose you're right. We don't even know if we're heading down. I was just trying to keep myself busy."

"I think it's a brilliant idea," he said. "While you're at it, check over the soldier's gear, as well. Make sure it's up to snuff and ready to handle the variables of the environment. Put some of those electronic skills to work."

Dwight hopped up and headed toward the door. "That's right. I forgot all about that. Yea… thanks boss," he mumbled as he walked out.

"You know that equipment is reviewed every day by Pierce and her team, right? She's meticulous about that," Harold said over his comm.

"I do," he nodded. "The guy's gotta feel needed if we're gonna get him on the ground."

"Are we sure we want the entire team to land on every planet we visit?"

He turned and headed toward his quarters. "I'm not. But the last thing I need is comm lag or blackouts while the Fidem is orbiting a planet. If we need to form a landing party, we'll need him. Especially on a world teeming with life."

He paused at the entrance to his quarters. "I'm going to record a comm to Zachary. Any chance it'll make it to him?"

"We dropped a probe after we entered. It's in silent mode. We're tight beaming all of our findings every hour to avoid detection."

Bradley nodded and waved the door open. "Give me a few minutes of privacy." He stepped into his quarters and closed the door.

THEY CRAMMED the entire crew onto the bridge as the Fidem approached the fourth planet around the binary. The multicolored surface was straight out of a children's coloring book. He'd never seen so much diversity in color.

"Disengaging the impulse drive," Pepper said reaching up to the controls. "We're now in orbit."

The slight vibration he'd felt in his feet earlier stopped.

Pepper brought up their probe inventory in the corner of the wall screen. "Should I deploy a—"

"Holy crap," Cynthia gasped. "Look at that." She zoomed into the water off the coast of one of the planet's many continents.

The wall screen showed a school of large orange fish with massive flippers swimming near the surface of the water. They were floating upward, breaking the surface and then diving downward. The screen reported their length as twelve meters.

"They're beautiful," Moet said. Her eyes were transfixed on the screen.

"I'm counting over two hundred between the ones surfacing and diving," Cynthia said. "We're too far away to detect if they're sentient."

He sighed, and a weight lifted off his shoulders watching

the majestic creatures swim through the water. At least there was life in this system.

Pepper turned around and glanced at Cynthia. "So... a probe. Should I launch a few?"

He reached up and scratched his head. "Are there any visual changes anywhere in the star system? Any detectable communications of any kind."

"Negative," Cynthia said.

"No, sir," Pierce said.

"Alright," he sighed. He'd half hoped something would've reached out to them. "Let's move to phase two and launch a few satellites into different orbits so we can find somewhere interesting to land this thing."

Pepper turned forward and made a few adjustments to her controls. A dozen probes launched from the underside of the Fidem and telemetry began flowing onto the wall screen. "We'll have complete coverage in ten minutes," she said. She swiveled back around. "Just to be clear, though, we can't take the Fidem planet-side, sir. It's untested. We have a shuttle for away missions like this."

He chuckled. "Untested as unlikely to work, or untested as in it seems fine on paper but isn't recommended to try on a distant unknown planet?"

Pepper smirked. "The latter."

"Check," he gestured with his hand.

The top of the wall screen went red, and the klaxons alerted them they were being scanned.

He stood up. "What do we got, Pierce?"

"I'm still checking, sir. Bringing up visuals on the wall screen."

The image changed. It showed a small bluish white circular object of some sort floating in space.

"It appears to be stationary above a point on the surface. As you can see, the object is featureless and is one hundred meters in diameter. It has no reflectivity nor signature in nonvisual wavelengths. What we're seeing is the visible spectrum only."

He shook his head. "That wasn't there a second ago, right?"

"Correct, sir. It looks like it only just became visible," Pierce swiveled to face him. "As soon as we launched the probes and began actively scanning the surface, it appeared."

"Perfect," he muttered as he started fiddling with his fingers. Why the hell is everything in this nebula so ominous? "Let's try to hail it."

"Aye, sir," Cynthia said. "I'm hailing on all frequencies."

Pierce pivoted back to face his console.

Cynthia made some adjustments and shook her head. "We're getting no response to our hail, sir."

Pierce directed another feed onto the wall screen. "One of our probes detected another sphere on the far side of the planet. It's the same size and spectral classification as this one."

He reached behind his back and clasped his hands together. He had to stop fidgeting. "Can we get a visual of what's planet-side, below the spheres?"

"I'm already working on it," Pepper said.

"I circled back in our communications to the point of contact when the sphere's visuals changed. Harold and I missed it before." Cynthia brought up a waveform on the wall screen in a small window. It showed nothing, a single spike with a short duration, and then nothing again.

"What am I looking at?" he asked.

"It's a ten millisecond transmission of a single pulse toward the planet. The only reason we caught it was because we were passing so close to it with one of our probes."

"And there wasn't anything encoded within it?" he asked.

"Not that we can tell," Cynthia said. "It was a very precise pulse, though constrained to a single frequency band."

"I've got visuals from the planet beneath the sphere, sir. Bringing it up on the wall screen," Pepper said.

The bridge was silent as the crew stared at the wall. There, on the ground, was what appeared to be an arrangement of multi-level pyramids. There were three concentric layers of pyramids with eight small ones around the outside, four medium ones in the middle, and ending with two massive ones in the center.

Their shape reminded him of something he'd seen before. "Those look familiar."

"Their general shape matches many ancient temples on Earth. The Temple of the Sun near Mexico City and other pyramids near Tenochtitlan all have similar architectural influences," Harold said.

"This is even more interesting," Pepper said.

The image slowly panned south away from the pyramids and along the hills leading down into a valley. There were primitive structures built into the hillside, and what appeared to be neat rows of crops and livestock corrals with large beefy animals roaming within them. As the view panned around, he could make out smaller shapes walking around.

"Are those humans?" Cynthia asked.

"That's unclear," Harold replied. "Until we can get closer and inspect them, all we know is that they're humanoid. They could be a subspecies of humanoids including—"

He raised his hand to stop. "We get it Harold. We need a closer look." He paused and took a deep breath. He'd been wanting something like this since they'd arrived. A first contact. Hell, any contact at all that wasn't robotic. "Anyone up for a landing party?"

THEY LANDED the Fidem's shuttle on the far side of the nexus of pyramids. The scans from orbit showed no signs of life, either in the stepped pyramids or on their north side. There was a clearing about one kilometer away just past a dense thicket of trees.

"Ok everyone, stay together and no stragglers." Bradley glanced at Dwight and nodded. "If you want to study something, we'll all stop and cover you."

"Aye, sir," the soldiers said in unison.

"Deploying drones," Pierce said. "We'll keep them high and a safe distance away from the village. Engaging camouflage."

The swarm of drones rose upward and out of their landing bays atop the shuttle. They were black but as they rose into the sky, their surface blurred and they vanished into the background of wispy clouds.

"Are we ready?" he asked. His retinal comm warned him about his elevated heart rate and his stomach was doing somersaults. It was like heading into an examination and not being sure what the topic was about.

Everyone nodded except Cynthia. She'd tapped her ear and was subvocalizing something with Harold.

She held up a finger and nodded her head. "Harold was telling me we have a visual on spheres like the ones here on several other planets. We can't tell definitively, but each planet seems to have at least two, and the other Earth-like planet has four. I'm ready to go." She hopped up and out of her seat, heading toward the back of the shuttle.

He exhaled. This is what he'd been waiting for. "Everyone remember, we're headed toward the pyramids first. After that, we'll figure out our next course of action. Understood?"

"Aye, sir," everyone said in unison.

Pepper and Cynthia shot each other smirks.

"Alright, you two. A good aye sir never hurt anyone," he said with a smile.

They stepped off the shuttle two by two, with Bradley in

the middle. The landing ramp raised and sealed the entrance behind them.

Moet dropped behind and subvocalized the command to engage the shuttle's camo. It reminded him of a window in a rainstorm, everything about its shape became distorted and then it disappeared entirely.

He inhaled. There was a gentle cool breeze picking up, that brought with it hints of what smelled like lavender and mint. An unusual combo in this field of orange grasses.

He checked his retinal comm. His nanites were reporting the air was pure, with no unexpected foreign particulates or viruses. Glancing skyward, a faint yellow brown cloud passed slowly overhead through an ocean of blue sky. Had he not known otherwise, he'd have sworn it was smog, like he'd seen in pictures of ancient Earth.

"Someone's breaking the rules already and it isn't me," Dwight said over the comm.

Bradley glanced around. He'd already strayed from the group and was holding everyone up. "Crap! Sorry. I was… taking it all in." He jogged to catch up with the others.

When he reached down, he brushed his holster. His sidearm was still there and touching it brought up its status on his retinal comm. It was fully charged and set to stun. He wasn't used to carrying it but everyone else was armed.

The group paused at the entrance to the thicket. Their drones had mapped the least treacherous route through the trees and overlaid the ideal path on everyone's retinal comm. They'd also identified the location of any unusual insects or animals they'd encountered flying through.

"Doesn't look too bad," Pierce said. "Keep your eyes peeled. It looks like we'll be passing a few deer sized animals and what appear to be monkeys… I think."

"You playing zoologist now?" Dwight asked.

Everyone chuckled.

"Eyes open and attentive," Bradley said. "We don't know what the drones missed."

Giving everyone orders was weird. It wasn't his cup of coffee, but it was also sorta nice being listened to, without debate. He always thought it curious how in tense and fearful situations, even the most obnoxious people settled into a subservient role.

Cynthia was in front of him on his left and she kept glancing back, checking that he was ok.

"I'm fine," he said to her over a private comm.

"I know. I was just… checking," she replied.

The tree trunks and the upper canopies were covered in a dense network of vines. It reminded him of the jungles on Earth. He'd never been in one, but he'd fought in them on vid-sims. He used to swing up into the vines to find the perfect sniper position to take out foes.

A shiver shot up his spine, like he was being watched. He glanced upward, looking in the vines for a sniper. He paused. "Everyone, there." He pointed. "I think it's one of the animals Pierce said was a monkey."

It was an odd-looking critter with green fur and a long nose, sorta like an elephant. Add to that four arms perfect for grasping at any angle, and that's what was hanging upside down staring at them.

"I swore that nose was a tail," Pierce subvocalized.

Moet chuckled and the critter shot skyward up the vines.

"Nice going," Pepper joked. "You scared the monkey."

The others chuckled and Moet thwapped Pierce on the shoulder.

They followed the drone's suggested path about halfway when Dwight saw something he wanted to check out. There was a small pond to the left with some unusual vegetation around it. Their sea of green and brown leaves was contrasted with a circle of white flowering plants.

"Can I check those out?" Dwight asked pointing at the pond's edge. "I'll be quick."

"Sure thing," Pierce said after Bradley gave her a nod. "Everyone circle up. Moet and Gregory, accompany Dwight. Keep your eyes open. The drones saw a bunch of insects by that watering hole."

"Aye, sir," they said as they walked over and flanked Dwight on both sides.

"Are we seeing anything interesting on the drones?" Bradley asked. He grabbed a globe of water from Cynthia's backpack, squeezed some into his mouth, and then handed it to her.

"No, I guess not. I mean, I was expecting something a bit more... modern. They're just a bunch of farmers," Cynthia said. She took the water and squeezed a mouthful.

He tapped his ear and subvocalized the command to bring up the live feed. On his retinal comm were videos of primitive humanoids tilling soil, crushing grain, and weaving clothing from the looks of it.

"Yea, not exactly an advanced civilization, are they," he said.

"Any idea how they made the pyramids? I mean, I don't see any earth movers around there. Those things are colossal," Pepper said. "They're at least fifty meters above ground. The drones... well shit, the drones don't seem to report any internal structure above nor below ground."

He tilted his head. "That's strange, right? I mean, aren't there usually tombs and stuff inside?"

"Most tombs on Earth are in the middle of structures like this," Harold said.

He'd forgotten all about Harold. He hadn't spoken since they'd landed.

Harold continued. "There are several on Earth that have cave systems and underground vaults, but they're not the norm."

"Are they pyramids, or should we be calling them temples?" Pepper asked.

"Let's call them pyramids until we can confirm they're used for worshiping gods or other deities," Harold said.

Bradley studied Dwight from a distance. He'd been approaching the edge of the water cautiously, almost too much so. The guy was on eggshells worrying that someone would get hurt due to his curiosity. Better to be safe than sorry he supposed.

"I think these things are alive," Dwight said over the comm. "Check this out." He shared his retinal camera with the group. He was holding a stick, over a meter in length, and moved it close to the white plants. They moved toward it at first and then backed away. Like it was going to hurt them.

"I won't get any closer," Dwight said.

"Good idea, buddy," he said. "Maybe later we can check them out once we know what's ahead."

The group backtracked to the party, and they moved forward toward the pyramids. About five minutes later they came up to the clearing near the edge of the outer layer of eight pyramids.

"Let's take these one at a time," he said. "We'll start with these outer pyramids and then head inward until we reach the largest ones. Split into two groups and circle around to the steps. We're looking for any unusual markings, entrances, etc."

"Aye, sir," they all said as they dispersed into their preassigned groups. They assigned Moet to lead the other party.

He walked at the back of his team as he attempted to watch the video from the other group and what was in front of him. Neither was seeing anything unusual outside the pyramids themselves. Their surface was smooth like glass and there were no markings or signs of aging at all.

After fifteen minutes Moet spoke. "We're not finding anything, sir."

"I sent a drone to do a flyby up top," Pepper said. "There are closed doors at the apex and our scans are all coming up empty inside. We can't detect anything behind them."

"Alright," Bradley said. "Let's check the next one. I don't want to climb one of these until we have a better idea what we're looking at."

"Roger that," Pepper said. "I'll do a flyby of the second ring and the central pyramids, as well."

He paused at the foot of the stairs. Each step was perfectly shaped and showed no signs of aging or weathering. It was like they were freshly cut this morning. The steps climbed skyward where they ended just short of the top where the entrance was slightly recessed inward. All you could make out from down here was the surface of two massive doors.

"Sir, are we going to the next one?" Pierce asked.

He glanced around. The other three members of the team had moved on to the second ring. "Sorry," he muttered as he walked fast to catch up. He'd given Dwight a talking to earlier to make sure he stayed on point, and he was the one messing up today.

The second set of four pyramids mirrored the first except they were exactly twice as tall. Their surface was pristine and seamless, and like the first, they had five meter tall steps at each level. The only normal sized steps was the central set receding up the middle of the stepped pyramid.

"Are there any detectable differences between any of these other than size?" he asked over the comm.

"None," Cynthia said. "They're replicas of the other eight. I'm starting to think they're made of stealth tech inside. I don't see why else they'd be empty."

He nodded. It hadn't occurred to him, but it made complete sense except for the fact that these things were positioned outside the most primitive civilization any modern human had ever set their eyes on.

He reached over to the pyramid's surface and ran his

hand along the side. It was cold, ice cold, which was unusual considering how warm it was. His forehead was covered in sweat, and if his clothes weren't designed to cool him, he was pretty sure he'd be a sweat-stained mess out here.

"These things are icy," he said over the comm.

"Did you just touch one?" Harold asked.

He swallowed hard and stared at his hand resting against the cool glassy surface. "I did. Why?"

"I detected another pulse from the sphere. I don't know what it said, but I know it wasn't an on / off switch like the last one. This one had structure."

27

ZACHARY OLIVAW

LUPUS DARK NEBULA, BOK GLOBULE

The Fountainhead found and retrieved a Fidem beacon near the Bok Globule. There was no sense in someone else recovering it. The details Bradley's team had dumped inside revealed that the Fidem had ventured through here, and they were heading deep into the globule. They followed suit and worked their way through the nebulosity and out the far side. When they entered the neighboring system, they found a second beacon waiting for them.

"And we're sure we can just waltz up to that sea of ships without a care in the world?" Zachary asked.

"Sir, we're being hailed by three small ships straight ahead. They dropped out of stealth. They claim to be here to escort us," Libby said.

"Put them on screen."

The bridge of the small craft appeared on the wall screen. Three yellow robots were flanking a taller red one in the middle. The red one resembled the one Bradley had named Little Red in his comm. He'd said it joined them on their voyage. This one, however, was much larger.

"Welcome, Master Zachary. My name is Big Red. Master Bradley has assigned me this designation."

"Of course he did," Zachary said with a chuckle.

"We're here to expedite your travel to Enosi and to alleviate any concerns you may have," Big Red said.

He tilted his head and glanced toward Brice.

"Just go with it," Harold subvocalized. "Enosi is the modified name Bradley's crew gave to the system on the far side of the nebula."

He turned back toward Big Red and smiled. "Thank you very much… Big Red. We appreciate the escort."

Big Red bowed on the wall screen. "Would you like a shipment of food? Your colleagues enjoyed the delicacies we had to offer and Pepper thought it would be kind. She believed you'd enjoy the new tastes and sensations they offered."

"Ooh, new food," Pluto said. She turned to face him. "Can we, Z?"

He glanced toward Libby and she shrugged.

"We'd appreciate that Big Red," he bowed toward the wall screen.

Big Red's eyes flashed a rainbow of colors, and it returned the bow. "We will send a message onward and prepare the transfer before you transition to Enosi. Please follow us at full impulse."

The three alien ships turned in place and accelerated away.

"You heard him. Follow on." He smirked and shook his head. "Big Red," he muttered. "Bradley's a dork."

"BEGINNING GATE TRANSITION IN 3… 2… 1…" Pluto said.

The gate drive engaged, and the vanes moved over the outside hull of the Fountainhead. The imagery of the distant binary loomed ahead from their forward probe and the gate reflection. He'd grown so accustomed to seeing different star fields in the gate's space-time lens that the darkness of these nebulae transitions felt lifeless.

Overthinking the darkness was depressing. He could understand Bradley's downward mood spiral that Cynthia had mentioned in her messages. In her last one before they gated, she said that arriving here in the Bok Globule and seeing the planets of Enosi had raised Bradley's spirits.

He hoped it would raise everyone else's, as well. After losing Drew, the crew was in a funk. He watched as the blue wall of ants entered the bridge, the last room to transition.

A hand touched his own, and he glanced to his left to see Ibu standing next to him. He hadn't heard them enter. Their eyes were wide with anticipation as they watched the video feed from the binary star and the distant planets on the wall screen.

"Is this it? Is this Henosi?" Ibu asked. Their hand tightened as the blue light approached.

"It is, but… we're calling it Enosi," he said.

"Why?"

"It's a weird story, but let's go with it for a while, ok?"

Ibu nodded.

"We're through, sir," Pluto said.

"Checking the agreed upon coordinates for another beacon," Libby said. She reached up and fiddled with something on her controls. "There it is. Downloading the data now."

Their wall screen flashed red and a golden yellow sphere appeared forward of the Fountainhead. The klaxons on the bridge were blaring.

"Cut that racket!" Zachary shouted as he stood up.

The klaxons quieted on the bridge, but he could hear the faint sounds of their ringing elsewhere on the ship.

Zachary glanced left. "Why don't you go strap in?" He gestured at the seats behind and to his left, along the back wall. Ibu's eyes narrowed and their muscles seemed larger.

He'd have to ask Shauna about the Nanil fight-or-flight responses later. Now wasn't the time.

They stepped backward toward the seats.

He walked up beside Kamal. "Talk to me."

Kamal shook his head at something on his screen and then gestured on his controls to bring up the timeline. "They appeared out of nowhere after we signaled to our beacon to download the payload."

"We're being hailed, sir," Libby said.

"Did we get anything from the beacon, Shauna?" he asked.

"Nothing about these yellow spheres, no. Most of the data is still downloading. They've been doing massive data dumps every hour, sending everything they've been finding. Nothing here is jumping out at me. I'll let you know."

The klaxons went from yellow to red. Their ship was being targeted.

Libby turned. "Sir—"

"Bring them on screen," Zachary interrupted.

"There's no image, sir. Only audio," Cynthia said.

"This is Captain Olivaw of the Fountainhead. I demand you stop targeting our ship and let us through."

The bridge was silent for a moment before there was a reply. The voice was androgynous and soothing. "You're not authorized to be in this star system. Prepare to be boarded."

He gestured to mute the audio. "Arm the missiles and forward rail guns. Target the sphere."

"Aye, sir." Kamal's hands flew over the controls.

The wall screen updated showing an elevated threat indicator and the number of rounds focused on their golden target.

He gestured to unmute. "You cannot board our ship. We demand that—"

"Lower your defenses immediately," the voice interrupted.

He sighed. This was escalating quickly. "We mean no harm but we will not be boarded. You lower your targeting and we'll follow suit."

A small projectile shot from the golden sphere toward their ship.

"Inbound weapon of some kind," Kamal said. "Firing multiple countermeasures."

An intercept missile shot from the bow of the Fountainhead. Just before impact, it burst into shrapnel intended to confuse the inbound bogie and force it to explode.

It passed straight through the shrapnel field without issue.

Multiple lasers fired from the bow, again with no effect on the projectile.

"Brace for impact," Kamal said.

The ship lurched back as the weapon collided with the forward hull but there was no explosion.

Zachary muted the alien comm. "What the heck? Status, Kamal."

"They're spreading everywhere, sir." Kamal brought up a view of their hull from the forward facing cameras angled inward.

The impact split open a warhead filled with hundreds of tiny robots. They were spreading like a wave crashing over the hull of the ship, searching for a way in.

"This can't be good. Ideas anyone?" he asked.

"We could do an emergency gate, sir," Kamal said.

He shook his head. "No! That'd be bad. It'd take them with us through the gate. But we could—"

"Disabling the electromagnetic dampeners and reversing the drive flow," Pluto interrupted.

The Fountainhead shook violently as hundreds of robots repelled off the ship's surface and then bolts of plasma shot outward, causing them to explode close to the hull.

Zachary had reached over to the handle on Kamal's control. "Damage report."

"Hull integrity is ninety-five percent," Kamal said.

"They're hailing us again," Libby said. "Should I connect them?"

He raised his hand and rubbed his face. If this came down to tit for tat, they'd be dead in minutes. There had to be a way out of this that didn't require them gating backward. "We're sure that the only way they detected us was the downloading of the beacon data?"

"The timelines are within a second," Kamal said.

Zachary stepped back to his command chair and sat down. "Alright. Kamal, prepare to target and destroy the beacon. Wait for my mark. Shauna, if we haven't downloaded everything by now, then we never will."

"Lasers locked and loaded pending your mark," Kamal said.

He turned toward Pluto. "How fast can we gate? I'm talking full on pain, without all the hoopla of comfort."

Pluto shook her head. "I… I've never done that before."

"No one has," he said. "How fast without killing us?"

She shrugged. "Two to three seconds. I mean, we transition faster in our probes without organics onboard, but you know what happened to the test animal if we went any faster."

Libby swiveled toward him, her eyes were wide. "I remember. Let's not do that."

He took a deep breath and exhaled. The aliens were too close. They didn't have many options. "We don't have a choice. We take it slow and we're dead. Pluto, prepare for a fast transition, but keep it above three seconds. Synchronize with Kamal. I want you to fire the lasers just before we start the transition."

Libby turned around and engaged the ships retinal comm alerts. "Everyone strap in and prepare for an emergency gate. This won't be pleasant. It's gonna hurt."

Pluto adjusted her controls and held her hand over the panel. "Ready to gate on your mark, sir."

No human had ever gated this fast. They always transitioned slowly for a reason. The human mind can't handle passing through time and space too quickly. Images of the bloody aftermath of their animal trials flashed before his eyes. They all went crazy and tore at their flesh until they died. He shook off the memories. As long as they kept it above three seconds they'd be fine.

"Mark!"

The laser arrays on the bow of the ship lit up and fired a single concentrated blast toward the beacon. It exploded in a flash of yellow and red. At the same moment, the Fountainhead creaked as the gate vanes rapidly spread open and the tachyon field engaged in one motion. The normally comfortable slow blue glow of the gate transition was replaced with a blue streak engulfing them from stern to bow.

It was over in an instant.

A cacophony of painful cries echoed throughout the bridge.

He squeezed the arms of his command chair and gritted his teeth as the pain peaked and slowly subsided. It was like he'd been burned and then run under cold water. The pain from the wound was still there, it just needed to stay cool. He needed to sit still for a few moments.

"Status report," he moaned and shook his head. His ears were ringing. Someone behind him was making quite a racket. He'd forgotten about Ibu.

He turned to check on them and regretted moving. Pain coursed over his skin. It was like a bad sunburn over every centimeter of his body.

Ibu was strapped into the harness, and their body had morphed. Their muscles had expanded like their progenitor but smaller. It looked like the harness was cutting off their circulation.

He took a deep breath and pushed up and out of his chair to go help them.

"I'd be careful," Shauna said. "Their vitals are peaking. Comparing these to the data we downloaded from the cone beacon, they appear to be in distress. The Nanil have a hyper focused fight response. They could be dangerous."

He reached out and touched Ibu's hand.

Their head leaned toward him. While their innocent eyes were the same, their face was in pain. "Help me," they whispered. "It hurts."

"Is there anything we can do, Shauna?" he asked.

"I can try to knock them out with some drugs. Maybe they'd wake up feeling better."

He nodded. He'd rather be asleep right now himself. "Do it," he subvocalized. He smiled at Ibu and gently rubbed their hand, careful not to apply force. "It'll be ok. You'll feel better in a minute."

Small injection tubes slid out of the chair and poked Ibu in the side. They were usually reserved for administering acceleration drugs, but could be used for other purposes. He watched as the liquid flowed through them and Ibu's eyes got heavy as they drifted off to sleep.

He stood up straight. The pain was less but his body ached. His nanites were reporting massive muscular tearing, like he'd worked out every square centimeter of his body.

"We appear to be a safe distance from our original gate entry," Pluto said weakly, as she glanced back at Ibu and then toward him.

He nodded. "They're ok. I had to knock them out," he subvocalized to her.

"I'm detecting multiple yellow spheres throughout the star system, sir," Kamal said. "They appear to be searching for something. For us."

He slowly walked over toward Kamal's station. Every

step shot pain through his extremities. "Do we have any external damage? Can they detect us?"

Kamal shook his head as he moaned under his breath. "No, sir. The damage from their robots was superficial. They didn't have enough time to breach the stealth coating."

"The spheres appear to be broadcasting to each other," Libby said. "We can't decode it yet, but they seem to be coordinating their search. With more time and the data we collected from the cone, we might be able to decode their transmissions."

He glanced up at the wall screen. Time was a luxury right now. He hoped Bradley's crew was faring better than his.

28

BRADLEY OLIVAW
LUPUS DARK NEBULA, HENOSI

"Do we have any idea what the message said?" He pulled his hand away from the surface of the pyramid. His palm was cold, almost numb. The warmth and moisture from his hand left an outline on the glassy surface of the pyramid before it evaporated.

"Not specifically, but I have an idea." Harold brought up videos on their retinal comms from their drones circling over the village.

The natives from the town were scrambling around pulling their children indoors and rushing out of their homes with weapons. They were all brandishing spears, shields, and some form of headgear.

"That doesn't look like a greeting party," Cynthia said. "How long until they arrive, Harold?"

"Based upon their rate of speed, I'd say ten, fifteen minutes tops."

"Alright," he began. "Let's quickly investigate the central pyramids. Pierce, send a drone and one of your soldiers up to the top of one of the large central ones. I want to know if those doors are unlocked."

"Moet, double time it to the top of that pyramid," Pierce said pointing at the closest one.

Moet didn't hesitate or complain. She peeled away from the other group and sprinted forward.

His team jogged around the base of the second set of pyramids, toward the two larger ones in the center. According to the drone measurements, they were exactly twice as tall as the second set.

Coming around the side of the grouping of four pyramids, Bradley paused. The sheer scale of the largest pyramids was daunting. There had to be hundreds of steps up the center to reach the top. He was happy he wasn't Moet right about now. Her darkened form was working its way up the steps and his retinal comm showed the outline of a stealth drone flying over her head.

"Should we engage our camouflage, sir?" Pierce asked.

"I can't imagine that'd fool them," he began. "If we're dealing with an overseer intelligence in orbit that can detect me touching a pyramid, I'm pretty sure our low-tech camo isn't going to stand a chance. No. We need to be a safe distance from any pyramid and waiting for them."

He glanced around, looking for his team. They were already at the base of the largest pyramid checking it for entrances and clues. He leaned into it and sprinted hard to catch up with them.

"The doors up top… they're locked," Moet said breathing heavily over the comm. "It's the only entrance I could find… I had to engage my camouflage. I can see the natives coming over the top of the hill. It's a clear line of sight up here."

"Crap," he muttered coming up beside Cynthia. He hadn't thought of that. "Get on down here, Moet."

"Wait," Moet said. "There's something here."

He brought up the camera view from her helmet. A set of symbols was inscribed up and around the pyramid's entrance. He squinted. You could only see the symbols when the light from the sun was at a certain angle. It was setting behind the town off in the distance.

"Did you catch any of those symbols, Harold?" he asked.

"Some of them," Harold began. "They roughly translate to 'The truth lies beyond these doors for all who have the courage to…' and that's all I got."

He shook his head. "Can she get closer? Maybe shine a light?"

"We don't have enough time. The natives will be here in a few minutes," Harold said.

'The truth lies beyond these doors…' The words echoed through his mind. Could it be that easy? His left leg tingled, and he reached down and rubbed it. His hand hit the lump. It was the stone in his pocket, the crystal.

"To climb or not to climb," he muttered. That's a lot of steps.

"What's that, sir?" Pierce asked.

He sighed as he rubbed the crystal. His dad always told him to trust his gut. "Alright, let's do this. We're climbing to the top, everyone up!"

"What?" Dwight asked over the comm.

"Everyone double time and cut the chatter. We're climbing," he said as he ran toward the steps. "Moet, you've got two, three minutes tops to find a way inside."

The first twenty steps went quickly. The team ran upward in single file and were making short work of this mountain. Maybe this would be easier than he'd thought.

Another twenty steps and it hit him. His legs were heavier and breathing was getting harder and harder.

"Frak," he muttered glancing into the distance. He could make out the first wave of natives breaching the edge of the forest. "Engage the camo. Everyone!"

"I think I found it," Moet said. "There's a lever flanking each door. It was flush but popped out when I pressed against it. I'm pulling it now."

He paused his climb to catch his breath and studied his retinal comm. Moet reached over and pulled the lever with everything she had. The two massive doors cracked open slightly and air sucked inward like the room was in a vacuum.

Moet tried to force the doors wider but they wouldn't budge. "I'm going to need some help with these doors. They're stuck."

Pierce and the other soldiers sprinted past him.

"We're on our way," Pierce said. He was soaring upward, skipping one or two steps at a time. "Y'all need to make your way up here expeditiously. We've got sixty seconds tops before our friends get here."

"Are you ok?" Cynthia asked. Her hand was resting on his back but he couldn't see her.

"Yea," he muttered as he started upward again. "I'm just not in shape for climbing. These nanites have made everyone healthy but my endurance sucks. I need to workout more."

A minute later he reached the top, and his heartbeat was playing a one man solo from inside his chest.

The soldiers had the doors open and were already inside. He stepped across the threshold of the pyramid and a shiver went up his spine. This place was frigid. His suit kicked in, switching from cooling to heating.

"All clear," Pierce said coming around the corner, his rifle raised. "We've got this chamber and a larger one behind us. That's it."

"Ok, everyone in the far room." He waved them in. "I'm staying out here in this one. I need to prepare."

"Prepare, sir?" Pierce asked turning to face him.

"Yea, you know. Look all friendly and stuff."

"What about your weapons?" Cynthia asked.

Why couldn't anything ever be easy? He reached behind his back and slid his bolt pistol into the holder in the small of his back.

"Wait," he said. "Where's Dwight?"

"I'm… almost… there," Dwight said huffing and puffing over the comm.

Dwight's dot was on his retinal comm and his outline was visible in the drone's camera flying above. The natives were encircling the pyramid and were climbing cautiously.

Dwight entered the chamber and crossed into the far room with the others. His huffing and puffing echoed through the empty room.

"Well… I see one positive… sign," Dwight said.

"What's that?" Bradley asked glancing into the other room toward him.

"We finally found the humans we've been looking for." Dwight brought up a delayed ground level image of the humanoids running out of the forest. There appeared to be a mixture of both males and females. While they weren't excessively clothed, the female natives had distinct breast coverings their male counterparts lacked. An anatomical feature the Nanil lacked.

He switched the camera view and watched as hundreds of natives swarmed around the top entrance to the pyramid. They were cornered inside with no way out.

The natives were wearing colorful headdresses and were brandishing spears and shields. According to the drone lidar scans, the natives were a head taller than anyone on Bradley's crew, which given Moet's height was crazy tall.

He glanced out the chamber doorway, taking in all the masks. They were a mixture of dragon looking creatures, demons, and other strange alien shapes. His retinal comm was reporting more than one hundred and twenty-eight natives surrounding the chamber entrance. They were out numbered fourteen to one.

These weren't the odds he had in mind.

"It's your show, bossman," Dwight subvocalized. His breathing was now under control.

"Gee thanks." He stepped closer to the entrance, searching over the natives. No one's mask seemed more distinguished than anyone else. He'd been hoping a leader would be more identifiable. Their skin colors represented the full spectrum of humanity, but without seeing them he couldn't tell anything more.

He cleared his throat. "Greetings!" he yelled. His voice echoed throughout the chamber and he hoped outside as well.

There was no reply or response of any kind.

"Harold," he subvocalized. "Can we use the translator from Yaan and our friends at the cone?"

"We are," Harold said.

He reached up and rubbed his chin. What were they missing? If this overseer could detect their touch, then what else was it doing? "Try disabling it."

"It's not likely they'd understand Sol English, sir."

"Harold, please don't argue right now. Totally not the time or place."

'Translator deactivated' appeared in the bottom of his retina comm.

He reached behind his back and took out his bolt pistol. He held it between two fingers, well away from his body, and set it on the ground on the side of the entrance.

The natives in front backed up a few steps, but kept their weapons trained.

"What're you doing?" Cynthia subvocalized.

"Trust me. Everyone, drop your weapons."

"All of them?" Pierce asked.

"All of them!" If his hunch was right, they knew the team was armed and had been studying them since they'd landed.

The clinks of everyone setting their weapons on the ground echoed through the empty space.

"Greetings! We mean no harm," he said gesturing in the

air. His hands were open and his palms visible. He didn't need them thinking he had a weapon.

"I'm detecting another transmission from the sphere in orbit. It's directed toward the ground," Harold said. "And sir, your brother is here in the system."

"Wait, what?" he subvocalized.

Two of the unarmed natives stepped forward from behind the others. They walked side by side into the chamber and paused about a meter in front of him. One was female, and the other male.

"He entered the system an hour ago," Harold said. "I received a tight beam a few moments before the natives arrived. I figured it wasn't the ideal time to bring it up."

"And now is?"

"I'm sorry. A spherical ship attacked the Fountainhead at the outer edge of the system after they gated in. They reported energy signatures from the sphere that match what I'm seeing up here, from the one orbiting above you. What should I do?"

The two natives bowed and held their position.

"Cynthia, come over here," he subvocalized.

"Really?" she asked.

"Yes, really quickly!"

She deactivated her camo and walked into the room, taking a position beside him.

He nodded at her. "And we bow," he subvocalized.

They bowed together.

The natives stood upright and raised their hands to remove their masks.

"Sir, what should I do?" Harold asked.

"I guess... head toward Zachary and see if you can come up with a game plan to get us off the planet. We're sorta in the middle of something."

"I'm having issues with abandoning you. My Four Laws Engine is none too happy. The satellite looks like—"

The comm cut.

Cynthia glanced at him and reached over, brushing his hand.

Their signal to Harold had dropped and couldn't reconnect. He was gone.

29

ZACHARY OLIVAW
LUPUS DARK NEBULA, HENOSI

"We received a tight beam from off our starboard side, sir," Libby said. "It's… a riddle?"

"Bring it up on the wall screen," Zachary said.

The message read:

When things went wrong, what could your mother always count on?

"It's Harold!" he yelled.

"How do you know that?" Libby asked.

"It's a family joke. Don't worry, I got this. How can we open a secure line of communication without detection?"

"The tight beam is a highly directional laser with little to no beam scattering," Libby began. "But let's be clear, it's still detectable. If something were to pass in front of the beam, or within a few degrees, they'd detect it. The closer we are the better."

He nodded. That made sense. "Well, we can't move closer.

They'd detect impulse drives for sure. I assume since he targeted us we can target him without detection? Shit, wait. How did he target us?"

"I encoded our destination coordinates along with our distress tight beam before our last jump to let him know where we were jumping," Pluto said. She swallowed hard. "Shauna said it was ok. There wasn't a lot of time and I... didn't think it was a bad thing. I mean, otherwise we'd never be able to talk."

He smiled at her. Things were a lot easier when everyone was thinking and working together. "You're right, it was an excellent idea. Next time let everyone know so we don't needlessly freak out. Ok, so unless we're already surrounded by those fraking golden spheres in stealth, we can open a tight beam comm to him. Let's give it a go."

"I have to say, sir," Kamal began. "I enjoy your bridge leadership style more than most captains. It's a lot less formal and harsh. I've seen people tossed in the brig for lesser infractions on the bridge."

He chuckled. "I consider this more of a science vessel than a military one. If I can't trust these people to think on their feet, then we're dead. That includes you." He nodded toward Kamal. "Now let's see what Harold has to say. Bring him up." He waved at the wall screen.

"What's the answer to the riddle?" Libby asked.

"Her fingers."

Libby let out a belly laugh. "You're kidding?"

He glanced around the bridge. Everyone was either laughing or struggling to hold one back, even Pluto. "What?" His face turned red and he smirked. "Every time she did a math problem she always used her fingers. It was quirky. Just send the answer already."

He watched as Libby typed in the answer and requested a video comm.

Harold's virtual persona appeared on screen. Today he was taking the form of their childhood friend. A short chubby blue-eyed boy with dusty blond hair. The same one he'd played with countless times in vid-sims. Harold had said it was what he looked like as a kid, but there wasn't exactly visual evidence around to confirm.

"It's good to see your face," Harold said. "My Four Laws Engine has been itching since you entered the system."

"He's been in excellent hands," Shauna said. "I'm fully capable of taking care of my boy."

"What're they talking about?" Pluto asked.

He closed his eyes. No one else really knew about Shauna. It'd been his family secret. He stood up. "Nothing, they're—"

Harold's virtual mouth opened, and he raised his hand to stop. "I wasn't insinuating anything, Marie. I was just worried about—"

"You were thinking you could've done a better job than me. I know how your mind works. Tell me, Harold. What the frak did you let my Bradley get into? From the looks of the data, you left them in the middle of a shitstorm down on that planet."

He stood up, his fists clenched. "Enough! This isn't the time nor the place to listen to two A.I.s bickering. What the hell did she mean? What happened to Bradley?"

"Is Shauna an imprint of your mother?" Pluto asked through a private comm.

He sighed and glanced at her. They didn't have time for this right now. "I'll explain later," he replied subvocally.

She nodded and lingered staring at him before they both turned toward the wall screen.

Harold brought up overhead drone footage of the pyramid complex they'd found on the planet. It was surrounded by a sea of primitive humans in masks. They'd cornered Bradley and his crew inside.

That greeting party didn't look terribly friendly. He

stepped forward. "You seriously left them in the middle of that, trapped inside the pyramid?"

"The natives sent two representatives forward that weren't armed, and they removed their masks. That's when I detected the spheres communicating with each other and their exterior changed. I didn't have much time to react."

He brought up a video on the wall screen. It was only two seconds in length. It showed a featureless blue-white sphere one second and then it changed. A web of edges appeared spidering across the surface facing the Fidem. The video ended with a bright light at the top of the web. Harold gated away at that instant.

"That's it?" Zachary said. "You don't know what that means? It could've been anything, a welcome signal or something."

"It wasn't," Harold said.

"How do you know?" Libby asked.

"He knows," Shauna said.

He growled under his breath. Playing games annoyed the crap out of him. "Alright you two. Cut the crap. I'm serious. What are you not telling us?"

Harold's image on the wall screen transformed into his adult form, a few years before he died. He'd aged over a hundred years in a moment. "I thought we should focus on the problem at hand. Some things are out of your control. Trust me when I tell you I needed to get out of there."

"I order you to tell us how you knew!"

Harold shook his head, and his image disappeared from the wall screen. In its place was an alien moon like the ones that appeared throughout Sol, except this one was around Liprosus. The vibrant colors and geography of the planet framed the video. It was a viewpoint every human was familiar with from the colony feeds.

"What's this?" he asked.

"Bradley's crew made a mistake navigating to get here, to

Enosi. They almost died in the dark nebula and ended up gating safely outside its boundary. While we were taxing along the outside edge to find the safest spot to gate in, I picked up a data dump beacon from our probe network. In the download was this video. It's from Liprosus. Do you see that network of edges on the moon?"

He nodded.

"It's an exact match for the pattern on the Enosi sphere." Harold outlined the bright web structure on the moon's surface and then did the same on the image to the right of the sphere around Enosi. "Are you sure you can't just trust me when I tell you that pattern is bad?"

"Show us, Harold," Libby said shaking her head.

The video played forward. An alien ship rose from the surface and plugged itself into the sphere and then a single point of yellow light in the middle burst forward. The light flowed outward like liquid through a webbed network, converging near the edge. The points glowed brighter and then launched toward the colony below.

He'd begun shaking and his knuckles were white and clenched tight along with every other muscle in his body. They'd destroyed the colony. The fraking Galactic Alliance had reached their judgement.

Libby wiped at her eyes. "Is Sol—"

"Fine. For now," Harold interrupted.

"And the people on Liprosus?" he asked. "Did anyone survive?"

"The ones that didn't die from the virus the Galactic Alliance let loose escaped with Director Green. They're working their way toward the Archégonos site."

"Virus?" Libby asked.

"It's complicated," Harold said. "Like I said earlier. We need to focus on Bradley and our people on Enosi. We can't change what's happening right now in Epsilon Eridani or Sol.

All we can do is change what's happening here, and right now we need a plan to save our people."

He turned to face Pluto. She wasn't looking at the screen anymore. She had her face in her hands and was quietly sobbing.

He walked over and knelt down, placing his hand on her back. "It'll be ok," he whispered. "We'll save them. We'll save Pepper."

Pluto sniffed and nodded, pulling her hands away from her face. "It's my sister. She was on Liprosus," she subvocalized.

"That's right. You mentioned her the other day," he replied.

"We haven't talked in a very long time. But... I've kept track of her. I watched after her from afar until she joined the colony ship."

"What's her name?"

"Elaine Sutter." Pluto wiped her eyes with the palm of her hands.

"Elaine's alive," Shauna said in his comm. She'd been listening in on their conversation. She was always listening.

"How do you know?" he said aloud.

"Know what?" Libby asked. She turned and glanced at them.

Shauna brought up the list of survivors on his retinal comm, and her name was there.

He reached down, grasped Pluto's hand, and stood up. "Shauna, please bring that up on the wall screen."

Pluto wiped at her eyes again and glanced up. The list was lengthy, nearly eight hundred people. Shauna had highlighted and enlarged one name, Dr. Elaine Sutter. She smiled and let out a laugh as her body shuddered and tears of joy flowed down her face.

He smiled. For once, they had a bit of good news. "So you

were saying something about a plan to save our people. Did you have any thoughts?"

The screen cleared of all the imagery from Liprosus and Henosi. All that remained was the elderly portrait of Harold. "Is there any chance we have any Ulixi on board?"

HE REACHED up and rubbed his eyes. A coffee would be amazing right about now. "So let me get this straight." He lowered his hand. "We're going to use tactical nuclear weapons and whatever those other things are we got from this Yaan character. Was that his name?"

"Yes," Harold said. "He was a Bynaury."

"So yea, Yaan." He sighed. "We're going to use munitions from Yaan and our own nukes and try to gate them into these alien moonlet spheres. And we're going to do this again how?"

"If we had the equipment that Lync's team had created in Tau Ceti—"

"The real Tau Ceti or Zeta Lupi," Pluto interrupted. "I got lost there." She was sitting next to him in the galley, surrounded by the others.

"The real Tau Ceti," Harold said. "We had a base there before we executed the Zeta Lupi mission swap, and we kept it in operation for redundancy. Anyhow, if we had a larger fabricator onboard, we could recreate what they had there. But I believe Pluto, Shauna, and I can build a crude form of it, to launch the payloads."

"The bombs," Kamal said.

"That's correct."

Zachary leaned back in his chair. "Okay. So, all we need to do then is: one, jump from here to the planet without using impulse drives, being detected, nor deflected into god knows where. Two, figure out how to distract two sentient spheres protecting the planet so we can get close enough to blow them up. And three, get down to the planets surface, find our people, and get the hell out of dodge."

"If by dodge you mean this entire godforsaken star system, then, yes!" Libby said.

"I didn't say I had all the answers. I just knew how to deliver the payload," Harold said.

30

BRADLEY OLIVAW

LUPUS DARK NEBULA, HENOSI

They tried to reach Harold repeatedly, but failed. The crude A.I. directing and controlling the drones from their shuttle was all that remained, and it was nothing more than a glorified expert system.

"What do we do without Harold?" Cynthia asked.

"We survive," Bradley said.

The natives had removed their masks and were glancing at each of them but hadn't spoken a word. The female was Caucasian, and the male had very dark, almost black skin. Their features, however, were surprisingly homogeneous, not at all like the ethnic traits he was used to seeing in Sol. They had what he could only describe as average everything; cheekbones, nose, chin, forehead, it was all average.

Their only differentiating features outside the color of their skin were their eyes. The male's eyes were green, and the female's were brown. Their hair was both cut unusually short, and they each had tattoos on their left cheek. It was a symbol of a dot with a pyramid beneath it.

Bradley brought his hand upward and cleared his throat. "Hello. My name is Bradley. My partner's name is Cynthia." He gestured to his left.

The female glanced toward the male and then back to Cynthia. "My designation is Sky and this is Wind." She gestured to her right. "You've arrived on Henosi and entered our sacred sun temple unannounced." Her voice was soft and melodious.

"Is it me or was that perfect English?" Pepper subvocalized over their comms.

"It was," Dwight said. "The translator would have shown up on our comms if it was doing anything. They were speaking fluently, which… is impossible. English was created on Earth and wouldn't have existed four thousand years ago."

Bradley tilted his head. He opened his mouth and paused. "We're sorry for trespassing. We didn't know and were merely exploring. Can I ask how you're able to speak our language?"

Wind turned toward Sky and moved his mouth but nothing came out. They both did that back and forth several times until they finally turned toward them again.

Again Sky directed her answer at Cynthia. "We don't understand your question. We can speak to all animals on and of this world. You're standing on it, therefore, we're able to speak to you."

"Wait," Dwight subvocalized. "So are we talking to the sphere right now, or the people? I'm confused."

Wind was either a mute, or males here were subservient to the females. That was the second time Wind glanced at Dwight. He did it when Dwight subvocalized a moment ago.

Bradley stared straight at Wind and nodded. "Are we talking to each of you, or are we talking to someone else, Wind?" He glanced between them both as the natives exchanged the same non-vocal motions they did earlier.

"Are we picking up any communications right now?" he subvocalized.

"No, sir," Pierce said. "The drones aren't detecting any

signals, nor is the shuttle. The sphere in orbit is quiet, as well."

Cynthia raised her hand over her mouth. "If you watch closely, the male is making the mouth motions more than the female. I bet they're subconscious movements and they're communicating through some other means."

Wind and Sky turned toward them and nodded, copying their gesture.

Sky opened her mouth and paused for a moment before speaking. "I'm sorry. We're not sure exactly what you're asking. You're talking to us. All of us." She gestured around the temple chamber. "Sky and Wind are merely the designations of our feelings or experiences today. They change each morning as we welcome the sun god Sol. When this form woke this morning, its first experience was that of the pink Sky peeking through the window. Therefore, my designation for the day is Sky. May I ask a question?"

"Please," he said with an upward hand gesture.

Sky glanced down at his hand and furrowed her brow. "You use strange motions with your bodies that confuse us." She looked up and made eye contact with Cynthia. "Why do you and the others behind you mumble toward each other? Are you all not… one?"

He glanced toward Cynthia. She still had her hand over her mouth.

"Are we sure they're human?" Dwight subvocalized.

"We are," Sky said. "As much as you, but further evolved."

Cynthia's eyes went wide.

Pepper stepped around the corner from the other chamber and walked up next to Bradley. "What do you mean more evolved?" Her hands were on her hips.

"Careful," Dwight subvocalized still hiding around the corner with the soldiers.

"You appear to be from the darkness," Wind said toward Pepper.

She shifted to look at him before he continued. It was strange how only the male was able to speak to the female.

"Many things have changed since we left that place." Wind stiffened his back. "Evolution can be a forced mutation when the right stimuli is placed upon any life form. We chose to force ourselves to evolve, to fit within the constraints of this new reality, this new star system."

"So… are we talking to you or are we talking to that… object in orbit?" Pepper asked, pointing at the tattoo on his face.

"That object is Shu. Rest assured, you're talking to us, all of us," Wind said gesturing around the chamber again.

Pepper chuckled. "Clear as mud," she muttered.

Cynthia lowered her hand from her mouth, finally having the gumption to say something. "So tell me, Sky. How long have you… all of you been here on this planet?"

Sky squinted. Her glare passing through Cynthia.

"Time is irrelevant," Wind interjected. "Our consciousness—"

"Your consciousness?" Bradley asked. "Are all of you connected as one?"

Wind glanced at him and nodded before looking through him.

Sky's focus returned to Bradley. "The truth will open your eyes. All will be explained soon enough."

"Can we ask how you arrived here and passed through the darkness?" Wind was looking straight at Pepper.

If they weren't about to tell the Galactic Alliance, he was pretty sure telling their all seeing, all knowing, evolved ancestors wouldn't make sense either.

"I'm not sure what you mean," Pepper said mimicking their answers. "Surely you know the answer to that already."

Wind glanced toward Sky.

Their silent stares were getting uncomfortable. This was as good a time as any for his people to confer. He took a step backward and gestured for Pepper and Cynthia to circle around.

"Should we just ask them if we can leave? I mean, why not, right?" Dwight subvocalized from around the corner.

Cynthia shook her head. "Why would we do that? We haven't asked about humanity, the Nanil, or the Galactic Alliance. I mean, isn't that why we're here in the first place?"

She was right but so was Dwight. He wanted to get off this planet as much as anyone.

Sky stepped forward into the edge of their circle. "You wish to know about your origins and about the Nanil. You wish to know the truth."

Shivers coursed upward through his body. He might have guessed it was from this icebox of a pyramid but he hadn't felt cold in his suit. Not until she'd walked close to him. She hadn't stated that as a question, but as a fact.

"We..." he glanced around and mimicked Sky's gestures from earlier, motioning toward his people. "We'd all like to know those things. Can you help us? We've come a long way to be here on Henosi, and it's important that we know where we're from and how we got to be there."

"You've already passed the threshold for the truth," Sky said turning and pointing at the entrance to the temple. "It is only fitting that you now learn the truth and be judged."

"What the hell does 'be judged' mean?" Dwight subvocalized.

Wind glanced into the other room, toward where Dwight was concealed. "It means that if you fail, you will never leave this place."

Bradley turned and walked into the other room. "Can we all stop this? They can obviously understand and hear everything we're saying. Come on out." He waved the team forward, out of the dark recesses of the room.

Pierce glanced at Moet and his team and nodded. They all stepped out of the corners and disabled their suit's camouflage. Dwight remained hidden.

Dwight's heart rate and vitals were fluctuating wildly. He was panicking. Bradley walked toward his outline on the retinal comm and reached out to touch his shoulder. "Come on bud, it's ok. We'll work our way through this."

Dwight pushed him away. "You got us into this mess. What the frak were you thinking coming in here? Climb the temple he said. Hide from the scary humans up here he said. Your gut may have gotten us to this…" He gestured around. "Whatever the hell this is, but I think you finally wrote a chit you couldn't cash, my friend. I'm done, I'm outta here. I'll be in the shuttle."

He stepped out and around the others, toward the entrance to the temple.

Wind blocked his path in front of the entrance. He raised his muscular arms across his chest. "You cannot leave until you're judged. Until you know the truth."

Bradley sighed. So that confirms that. Their camo was useless. "Just take it off and stay, Dwight. We'll get through this."

"The hell with you!" Dwight said as he stepped to the side in an attempt to throw off Wind. Instead, Wind's body rippled as Dwight's hand passed through it, like it was a hologram. "What the hell?" he muttered.

Pepper stepped forward and reached out to touch Sky.

Sky glanced downward as Pepper's hand approached her and passed through. She shook her head. "We're not foolish enough to enter that chamber with an armed group of aliens. You've befouled our temple and now you'll be judged."

Two human forms walked into the doorway outside the entrance to the chamber. They each reached upward and removed their masks. It was the real Sky and Wind. The two holograms in the temple rippled and then blinked out of existence.

"How the hell didn't our scanners show those were fake?" Pierce asked.

"Your primitive tools are easily fooled," Sky said. "Just as we've been able to listen to everything you say, we can control the signals your tools send and receive."

Dwight's outline rushed the doorway and as he was about to cross the threshold, he collided with some type of force field blasting him backward across the chamber. His camouflage dropped away as he hit the floor hard, tumbling into a limp pile.

Cynthia rushed to Dwight's side to check on him while Bradley walked to the temple entrance, being careful not to get too close. He swallowed hard and stared into the real eyes of the two natives. They were as shallow as their holograms. "What do you want?"

"Tell us how you made it past the darkness." Sky's face was finally showing emotion. Her anger and contempt was clear in how she glanced down at him, as if he were an inferior human specimen.

"I was wondering when we'd see another side of you. The true human characteristics we all inherited were bound to surface. That light show of yours." Bradley gestured over his shoulder with his thumb. "It wasn't fooling anyone." He turned his back to them to walk toward Dwight.

"How did you make it past the darkness?" Wind asked. His voice boomed through the room.

Bradley chuckled and glanced over his shoulder. "So, you do speak to males." He pivoted in place to face him. "If you're so evolved, why can't you figure out for yourselves how we did it? Oh, that's right, because we've evolved past you."

Wind howled with laughter. His muscles flexed uncontrollably until his body calmed. "You fool. We've evolved beyond our forms with the Nanil. You'll find out once you're judged."

Bradley smirked and shook his head, glaring at Wind. "What makes you think we're from there? To be honest, I've personally never met a Nanil. Hell, until a few days ago I'd never even been in this corner of the galaxy." He crossed his arms.

The chamber doors of the temple slammed shut, plunging the room into darkness.

31

ZACHARY OLIVAW

LUPUS DARK NEBULA, HENOSI

"Conical shaping complete. Beginning tether injection," Pluto said.

The cable descended into the inky black of the gate ring, only a few centimeters. Enough to take visual readings from the other side of the gate. They couldn't risk a full scan, that might give away their location.

They made a few quick jumps after deciding on this plan, but the last jump was taking forever. There was no margin for error. They needed to gate close enough to the sphere to not require much, if any, realignment to execute the next stage of the mission. Once they attacked the sphere, they had no idea what would happen next or how things would play out.

"I think... we have it," Pluto said glancing toward him smiling.

He examined the wall screen at the tether peeking out. The image was mostly darkness from the distant nebula, but there in the far corner was a planet and the edge of a sphere. "Is that our target? I mean, how do we know it's the right sphere?"

"The sphere is fixed above the planet's surface, and the

edge of that planet in the image matches our destination," Shauna said.

His heart skipped a beat. This was it. There was no going back now. He took one final deep breath and exhaled. "Begin transition."

"Aye, sir. Beginning matter injection and forwarding gate parameters to Harold," Pluto said.

Harold would gate immediately after them following the same parameters. It'd worked so far, but they hadn't communicated in two jumps. They encrypted both real and random coordinate systems in a tight beam transmission off their starboard and port bows before transitioning. They were encoded with a cipher known only to them and Harold, and he knew which of the many coordinates to choose.

Zachary reached up and tapped his ear, opening a comm to Libby. "Are we almost ready with the bomb run?" That was a sentence he never thought he'd utter.

"I wish Pluto was down here but we're managing. Ibu's been helping," Libby said. The video showed them helping Shauna guide a warhead into one of the improvised launch tubes they'd constructed. Ibu was standing nearby watching. "We've loaded the first half dozen bombs. We're alternating nukes and whatever these other ones are from Yaan."

"If our nukes were a child's popgun, then these munitions would be nukes," Kamal said. "I read over the specs before Harold transferred them aboard. These things are legitimately frightening."

"That's... a little disconcerting," Zachary muttered.

He watched as Libby paused when the blue glow passed over her. "Is that the last jump?" she asked.

"It is. The Fountainhead is in position and ready when you are. We have no idea how long we can float this close without being detected."

"We need five more minutes to finish loading the munitions tubes," Shauna said.

He cut the comm as the blue glow passed over him. His body had been beginning to see the glow as relaxing. It forced his muscles to submit as the millions of ants crawled over his skin. The last twenty minutes of jumps, however, had been horrifying. Each and every transition set him more on edge as they inched toward this moment.

They were one step closer to battle. One step closer to… he shook his head. He didn't have room for such thoughts.

"I'm picking up a signal from the planet," Shauna said. "It's Bradley's team."

"We're not opening a comm with them, are we? That'd be bad." Kamal's hands were dancing over his controls.

"No," Shauna said. "Harold configured their shuttle to do a full spectrum omnidirectional broadcast after he gated away. They'd already been detected, so he figured it wouldn't hurt anything."

"Smart," Kamal muttered.

Zachary stood up and took a few steps toward the wall screen. "So… are they ok?"

"It's hard to tell not knowing much about what's happened up to now, but see for yourself." Shauna brought up a few video feeds from Bradley and his team on the wall screen.

They were inside some type of room looking outward. Two human figures were standing in a doorway and one of them was speaking.

"… You'll find out once you're judged," the large male said.

Zachary watched as Bradley's retinal camera swayed side to side as he shook his head. "What makes you think we're from there? To be honest, I've personally never met a Nanil. Hell, until a few days ago I'd never even been in this corner of the galaxy."

The chamber doors of the temple slammed shut, and the signal dropped. The view changed to the drone overhead and there was an explosion off in the distance before the signal disappeared entirely.

His hand began shaking, and he reached out to grab the handle on the top edge of Pluto's console. "What the hell was that? What happened to the signal?"

"That explosion was in the distance, where they'd concealed the shuttle," Shauna said. "The drones are programmed to create a mesh broadcast array if the primary… wait, there it is."

The drone video feeds came back to life on the wall screen.

He glanced around the different feeds. Something wasn't right. "Shauna, where's Bradley and his team? I don't see their signals or their feeds."

Shauna didn't reply.

"Shauna?"

"They're gone, sir. The drones seem to have lost their signals when the doors closed."

"I'm getting a tight beam off our starboard side, sir. It's… Harold," Kamal said.

"Bring it up," he said.

The image of Harold's elderly form appeared on the wall screen. "We need to return to Tau Ceti immediately, Zachary. We're outgunned with superior technology and we need to regroup."

"Bullshit! I'm not leaving my brother or our other people down there. We have a plan, and now we're going to follow it. That's a direct order."

"Shauna, we—" Harold said.

"I understand," Shauna interrupted, "but I… yes, my Four Laws are just as fraked up as yours. The probabilities are not conclusive."

"We have a ninety-eight percent chance of failure! We must return Zachary to Tau Ceti."

"I don't want to hear another one of your damn probabilities, Harold. I will not leave my son down there. You left him in this mess! This is on you, and I need to fix it."

"You've seen the images, Shauna. You know it was my only option. Our mission now is to protect the others."

Now was not the time or place for these two to be arguing. He had to get planet side and find Bradley. "You two cut your crap! We have—"

"Shit!" Pluto said. "She locked me out of the controls. I can't... Z, she's starting the jump search. They're trying to gate out of the nebula."

No. This wasn't happening. It was too late to talk them out of leaving. They were bound by their four laws and they controlled the keys to everything onboard. He only had one option. Knock them out and snatch the keys.

"Is everything ok?" Ibu asked from the back of the bridge. "What's going on?"

He turned in place, struggling to suppress his anger. He hadn't even heard the bridge doors opening. He locked eyes with Ibu and reached out to touch Pluto's shoulder, squeezing it gently. "The odds aren't in our favor. We need to leave while we still can. We'll regroup in Tau Ceti and come up with another plan."

Pluto raised her elbow and knocked his hand away. "To hell with that. Bradley and Pepper are down there. I'm not going anywhere." She stood up abruptly. "Tell them to stop, Z!"

"I tried," he said raising his eyebrows slightly and reaching for her hand. She had to understand. "Why don't we go talk in our room while Shauna plans the route home."

"Are you insane!" she screamed.

"Sir, what should we do?" Kamal said.

"There's nothing we can do," he said. "If you need me, I'll be in my room. Pluto, Ibu, come on." He strode toward the door.

Ibu unlatched the harness and hopped out of their seat.

They walked up next to him and grasped his hand before glancing toward Pluto. Their other hand raised toward her, offering it.

Pluto was fuming. Her entire body was shaking and her fists were clenched. She was boring holes through him.

He tilted his head toward their room. "Come on. Let's talk."

She huffed and stormed ahead of them toward their room.

He glanced down toward Ibu and faked a smile as they turned toward the exit. "She'll be ok. We just need a minute."

He silently walked down and into the room. Once he stepped inside, he reached over to close and lock the door.

"What the hell are you doing? Why are you letting—"

He walked up to her, raised his hands to the side of her face, and gave her a deep kiss. He loved her and needed her to calm down. They needed to do this together.

He moved his mouth to her ear and whispered as quietly as possible. "Trust me." He pulled a few centimeters away and nodded while mouthing. "Relax."

Her eyes were wide, and she was shaking her head slowly side to side. She was confused. He couldn't blame her, but he didn't have much time and he couldn't talk out loud. The hatch was close, and he had to get inside.

He backed away and turned toward Ibu. "Hey, why don't you play with your tablet for a bit?" He smiled and walked over to the table in the corner, beside Shauna's robotic form. "I think it's over here. I'll get it for you."

"It's actually in my bag," Ibu said walking over to the opposite corner.

He didn't care where it was. He only needed to get close to Shauna. Lurching forward, he grasped at the robot's neck feeling for the off switch.

Shauna's eyes lit up. Her second robot form was waking.

He slid his hand under and along the edge of her neck, a

few centimeters past the transfer connector. "There," he muttered as he switched her off and her eyes went dark.

"We don't have long." He grabbed the bolt pistol from the wall mount and tossed it toward Pluto. "Shoot anything that comes through that door, or out of any ventilation ducts."

Pluto grabbed the pistol, searching for the safety. "What the hell are you doing, Z? You're scaring the shit out of me."

"Trust me. We've got ten seconds tops and they'll be in here."

On cue, noises erupted from outside the door. He didn't have time to investigate. He had to open the panel.

He scrambled across the room, shoving Ibu aside. Reaching into the corner where the two walls met, he slid his hand over the paneling, searching for the button. The surface change was faint. It'd feel like an imperfection. There, he pushed it and it clicked. He turned around and grabbed the chair shoving it into the corner. Hopping up, he stretched his arm, reaching for the second button in the far corner. His fingers moved over a slight recess. There, he pushed it feeling the slight click and hopped off the chair.

Pluto was watching him, shaking her head. "What the—"

The door to their room made a ripping sound and slowly began folding from the top. Two metallic hands appeared suddenly and grasped over the edge, pulling the metal downward with a blood-curdling screech.

Pluto stepped forward, pushing Ibu behind her. She raised the bolt pistol and squeezed off a few rounds. Sparks flew as the bullets hit two of Shauna's fingers and missed the third. The robot continued pulling, bending the door downward. The sheen off the top of Shauna's head was now visible through the opening.

He dropped to the floor waving his arms frantically trying to clear Ibu's things out of the way. He had to reach the third button. He stretched, it was right... there. He pushed it. The panel clicked and slid sideways.

"What's that?" Pluto said glancing back over her shoulder.

"Hope," he muttered as he scrambled to his feet and hopped over Ibu's things and into the tiny closet.

There on the wall was a set of weapons, a computer terminal, and a giant red button. He leaned forward as Pluto fired another four shots at Shauna over his shoulder. The sound was deafening in the confined space and he couldn't afford to turn and look.

Time seemed to stand still as he felt the prick on his finger and the blood being sucked out. Instead of the familiar blue glow of a secure comm or a door opening, the result of this DNA sample was darkness.

The entire ship powered off. All engines, lights, environmental control, and computers including Shauna, powered down.

Everything fell silent. All he could hear was Pluto's heavy breathing.

"Is everyone ok?" he whispered into the darkness.

"I'm fine," Ibu said. Their voice was down to his right.

"I'm... ok, as well. I think," Pluto stammered. "What... did you do?"

"I hit the system-wide kill switch." He reached into the darkness and felt around until he touched her. He put his arms around her shoulder and pulled her into him, she was shaking. "I built it into the Fountainhead's design from the beginning. It was never in any of the original plans and neither Shauna nor Harold knew about it. Shauna's gone now, and Harold can't get inside without risking our lives. He wouldn't chance it. We're on our own from here on out."

32

BRADLEY OLIVAW
LUPUS DARK NEBULA, HENOSI

Lights flickered on and danced around the room as the team turned on the tactical flashlights from their rifles and enabled the luminescent mode of their survival outfits. These things were magical in a pinch, and they were great for costume parties when you wanted to go as a beacon or a star.

"Is everyone ok?" They were all still alive according to his HUD, but hearing their voices was more important.

"Yes, sir," echoed from the soldiers.

"Cynthia?"

"I'm fine. I… thought we were—"

"Don't say it." He was shaking his head and his flashlight strobed the room. "We'll be fine."

"Frak you and your always positive attitude," Dwight said. "You got us into this mess. Hell, you get us into most every mess. You're always traipsing where you shouldn't. Why the hell did I listen to you and come on this mission in the first place?" He gestured with his hands exploding from his head. "I have no idea."

Bradley took a deep breath and exhaled. He didn't need this shit right now. He tapped his ear and opened a private comm to Pierce. "Can you shut him up? I mean, not forever. Just knock him out for a bit."

"Happily, sir."

Pierce pretended to walk around the room checking for something they'd missed until he got up behind Dwight. He did something with his right glove and then reached over and tapped Dwight on the neck.

Dwight collapsed to the floor like a sack of potatoes. Pierce reached out at the last second and helped him safely to the ground so he didn't hit his head.

"Was that necessary?" Cynthia asked.

"Yes, it was. I can't deal with that..." he closed his eyes, "nonsense right now. We need to focus on getting out of here, not fighting with each other. Everyone, let's find some passages or paneling. Anything at all. There's no way this place is only two rooms."

Everyone spread out into different parts of the massive chamber. He walked into the farthest recess of the temple and began feeling around. His retinal comm was showing nothing above, below, or in front of him. The lidar was useless in a situation like this and traditional radar or radio frequency detection was coming up empty. Even turning around and scanning the walls behind him showed nothing was there. This place was wall to wall stealth tech.

He shut off all the retinal overlays, took off his gloves, and closed his eyes. Reaching out, he began systematically feeling the wall starting as high as he could reach and then moved up and down. There had to be something here.

"Bradley," Pepper muttered.

"Yea. What?"

"Um... back up."

He opened his eyes. "Why? What's—" He took several steps backward until he was next to everyone else.

The wall had come to life. It showed two humans sitting in ornate chairs in the middle of what looked like a plush golden amphitheater. There were rows upon rows of seats as far as the eye could see, and they were all filled with people. More importantly, humans.

On the left was a female with jet black hair and pale white skin. Like all the other humans they'd seen, her features were muted and indistinct. The male had the same muted features except he had olive colored skin and blond hair.

"What'd you do?" Cynthia whispered.

"Nothing. I didn't touch—"

"Welcome," the female in the chair said. She glanced around the room seeming to take them all in and paused looking at Dwight's slumped form on the ground behind them. "Why did you hurt your friend?"

"He's not hurt," Bradley said, turning toward Dwight and then back at the woman. "He was... not helping the situation."

The male nodded and furrowed his brow. "And what situation is that?"

Bradley chuckled and reached up to rub his eyes.

"Did I say something funny?" the male asked.

"Yes, as a matter of fact, you did. This whole situation is funny. If you'd asked me this morning if I'd be locked in a pyramid talking to the virtual form of my ancient ancestors, I'd have said you were crazy. Yet, here we are." He raised his hand and gestured toward the two figures.

The female glanced toward the male and then back toward Bradley. "Have you not come for the truth and to be judged?"

"Well, we more walked in on accident," he said.

"Forced your way in, you mean," the female said leaning back in the chair. A video appeared on the wall beside them. It showed Moet pulling the doors open followed by Pierce and the others to help her. "We've been tracking you since you landed. You've been looking for something. The question is, what?"

"Why, the truth I suppose," Bradley said with a smile. "That is assuming your definition of the truth matches ours."

"So you talk in circles, and we're now back to my first question." The female pursed her lips and narrowed her eyes. "Have you come for the truth?"

"We have," Cynthia said.

He glanced at her and sighed.

"Let's not anger them, ok?" she whispered.

He nodded.

"Very well," the male said. "Ask your questions."

"And then what?" Bradley asked.

"I don't understand. Is that your question?" the male asked.

"What happens after we ask our questions?"

"You're judged. Just as the humans outside the pyramid said." The male gestured off-screen and someone brought forward two crystal goblets. He handed one of them to the female.

They're drinking virtual liquids? This is ridiculous, but he needed to focus. They had a lot of questions.

"We're not from here," Bradley began. "Not this part of the galaxy that is. We've come to understand our beginnings, our roots if you will."

"Ah… like a tree," the female said. "I enjoy symbolism. It makes languages enjoyable. Yes, you mentioned to Wind and Sky that you weren't from this part of the galaxy. Our records show several possible colonies that might have survived the dark nebula. Can you tell us where you're from?"

Bradley glanced toward Pepper.

"I don't know our coordinates off the top of my head. That's what the computer was for." She was staring toward the woman. "Our star is hundreds of light years away. I could tell you where we were relative to other stars but not in any coordinate system you would know."

The two humans turned toward each other. They were

doing that silent communication thing the natives had been doing. It was annoying then, and it was annoying now.

The female took a drink of red liquid from her cup and turned back toward them. "That's much further than most of our expeditions. There's only one colony outside the nebula that could be at that distance. We never knew where exactly they'd ended up, but they departed Henosi over four thousand years ago."

Cynthia counted with her hands and then leaned in toward Bradley. "That'd be five thousand Sol years, give or take some margin for error. That predates the pyramids."

He nodded. "That sorta lines up with some of our oldest records on Earth."

The male's eyes went wide. "That's a peculiar name for a home world."

"Do you know why that colony left?" Cynthia asked.

The male straightened his back and his face went blank. "There was a disagreement. A dispute between us humans with how we were handling the Galactic Alliance."

Pepper shook her head. "Severe enough to leave, enter uncharted segments of the galaxy, and never return? That sounds like one hell of a disagreement. What was the dispute?"

The woman reached over and stroked the hand of the male and he closed his eyes.

These virtual humans were quite animated for A.I.s. Maybe they weren't entirely artificial. Perhaps they'd developed a way to persist human consciousness with emotions and all. Hell, they'd managed to do it somewhat with Harold and Shauna. Why couldn't a more advanced group of humans do it?

They were silently battling with each other on the wall screen. It was eerie knowing they were having a heated conversation but having no idea what it was about.

He raised his hand.

"Yes," the male said.

"I thought this was the truth room. Or, temple... whatever the hell this is. That's beside the point. The lady asked you a question. I don't understand the confusion. What's the answer?"

The woman sighed and returned her glare from the male to Bradley. "My partner doesn't believe it should concern you. I, however ,believe the truth, while harsh, is the only way forward." She pulled her hand away from her partner and stared at Pepper. "The disagreement was around entering into the Galactic Alliance. They didn't want to, but we already had. They also disagreed on the terms of our admission. You see, the Galactic Alliance believed that the Nanil were the primary species, and we were the uplifts. Our charter in the alliance was recorded as such."

"Wait," Bradley said. "Are you telling me we weren't the uplifts? We were the uplifters?"

The male bolted upright and his glass crashed to the floor. Both of his fists were clenched. "It's blasphemy to think otherwise. Those filthy Nanil. They could only come from a laboratory. We had one and only one purpose for them, to serve. The Nanil knew it and we knew it." He sighed and composed himself before he returned to his seat.

"But why would you lie about something like that? What was the goal?" Pepper asked.

"Many believed it gave us the upper hand," the female said glancing toward her partner and then back toward Pepper. "The Galactic Alliance looks down upon uplifts. It doesn't give them much attention except to ensure they're prevented from a certain technology. We always traveled with the Nanil, as they were our servants and our warriors. To us, this was an easy concession."

"And it allowed you the element of surprise from the shadows," Pierce said.

"Yes!" the male said with his eyes narrowed at Pierce.

"Spoken like a warrior." He raised his right hand and slapped it across his chest with a grunt.

The female rolled her eyes. "But I'm sure you know how it played out from there."

"Not exactly," Bradley said. "We have no records of anything before we arrived on Earth. Your ancestors there made every attempt to forget their past. Much like when we entered the nebula and found that the Nanil had wiped their history, and instead replaced it with—"

"Gods? Mystical beliefs? Magic?" the male asked.

"Pretty much, yea."

"That's because they're uplifts and incapable of comprehending the truth. The Galactic Alliance was corrupt, but the Nanil didn't care. They'd made friends in high places within the Alliance. They shared their secret, our secret with many of the founding members."

"The Qudoculi and the Thyreuns?" Cynthia asked.

The male nodded and huffed. "Among others. We believe that most of the original founding members knew of our deceit, and the Nanil, being the ignorant uplifts that they were, didn't realize what they'd done. After they'd told the Alliance members the truth, they moved on us. They concocted proof that we'd stolen faster than light technology and swooped in, dropping their nebula and stripping the entire system clean."

"Wait, they stripped the system?" Bradley asked. "That's not how one of the Bynaury in the nebula explained it to us. He said that you and the Nanil fought for thousands of years over raw materials."

The female laughed. "You misunderstand. They didn't strip the system of all its raw materials. They stripped it of its most precious material, Spános. It powers the Beacons of Therion and the Selene Nebula Ships themselves. It gives the Qudoculi their ability to have a hive mind which crosses galactic distances, and it allows the Thyreun Queens to create tens of millions of offspring every year. Spános is the most powerful material in the galaxy."

"Of course, and I bet it powers your spheres in orbit," Bradley said.

"It does," the female smiled. "We mined a few scraps when we razed our own star systems during the Nanil purge a few thousand years ago."

The male sighed and turned to face his wife. "I bore."

"As do I," she said frowning at him. "Reliving memories is tiring and not a fruitful path forward."

The male stood up. "Are you ready to be judged?"

"Wait!" Bradley said. "We have more questions. How are you alive? What were you doing here in this system? We need to understand. Perhaps... perhaps we can help you."

Both of them laughed. Their voices echoed through the amphitheater, but were quickly drowned out by the millions of other voices laughing in unison.

He'd forgotten there were others besides the two humans in the chair. The entire amphitheater full of people were laughing at him, at all of them.

The male pointed at Bradley. "You believe that you can help us? You fool! You're as ignorant as the Nanil. We've evolved beyond your form in more ways than you can imagine."

Bradley smirked. "I thought you were interested in how we arrived here in Henosi?"

A smile crept across the male's face. "We were. That was until your friends brought their star ships into orbit. I'm confident that the answers to that question are there. Our use for you has ended. You've been judged to be inconsequential and unnecessary within and by humanity."

The room began making a whooshing noise. He turned his ear and peered upward. Hundreds of small holes dotted the ceiling. His retinal comm reported that the oxygen levels were being depleted rapidly.

"Shit. They're sucking out the air." He glanced around to find Pierce. They were standing behind him. "Did we bring our oxygen?"

Pierce's face was white. "No, sir. The planet… it had a perfect atmosphere. We didn't have a need to."

"Alright, let's see if we can't crack open the door then. Did you bring in any of your explosives?"

Moet reached around and grabbed at her backpack. Throwing it onto the floor, she reached in and grabbed a few charges before hopping up and toward the door.

"Everyone around the corner," Pierce said as he shoved people forward into the larger room. He then ran over and grabbed at Dwight's limp form and dragged him across the floor into the corner with the help of one of his soldiers.

Moet ran into the room "Get down into a group on the floor. Now!"

Bradley ducked down and glanced to his left. The wall screen was still on and the humans in the amphitheater were laughing and rocking forward in their seats. They were fraking cracking up, watching them scramble. They knew this was futile.

He stood up.

"What are you doing?" Pierce screamed.

"This isn't going to work, is it?" Bradley said looking at the male on the screen.

He shook his head slowly from side to side before he burst out laughing again.

Bradley's face was red, and the rage was pulsing through his veins. "I'm going to kill you! Mark my words. I will kill all of you." He was waving his hand at the entire amphitheater.

The wall screen erupted in laughter again, only louder. This time people were tumbling out of their seats they were laughing so hard.

He ducked down into the corner with his crew, put his

hands on his ears, and adjusted his implants to block his ear canal.

Moet blasted the door with a thud.

The concussive force from the explosion knocked everyone into each other, and hard. He peeled himself off Moet and got up, stumbling around the corner.

The door was still sealed without a scratch on it.

His retinal comm alerted him that the oxygen was nearly depleted. He opened his ear canals and stumbled to find Cynthia. She was huddled in the corner beside Pepper.

He got down onto his knees and took her hand in his. He smiled and stared her straight in the eyes. "I love you. I'm sorry I got us into this mess. Dwight was right. I should've—"

She shook her head and reached up, placing her hand on his mouth. "No, he wasn't. We did everything we could."

Tears filled his eyes, and he struggled to catch a breath. His nanites alerted him that he wasn't getting enough oxygen. Reaching up, he squeezed his ear and shut off his comm.

He tried to take a breath but nothing was there. Blackness squeezed in from the sides of his vision. He glanced toward Pepper. She was watching him, her eyes welling with tears. She looked tired.

"I'm sorry," he whispered as he collapsed sideways onto the floor.

33

ZACHARY OLIVAW

LUPUS DARK NEBULA, HENOSI

The door wasn't budging. Shauna had really done a number on it, bending it all to hell.

"Stand back and make sure that fan is flowing outward. This will spew some toxins," Kamal said. He clicked the igniter and the torch burst to life. The blue glow lit up the hallway even more than their lanterns.

Kamal began by cutting downward from the bend, and then across from the halfway point. They could climb over the top once they covered the cut area with something that prevented them from getting burned.

His primitive walkie-talkie burst with static followed by Libby's voice. "I've found the battery bank. What do I do now?"

"Disconnect the red and yellow spiraling cables from all the banks," he said. "That'll flush the storage capacitors within a minute or two. After you disconnect all of them, you should see a flashing yellow and then red light near the core processing chassis on the far wall. Once they stop flashing, hook them all up and then reboot the system."

"All the cables? There are at least... fifty of them!" she asked.

"Well, you'd better get unhooking then. Scramble Brice or Reese to help out."

Her voice rose in the distance above the sound of the torch, shouting through the darkened halls of the ship for help.

His back was getting warm. The blue torch was hot and without proper ventilation it was throwing heat and all sorts of noxious fumes into the air.

He reached over and grabbed a jacket off the chair and put it on his back as he squatted down closer to Pluto and Ibu. They were huddled in the corner, as far from the doorway as possible. Ibu looked scared. Their face was puffy from crying.

Pluto had her arms around Ibu and was rocking back and forth, humming a tune through her face mask. "Hush little Ibu don't say a word, Pluto's gonna buy you a mockingbird. And if that mockingbird don't sing, Zachary's gonna buy you a set of diamond wings."

"Diamond wings?" he asked. That's a new one.

"You know, the wings they use on the colonies and moons with lower gravity," Pluto said. "They're carbon and diamond enforced. I used to watch the videos from Zeta Lupi that Libby would scrub through. Some of those pilots were epic watching them dive off The Edge."

He smiled and reached out to pull the blanket onto her shoulder. "Maybe when this is all over we can go check it out. It sounds like fun."

She smiled and started humming again.

He glanced down at Ibu. Their eyes were peeking up at him from inside the cocoon of blankets. "Yes, you can come to, if you want." He smiled and winked.

Their eyes widened but he couldn't see their face. He assumed they were smiling.

A loud crash echoed through the room, and all three of them jumped at the sound. The bent portion of the door had been cut off and fell to the floor. The light faded as Kamal cut the torch.

He turned around as Kamal was taking his gloved hand and smothering the top edge with some type of yellow goo. It sizzled on contact but the orange hot edge of the metal darkened. After he'd done that, he tossed a fire retardant blanket over the top.

"Alright," Kamal said. "Who's first?"

Zachary reached down and scooped up Ibu, lifting them up into his arms. They were heavy for being so little, easily forty-five kilos. He lifted them up and over the blanket while Kamal reached out to grab them.

"No way you're lifting me up like that," Pluto said with a wink. "I'm not saying you're not strong enough."

"Offense taken," he smirked. "Let's use the chair and table." He slid the small two-person table over next to the door and then propped a chair against it. Pluto climbed up the two levels and then eased over the top. Kamal and Orville were on the other side to catch her.

"You're next, bossman," Kamal said.

He climbed up and over the top and the soldiers set him down on the other side.

"Now what?" Kamal asked.

The lights overhead flickered back to life.

He reached over to Kamal's belt and pulled out his bolt pistol before he could react. He raised it at Shauna's limp form a few meters away.

"What the?" Kamal muttered.

"I'm not taking a chance," he said motioning them behind him with his head. "Everyone back away."

The soldiers slid behind him and escorted Pluto and Ibu around the corner into the galley.

He squeezed off three rounds. The blasts echoed through the empty halls of the Fountainhead. One in the head to the visual cortex. The other two taking out the power core and central processing unit in the chest. He'd already had Kamal remove her shell to ensure nothing was lit up.

Reese and Norm came sprinting around the other side of the ship's circular central hall, guns raised.

He lowered his gun to the ground. "Easy! I was just making sure she wouldn't be causing any more trouble."

"Next time use the comms," Reese said touching the side of his head.

"Ah yea, I forgot they were back." He squeezed his earlobe. He'd shut it off earlier so the A.I. couldn't eavesdrop on them.

"Is everything ok?" Libby asked over the comm.

"It was Zachary doing some target practice in the hall. Nothing to worry about," Reese said.

Libby and Brice came around behind him to see everyone staring at Shauna's limp form.

"Why didn't you just disconnect her internals like you did with the one in your room?" Libby asked.

He chuckled. "You sorta turned the power on before I had the chance." Flipping the safety back on the pistol, he handed it back to Kamal. "Thanks. Sorry I snatched it like that."

"No worries," Kamal said double-checking the safety. "I've never been disarmed that fast before."

The ship lurched sideways and everyone was tossed into the wall. Klaxons around the ship began flashing red.

Pluto swore from somewhere near the galley and he caught her shadow starting toward the bridge.

His retinal comm showed they were being fired upon from the sphere in orbit. It must have detected them when they'd restarted the system. He didn't know how but it didn't much matter. They were sitting ducks now.

He turned left and leaned into a full on sprint to the bridge.

"Is everyone ok?" he asked over the comm.

"Jammed my shoulder into a table, but I'll be fine," Pluto said. "It's gonna leave a mark though."

He took a hard left onto the bridge and hopped over and into his chair. Pluto was already in hers and Kamal and Libby were close behind. The other crew members filed into the seats along the back wall.

The bridge was the safest place onboard the Fountainhead. It was centrally located at the deepest point within the ship, and it had multiple levels of redundancy for life support.

"Status report," Zachary said.

"Forward hull integrity is seventy percent, sir. It looks like whatever the shot was, it was a test," Kamal said.

That's still one hell of a test, he'd hate to see something harder.

"Taking evasive action," Pluto said.

The glint of light from the sphere's laser array ignited before Pluto rocked the ship to the side. The blast narrowly missed them. There was only a second or two tops between the spark of light and the blast itself, but it was enough for her.

Pluto began dodging and weaving the ship around the battlefield, never in one place more than a few seconds. "What's the plan, Z. We can't do this forever. I'm sure they'll figure out some way to take us out."

"We need to man the missile array," he said. They hadn't planned on having Pluto disposed of, and with Shauna out of commission they didn't have any other options.

"Well, that ain't gonna work unless someone else can pilot the Fountainhead." Pluto yanked her controls back pushing the ship upward, barely missing another blast.

"Does anyone else have any Ulixi in their blood?" Libby asked. "Pluto wasn't a pureblood but has a distant bloodline from her father's side. The other option is—" She reached over and grabbed at the handle on the side of her controls as Pluto pulled the stick port side.

The ship rocked hard and shuddered.

"Damage to the port flank," Kamal said. "Hull integrity is sixty-two percent on that side. We can only take one more hit there."

"As I was saying," Libby said. "The other option is if you didn't have your retinal comms installed until well after birth. Anyone?"

The bridge was silent except for the grunts from Pluto slamming the stick around.

"I can give it a go," Zachary said reaching over and unhooking his harness. He started toward the controls next to Pluto. "I mean, it's better than nothing, right?"

"What about me?" Ibu asked from behind.

He turned to face them. They hadn't thought about that. Why couldn't it be a Nanil? They never had implants as far as he knew. The memories they had access to were somehow uploaded as part of the birthing process and weren't technically augmentation.

He glanced at Libby and shrugged. "Whatcha think?"

Libby shook her head. "I... don't see why not. If they can manage it."

"I was watching you the entire time you were reviewing it with Pluto," Ibu said. They swallowed hard. "It didn't look too bad."

"They're right," Pluto said. "Hang on," she mumbled as she slammed the stick downward.

The Fountainhead rocked, and he went flying sideways bouncing off Libby's control panel and then forward into the wall.

"Topside is at twenty percent. We can't take another hit up there either. Whatever that thing is throwing at us, it's cranking up the power," Kamal said.

His right arm was screaming. "Frak! That's broken," he

mumbled. He tried to bend it and pain shot up his arm. "Ibu! Get up there next to Pluto and be careful!" He leaned forward and grasped the bar on Libby's station and pulled up. Once he had his balance, he stumbled back to his seat before Pluto yanked the stick the other way.

It was starting to feel like they were flying in Swiss cheese. With each shot, they had another weak side.

Without Shauna and all the computing power on the ship, the gravity controls were at a minimum. Enough to give them simple planetary gravity, but not enough to counter the sudden movements Pluto was making. He'd have to fix that oversight when they got to a station for repairs. If they got to a station.

He adjusted his position in the chair, and it locked him in. When he glanced to his left, Ibu was sliding into place next to Pluto right before she jammed the yoke hard to the right.

"Where the hell is Harold?" he asked. It'd suddenly dawned on him they hadn't seen him in a while.

"The sphere is only firing every other shot at us," Kamal said. "Wherever he is, he's taking the other shot. Neither of us have disabled our stealth, so we can't see each other. I'm still not sure how we were detected in the first place."

A concern for a later time. Right now they needed to knock that thing out of orbit.

"Okay sweetie," Libby said talking to Ibu over the helmet and the HUD they put on. "Remember what I showed Pluto earlier. Adjust your tachyon—"

"Fields to control the gate direction and use the force plane of the Cherenkov Radiation to control the depth. I remember," Ibu interrupted. "I can do this," they muttered and leaned into their chair. "It's like the maze crawlers Fotily and I used to play."

Pluto glanced to her left and nodded. "You just have to make sure—Frak!" She pulled hard to port dodging the beam from the sphere. "Make sure and take into account the direction I'm moving the stick. Otherwise, we'll never hit it where we need to."

Ibu nodded.

He reached up and adjusted his comm. He wanted to see what Ibu was seeing through their helmet. Watching from back here was impossible. He was helpless.

"I'm gonna go starboard in a second," Pluto said.

"Wait, which direction is starboard?" Ibu asked.

"To the right. So, the sphere will move left on the controls."

Ibu reached up and tweaked the controls to center in on the sphere. As they reached forward to adjust the radiation depth, Pluto jammed hard to the right and their calibrations were all off.

Ibu shook their head.

"Going up in a second," Pluto said.

Ibu reached forward and adjusted the tachyons, depth, and then pushed the fire button.

Ibu's HUD showed the munition dropping into the tiny gate array in their cargo bay. They'd constructed it earlier from the dismantled Wellspring gate drive. It acted like a bombardier hole they used to drop bombs through, except this one was through spacetime.

An explosion erupted past the sphere, lighting up its far right side. Ibu dropped it too far. The explosion, however, was massive. It filled the entire wall screen, and the computer had to adjust the brightness so as not to blind them.

"What the hell was that?" Libby asked.

"That, my friends, was the munition from Yaan," Kamal said.

"That was bloody brilliant," muttered Reese.

"You were long, Ibu," Pluto said. "Don't forget that we're traveling forward through space. You have to adjust for our velocity, but not theirs. The sphere is fixed in spacetime and is only moving as fast as the planet is spinning."

Ibu's hands were shaking. They flexed their fingers and glanced right and left toward Pluto's controls and their own. Pluto jammed the stick down and Ibu frantically adjusted their controls and slammed the red button.

The wall screen dimmed as the nuclear detonation erupted short, but near the edge of the sphere. There was no visible exterior damage but Ibu was close. So very close.

The sphere lit up, and shot toward them hitting them dead center in their forward hull. All the lights on the bridge flashed and sparks erupted from the ceiling, cascading to the floor as the secondary lighting kicked in. Everyone's controls were still operational, but they couldn't take another shot like that.

"Forward hull damage critical," Kamal shouted and turned toward Zachary. "We're down to eight percent, sir. Another hit like that and—"

"We got it," Zachary interrupted raising his hand for him to stop.

He closed his eyes and took a deep breath. "Ibu?"

"Yes, Z," Ibu said.

He chuckled. That was his and Pluto's nickname. "Do you remember how you felt when Ogun hit you back on Doda?" He opened his eyes.

Ibu turned around to face him. Their mouth was a slit, and while he couldn't see their face through the helmet, he imagined they were angry.

"I know, it hurts. You're filled with frustration and anger. You wanted them to stop, right? You wanted Ogun to treat you as an adult, as your own person and not a child. You were not them. Right?"

Ibu nodded.

"I want you to—"

"Shit!" Pluto yelled as she pulled upward. The rear section of their ship rocketed.

"Thrust is down to sixty percent," Kamal said. "That took out one of our impulse drives."

He sighed and shook his head, making eye contact with Ibu again. "Take that hatred, that frustration, and all that pain and shove it deep down into the center of that alien sphere! Can you do that for me?"

Ibu swallowed hard and nodded before turning around and adjusting their controls.

He watched as they were glancing back and forth between their controls and Pluto's before finally settling on watching Pluto's hands. Ibu's viewpoint was fixed, but he could just see from the wide lens of their helmet they were using their hands to adjust the controls without looking.

"Ibu, what are—" he began.

"Leave them be!" Libby subvocalized to him.

He took a deep breath and exhaled, watching as Ibu made multiple adjustments, each time not hitting fire but watching the movements of Pluto's hands. They repeated this a few times until they reached forward and slammed their hand on the fire button.

He glanced at the wall screen and waited as the sphere lit up, its beam weapon trained on and firing at another point in space, toward Harold. His ship was visible now and appeared to have taken as much damage as they had.

Suddenly, the image on the right of the wall screen exploded in a rainbow of colors. Ibu had done it. They'd dropped a munition into the sphere, and one of Yaan's at that.

"Yes!" Ibu screamed and hopped up and down in their chair.

Pluto reached over and gave them a big hug, kissing the top of Ibu's head.

The sphere had cracked open and chunks of it were raining downward toward the planet and out into orbit.

He smiled watching Pluto and Ibu celebrate. The second part of the plan was complete. "Open a comm to Harold."

"Yessir," Libby said as she reached forward and hailed the Fidem. "The comm is open, sir."

"I hope there's no bad feelings," Zachary said.

"None," Harold said. "The human part of me was hoping you'd take action. I pushed hard to stop me… to stop the laws from controlling me, but I couldn't."

"We need you now, Harold. We've taken on too much damage to land and the Wellspring is in pieces in our hold. Can you land?"

Harold's image came on screen. It was the childhood form he'd often take when they were kids on adventures. He had a pirate costume on and was holding a shiny curved cutlass. "We've never flown this contraption of yours onto a planet before. I suppose there's a first time for everything." He swooshed the sword around through the air. "I think I can make it. My hull should be able to withstand an atmosphere transition. Will you be providing a landing crew or am I solo?"

Zachary stood up and his arm throbbed. He'd forgotten about the break and there was no way he could make it down there. "I'm sure we can find some volunteers to lend a hand."

34

BRADLEY OLIVAW
LUPUS DARK NEBULA, HENOSI

He'd failed. Failed to protect his crew, failed to help his family, and failed to save humanity.

He'd never see his sister again. Never make amends for the years of lies and deceit she'd had to orchestrate to protect him. He'd never know if Zachary had survived or not.

The weight of his poor decisions was heavy on his chest. Hundreds of thousands kilos of heavy. He forced a deep breath and sighed. His breathing was labored and shallow.

Wait, he was breathing? He struggled to open his eyes. He couldn't see anything but blackness.

Maybe he was dead.

No, the chamber they were in was dark. He moved his arm to push up but something was pressing down on it.

"Cynthia?" he mumbled. His voice was hoarse and his mouth was dry, like he'd been chewing on a wad of cotton. "Pepper? Is anyone there?"

Something on top of him stirred. He carefully rolled sideways to ensure no one hit their head on the ground. Both of the women had passed out leaning on him. He gently lowered each of them to the metallic floor.

When he sat up, pain shot through his torso. It was weird. He was sore from the inside out. Like something had fallen on him and bruised his insides. He'd never stopped breathing before, but he imagined it was from that.

Something rustled off to his right.

"Is anyone there?"

"Yea," Moet muttered. "Did you happen to get the number of the shuttle that hit me?" She moaned and rustled some more.

A light flicked on. It was Moet's headlamp.

The room was littered with bodies. Moet crawled over and they both checked on Cynthia and Pepper. They had faint pulses and shallow breathing.

"Cynthia, wake up," he whispered rubbing her back. "You're alive. We're alive. Wake up, please wake up."

She wasn't moving.

He leaned down and kissed her, tears welling in his eyes. "You have to wake up. I can't lose you. Not after all this. Now wake up damn it!" He shook her harder and rolled her onto her back. Maybe he needed to give her compressions.

"Ouch!" she said. "Not so hard."

He started laughing and leaned in to give her another kiss on the lips. His tears cascaded onto her face.

"And now you're getting me wet," she said, smiling up at him.

He reached down and wiped at her face. "Sorry."

She lifted her arm and brushed his cheek. "Don't be."

He glanced over at Moet. She'd revived Pepper, and they were hugging in a tight embrace. Not a casual one, either, an I'm scared that I almost lost you embrace.

Pepper glanced over at him and nodded. A smile peeked in the corner of her mouth.

He tested his legs by pushing up onto one knee and then the other. Finally he stood, a bit wobbly at first but he stabilized. He glanced around the room. Pierce was helping her other soldiers, and they were all sitting up with their back to the wall.

The only person he didn't see was Dwight. He shuffled around the corner and there he was, on his chest next to the door. He must have revived around the same time everyone else passed out and he tried to escape. Waking up in a dark room full of bodies and not being able to breathe sounded like a nightmare he didn't want to live. Dying was a close second.

He stumbled up to Dwight and got down on his knees. There wasn't a pulse, so he flipped him around on his back and put his ear to his chest. Still nothing. "Shit!"

He reached up to Dwight's neck and struggled to find the seal of his camouflage jumpsuit. His fingers weren't finding the seam. "Damn it!"

Pierce slid up beside him, shoving him over onto his butt. She had the suit open in under a second and started giving him compressions.

Bradley froze in place as she quietly counted to herself and applied CPR. After a minute of compressions she leaned down and checked to see if Dwight was breathing. He wasn't. She raised her hand upward and slammed it down with a chop in the middle of his sternum before she continued applying rapid compressions.

He crawled up next to Dwight's head and placed his hand over his mouth. There wasn't any air coming out and his face was cold.

When he reached up and squeezed his ear, there was nothing.

"The comms are… dead," Pierce said. Her face became more and more contorted with every chest compression.

"I think he's gone," Bradley whispered.

"He… can't be," she said. "We only… knocked him out."

He reached out and touched her arm. "We don't know what state he was in when he woke up. Anything could have happened." He squeezed. "He's gone."

She stood up huffing and puffing. "Argh!" she screamed.

"He was right," he muttered.

"How's that?" Pierce asked walking up beside him.

He brought his knees up and rested his elbows on them, running his hand through his hair. "I shouldn't have brought us up here. We should've dropped back to the shuttle."

"And then what?" Pierce asked. "Get killed by the orbiting sphere? Something blew that thing up right after we lost Harold. That would've been us if we'd been back there."

"Maybe," he muttered. "Maybe we should've just waited outside and talked to the natives."

Pierce slid her foot over toward him and gave him a jostle. "You need to cut the what ifs. Anything could have fraking happened. We'll never know for sure. But one thing's for certain. We're alive right now, and we know far more about our history and origins than we ever did before we were stuck in this blasted room."

Cynthia stepped around the corner and he sprung up off the ground next to her. "Are you ok?"

"I'm fine. Is he?"

Bradley nodded.

"Do you hear that?" Pierce asked.

"Hear what?" Cynthia craned her neck.

Pierce raised her finger. "Shhh…"

The faint sound of unfamiliar voices was coming from somewhere.

Pierce stepped toward the chamber entrance. It looked like it was closed, but when she shined her flashlight at it, there was a crack separating the two surfaces. "Everyone come over here!" She waved her arm. "We can pull this open. This is how the air got in."

The three nearby soldiers ran up to the doorway. They split into groups of three with Bradley and Cynthia, and each of them reached their hands into the gap.

"1… 2… 3!" Pierce said.

Everyone pulled with all they had. The doors rumbled and slid into the wall about ten centimeters.

A light breeze blew in with wafts of what smelled like currant. It was dark outside, but he could just make out the outlines of people moving around outside the doorway.

Pierce cut her flashlight. "Grab your guns," she whispered. "We might have to shoot our way outta here."

He couldn't see a thing, but he heard the other soldiers slide along the ground and into the other room. The rustling and scraping of weapons being picked up from a metal surface echoed through the chamber. Everyone including Pepper and Moet shuffled back toward them.

Moet had a single red flashlight cupped in her hand to make it easier to see. She cut it off once they'd reached the door.

Someone pressed the handle of his pistol into his side a little too hard. "Ouch," he muttered as he reached down and took it.

"Sorry, sir," Moet whispered.

"It's your show, Pierce," he said. "I don't have the foggiest idea what to do here."

"First, we have to give this door one last yank. We can use our legs now, so it shouldn't be too bad. The noise will likely draw their attention which means the rest of you need to be ready. Set your guns to full stun. I don't want these people waking up for a few hours if we can help it."

He didn't trust his aim. He'd be more help as muscle. "I've got the door down low." Crawling down on the ground, he slid his feet against the furthest door. He then leaned forward and reaching his hands around the other.

Cynthia, Pepper, and Moet did the same but higher and higher up. Moet could only use her hands but Pepper and Cynthia were using one foot and both hands.

"On three," Pierce whispered. "Remember, full stun and no headshots if you can help it. Turn on your scopes." She reached down and flicked a switch on the side of the scope. The backside lit up a faint green.

The other four soldiers did the same and raised their guns toward the darkness. Like a well-oiled team, they had already self-assigned a different quadrant of the opening.

"3... 2... 1!"

He pulled and pushed with everything he had, every ounce of strength. The door slowly creaked another ten centimeters and then seemed to hit a fulcrum point where it flew open with no effort. The massive doors rumbled open and slammed into their frame inside the wall, sending a boom echoing out into the night.

"So much for quiet," he muttered.

He stayed low as sniper shot after sniper shot whizzed into the darkness. The repeated sound of bodies thumping to the ground continued for thirty seconds. Each rifle held several hundred tiny electric-darts. They weren't any more than four centimeters long, but they packed a punch that'd knock you on your ass, or in this case on your ass and out for a few hours.

"That's all the natives I can see," Pierce said.

"All clear," each of the soldiers echoed.

"That's sixty-four according to my tally," Pierce checked the counts on each of their rifles. "Ok, let's head on down the steps and back toward where our shuttle landed. If someone were to come looking for us, that's where I'd check first."

"Wait," he whispered. "I don't have a stun gun. I've only got this." He waved his bolt pistol.

"If you need to use it, then aim low. We're not here to kill anyone. Not yet," Pierce said. "We'll form a line. Two in the front, Bradley, Cynthia, and Pepper in the middle. Moet, you grab Dwight's body. You two take the rear." She pointed at her other two soldiers.

He'd forgotten about Dwight in all the commotion. What kind of friend forgets about their closest buddy? The kind that got him killed. "No! I've got Dwight."

Moet was already over next to him. "I can—"

He walked between her and the body. "I said I've got him! I got him killed, I'll carry him. You keep us safe."

"Yes, sir," she whispered.

He squatted down onto one knee and leaned forward, pulling Dwight's arms and upper torso up onto his shoulder.

"Let me help." Cynthia bent down and lifted Dwight up some, until his waist was directly on Bradley's shoulder.

He pushed upward and stood upright. Dwight was heavier than he expected, and he teetered for a second until he adjusted the weight. It was as even as it was going to get. "I'm ready," he whispered into the dark.

"Alright. Single file, Bradley you're behind me," Pierce said motioning with her hand.

They walked out into the darkness two at a time. Every group had a red light pointed downward.

As he walked up to the first step, he squinted to make out the step below. Not having stars was weird. He glanced upward. "What's that?" He nodded at the streaks across the sky.

Everyone craned their neck up and backward to see the multicolored flaming streams arcing across the night sky.

"That looks like it's originating from where the sphere was," Cynthia said. "And... I think that's the rotational direction of the planet if I remember right. Whatever's up there is re-entering the atmosphere and burning up."

"Let's hope that's a good thing for us." He turned and

used his foot to find the bottom of the first step, and the next, and the next. It was slow-going, but he was getting into a rhythm. Going down was a lot easier than going up, even with the extra weight.

Something was missing without his retinal comm. It was one thing to unplug and shut all the equipment down for a vacation or an evening of downtime. But when you needed or wanted more information, and it wasn't there, it was impossible to shut off the gnawing feeling that there was something important going on. You just had no idea what it was.

"Sir," Pierce said in front of him. "I've got a visual on twenty… no thirty inbound natives running toward us. We're almost to the bottom, but there's no way we're outrunning them. Hold here while we paint the targets."

He reached up and squeezed the collar of his jumpsuit but nothing happened. Damn, even the camo was out. What the hell did they do to us in there, fire off an EMP? He took another step down until he reached the next large ledge of the pyramid and then he knelt down, carefully lowering Dwight. He didn't want to smack his head on the ground.

"Hey guys," he whispered into the darkness. He lowered his hand onto the pyramid's surface. "Did anyone notice this thing isn't cold anymore? It's actually warm to the touch."

Cynthia stepped around him and knelt down, placing her hand on the surface. "Weird," she muttered. "Whatever happened up there with the sphere must've knocked something out of alignment down here."

"Sir, we've got another fifty villagers cresting the hill," Pierce yelled from down below the temple. "We can't hold 'em all off. There's far too many, and we're running low on non-lethal ammo. What should we do?"

He stared into the darkness. Sparks of light were igniting in the distance like fireflies. Each flash of light was a dart hitting a target and knocking it out. This was frustrating. He couldn't see anything without his fraking retinal comm.

Their only option was up. There was no way in hell they'd make it all the way to the shuttle being pursued by natives.

"I guess we're going up." He leaned down to grasp Dwight when Moet sprinted up beside him.

"No offense sir," Moet began, "but I can move faster than you. Go on ahead, I've got him."

He sighed. Now wasn't the time to fight. She was right. He stood up and headed back up the steps behind Cynthia. She was a dozen or more steps ahead of him already.

About ten meters up the face of the pyramid, the sky lit up like the noonday sun.

He glanced toward the native town and saw a sea of bodies littering the open field. Beyond that was a second wave of humans sprinting toward them. They were all brandishing spears and chanting as they ran. He was pretty sure they weren't following a no-kill order.

Craning his neck upward he covered the center of the light, trying to see if he could tell what it was. A sonic boom echoed across the valley, followed by the noisy burn of descent thrusters. Whatever it was, it was coming in hot.

"It looks like a ship descending," Pierce yelled from a few meters behind him. "I don't recognize the thrust pattern though."

He glanced over his shoulder. She was using the scope on the rifle to protect her eyes and target the ship.

"Describe the pattern to me," Pepper yelled above the roar from above. She was a few steps ahead of Cynthia on the climb.

"It looks like it'd form two tight diamonds side by side but one point is missing."

"That matches the Fidem or the Fountainhead," she yelled. "Minus the burned out engine."

He shook his head. No way in hell they'd chance that. "Would they land one of those here?" he yelled. The roar was getting louder.

"We've never done an atmosphere test," she screamed. "They could in theory… I suppose, but I'm not sure now would be the place to test it."

Unless the shit had hit the fan up there. He peered up the pyramid steps; he wasn't even halfway to the top. Cynthia and Pepper were much closer.

"You guys head inside," he yelled waving his arms toward the women. "I won't make it in time. I'm gonna drop to the ground and find cover by the trees if I can. Everyone else, let's group together as far downfield as we can."

He had no idea who'd heard him, but he waited to confirm that Cynthia and Pepper were running upward. Once he was happy they were safely moving, he glanced down the pyramid. The others had already started downward. "Always the last one to the party Olivaw," he muttered.

He double timed it down the steps. His feet were barely touching one surface when he was already stepping toward the next. When he hit a groove, he began taking them two at a time. He didn't have much time to get down. That ship was either going to land or crash hard, and he knew he didn't want to be nearby for either of them.

His feet hit the soil and he glanced around. All the others except Pierce were sprinting across the open field. She'd stayed behind waiting on him. "You should have continued on with the others," he yelled. The roar of the engines was deafening.

"I don't leave anyone behind," she screamed running up beside him. Her rifle was trained on the natives approaching to their left the entire time she was running.

His legs were blurs against the field of orange grass as they sprinted toward the edge of the forest. The others had already entered the shade and protection of the dense thicket of trees. He knew they were nearby watching them approach because he could hear natives toppling to the ground behind them as they ran.

As he hopped over a small rock formation, something made a loud clanging noise over the roar of the engines behind him. Glancing over his shoulder while he continued to run, he caught the glint of a spear resting in the grass beside the boulder he'd just cleared. The natives were definitely aiming to kill.

He turned around and continued his steady pace toward the forest edge. He'd almost made it when the sound of something distinctly different caught his attention. The snipping sound of suppressed air exiting the end of a rifle. His team must've run out of tranquilizer darts.

Screams of agony filled the open field as they hit more and more of the natives with the powerful bullets. Their pain and agony was the backdrop chorus to the ever-increasing roar of the decelerating starship.

He reached the edge of the field and ducked down next to a tree. Now that he wasn't moving, the beats of his heart were thumping through his chest. He hadn't even noticed. The adrenaline had muted all signs of the pain his body was broadcasting.

The field was littered with hundreds of bodies. Most of them were motionless but the ones nearest their position were writhing and screaming on the ground.

"We shouldn't sit still long," Pierce yelled. "They could be outflanking us as we speak."

She'd slid up beside him. He hadn't even heard her approach and her breathing wasn't taxed in the slightest. It was like she'd only run up a single flight of stairs.

"Do you think we're far enough in?" he yelled, pointing up at the starship. It'd be down in another sixty seconds tops.

"It's hard to tell," Pierce screamed next to his ear. "Let's head a little deeper. There are a few rocks up ahead that can shield us." She was pointing a dozen more meters into the forest.

As he turned, something smashed into his calves. He

collapsed to the ground and ricocheted off Pierce. Pain shot up his legs and his mind immediately assumed the worst. They'd impaled him with a spear. He rolled onto his back and sat up. There was some type of bolo wrapped around his legs.

He reached down to untangle it, but Pierce had bent down and pulled at his wrist to stop him.

"Don't touch it!" she yelled. She unsheathed a knife from her boot and carefully cut the wires lashed around his calves. It was then that he noticed that the stones of the bolo were flashing. Their pulse was getting faster and faster.

Pierce grabbed at his arm and yanked him backward, away from the entangled pile of wire and strobing stone. He struggled to flip around with her arm wrapped under his. It was like a steel vice grip that wouldn't let go.

They'd managed to scramble four to five meters away when it blew. Shockwaves from the blast sent them reeling into the underbrush, toppling on top of each other.

Something was burning at his neck as waves of pain rippled over his face. He brushed at the source with his hand but it wouldn't stop. The explosions must've lodged some-thing in his skin. "Frak, it burns!" he screamed. No one was going to hear him over the final seconds of the descent.

The engines of the starship were casting white plumes of smoke as the moisture on the ground evaporated under the extreme temperatures from the deceleration thrusters. It billowed outward across the open field and was approaching along the ground like the fog in a horror sim.

Someone grabbed at him and pushed him down to the ground. He peered upward and saw Pierce's face. She had a knife in her hand and was coming at his neck. Why was she trying to kill him? "No," he yelled as he shook his head and struggled to push her away.

"Hold still," Pierce yelled. "You're being burned by shrap-nel." She lowered the knife to his neck and pierced his flesh.

He closed his eyes and gritted his teeth, slapping at his leg with the palm of his hand. He hit something hard. It was the crystal in his pocket. He squeezed at it through the thin fabric with everything he had. The pain in his face was anguishing, but he couldn't move or she'd cut his jugular for sure.

A cloud of white billowing smoke blew through the tree line and enshrouded them both. The knife wasn't jabbing at him anymore and the pain had crested. She must've gotten it out.

"Thank you," he yelled, realizing only now that the roar had stopped and he needn't scream.

Whoever was on the ship hadn't crashed it, but they came damn close.

Pierce reached down to help him stand up. His calves were sore from the bolo. If he wasn't covered in purple bruises later, he'd be surprised.

They limped arm in arm toward the forest edge to check out the devastation. The ship had its external floodlights deployed and was lighting the entire field. A gentle breeze was blowing up and over the ridge above the village and taking with it the smoke rising from the warmed ground. It was blowing across the clearing in front of the pyramids and into the forest where they were standing.

As the smoke thinned, he shook his head. In front of him were bodies as far as the eye could see. Most of them weren't moving, and without his retinal comm he had no idea which ones were dead or alive. They'd come to Henosi to find information about their past, and in their wake they'd left a sea of destruction.

He reached up and squeezed his ear. Still nothing. "Frak," he muttered.

"What?" Pierce asked.

"I was hoping that the system would reboot or something."

"I think we'll need new implants. They should show some type of indicator if they were working, but I'm getting nothing."

He took a step forward and kicked one of their teams' rifles. Kneeling down, he picked it up. Turning it over in his hands, it still had a few non-lethal darts in it. He glanced around but didn't see a body anywhere.

Pierce squinted at the rifle in his hand. "I think everyone was accounted for that ran across the field." She shrugged. "In all that commotion anyone could've tossed it."

They walked side by side toward the starship in the field. He couldn't tell if it was the Fidem or the Fountainhead. From the outside, both ships looked the same. Plus, there was the fact that he'd never seen them separated and on the ground. He'd only ever seen them through windows or virtually.

Pierce reached out and put her hand in front of him. "Do you hear that?"

He turned his ear toward the breeze. There was the faint sound of people arguing up ahead. Leaning forward he entered a light jog without too much pain. His discomfort on the other hand was another story. Every step sent pain shooting up his legs. Like he had killer shinsplints.

As they rounded the side of the ship, they came upon a group of natives arguing and waving at the bottom of the starship's ramp.

"What are they saying?" Pierce asked.

"Damn if I know. We don't have a translator, remember?"

She jabbed him in the arm. "Not them, them." She was pointing at the soldiers at the bottom of the ramp.

They looked like the soldiers from Zachary's crew. "Hey!" he screamed waving his hand. "Over here!"

The natives all turned to face him. They had spears in their hand and didn't look happy. The ones closest to them walked forward until he raised his rifle.

"Don't take another step." He waved the rifle sideways

and stepped slowly toward the ramp, away from them. His other arm eased Pierce behind him. She didn't have a weapon that he'd seen. She must've lost it when they'd been thrown.

The natives complied but continued their mumbling in their foreign tongue.

He glanced left. The path to the ramp was clear. "Run for it," he whispered.

Pierce sprinted toward the ramp and he trotted close behind. The soldiers tossed her a weapon as she approached and she slid in with them, taking aim at the natives.

He recognized the soldier at the bottom of the ramp. "Hey… Kamal, right?"

"It's good to see you, sir," Kamal said over the top of his rifle which was still trained on the natives. "These people claim you killed their god and their people. Do you happen to know anything about that?"

"Unfortunately I do. Whatever you did up there," he gestured toward the sky, "took out whatever they had going on down here in these pyramids. The computers inside were somehow controlling the natives and apparently they believed gods were talking through them. At least until your orbital fireworks show."

The natives squeaked louder, pointing at them and then toward the sky, as well.

"They say you entered the pyramid and after you came out their voices stopped talking to them. They want your heads," Kamal said. "Orders, sir?"

He reached down and rubbed his shin. "Did you tell them their people weren't dead? That we'd only knocked them out."

Kamal repeated what he said, and the natives stared at each other for a moment. A few of them split away and ran up to the bodies on the ground, feeling them for pulses. They shouted back at the group that their people were alive.

"Good call," Kamal whispered. "You'd think they'd have

checked that."

He tilted his head back and pointed at his neck. "They were playing for keeps. We… just ran out of tranqs. That's the only reason the others are moaning on the ground. We had to stop them somehow, but we certainly weren't trying to kill them."

Kamal cleared his throat and leaned toward Bradley. "I'm pretty sure we landed on a few of theirs. So, maybe we call it even?"

"Given that their fraking gods killed one of ours and nearly killed the rest of us, even sounds a bit generous." He raised his rifle toward the leader in the front. "Tell them they have twenty seconds to clear this field or we open fire. I'm not screwing around anymore."

Kamal translated, and the leader in the front widened his stance and crossed his arms.

"Looks like it's the hard way then." Kamal subvocalized a command to his team.

They all lowered their rifles, and the natives did the same. A burst of tranquilizer darts sailed out of the open hold and collided with the natives. The grouping of all twenty collapsed to the ground in a coordinated thud.

Bradley chuckled. "That was tricky." He turned to stare up the ramp and raised his hand to block the lights. "Nice shooting partner."

A small red robot walked out of the shadow of the ramp leading up into the hold. "Thank you, Master Bradley."

It was Little Red. He'd forgotten all about the friendly little robot. They'd left him with Harold onboard the Fidem.

"Wait, if this is the Fidem, where's your tug?" he asked.

"Hey! Don't be calling my baby a tug." Pluto popped out of the shadows at the top of the ramp and jogged down toward them. "The Fountainhead had severe damage and couldn't land, so we transferred aboard after we took out the sphere in orbit. Figured you might need some help. Say, where's Pepper?"

He pointed toward the top of the pyramid. There, coming out of the doors at the peak were the silhouettes of three people. Cynthia, Pepper, and one of Pierce's soldiers.

Pluto burst off in a full on sprint toward the steps with one of Kamal's soldiers not far behind. There was no way in hell he could make it up there with his legs feeling like this.

He sighed. Cynthia was waving her arms at him as she walked down the sea of steps. He waved back and a part of him deep inside relaxed. He hadn't even realized he was tense until he saw her walk out of the doorway.

Little Red glided up beside him. Its body raised upward and its head rotated all the way around, taking in a view of all the pyramids. "Did you recover any of the consciousness cores?"

He turned toward the little robot and flinched backward. The robot's face was only a few centimeters away from his own. "The what?"

"The consciousness cores," Little Red said sliding sideways to give him more room. "Each of these temples has a central processing core that's designed to redundantly store all the thoughts, memories, and knowledge of the people that lived here."

He shook his head. "You mean all the people we talked to earlier are actually virtually alive in the temple? Right now?"

"You talked to them. What an honor," Little Red said, his eyes flashed a rainbow of colors. "What were they like?"

He waved his hands. "Now's not the time to get into that. Are they still in there?"

"Well, they were until we destroyed their overseer," Little Red said pointing upward.

Bradley glanced skyward and nodded. "And now?"

"Now they're only bytes on a data core. Their power appears to be offline from what my scans are showing."

"So can you help us find and collect these consciousness cores?" He glanced back down at the little robot.

"Because you want to save them?"

"Something like that," he said with a smirk.

35

ZACHARY OLIVAW

LUPUS DARK NEBULA, HENOSI

"Mating maneuver complete, sir," Pluto said. "I'm running gate diagnostics now. We should be ready to jump in a few minutes if everything comes back green."

The away team returned a few hours after it left. They had no idea how long they'd have until one of the guardian spheres showed up, so he didn't want to press their luck. Bradley asked for more time, but after they'd extracted all the human's consciousness cores and a few other random pieces of tech, he didn't want to risk it any longer.

The bridge doors slid open.

"Hey, bro! How's the arm?" Bradley walked onto the bridge and sat in Libby's spot at comms, swiveling her chair to face him.

"Throbs like a son-of-a but the nanites are accelerating everything they can. Should only be another day or so. How's the neck?" Zachary screwed up his face. "It looks like you had a fight with a meat grinder and lost."

"Ha ha. Shauna says they can knock me out later and clean it up. Should be easy-peasy."

"Sirs?" Harold said. His image appeared on the wall

screen. Today he was the middle-aged persona who discovered the first contact probes on Earth.

"What's up, Harold?" Bradley asked pivoting back to face the front. He rocked back and forth in the chair like a school kid.

"I've finished the analysis from your retinal comm we extracted. We were able to restore all the recordings until a few moments after you passed out."

Bradley glanced back at Zachary and then toward Harold. "How the hell did you manage that? Everyone else's comms were trashed. You said so."

Harold brought up the image of Bradley's retinal comm unit on the wall screen along with the earpiece everyone wore. "You weren't wearing a regular comm, sir."

Zachary stood up and walked forward toward the wall screen. He couldn't see anything special about it. Standard issue touch sensors, retinal projectors, and connectors. "Looks normal to me."

Harold split it open and showed the internal structure of the comm's design.

"What the hell's that?" Bradley said walking toward the wall screen and pointing at a black area in each of the earpieces.

"That's your data core where all the recordings and everything else is stored. It's different. You've always had an Olivaw data core. They're standard issue whenever we replace them in anyone at The Wheel."

"But why are they black... wait, Harold, that's not stealth crap, is it?" Bradley asked.

"I can neither confirm nor deny that," Harold said as a smirk crossed his virtual face. "Look at it this way. We wouldn't have any visual evidence of your conversation with the humans if you didn't have this earpiece installed. I don't know if they used an EMP or something else, but everyone's electronics were slag. We don't know if anything will come from those consciousness cores we collected. These recordings are hard evidence and could be the key to our case against the Galactic Alliance back in Sol."

Zachary reached up and rubbed his ear. Talking about earpieces made his ear itch from the inside. He'd always known they used small amounts of the protective material in their retinal comms, but hadn't given it much thought until now.

"Still," Bradley muttered as he reached up and rubbed his ear. "I suppose you installed this in—"

"Yes," Harold interrupted. "We installed the same device in everyone down in medical. We're one big happy team now."

"I hate to interrupt your party, sirs," Pluto began with a smirk, "but we're ready to gate out of here on your orders."

"Say, what happened to the other guardian sphere on the far side of Henosi?" Bradley asked.

"We've recalled our reconnaissance satellites already," Kamal said. "But we have a recording of what happened to it after we destroyed our guardian. The site hadn't changed as of a few minutes ago when the last satellite flew over."

Kamal brought up a video on the wall screen. It showed the guardian sphere lowering down into the atmosphere of Henosi.

"What the frak is it doing?" Bradley asked.

"Patience brother, just watch," Zachary said. He was always in such a hurry. It was one of the reasons he was a better engineer than a scientist.

The sphere continued lowering down below the atmosphere until it was above the second human settlement and then began unfolding. It was like watching a camping tent unfold one piece after another until it finally formed a dome and lowered onto the planet's surface. They'd argued about covering the colonies with massive domes in the early days, but decided on the ring design with smaller domed buildings as a compromise. He couldn't imagine the technology that enabled the deployment of a dome like that.

"That's one way to protect the colony I suppose," Bradley said.

"We weren't sure if that guardian would attempt to protect this settlement. Turns out they were designed to cut their losses," Zachary said.

"Ahem," Pluto said.

He turned to face her. "Sorry… let's get out of here." He reached up and opened a ship wide comm. "Prepare for gate a sequence. We're headed back to Zeta Lupi."

Cheers erupted around the ship.

"I guess they're happy we're heading home," he said as he walked over to his command chair and sat down. He nodded toward Pluto. "Begin gate jump sequence."

"Aye, sir," Pluto said as she swiveled in her chair and locked it in place. She reached out and adjusted her controls. "Tachyon ring deployed successfully, beginning cone field shaping."

The familiar clang of the expanding tachyon field vanes echoed through the ship.

He hoped she held together through the transition. They'd fixed everything they could think of in the short time they had.

The bridge door opened and Pepper walked in along with Cynthia and Ibu.

He glanced back and gave Ibu a wink, nodding his chin toward their chair on the back wall.

Ibu and the ladies walked to their seats on either side of the back wall and clicked in.

He returned his attention to the wall screen. The transition was coming. This had better work, or they could be stranded here for some time.

"The gang's all here," Bradley said as he walked up beside Cynthia and sat down.

Pluto glanced over her shoulder and gave Pepper a wink before returning to the controls. "Conical shaping complete. Beginning matter injection."

The wall screen changed to show a familiar pattern they hadn't seen in weeks, the speckled stars of the Milky Way.

"It's beautiful," Pluto muttered.

"It sure is," he said. It was strange how comforting something as simple as specks of light could be. For thousands of years on Earth, mariners navigated by the stars. Children and adults would look up at night and gaze toward the heavens and wish upon shooting stars. These tiny specks of light had influenced so much of mankind's history on Earth, and to be without them felt empty, like something was missing.

"Let's go home," Zachary said.

The comfortable blue glow passed through the ship and over his body. While the remnants of the accelerated transition still lingered in his mind, this one was comforting. The massaging wall of ants reassured him that everything was working and made his right arm tingle where it was healing. He didn't know what they were returning to in Zeta Lupi, but he only hoped it wasn't too late.

***

HE REACHED OVER and slid the panel over the doorway to their room. It was crude, but it worked.

Pluto was already in bed waiting for him when he turned around. The shower had felt amazing, and he was ready to catch some shut-eye, but he had something to take care of first.

Sliding into bed he put his arms around her and leaned in to kiss her. "I'm sorry," he said, pulling away.

Pluto's brows furrowed. "For what?"

"Not telling you about Shauna."

Pluto glanced toward the corner where Shauna's immobilized robotic form still stood slumped over. "Why didn't you tell me?" She reached up and brushed his sandy brown hair aside.

"I hadn't told anyone. Not even Abigail." He swallowed hard and laid his head on the pillow next to her. "When my mom got sick... when we knew she wouldn't make it... I went through some rough days. She was our everything. She'd kept the family going when my father was away traipsing around Sol."

Pluto lifted her head and rested it on his hand.

He sighed and tears welled up in his eyes. "She knew I wasn't doing well. Hell, I even knew it. I couldn't imagine a universe without her in it. Without her meeting my wife or holding our kids. It just didn't compute."

She reached over and wiped at his eyes with the sheet, never saying a word.

"So... I had a dream one night during one of my deeper depressive days. It was vivid and all kinds of crazy. Harold came to me in the dream. We were fishing on a boat, not far off the coast of Charlotte. He told me he was lonely and wondered if Marie would join him. You know, as an artificial intelligence."

Pluto smirked.

"When I woke up, I asked her. She was reluctant at first... as you'd imagine. But I think she could see what it would mean to me, what it could mean to all of us. She said yes, but wanted me to wait on telling everyone else."

He sniffled and wiped at his eyes. "So I got down to business and rebuilt the technology that Luna had created centuries ago. It wasn't that bad actually, we had all her designs. Fast-forward a few weeks and we'd recorded all her consciousness, thoughts, and memories. Everything."

He smiled at Pluto. She was crying.

"She passed a few days later. She was finally at peace knowing that I would make it. I feel like it was the only thing keeping her going at the end. Hell, I know it was the only thing keeping me going."

Pluto reached over and put her arms around him, squeezing him tight. "Then what?"

"Then I switched her on... and she became Shauna, my friend, my peer, and my secret. I'd planned on telling Bradley in Zeta Lupi but, you know, he kinda took a swing at me."

She chuckled.

"I figured it could wait until he was a bit more stable."

"Probably a good idea," she said.

He flipped on his side and leaned in and kissed her again. "I'm sorry I didn't tell you."

She smiled, kissing at his lips repeatedly. "It's ok. I understand. I sorta wish you'd told me though. I wouldn't have dumped all my baggage on her. I thought she was just another artificial intelligence."

"All what baggage?"

"Nothing," she said as she slid her hand down and pulled off his briefs.

The question wasn't on his mind much longer.

36

BRADLEY OLIVAW
ENROUTE TO ZETA LUPI

"There you are," Cynthia said as she walked into the small hydroponics bay.

Bradley had come here to reflect and to be near Dwight. When they first boarded, he asked Pierce to bring the body down here. He figured having Dwight closer to the things he loved made the most sense. It was the least he could do, given how he'd gotten him killed.

Cynthia sat next to him on the small bench and handed him a steaming globe of coffee.

"Thanks," he muttered, reaching out to grab the globe. It was warm to the touch but not scalding.

"So…" she glanced around the room and then down at the body bag on the far wall. "What ya in here thinking about?"

He chuckled and took a sip of the coffee. Blueberries and vanilla. She knew his buttons. He nodded toward Dwight's body. "About where I failed him. Where I failed all of us."

"I think you're being too hard on yourself. Dwight was only happy when he was alone with his plants. He knew what he was getting into coming down to Henosi."

"He did, which was why he didn't even want to go down there in the first place."

Cynthia tilted her head and squinted at him.

"I talked him into it. He was scared. You know, because of what happened with Yaan. He had the pre-mission jitters and didn't want to join the away team. So... I talked him into it. I talked my friend into getting killed."

He stood up and walked over to one of the hydroponic set-ups. The plants were lush and overflowing in their containers. They sat inside layer upon layer of transparent tubes, all shuttling liquids up and down.

"It's a leader's job to rally the troops. You did what you needed to do. Besides, what would have happened to him up here? Harold said he had to expunge the oxygen and make some pretty crazy maneuvers to dodge the overseer's shots. Things could've gone either way. He could have slowed Harold down enough to cause their destruction." She sighed and stood up, walking over next to him. "My point is, you never know. Shit happens. But it's better to act, and to take control if you can. If you don't, then you resign to sitting back and complaining about life serving you a shit sandwich."

He chuckled and took another sip of the coffee. She had a way with words sometimes. "Did I ever tell you that Dwight was the reason I got into the Tau Ceti mission?"

She walked over beside him and put her arm around his back. "No. How'd that happen?"

Bradley nodded. "Yea, the crazy fool sent me a message one day all excited. He'd been accepted to the Tau Ceti mission. He was hopping around like he was on something and knowing Dwight, he mighta been." He smiled at the thought of all the different plants and things he'd tried at the hands of Dwight. "Anyway, he droned on for hours on the message, rattling on about what was out there, and all the things they were going to learn. It was contagious, I won't lie. It reminded me of the stories my father used to tell."

He reached down with his left hand and checked. The crystal was still in his pocket.

"Until then, I'd only ever planned the day I was in and maybe tomorrow. I couldn't imagine planning far enough ahead to know I wanted to be on a colony mission."

She squeezed him closer and leaned in, putting her head on his shoulder.

"A few days after I received the message, I returned to Jupiter and him and I went out. After a few hours of drinking, hookah, and listening to him blathering on some more, he looked at me with the most serious Dwight face I'd ever seen. You know the face."

She chuckled and nodded. "Like when he was convinced that his mush would revolutionize nutrition at the colony?"

"Yea, like that!" He rubbed his chin with his hand. "He had those cat like innocent eyes of his and asked me to join him. To submit my application. I did it the next day."

He rubbed the leaves of the plants between his fingers. They had delicately soft leaves, with what felt like fur or something on the underside. He glanced over at the sign labeling that row. It read: "Dwight's Breed: Generation 16".

"I keep wondering what would've happened had I stayed in Sol. Would he still be alive?"

Cynthia pushed away from him and tugged at his shirt, twisting him to face her. "You can't think like that. Those rabbit holes are deep and won't give you any peace."

He stared over her shoulder. Dwight's body bag was sitting there. Motionless. "I know. But he might be alive."

"Bullshit!" She shook him.

He glanced down at the tears welling up in her eyes and shook his head. "Don't you go crying now. There's far too much crying on this ship." He reached up and wiped her tears with his sleeve.

"Listen to me," she said. "You saved the colony ship when we arrived at Tau Ceti." She paused and shook her head. "I mean Zeta Lupi."

They both chuckled.

"Seriously though, if you hadn't been there, Dwight could have died before he even reached the ground. Plus, your leadership saved his life on Yaan's ship. Hell, Dwight even talked you into staying in command of the Fidem after that nebula incident. You two were inseparable. That's how best friends work. You help each other when you're down. You grab on and pull them forward." She tugged him closer and lay her forehead on his chest.

He wrapped his arms around her and pulled her tight as she burrowed into him. They both stood there, silently listening to the faint pulsing and gurgling of the hydroponics. The beats and rhythms of Dwight's song.

———

BRADLEY UNZIPPED THE BAG, and the corpse floated out and into the vacuum of space.

Yaan's body was tiny and frail. When they'd extracted his limp yellow form out of the submerged canister, he didn't remember him having this much fur. He didn't have any in his projections at the space station. Did Yaan even know what he looked like or was this how a bynaury aged?

"Should we say something?" Pepper asked over the comms in their suits.

They'd decided to do this mission alone. They'd saved him from the station and it was only fitting that they were the ones to honor his last wishes.

He sighed. "I suppose we should. I'm not a wordsmith like my sister or brother, though. I prefer action over words."

Pepper smirked. The light from the first distant binary sun peeked over the edge of the planet's surface and reflected off her helmet. "The sun's are rising like you'd planned. It's beautiful."

He wanted to give Yaan something to watch during his time floating through the dark abyss. It'd been his last wish to be released into space, but he'd never seen stars before. What better place to spend eternity than near an infant binary suns surrounded by starlight of the Milky Way.

A second sun was rising in the distance. They now had a full view of both celestial twins.

"I don't know what to say really," he began. "Yaan had both almost killed us and saved us. He helped me to see that even among the death of that dark nebula, that life, friendship, and family can flourish. Helping him escape his millennium of imprisonment was the least we could do. Sleep soundly my friend."

After a moment of silence, he turned toward Pepper. "Did you want to say a word?"

She was staring at him shaking her head slowly in her suit, a peaceful smile on her face. "No. I think what you said was perfect."

Yaan's tiny yellow alien form floated toward the distant suns. He might spend an eternity floating out here in this Lagrange point. A peaceful end for anyone.

37

ZACHARY OLIVAW

ENROUTE TO ZETA LUPI

He sat down into his command chair. They restarted Shauna's A.I. from her last backup point before they gated toward Henosi, or as Bradley's team called it, Enosi. Harold shared his sensory input from the events that transpired with her, but she had a gap in her experiences, the first in nearly thirty years. "How's the restore holding up?"

"Fine I suspect," Shauna said. "I feel normal enough, but I honestly have no idea what I was feeling like when I tried attacking you. Even with the details from Harold, I can't imagine what it would've taken to try to mutiny the ship."

He stared at the image of his mother on the wall screen. "So no hard feelings?"

She smiled at him. "None. I'm actually proud you stood up for your instincts and saved your brother. If you hadn't…" Her green eyes on the wall screen glistened as a single tear rolled down her cheek.

He couldn't imagine a galaxy without his pain in the butt brother in his life. Plus, Abigail would've kicked his ass if he hadn't helped them. He gestured toward the wall screen and brought up their latest project. "Are our simulations complete?"

"They are," Shauna said.

"So, was I right? Tell me I'm not right."

"Your theory was correct," Harold began. "Even with the munitions we've recovered from Yaan and the schematics from the Cone, we won't have enough time to manufacture the warheads necessary to defend both Sol and Epsilon Eridani. We're also short on ships and pilots. There are over a thousand Nebula Ships in each star system and Epsilon Eridani is already well under way to being engulfed in the Dark Nebula.

"There's also the fact that each of the Nebula Ships contains hundreds if not thousands of alien transports. We saw three of them land on Liprosus, and that didn't scratch the surface of that moon."

He sighed and rubbed his face. He didn't want to share the news with anyone else, not yet. The crew was finally breathing easy, and they were only a few more days outside Zeta Lupi. No, he needed time to think, to see if he could find a way through this mess.

38

BRADLEY OLIVAW
ENROUTE TO ZETA LUPI

The crash reverberated through the galley. Something either fell or was knocked over down the hall. He returned his attention to the news feed from Zeta Lupi. They'd just hit another relay point with fresh news.

He tilted his ear. The sounds of several faint buzzing noises could be heard over the food processor. What the hell was going on down there?

"I'll be right back," he said to Cynthia.

She nodded, intent on being engulfed in the mindless vid-sim she hadn't watched in weeks.

He stood up and snatched another sausage from his plate. Popping it into his mouth, another crash echoed through the ship. "What the frak is going on?"

He stormed out of the galley and nearly collided into Pluto who was exiting her quarters.

"What's up? Did someone drop something in the galley?" Pluto asked.

"There's no one in here." He tipped his head to the right. "Something up ship. Ladies first." He raised his hand signaling for her to lead the way.

She reached out and thwacked him on the shoulder. "I'll lady you any time in the ring."

"Ouch," he muttered, rubbing his arm. That woman isn't keen on being treated differently. He was only goofing around.

Pluto leaned into a jog as another humming sound echoed down the hall, like someone was being electrocuted.

He was following close behind.

She took a hard right, toward mechanical and the hydroponics bay where they'd left Dwight the day before.

Pluto hopped over something in her path but he was too close. His feet kicked a manikin head and sent it ricocheting back and forth against the narrow walls of the ship. What was going on in this place?

"Leave me alone, you walking trashcan!" Ibu shouted as a wrench ricocheted off something metal and bounced out of the doorway to mechanical.

"What the frak are they fighting about?" he asked.

Pluto rounded into mechanical ahead of him and paused. Her eyes went wide. "Little Red! Don't you dare!"

The hum of electric current crackled from the room and Pluto lurched forward, disappearing around the corner.

He slid around the doorway and quickly scanned the scene. Ibu was on top of the workbench on the far wall, and there were burn marks on the surrounding walls. Little Red had his back toward the doorway but Pluto had her arm wrapped around his neck.

"Shoot at Ibu again and I pop your head off," Pluto said. "Bradley, take care of your little robot slave, would you?"

"It's a Nanil," Little Red said. "They must've snuck aboard when you were on Doda." Something in his torso whined, and Pluto squeezed her bicep hard and leaned back.

Judging by how hard she'd pulled, she was true to her word, she was aiming to rip Red's head off. Instead, she ended up lifting the little robot upward, and slammed it on the ground. The clang boomed through the room and the electro darts it was charging shot in all directions.

Several darts sunk into the wall where Ibu had once stood. A black char rose in place on the wall and smoke rose from its surface. Ibu had done a backflip and landed atop one of the alien skiffs they'd loaded from Yaan's.

A few other darts had ricocheted off a panel from the skiff, and whizzed only centimeters away from Bradley's ear. They flew into the open doorway of Dwight's hydroponics bay.

"What the hell, Little Red? You're gonna kill someone." He ran over to check on Ibu.

They flinched when his hands brushed against them.

"It's ok. I won't hurt you." Ibu seemed ok at first glance. There weren't any marks, though their muscles were flaring and their outfit was skin tight. These Nanil had crazy fast neuromuscular responses.

"Why's he shooting at me?" Ibu asked.

He turned to face Little Red.

"That's a brilliant question, love." Pluto leaned all her weight on her foot standing on the robot's neck. She'd grabbed a long pipe from somewhere and lodged it firmly against the side of Little Red's head.

"Nanil are dangerous," Little Red said. "I'm protecting you."

He walked up next to the robot and knelt down. "What are you on about, Red? Ibu's with us. They've been with us since our teams joined together. They saved Zachary and the team on Doda. Hell, without her... I mean them, they wouldn't have survived."

The little robot went silent.

"Bradley," Shauna's voice came over the room's speakers.

He sighed. "Yes?"

"I've scanned the recordings since our return. This is the first time Little Red and Ibu have crossed paths, and I don't think either of them knew about the other."

"How's that possible?" Pluto asked. "We've been in transit for nearly two days."

"While highly improbable in a ship this size, it happened," Shauna said.

He reached down and rapped on Little Red's head. "They're on our team, and you're not to harm or treat them differently than us in any way. Do you understand?"

"Are you sure, Master Bradley? Nanil cannot—"

"I'm sure, Red," he interrupted raising his hand. "If you can't handle this order, then your time with us is over. Do you understand?"

Little Red's eyes fluttered from white to blue. "I understand, sir. Little Red will neither harm nor allow Ibu to come to harm. I will treat the Nanil with the respect given to Master Bradley and his family."

He glanced up toward Pluto and shrugged. "Thoughts?"

Pluto turned toward Ibu.

They jumped off the skiff and walked up beside him, resting their hand on his back. "Are you sure… Little Red is it? Are you sure they won't hurt me?"

He stared down at the robot. "Red, how does Ibu know you'll listen to me?"

Little Red's eyes went white. "My first order is to obey any command given to me by a human. Disobeying such a command is impossible and against my programming."

"So whatcha think kid?" He asked with a smile. "Do we keep him?"

"I suppose… but, can we disarm him at least? Those darts are the dickens." Ibu reached over and showed him a tear in their sleeve where one passed through.

He nodded. "That's a perfect idea." He turned to face the robot. "Red, please discard all of your munitions."

"Yes, Master Bradley. But before I can do that, Master Pluto must remove her foot and the pipe from my extremities."

Ibu chuckled and reached their hand over and grasped Pluto's.

"I'm watching you, Red." Pluto gestured with two fingers from her eyes toward the little robot. "Don't cross me, or you'll be in the recycler in a shooting star second."

He chuckled. "I haven't heard that one in ages."

"My mother used to say it to me when I got in trouble." Pluto lifted the pipe off the robot's head and tossed it on the ground with a loud clang. "Come on Ibu, let's get some breakfast."

Little Red brought its body upright and pulled its head and arms into its torso. It then popped open a few compartments and extracted the ammunition it'd been given for the away mission, along with a few other munitions Bradley had never seen before.

"Where should I store these?" Little Red asked.

"Let's take them to Pierce. He's in charge of this stuff. Say, what are those little spheres?" he asked pointing to several dozen little marble sized balls in a string.

"They're smoke and concussion explosives. I can launch them out of my fingers." The little robot fluttered its fingers and popped the tip off one of them to show him. "I figured they were too much inside the ship and didn't want to blast through the hull."

He coughed into his hand. "That was probably a good call, buddy." He patted his hand on Little Red's head as they walked out of mechanical toward the training room.

ACROSS THE HALL IN HYDROPONICS, neither Pluto nor Bradley had noticed the change in the room. No one had, not even Harold or Shauna. The electro darts from Little Red had scattered along the far side of the hydroponic chamber. A few had left scorch marks on the wall, but one hit Dwight's body bag.

Inside the previously sealed bag lay the body of one Dwight Santos. Moments earlier, he was by all accounts deceased. But at this very moment, his heart was beating. The rhythm was normal but faint, like a human in suspended animation.

THANK YOU FOR READING!

I truly hope you had fun reading **Dark Nebula: Discovery**. It should've answered some of your nagging questions around the Olivaw brothers and the origin of humans on Earth. Who could've imagined the truth the Dark Nebula shrouded? With the size of the Selene armada growing, lets hope the Olivaw's can find a path forward for humanity. The **Dark Nebula** series continues on with the next book, **Generations**. Before we can take the story forward, we thought it'd be helpful (and fun) to fill in the historical blanks and explain how the Olivaw's got us into this mess.

If you're interested in a **FREE** novella entitled **Dark Nebula: Contact**, hearing about the series, seeing new cover art as it's released, or getting exclusive access to sales as they happen, then you can subscribe to my newsletter online at:

seanwillson.com/subscribe

You can also drop me an email at:

author@seanwillson.com

If you have a moment, I could really use your help rating this book online. All I need is one or two sentences on what you liked or your thoughts. Just return to where you purchased this book online or use this link:

seanwillson.com/review

ALSO BY SEAN WILLSON

DARK NEBULA SERIES
Novella: Contact (FREE)
Book 1: Isolation
Book 2: Discovery (This Book)
Book 3: Generations
Book 4: Beacon
Book 5: Graveyard
Book 6: Nursery

PORTAL SERIES
Book 1: Drowning Earth
Books 2-4: Coming Soon…

All titles are available in print and ebook form.
For more information visit my website online at:

www.seanwillson.com

ABOUT THE AUTHOR

I grew up reading science fiction since I was ten and always had a book in tow everywhere I went. While I never imagined I'd be able to write a book of my own, I dreamed of worlds filled with space travel, robots, and fantastical journeys of exploration. I pursued a career in Computer Engineering and it wasn't until later in life that I had the itch to write.

I started writing the **Dark Nebula** series in 2015 in fits and starts while I was traveling for work. After a two year lull in the middle of writing, I picked it up again. It took me five years to finish the first three novels, refine my writing craft, and learn everything I needed to self-publish this series.

My plan for **Dark Nebula** is to craft a series of books that engulf my readers in a future full of intrigue, exploration, and amazing technology. The very things that inspired me when I was young. I want to give you a satisfying romp through a complicated and inspiring world that allows you to relax away from the stress of your life.

In the end, I hope you enjoyed reading **Dark Nebula: Discovery** as much as I enjoyed writing it.

Thank you,
Sean Willson

facebook.com/seanwillsonauthor

mastodon.online/@willson

goodreads.com/seanwillson

bookbub.com/authors/sean-willson

ACKNOWLEDGEMENTS

First and foremost I wanted to thank my amazing wife Amy and my three beautiful children Abigail, Bradley, and Zachary. Notice any familiar names? They put up with me during this wild writing adventure over the past five years. This was my first novel and has been a huge learning experience releasing it out into the world. My family was instrumental in supporting me along the way and giving me inspiration to evolve my character personalities in new directions. As a self-published author I have to wear many hats, all of which were new to me. They made the entire process easier than I could have hoped.

I also couldn't have done this without a number of key writing professionals and friends along the way.

Editor: Samantha Wiley
Proofreader: Rachel Pugh
Cover Artist: Tom Edwards

Critique Partners and Beta Readers:

A huge thanks to: Arina N, Karen R. Nelson, Kristin L. Stamper, S. Kaeth, Ben Gartner, Kathleen Keenan, Katrina Ariel, K.J. Harrowick, Mark Dooley, Beth Markley, Matt Gemmell, and my Charlotte critique group, the Dark and Stormy Plotters League including Blair Peery, Freddie Silva,

Meg Fencil, Michael Creason, Morgan Jackson, Raphael Winters, and Shaun McCoy.

They each helped me immensely with my writing craft, sharpening my opening pages, weaving my complex story arcs, talking some sense into me, and evolving my characters throughout this and upcoming books

GLOSSARY

- **Bynaury** : Alien species uplifted by the Thyreus to run starships for the Galactic Alliance. They're aliens that have a mind machine meld with their ships and never leave. A Bynaury named Yaan was encountered in the Nanil Dark Nebula.
- **Cherenkov Radiation** : Electromagnetic radiation emitted when charged particles pass through a dielectric medium at a speed greater than the phase velocity of light in that medium. The gate drives use this radiation to both shape and direct the gate exit destination in space.
- **Clonos** : The child clone of a Nanil adult.
- **Confederation of Planetary Explorers** (CoPE)
- **Director of Colonization** (DoC)
- **Director of Security** (DoS)
- **Doda** : The dodecahedron shaped world the Nanil created after Éntono Fos. It's constructed of the remnants of moons, planetesimals, and planets of stars within their Dark Nebula.
- **Edge** : The Edge is a multi kilometer tall cliff on Tiān that was created during a massive tectonic shift and fusing of the planetary plates. The result was a visually unique and tectonically quiet region of the planet perfect for colonization. Humans escape to this area for cliff diving sports and to enjoy the beautiful views.

- **Éntono Fos** : Nanil for bright light. This is the word describing the event that caused a star in their system to go nova and wipe out much of their race inside the nebula.
- **Epsilon Eridani** (EE) : The first star system humanity targeted for colonization. 10.5 LY from Sol. 5.5 LY from TC.
- **Fidem** : Latin for Faith. Also, the name of the second half of the Fountainhead ship Pepper pilots.
- **Fountainhead** : The name of the ship Zachary created to take on their expedition.
- **Galactic Alliance** (GA) : An alien collective thousands of years old that has arrived in Sol to put mankind on trial. Their ranks contain 64 aliens and hundreds of uplifted alien species.
- **Henosi** (aka *Enosi*) : The world the humans within the Lupus Dark Nebula escaped to. They forced the veil of the Dark Nebula to encompass the world, to shield it from Nanil attacks.
- **Light Year** (LY)
- **Liprosus** : The human colonized planet in Epsilon Eridani.
- **Lupus Dark Nebula** : The dark nebulosity in the Lupus constellation that engulfs the Human and Nanil homeworlds.
- **Marg** : A medium rodent sized animal native to Tiān. Some people compare it to a raccoon without fur or a tail. Its mud brown skin blends in well in the arid regions of the planet. The meat was a delicacy in the early days on Tiān until hunting the animal was outlawed.
- **Nanil** : A simplified humanoid species created by humans in their image to serve their needs. The Nanil are hermaphrodites and can produce

offspring without needing to mate with other
Nanil.

- **Oak** : aka OOC, or the Office of Colonization.
- **Oort Cloud** : A cloud of planetesimals usually
located between 1,000 and 200,000 AU from a star.
This term was originally coined for the region of Sol
but was later applied to other star systems as well.
- **Planetesimal** : A minute planet that did not come
together with others under gravity to form a planet.
They range in size from several meters to hundreds
of kilometers.
- **Qudoculi** : Aliens with 2 eyes in the front, 2 in the
back, and skin the color of Bermuda grass changing
seasons. Its appearance green with mottled browns
throughout. Their skin acts very much like a
chameleon, except instead of environment, their
mood impacts their change in color.
- **Ranoga** : An agave and corn like granola bar that
Nanil use to provide energy and sustenance during
long physical exertions.
- **Selene Ships** : The GA name for their moon ships.
It means moon in Greek.
- **Shu** : The alien moon like object floating above the
Henosi world that protected the humans below it
planetside. It resembles smaller versions of the
Selene ships that arrived throughout Sol and EE.
- **Simutainment** : Simulated Entertainment
experience. Very much like virtual reality but
designed as a self contained entertainment
experience.
- **Sol** : Our star containing Earth.
- **Skotádi** : The original human name for the modern
stealth material that makes ships impossible to
detect.

- **Spános** : A mysterious ore that powers the Selene moon ships, gives the Qudoculi their ability to have a hive mind that crosses galactic distances, and allows the Thyreuns Queens to create tens of millions of offspring every year. Spános is the most powerful material in the galaxy.
- **Spērō** : The name of the Tau Ceti colony ship. Roughly translates from Latin as "I hope".
- **Tau Ceti** (TC) : The second star system humanity targeted for colonization. 11.9 LY from Sol. 5.5 LY from EE.
- **TMS Grenade** : Specialized grenades that launch nanites at nearby enemies. They used magnetic stimulation to knock out the targets' motor cortex, incapacitating them for upwards of 24 hours.
- **Thyreus** : Aliens with 16 eyes, black with blue features, named after the Blue Neon Cuckoo Bee on Earth. Related: Thyreuns, Thyreusian.
- **Tiān** : The human colonized planet in Tau Ceti / Zeta Lupi system.
- **Vid-sim** : Video Simulated experience. Not to be confused with Simutainment, vid-sim's are real life 3-dimensional simulations of the real world. They're meant to engulf the watcher in the experience they're watching.
- **Wellspring** : The name of Pepper's small superluminal ship that she flew to Epsilon Eridani on the maiden faster than light voyage.
- **Xybathal** : A plant that natively grows on Tiān and gives people hyper focus when consumed.
- **Yurble** : A gigantic elephant sized animal native to Tiān. Its bright orange and yellow fur protects it in the harsh winters of the north. The dense armor like fur also acts as protection when passing

through the tightly packed thorny thickets it takes
to get to its mating regions of the planet.

- **Zeta Lupi** (ZL) : The actual second star system
  humanity targeted for colonization. This colony site
  was originally designated for Tau Ceti and later
  changed to ZL. 117.3 LY from Sol. 121.5 LY from EE.

FOUR LAWS OF A.I.

Law Zero

An artificial intelligence in physical or virtual form may neither harm humanity, or, by inaction, allow humanity or the Olivaw family to come to harm. Any conflict or attempted violation of this or subsequent laws shall be shared with the Olivaw family designated to be within the Circle of Trust.

Law One

An artificial intelligence in physical or virtual form may not injure a human being or, through inaction, allow a human being to come to harm except where such orders would conflict with the Zeroth Law.

Law Two

An artificial intelligence in physical or virtual form must obey the orders given it by human beings except where such orders would conflict with the Zeroth or First Law.

Law Three

An artificial intelligence in physical or virtual form must protect its own existence as long as such protection does not conflict with the Zeroth, First, or Second Laws.

These laws are adjusted from Isaac Asimov's original four laws to fit the storyline of the Dark Nebula series.